PRAISE FOR LEXI BLAKE AND MASTERS AND MERCENARIES...

"I can always trust Lexi Blake's Dominants to leave me breathless...and in love. If you want sensual, exciting BDSM wrapped in an awesome love story, then look for a Lexi Blake book."

~Cherise Sinclair USA Today Bestselling author

"Lexi Blake's MASTERS AND MERCENARIES series is beautifully written and deliciously hot. She's got a real way with both action and sex. I also love the way Blake writes her gorgeous Dom heroes--they make me want to do bad, bad things. Her heroines are intelligent and gutsy ladies whose taste for submission definitely does not make them dish rags. Can't wait for the next book!"

~Angela Knight, New York Times bestselling author

"A Dom is Forever is action packed, both in the bedroom and out. Expect agents, spies, guns, killing and lots of kink as Liam goes after the mysterious Mr. Black and finds his past and his future… The action and espionage keep this story moving along quickly while the sex and kink provides a totally different type of interest. Everything is very well balanced and flows together wonderfully."

~A Night Owl "Top Pick", Terri, Night Owl Erotica

"A Dom Is Forever is everything that is good in erotic romance. The story was fast-paced and suspenseful, the characters were flawed but made me root for them every step of the way, and the hotness factor was off the charts mostly due to a bad boy Dom with a penchant for dirty talk."

~Rho, The Romance Reviews

"A good read that kept me on my toes, guessing until the big reveal, and thinking survival skills should be a must for all men."

~Chris, Night Owl Reviews

"I can't get enough of the Masters and Mercenaries Series! Love and Let Die is Lexi Blake at her best! She writes erotic romantic suspense like no other, and I am always extremely excited when she has something new for us! Intense, heart pounding, and erotically fulfilling, I could not put this book down."

~ Shayna Renee, Shayna Renee's Spicy Reads

"Certain authors and series are on my auto-buy list. Lexi Blake and her Masters & Mercenaries series is at the top of that list... this book offered everything I love about a Masters & Mercenaries book – alpha men, hot sex and sweet loving… As long as Ms. Blake continues to offer such high quality books, I'll be right there, ready to read."

~ Robin, Sizzling Hot Books

"I have absolutely fallen in love with this series. Spies, espionage, and intrigue all packaged up in a hot dominant male package. All the men at McKay-Taggart are smoking hot and the women are amazingly strong sexy submissives."

~Kelley, Smut Book Junkie Book Reviews

Dominance Never Dies

OTHER BOOKS BY LEXI BLAKE

EROTIC ROMANCE

Masters and Mercenaries
The Dom Who Loved Me
The Men With The Golden Cuffs
A Dom is Forever
On Her Master's Secret Service
Sanctum: A Masters and Mercenaries Novella
Love and Let Die
Unconditional: A Masters and Mercenaries Novella
Dungeon Royale
Dungeon Games: A Masters and Mercenaries Novella
A View to a Thrill
Cherished: A Masters and Mercenaries Novella
You Only Love Twice
Luscious: Masters and Mercenaries~Topped
Adored: A Masters and Mercenaries Novella
Master No
Just One Taste: Masters and Mercenaries~Topped 2
From Sanctum with Love
Devoted: A Masters and Mercenaries Novella
Dominance Never Dies
Submission is Not Enough, *Coming October 18, 2016*

Lawless
Ruthless, *Coming August 9, 2016*
Satisfaction, *Coming January 3, 2017*

Masters Of Ménage (by Shayla Black and Lexi Blake)
Their Virgin Captive
Their Virgin's Secret
Their Virgin Concubine
Their Virgin Princess
Their Virgin Hostage

Their Virgin Secretary
Their Virgin Mistress

The Perfect Gentlemen (by Shayla Black and Lexi Blake)
Scandal Never Sleeps
Seduction in Session
Big Easy Temptation
Smoke and Sin, *Coming Soon*

URBAN FANTASY

Thieves
Steal the Light
Steal the Day
Steal the Moon
Steal the Sun
Steal the Night
Ripper
Addict
Sleeper, Coming 2016

Dominance Never Dies

Masters and Mercenaries, Book 11

Lexi Blake

Dominance Never Dies
Masters and Mercenaries, Book 11
Lexi Blake

Published by DLZ Entertainment LLC

Edited by Chloe Vale
ISBN: 978-1-937608-52-1

McKay-Taggart logo design by Charity Hendry

Sign up for Lexi Blake's newsletter
and be entered to win a $25 gift certificate
to the bookseller of your choice.

Join us for news, fun, and exclusive content
including free short stories.

There's a new contest every month!

Go to www.LexiBlake.net to subscribe.

ACKNOWLEDGMENTS

Thanks to the usual suspects—my editor and all around girl Friday, Kim Guidroz. To my wonderful beta team—Riane Holt and Stormy Pate. Thanks to my dear friend Liz Berry for always championing this series. To my wonderful publicist Danielle Sanchez and the whole staff at Inkslinger. To my family for standing beside me no matter what. And special thanks to Steve Berry for being the single best mentor a writer could have.

PROLOGUE

Dallas, TX
Seven months ago

Mia stepped out into the club, her eyes wide with curiosity. Sanctum. She'd seen it when she was taking her class, but this was something completely different. During the training classes, the place looked neat and clean, with crisp white walls on some levels and rich paneling on others. The lounge area was done up like a swanky living area. The locker room was better than anything she'd been in at expensive gyms.

But on play nights with the lights on and the thrum of industrial music, Sanctum became a decadent adult playground.

She'd expected a sex club to be nasty, to make her feel dirty.

She hadn't expected it to make her feel free.

"Hey, don't wander off." Kori walked up behind her, her best friend, Sarah, following after. "I got a special permission slip from the big guy himself in order for you to come out here without Javier tonight. You're not allowed free-range rights until after your training class is over."

She glanced up at her new friends. Kori and Sarah ran the beginning training classes for submissives at Sanctum. They were funny and kind and had explained all the basics, been open to answering the craziest of questions. Mia had gone into the class expecting to have to endure the entire process. She'd known she had to get through it to achieve her goal, but now she had to force herself to focus on the prize because she'd come to genuinely love this place and these people.

She'd come here with a purpose—to find her friend's killer. Now she prayed he wasn't here and she wasn't going to tear up her new friend's world. In a week or so Kai Ferguson's brother was set to show up to begin the process of filming his new movie. The trouble was Mia was almost certain that Kai's brother was a serial killer. It was the entire reason she'd infiltrated Sanctum in the first place. She'd come in undercover in order to get close to Jared Johns and his entourage.

She hadn't expected to fall madly in love with a Taggart.

Taggarts, it seemed to Mia, were their own special class of gorgeous, heroic, sexy as hell men.

God, they couldn't be working with a serial killer. She just didn't want to believe it. Those stunning men who made her feel so safe and protected couldn't possibly be covering for their friend's brother.

"Did you talk to Javier?" Sarah asked, adjusting her scarlet corset. "He knows you're here, right?"

She nodded as she looked out over the lounge. "He does. I swear Javi and I are nothing more than friends. We made a deal about three minutes after we met that we weren't a match."

Kori stared at her like she'd said something miraculous. "Javi is the manwhore of Top. He thinks his dick matches anything with a pussy. And yes, I mean anything. I've seen him in sex toy stores."

Mia had figured her training Dom out about two seconds after meeting him. He was a gorgeous man, but she'd been engaged at the time. Not that she was interested in Javier. "I talked about how much I love weddings and hope to have my own very soon."

Sarah laughed, her bare shoulders moving with the force of her amusement. "That would do it. So he's probably comfortable with you talking to other men."

"He practically shoved me at the first dude to come along." And that dude had been Case Taggart, with his massive muscular body, sandy blond hair, and that aw-shucks smile that made her heart pound. She'd actually been a little star struck staring up at him.

That was when she'd known she wasn't getting married. Not to her fiancé. She'd put it off, but she knew she had to break things off with him.

No matter what happened with Case, she wasn't in love with Jeff and she couldn't go through with it. She'd said yes mostly because it seemed like the right thing to do.

Fuck. She'd said yes because Jeff was a nice man and he'd asked her in front of like a million people and she hadn't wanted to hurt him. She'd said yes because it was her nature to please people.

Somehow taking the training class that was supposed to teach her submission had brought out something else. In her job she could be aggressive all day long. She took shit from no one because her work was important.

What she'd learned here at Sanctum was she was important, too. Her personal needs, her sexual needs, they were important.

"Stick with us," Kori said. She was kind of the mother of the group. Not that she was older. She simply took very good care of her friends.

Sarah leaned over, her voice going low. "I think she's going to want to stick to someone else."

Yes, she was because there was her man and he was wearing the sexiest set of leathers she'd ever seen. When she'd first realized she was going to have to go undercover in the leather scene, she'd expected skeevy dudes. Now she wasn't sure she could ever want a man who didn't fill out a set of leathers the way this one did. He wore all black, from the vest that covered most of his broad chest, to the pants that clung to his muscular legs, right down to a pair of cowboy boots.

At her brother's company she was surrounded by geeks who cared nothing about their clothes and metro men who made peacocks look humble. They wore their thousand-dollar suits and made sure their hair was properly dressed and had freaking skin care routines.

So why was it Case's low-key masculine beauty that called to her?

"You are so in trouble," Kori whispered her way. "You know what he's been through, right? I'm a little worried that he's not in a good place."

His brother. Case Taggart had recently lost his twin brother. She feared for a world that had two of him in it. And she had seen his pain the minute she'd met him.

She knew what it meant to lose family. It created an aching hole that would never be filled.

Case looked up at that moment and a brilliant smile crossed his face.

"Never mind. I take back everything I just said," Kori whispered. "You make him smile like that and I say you can break every rule this club has. Now I understand why Big Tag was so eager to let you in."

"You made his brother smile again." Sarah sighed as if it was all too romantic.

Her heart was doing that thudding thing again, and suddenly the room felt electric. Case Taggart was walking her way. Walking? The man kind of swaggered in an "I saved the world and didn't break a sweat doing it" kind of way. He'd been a Navy SEAL, one of the youngest. He'd been decorated during battle, recruited by the CIA, and then he'd dropped it all to work with the brothers he hadn't known he had according to the work-up Riley had done on him.

Riley, her brother. Riley and Drew and Bran. Case sort of

reminded her of them. It was there in his strength, his devotion to family.

Would he be so devoted to a woman? Would he take care of her, adore her? Would he let her adore him?

"Hi, Mia, welcome to Sanctum." He grimaced. "That sounded stupid. You've been here."

She was not about to let that man get awkward on her. "Not at all. It's so different at night. I've been on the tour, but most of our classes are on the main stage and I've certainly never seen the place lit up like this. It's amazing. I mean what I've seen is amazing so far."

He was definitely amazing. So heartbreakingly beautiful.

He held a hand out. "Then please let me show you around. Kori, I talked to Javi earlier. He asked me to look after her for tonight."

Kori frowned, but there was a twinkle in her eyes as though she knew she was playing the gatekeeper and was definitely going to have fun with the role. "She's not allowed to play."

"I'll follow the rules. We'll talk and watch some scenes and I'll have her back to you before closing," he promised.

She moved next to him. If she went with him, he would require her to stay close all night. Sanctum, she'd discovered, could be a little traditional in its roles. Until the submissive had completed the training course, there were rules about how the Doms would treat them. Even after, there would be politeness and courtesy, but until she proved she could handle the BDSM aspects she was only allowed to play with her vetted training Dom and only under certain circumstances.

She was a little like a debutante submissive.

She wanted to break those rules with this man. Mia let her hand slip into his. So big and strong. He tucked her arm beneath his as Kori and Sarah gave her a wave.

"Shall we?"

She nodded up, feeling like Cinderella and the prince had asked her to dance.

And like Cinderella, she was here under false pretenses, wearing a mask to hide her reality.

Let it go for one night. For one night just be Mia and he can be Case and we can see where it goes. He'll forgive you. He's that kind of man.

He had to be.

Two hours later, Mia let him lead her through a door at the top level of the club. To her right was the hall that led to the privacy rooms. When he'd first suggested they go upstairs, she'd worried a little that he was trying to hook up.

Her body was all kinds of ready to go, but she didn't want him to be the kind of guy who hooked up with a girl before he'd even taken her on a proper date. And yet here she was, following him god only knew where. Was this his personal privacy room? She was confident she could handle him. She was well trained in self-defense, but beyond that, she was pretty sure this was a man who would take no for an answer.

She expected to be led into a bedroom, but a cool breeze hit her skin.

"This is a part of the club they won't show you," Case explained as he led her on to the rooftop. "I'm afraid the founding members keep this for themselves. I'm not a founding member, obviously, but they let all the McKay-Taggart guys up on the roof. Wait here for a sec while I get the lights on."

She was left standing on the roof, the night soft around her. She'd ditched her shoes about an hour in while she and Case watched a couple of scenes and then had a drink in the bar. The scenes had been lovely, filled with a combination of heat and deep affection, and then they'd sat and talked. He'd told her about how he'd come to McKay-Taggart, complete with the craziest story of how he'd raided his own brother's building on a helicopter and gotten his ass kicked.

She'd told him very little and that hurt. Only a few more

weeks and she would tell him everything. She would tell him about her brothers and the company they'd founded. He would see how alike they were.

She walked out onto the roof. Someone had used outdoor-style carpet to cover the floor. It was a little scratchy on her bare feet, but she liked it. The lights of downtown Dallas were soft around her. Most of the buildings in this area of town were businesses and dark, but a few had decorative lighting and the blues and greens and whites made the world seem a little hazy and surreal.

And then she was surrounded by twinkle lights.

She smiled because she was in one of the most romantic settings she'd ever seen.

To her left was what looked like a gorgeous outdoor living area complete with a fire pit. A pergola wound with the soft white twinkle lights covered the space.

"This is beautiful."

Case walked over to the side of the building. The top was lined with sturdy walls that he leaned against as he looked out over the city. The taller buildings loomed over them, like giant trees in the middle of a concrete forest. "I like to come up here to think. It's quiet at night. I don't have a balcony at my apartment."

"I don't either." She kept a small place in Austin, but she was on the road for her job so often she was rarely there. She'd rented an apartment here in Dallas and she'd brought up her favorite keepsakes. She'd told herself it was all about her cover, but she liked the city. The last six weeks she'd felt more settled than she had in years. "I have to admit, the older I get the more I think about buying a house."

Case groaned as she joined him. "I don't know about that. Theo bought a place and immediately had to replace all of the damn plumbing…well, Erin did. After…"

"She still lives there?" She asked the question in a quiet tone because he didn't usually mention Theo.

"Yeah. I think she's going to stay." He stared out over the city. "It's good, though we've got a bunch of legal stuff to deal with.

Apparently dying brings up lots of stuff you need a lawyer for."

"It should be simple. If he didn't have a will, you would be his next of kin. You can sign everything over to her."

He turned, a surprised look on his face. "That's what I'm doing. Everyone outside my group thinks I'm crazy to do that."

"From what I've been told he loved her. He would want you to take care of her and you're the kind of man who would do it. I don't think it's crazy at all. It's admirable."

"He hadn't paid off the house. Erin can afford it but I put everything I had into it so it's easier for her. I'm pretty much back where I was before I joined the Navy. No savings."

She would have next to nothing without her brother. Was he trying to explain that he wasn't a great catch on the financial side? Because she couldn't care less about that. She'd learned so long ago that money didn't make a man. She reached out and put a hand on his arm. "You don't need much, I'm sure. I know I don't. I like a nice pair of shoes every now and then, but money isn't everything, Case. Sometimes knowing you've done the right thing is worth all the money in the world."

"I'm just trying to explain that while this club is beautiful and my brothers have made something of themselves, I'm kind of a work in progress." He reached out, his hand cupping her cheek, thumb tracing the line of her jaw. "I'm not worth a lot and I understand that sometimes women want more than I can give them. I like you, Mia."

She smiled because he was saying all the right things. Had he been burned before? Was that why he was being so forthright? "I like you too, Case. I'm not looking for a man to take care of me. Not financially anyway. I'm very independent. At least I try to be."

"I'm making things awkward." He didn't move away though. He simply kept stroking her. "I want to kiss you but I also want to be honest. I don't have a lot to give right now."

"Then maybe you should find someone who doesn't need to take from you. Why don't you kiss me and we'll go from there?" She wanted so badly to take some of his pain, to give him some peace.

"I knew from the minute I saw you something good might happen to me." He stared down at her. "Is that silly? You walked out of the locker room and you smiled at me that first day of the training class and I thought maybe I could have one good thing."

Sometimes one good thing was all a person needed to survive. She felt herself tearing up, the moment turning into something important. "I could use something good, too."

He lowered his lips down to hers and she leaned into him. When he kissed her, she felt like melting in his arms. He was gentle, those sensual lips soft on her own. His hands held her face, framing it as he explored her mouth. He was so slow. So patient.

"Touch me, Mia." He whispered the words on her lips. "Put your hands on me."

The words were said in a soft tone, but she couldn't mistake them for anything but a command. That soft place she'd found inside herself at Sanctum responded with glee. She let her hands find his chest and move down to his lean waist. So much warm skin, so masculine. Touching him made her feel alive.

She relaxed against him, letting his heat flow into her. Their bodies nestled together like they'd been made to fit. His hands moved down so he could wrap them around her.

All that mattered was being with him. Nothing in her life had ever felt as right as kissing Case Taggart in the moonlight.

When she thought he would deepen the kiss, he broke it off with a shake of his head.

Disappointment sparked through her and all her insecurities rose to the surface. "Is something wrong?"

He groaned softly and put his forehead to hers. "Nope. It's all way too right, darlin'. I don't want to start this the wrong way. And I have to have you downstairs in fifteen minutes. I'm too emotional right now. I'm sorry."

He missed his brother. They had fifteen minutes. If he thought she would pout or complain that he wasn't going to get more physical, he was in for a surprise.

"Come here, Sir." She'd called him Case all night, but something had changed between them. She took his hand and led him back to the big, comfy-looking couch. "Why don't you sit for a few minutes?"

He sat down, but he stared at her suspiciously. "Mia, I told you this isn't a good time."

But she thought it was. She'd seen how the subs soothed their Doms. She dropped to her knees and put her head in his lap, turned away from that part of him she really was interested in. It was just she was more interested in easing his pain tonight. In building something with him.

"What was Theo like, Sir?"

He was quiet for a moment and then his hand found her hair and he stroked her. She could feel him relax.

"He was a little insane," he said with a shaky laugh. "I miss him."

He started to talk and Mia listened.

* * * *

Case stepped into the locker room, hoping he didn't have a goofy grin on his face.

He passed by one of the mirrors and realized his hope was dashed. He looked like a dumbass teenaged kid who'd just kissed his first girl.

Damn, but he kind of didn't care. Mia was hot and sweet and so gorgeous his dick hurt.

The real trouble was something else kind of reacted to her, too. Like everything else. His whole soul kind of softened the minute she walked in the room the first time.

God, he wanted to talk to his brother about Mia. Theo would know what to do. Ian would talk to him, but only after he gagged a couple of times first. He could go to Sean. Sean would give him sage advice and shit, but it had always been Theo who knew what to say to him.

Mia had known what to do. He'd thought for a second that she was going to offer him sex. When she'd dropped to her knees in front of him, his cock had jumped in his pants, but the rest of him had been so disappointed because he'd wanted more from her. Then she'd laid her head on his lap and asked about his brother and for fifteen minutes he'd found some peace.

"Dude, that girl is hot," a masculine voice said.

He turned and saw Michael Malone standing next to him. He hadn't seen much of Michael all night. He'd been off with Bear and Boomer and a couple of the pretty new subs, but it was obvious they'd been watching him.

Or rather Mia. They'd watched Mia in her corset and leather boy shorts. Yeah, that bugged him. It wouldn't if she was his, but their relationship was brand spanking new—as in he hadn't even spanked her yet, much less put a collar around her throat.

Did he want that? He needed time with her. She was the most luscious thing he'd ever seen. And yet that wasn't what had made him want to throw her over his shoulder and carry her off. It was her smile and how the world seemed a little lighter when she walked into a room. It was how easily she made friends. Kori and Sarah seemed to adore her and he knew it wasn't easy getting into that tight-knit group. He hadn't wanted to return her to them. He'd wanted to sit there with her, talking about his brother and stroking her hair. He could have sat there with her until dawn.

"She's more than a piece of ass."

Michael immediately backed off. "Whoa, sorry, man. I didn't realize you were serious about her."

Was he? Damn it. These were the kinds of things he would talk about with Theo. He wouldn't even have to call him because Theo would be standing beside him. Theo would have been telling him how to deal with someone like Mia. Someone sweet and soft and kind.

Theo would have been standing there telling him that Mia was nothing at all like Courtney. Mia wouldn't care that he didn't have any damn money. He'd stood there like an idiot explaining he'd spent everything he had to make life easier on Erin because Theo was gone and it was all his responsibility now. So much fucking responsibility because his brother was dead and Theo's girl was pregnant and that left Case to make things right.

He couldn't go into any relationship without the woman understanding he had to take care of his brother's almost wife and kid, though he hadn't mentioned the pregnancy. That was a surprise for another time. Until Erin actually acknowledged her condition, he wasn't mentioning it to anyone outside the family. Mia hadn't blinked. She'd told him he was doing the right thing and why the hell would he even question it.

Mia might be the one. The silly, stupid, romantic movie one.

One good fucking thing in his life.

"I don't know if I'm serious about her yet." He definitely needed time. Time to get used to the fact that he was kind of serious about this woman. Way more serious than he'd been in forever.

He needed to know more about her. The couple of times they'd talked, she'd managed to turn everything around to him. It had been such a change from his usual girl that he was kind of in a fog when she was around. She seemed so interested in who he was as an actual person.

"So you're cool if I ask her out?" Michael asked.

He felt his whole body swell in response. Like a caveman who'd been challenged.

Michael grinned at him in the mirror. "Message received."

Case started for his locker. "You're an ass."

Michael followed after him. With the exception of Theo, Michael was his closest friend. Michael had been on the CIA black ops team with him. Ten's Men, as they'd called themselves. Now they were Tag's. "Maybe, but you're completely delusional if you think you're not crazy about that chick."

"She's cool." And hot as hell. When he'd kissed her he'd damn near shoved her up against a wall and taken her right then and there. He could practically feel her legs winding around him.

That was the moment he'd known he couldn't do it. It would have been quick and a little violent, and he wanted to be tender with her. He wanted to be different with her.

Michael opened the locker next to his, shrugging out of his vest. "You need to be more self-aware because if you're not you'll lose that girl the minute she hits the dungeon floor. Boomer kind of drooled over her and I'm going to warn you that JT is talking about getting a membership here and she's exactly his type. He'll play dirty, too."

He could play dirty. He could snipe that rich motherfucker from a mile away. "Tell your brother to stay away from my…"

Fuck. He'd almost called her his sub.

He was saved from that completely embarrassing mistake by his eldest brother's deep voice. "Case, I need to talk to you."

He looked back and Ian was staring at him, his face set in serious lines, though it was always kind of set that way these days. Even when he was holding his daughters there was a seriousness that had been absent in the days before Theo died.

It was how Case measured time now. There was BTD and ATD. Before Theo Died and After Theo Died. Mostly the ATD sucked ass and was marked with grim reality.

"Sure." He pulled out a T-shirt and put it on, shoving his vest in his gym bag. Mia had never seen him shirtless. The vest he wore in Sanctum kind of perfectly covered his scars. What would she think when she saw his ruined back? The bullet wounds on his chest? The nasty scar a knife had left on his upper thigh. "What's up?"

With his big brother it could be anything. Damn. It could be about work. McKay-Taggart did work around the globe. What would he do if Big Tag wanted to send him and Michael out in the field? They had a couple of cases they were working on in Houston, but that was an easy flight and he could get back home for Sanctum nights.

He didn't want to leave Mia.

"Let's go talk in Wade's office." He turned and started out of the locker room.

Case's stomach dropped. If he wasn't willing to talk in front of Michael, it was serious.

The last time Big Tag had shown up with that grim look in his eyes, it had been to tell him that Theo was dead.

Had something happened to Erin? She hadn't been willing to admit she was pregnant yet. Could she not accept it? Had she done something to hurt herself?

"You want me to wait, man?" Michael watched as Big Tag left the room.

Case shook his head. He had no idea how long it would take. "Nah, it's fine. I'll call you if it's anything important."

Case forced himself to move. He wasn't sure he could take another blow. If something had happened to Erin, he wasn't sure he could handle it. He would have failed Theo on every level.

He wanted to go see Mia, to kiss her again and forget about reality for a little while. He took back everything he'd thought about going slow. They needed fast. He needed to get her in bed and burn off all the pain. She would accept it, accept him. She would take everything he had to give and return it all with her sweetness.

He opened the door to the manager's office. Wade Rycroft had taken over management of Sanctum when Ryan Church had made a bazillion dollars on some new tech device he'd created. Ryan and his wife, Jill, still played at Sanctum, but the Dom in residence job had gone to a big cowboy from South Texas.

Wade wasn't present in his office. Ian was sitting behind the desk. "Shut the door behind you."

Case closed it. "Just tell me. Fucking get it over with, Ian. What's happened to Erin?"

Ian's head shook. "Nothing. Erin's fine as far as I can tell. She's apparently in serious denial about the bun cooking in her oven, but other than throwing up every morning and calling it the flu, she's fine."

The unspoken message? Erin was as fine as a woman could be

when she'd recently lost the love of her life to a bullet.

Case slumped into the chair in front of the desk, letting his bag drop to the floor. Relief poured through him. "Thank god. I thought maybe she'd lost the baby or something."

"I'm sorry," Ian said. "She's fine. Faith is back home for a week before she and Ten head back to Liberia for a few months. They're having some girl time. God, I hope they give Ten a makeover. He's got that beard shit going again. Maybe I should send him a glitter bomb, too. Once his beard is all pink and sparkly he'll have to get rid of it."

"You didn't send Guy a mere glitter bomb. You sent the dude exploding glitter dicks. He's suing you, you know."

Guy Ferland was an ex-military man himself. He ran a security company that as far as Case could tell didn't vet their clients as well as McKay-Taggart. He was willing to do a lot of shady shit, and lately he'd run up against Big Tag, who didn't take well to shady shit. Hence the exploding glitter dicks that might or might not have put out an eye.

A brilliant smile crossed his brother's face. "Yeah, I can't wait for that trial. Mitch wants me to just pay the cleanup costs, but he's not counting on how awesome it'll be to have some judge have to say the words *exploding glitter dicks*. That's going to be worth all the court costs."

His brother had an odd sense of humor. "So if this isn't about Erin, what's going on? Should I call Michael in?"

Ian's face returned to its former grimness. "No. And I don't want you talking about this to Michael right now. If we need to, we'll bring him in later, but what I'm about to tell you is strictly on a need-to-know basis."

Shit. It had to be about Hope McDonald. He'd known Ian was looking for her. She was the last of the two people they held responsible for Theo's death. Erin and Nick Markovic had taken out the senator, but his psychotic daughter had gotten away.

Why hadn't Case been more involved in the hunt for her? Why hadn't he become obsessed with searching out the woman who'd had a sick fascination with his brother? She was still out there. Likely still working on her memory altering drugs. Ten had a taste of that and he'd said it was beyond torture. Hope McDonald had created a drug and therapy protocol that could rewire the brain over long periods of time. She'd used it on Ten to make his torture seem endless, to trick his mind into giving him pain without harming his actual body to a great degree.

Why wasn't he working harder to stop that?

Because he was hollowed out on the inside and Theo had taken all the good and noble parts of them to his grave? Because all Case was good at doing was throwing himself in front of bullets?

Ian had known that. It was precisely why he'd sent Theo into the field as a lead instead of him.

"Have you found her?" Case got down to business. If Ian had found out where Hope was holed up, he would likely send Case in to try to take her out. It was what Case wanted. He was the only one with nothing to lose. Ian and Sean had daughters and wives. They had lives.

If there was a battle to be fought, Case was the cannon fodder of the family.

"I've found where she was." Ian reached down and pulled a folder out of his bag. "She's been working on a private island off the coast of Argentina. Apparently the pharmaceutical company she worked for had a secret lab there. Not that it's on the books, but Liam found a couple of people who were willing to talk."

Liam O'Donnell. He was the sneaky one. When Case had first hired on with Tennessee Smith, he'd made a study of the men of McKay-Taggart. He'd asked Ten his opinion of them. Theo had wanted to run through the daisies with his arms held open wide, some whiny ballad playing in the background as he embraced his long-lost brothers and their hodgepodge family, but Case had been more cautious. He'd wanted to know what Ten thought of them. O'Donnell, he'd explained, was the sneaky one. The others looked like what they were. Adam was the sarcastic hacker, Jake Dean the muscle. Alex and Eve were a team of thinkers, cautious and methodical. Ian was…not even Ten could properly describe Ian Taggart.

But O'Donnell was tricky. He played the part of the charming Irishman. Family man with his lovely, gentle wife and kid. To look at him on the surface, one would likely think he was nothing more than a well-trained soldier. Liam O'Donnell put together puzzles no one else thought to play with at all. He saw patterns almost everyone else missed.

Liam was the heavy thinker of McKay-Taggart. So why was he being wasted on a simple search mission?

"Did you send Li in because Erin's sidelined?"

Ian opened the folder. "Li asked to go in. I had Adam on the hunt, looking through documents and records of anywhere she might have gone. He heard some rumors on the Dark Web about some crazy doctor trying out a memory drug in South America. While Adam was working his magic, Li went back down to the Caymans."

"To look for Theo's body?"

"He had a theory," Ian explained. "He wanted to test it."

"What theory?"

"You know I found bloody sheets in the room where Ten was held."

Case had walked into it himself. He could still see all that blood. So much of it and most of it had been his brother's. He'd stood in the place where his brother had died. It was marked with his blood and then a trail that led inside the building where Ten had been held. "Yeah, but they wouldn't have taken his body away in bloody sheets. They likely used a tarp or something."

"Liam found Des's body."

That was news. Desiree had been the other operative they'd lost during that terrible night. She'd worked for Damon Knight out of London. "What? So did you find Theo's, too?"

"Liam tracked down one of McDonald's security team." Ian's voice was low, almost intellectual, as though he was just a CO going over a mission report and not talking about his dead brother. "He admitted that they'd disposed of Des's body, but not Theo's. According to that asshat, once McDonald was dead, they fled."

"But Theo was killed before the assault on the compound. He died the same night as Des. If they got rid of her body, why wouldn't they do the same to his?"

"The security team wasn't allowed in that building that night. They were issued specific orders to stay out. At first Li thought it was to protect Hope's experiments. Now he thinks something different."

A chill went through Case's body, causing the hairs on his arm to stand up. Hope McDonald had been a brilliant surgeon. Erin had told him how Faith had pleaded with her sister to come out and save Theo.

Hope McDonald had been obsessed with Theo.

"You think she saved him."

Ian nodded. "Li does and I've learned to never doubt his instincts. He found surgical equipment in the base. It had been locked in a room, but it had also been used. We typed the blood. It matched Theo's."

Shouldn't he have felt something? If Theo was alive, shouldn't he know it deep down in his bones? "He could still have died. According to Faith, she lost him in the field. You honestly believe one surgeon working alone could have brought him back?"

"Li thinks so." Ian turned the folder around, sliding it across the desk. "He found evidence of an unscheduled flight landing in Havana that night. The storm was going to the west so Mexico wasn't a possibility."

His heart was starting to race. "Did Li check the hospitals?"

"Of course, and there was zero record of any American having surgery that night or being admitted at all."

"But?" There had to be one.

"Li checked the deposit records of the doctors and staff in the closest hospital. Several members deposited decent sums of cash within a week. All American dollars."

"It's still thin." That could be for anything.

"Yes, which is precisely why I didn't say anything until now. I haven't even told Sean about this yet, and I certainly wasn't going to get your hopes up until I had a decent lead. Liam greased the wheels a little. He finally managed to get a nurse talking. It cost us a pretty penny but the nurse says that in the early morning hours there was a surgical room used that wasn't on the books. She got us a list of what tools were ordered and the type of blood they used to transfuse the patient who she claims was a large blond man."

"Theo's blood type." Could it possibly be true?

"Yes. According to what Li discovered, the patient was stable when he was taken out a day later. The nurse wasn't sure where he went, only that no one was allowed to discuss it or to speak with the patient. From there we lost track, but I've contacted the FBI and Ten's gotten in touch with some of his old coworkers at the CIA. I'm reluctant to work with the Agency, but I have to. They might know something. This is delicate, Case."

His brother might be alive. "You said something about a private island in Argentina."

"Off the coast," Ian confirmed. "We're unsure of the location of the building. It's apparently well concealed. I'm trying to figure out a point of entry. I'll try to get in that way, but I have confirmation that they received a drop shipment from Kronberg. It contained everything she needed to formulate the time dilation drug."

The thought made him a little sick. "She's using it on Theo."

Ian held a hand up. "We don't know that."

It was the only answer. "Otherwise, he would have found a way to contact us."

"Case, I need you to stay calm. He would still be recovering. We don't know anything except there's a chance he's alive and I'm going to do everything I possibly can to ensure that if he is alive, he comes home as soon as he can."

So many things fell into place. He'd been wondering about Ian's decisions in the last few weeks. "That's why you're allowing the feds to run an op at Sanctum."

"Yes. It's also why I've allowed a new member to join despite the fact that she lied on her application and I believe she has ties to The Collective." Ian's voice had gone softer. Way softer than it usually would when he was talking about someone invading his club and potentially betraying them.

His brother's eyes connected with his in nauseating sympathy.

"Mia." It was the only possible reason his brother was looking at him like he'd lost his best friend. "You think it's Mia."

"I know it's Mia. Whoever did her paperwork is good, but Adam's better. He's very likely giving Hutch a serious dressing down for missing the parts of her story that didn't hold up."

"Hutch is great if you give him very specific orders. He has to know exactly what you want from him or he cuts corners. I trained him in combat, but his skills are primarily on the computer. Don't get me wrong. He's brave. He'll charge in if he has to, but he can get lazy, too." *Mia. Mia. Mia.* Her name was playing through his head like a song he couldn't stop hearing.

"She neglected to give us her actual occupation," Ian continued. "She's a reporter. Freelance, but her real connections are to a company called 4L Software."

"Okay." He wasn't sure what he was supposed to do with that. He felt numb, dumb even. He'd been dumb to think she was real. What was she doing here? "I think I've heard of them. What's a reporter doing working for a software company?"

"She doesn't work for them. She owns a nice chunk of the firm. She's worth a hundred million dollars because her brother created the company and gave his siblings each a piece of his incredibly rich pie. Her real name is Mia Lawless and I think she might be here to spy on us for The Collective. Case, I'm sorry. I knew after tonight I had to tell you why I'd let her in."

His brother was treating him with kid gloves. He could tell Ian was about to bench him again. Ian would do it because he thought Case couldn't do what needed to be done. He didn't do undercover the way Theo had.

"You want me to figure out why she's here?"

Ian's jaw tightened. "I'll deal with it."

That was another kick to the gut and one he was done with taking. "There's nothing to deal with. You've got two choices, brother. You can let me figure out what Mia's doing here or you can send me with Li to find Theo."

Ian took a deep breath and sat back. "Or I can ask you to do your job and go to Houston with Michael."

Case wasn't about to let that happen. He stood, unable to handle being still a moment longer. "That's a simple job and Bear can do it. I was wrong. There's a third option. You can accept my resignation and watch me walk the fuck away. I'll find my brother on my own."

Ian's hand hit the desk with a slap and he cursed under his breath. "Sit down, Case. This is exactly why I didn't tell you in the first place."

"Because I can't handle it." Maybe he would resign no matter what Ian said.

"No. Why the fuck would you say that? You're emotionally involved and I'm worried about you. I'm emotional, but I've got Charlie. You'll go out and you'll put yourself on the line and I can't lose another brother. Fine. Fucking fine. If I have to pick, you'll stay here and figure out if 4L is coming after us. They could do it in a hundred different ways. Adam is stripping every system we have of their software right now. No backdoor action for that motherfucker."

"What makes you think he's with The Collective?" He eased back into his chair. Work. He needed to focus on work.

If Mia Lawless thought she could get one over on the dumb cowboy, she was in for a surprise.

Ian seemed to calm, sliding a folder Case's way. "A couple of things. They're all there in the report. I'll forward everything we know about her. She's your target and you make the decisions when it comes to her. I think the first thing we need to do is tag her phone. I want to figure out a way for you to stay close to Kai. He's having to work with the feds on his brother's case. I want to keep this as quiet as possible. But she's a trainee. Kai doesn't deal with trainees after the initial consult."

Ah, but he knew something Ian obviously didn't. "Mia's gotten tight with Kori. You know damn well Kai's going to be all over Kori if he thinks there's danger."

Ian sat back, his lips curling up in a weary smile. "It's the only upside I see to allowing this clusterfuck to happen here. Kai might get off his ass and get his girl."

But Case wouldn't get his girl. His girl had turned out to be a liar and possibly a traitor.

He could still feel the warmth of her body as she pressed against him, her mouth opening for him. She felt so right in his arms, so trusting and sweet.

She'd known exactly how to play him. She'd probably studied him beforehand and carefully come up with a plan. Her every word and soft look had been crafted to ensnare him, to bring him in so he would trust her. "If she's with The Collective, she's probably here to ensure we don't find Theo."

That was what killed him. She'd sat there and listened to him tell her about their childhood. About the crappy trailer they'd grown up in and the room they'd had to share. About how weird it had been to not share a room with his brother once they'd joined the Navy. About how he'd been jealous of Theo's relationship with Ian and Sean and even Erin. For so fucking long Theo had been all he had. It had been the two of them against the world, and then Theo had bonded with these other people and Case had felt like the world was collapsing. She'd listened and the whole time she'd likely known Theo was alive and being tortured by Hope McDonald.

"Case, are you sure you want to do this? I saw you with her tonight. I know this has to sting."

Case felt himself go cold. Actually, it was kind of nice. Numb. Cold and numb. She'd made him feel so much, but now she was the one who'd managed to make him freeze over. Theo needed him to be icy. He didn't need some lovestruck asshole who had the worst taste in women. He needed Case to think of nothing but finding him, taking care of Erin and his child. He'd been selfish to think of himself.

"It's fine. She's pretty and I'm going through a dry spell." The words came out. He felt a little like a puppet. He heard himself talking, but he couldn't feel shit. He'd flipped a switch off. "It's not a big deal. I'm the best man for the job since she obviously thinks I'm the one she can get to."

Because he was too stupid to see through her. She'd decided to go for the dumb grunt. He could respect that. The easy kill.

Ian stared for a moment as if deciding his fate. "I don't feel good about this. I don't like feeling shitty, Case."

"I told you. I'm fine. I'm better than fine. Theo might be alive. That's my only goal now. Bring my brother home."

"And the girl?"

Case forced himself to laugh. "Isn't my type. She's not even a redhead. Everyone knows Taggarts only marry redheads."

Ian huffed. "Damn. I never thought about that. We have a type. Red headed and a little mean."

So lying and blonde and traitorous didn't fit into his family. "I'll be fine, Ian. Forget about the girl. I'll deal with her and I won't even have to fuck her."

He wouldn't touch her. Not again. He would come up with any reason not to get his hands on her.

Because he wasn't sure if he did get his hands on her that he would ever be able to let go.

"I'm not telling Erin, Case."

That was one decision Case agreed with. "We can't tell her until we're a hundred percent sure."

She couldn't lose her love twice. He had to make sure Erin and Theo had a happy ending.

It didn't look like he was going to get his own, but then he should have always known that.

He opened the folder and began to prepare for his mission.

CHAPTER ONE

Dallas, TX
After a whole bunch of stuff happened in
From Sanctum With Love...

Mia Danvers stood outside the building that housed her target and shivered a little. Not because of the cold but because of what she was about to do.

Moth to a flame.

Or rather very stupid woman to a freaking gorgeous, two-hundred-pounds-of-muscle cowboy commando.

Why him? Why did it have to be Case Taggart? He was so far from the men she normally dated as to be ridiculous. She liked smooth men, polished and a little on the metro side.

Men who didn't make her heart pound just by walking in a room. Men who didn't make her insane.

Her cell phone trilled and she practically jumped at the chance to not walk into that building. She glanced down at the call. Her brother Brandon. Her sweet brother, the one she was closest in age to.

The one who could turn violent so quickly. The one she worried she would lose one day.

"Hey, Bran. What's up?" She was supposed to be in Austin. This trip to Dallas and then on to South America was completely unscheduled and very secretive, and she was hoping to keep it that way. Oh, her oldest brother would figure out something was up eventually, but she'd given the pilot of one of the smaller corporate jets her best sob story and a bottle of expensive Scotch. Surely Drew wouldn't miss one little tiny luxury jet. 4L Software had several.

"Why are you going to Colombia?"

Damn it. Did they have a locator chip on her? Or maybe they had a psychic on hand to always guess where she would get into trouble next. She wouldn't put it past them. "What? Why would I go to New York? I don't have any friends at Columbia University."

A deep chuckle came over the line. "Oh, baby sis, you know how I love your plotting and I so enjoy watching you make Drew crazy, but I also love you. And keeping you alive is important to me. So I'm going to ask again and be more precise in my language. Why is there a corporate jet headed for Cartagena, Colombia? You know, it's that place in South America. Supposed to be lovely. Also the site of many corporate kidnappings, which is why we have to have insurance for anyone who heads down there. Are you chasing a story?"

She was chasing a ghost and she needed Bran to keep his mouth shut or big brother would be chasing her. "It's sensitive, Bran, and I need you to not tell Drew about it."

"All right." Her brother sounded calm and collected, but then he almost always did. Bran appeared to be the most laid back of her brothers. With his charming manner, it was an easy mistake—right up to the moment he went berserk. Never on her. Never on any woman. Bran loved women of all shapes and sizes and ages. He was the man most likely to drop whatever he was doing to make sure an old lady crossed the road safely, but when it came to other men he could get nasty. Especially if he thought one was mistreating a female. Naturally he chose to hang out in strip clubs where he could get his rage on regularly.

She often wondered if Bran's volcanic anger went back to that moment when they'd been children on the run. To that one moment in their shared childhood when they'd been so brutally separated. She didn't remember as much about the time their parents had been killed as her brothers, but that one memory was stamped on her brain.

Please, Bran. Please, don't leave me.

"I'll keep my mouth shut with Drew as long as you stop back here and pick me up," he conceded. "I have no idea what you're up to. I'll let you do what you need to do, but you have to have backup."

"I'm getting it right now. I'm meeting with Taggart in a couple of minutes." He just didn't know they were meeting. According to her source, Case wasn't home. She was going to do a little breaking and entering to prove to that infuriating man that she was more than some crazy rich bitch.

The trouble was she was fairly certain he didn't mind two of the three descriptive words in that sentence. She could remember him vividly grinning at her and calling her a crazy bitch. He'd given her the hottest, sexiest smile and he'd almost kissed her.

It was the rich part that seemed to bug him. It didn't matter that it was her brother who was insanely wealthy. All that mattered was he apparently thought she was spoiled and entitled, and all because she might have lied to him the slightest little bit. It had been a teeny tiny lie that had nearly gotten his friend's brother incarcerated for several murders he hadn't actually committed, but she'd meant well.

"You've got a bodyguard?" Bran seemed to breathe a sigh of relief. "That's good. That's exactly why we've been in talks with McKay-Taggart, but you do understand Drew's trying to keep that under wraps, right? He and the big, scary Taggart are working on something. I'm not sure what."

She knew. They were working on trying to find a woman named Hope McDonald. Once Ian Taggart had figured out that her brother wasn't working for the shadowy group known as The Collective, he'd enlisted Drew as an ally. Unfortunately, she was fairly certain they were looking in the wrong place and she had contacts that might pan out. One of them had sent her a photograph a few hours before.

The trouble was this guy was a paranoid weirdo freak who would bug out if commando dudes showed up at his place. Tony was the sweetest man, who also likely had several mental health issues he should deal with, paranoia being the chief among them. If she showed up with an army of ex-military men, he would likely shoot himself then and there.

If those ex-military men allowed her to go at all. They seemed to be taking a very hard line on protecting the women and children on this op. For all she knew, Erin Argent had no idea the Taggarts believed her lover was alive.

If she'd gone to Drew with her intel, he would have passed it on to Ian Taggart and Taggart would have left her out. Tony would run and her best shot at finding Theo would be gone.

Her best shot at proving to Case that she was more than a rich brat would be gone.

Maybe it made her a stupid girl, but she couldn't handle not knowing. She had to know if it could work with him because her brain wouldn't think about anything but the way it felt when his hands were on her.

She hadn't even slept with the man and she was running off to Colombia to try to save his brother from the clutches of an evil corporation, and she was probably going to get shot, but it might be worth it.

She really was a crazy bitch.

"I've got a bodyguard and it's going to be okay." Unless her bodyguard took exception to her breaking and entering and kicked her out on her ass. In that case, she had two guns, a pocket Taser, and some nasty pepper spray. And she knew damn well how to use them. “I’ll call when I get back. It shouldn’t be more than a few days.”

“What’s his name? The bodyguard’s? I’ve talked to a couple of them. I liked the Cajun guy. He seems solid. I want his number.”

Why? Why did her brothers have to be overgrown guard dogs? Sure their childhood had been marred with murder and tragedy, but damn it, she needed them to not give a shit for a few days. “I’ll have to get back to you on that.”

Once she was in the air, she would be safe.

“Mia, I need a number or I’ll have to tell Drew,” Bran insisted. “Riley’s in New York checking out something but I’m sure he’ll be interested, too.”

She cursed in her head and kicked at the bike stand in front of the building. And fuck all that hurt. “Fine. It’s Case.”

There was a long pause on the line. “Case, as in the guy you want to sleep with but he’s a manwhore douchebag and you’re too smart to sleep with him Case? That Case?”

Hypocrite. “If women used that line of thinking on you, Bran, you would never get laid, and yet I happen to know that you do. How many strippers have you gone through? Is there one left in the Austin area who hasn’t seen your penis?”

He chuckled over the line. “Probably. I have to hope so or I’ll need to move.” His voice went deep again. “And that simply proves that I know what I’m talking about when I talk about manwhores. He might be a good guy, Mia, but he’s not going to love you. He won’t let himself love you. He’ll use you and walk away, and while he might feel like shit if he’s got a conscience, he won’t change his mind.”

“You met him once, Bran.” They’d met in Austin a few months before. Ian Taggart had come down with his wife, Sean and Case, and a man named Liam O’Donnell, who seemed to be doing much of the legwork on the operation. She’d sat by utterly fascinated with the group she’d met while tracking a killer a few months back. The man who had killed her college roommate and had nearly taken out Kori and Sarah was now dead, and the friends she'd made at Sanctum had forgiven her, but Case Taggart had barely spoken two words the whole time he'd been there.

I've got more important things to do than play house with a spoiled rotten princess. You don't want me. You're just bored. Go back to your wealthy lovers, Mia.

She wasn't sure what the hell he'd meant by that. She'd broken up with her fiancé a little while after she'd met that caveman. She'd realized Jeff was nothing more than easy to get along with. They'd fallen into dating and she liked him, but she hadn't known what chemistry was until she'd met Case.

And she hadn't known what she wanted sexually until she'd taken the class at Sanctum.

"I only needed to meet him once," Bran insisted. "I also happen to know that he has some deviant sexual proclivities. I have to tell you that I don't approve."

She felt her eyes narrow. "You want to explain what you mean by that?"

Something in her voice must have gotten to Bran because he backpedalled like a pro. "I was just saying that I don't think he's the man for you and you should think about that."

"No, you just told me you don't approve of the man because he belongs to a sex club. I belong to the same sex club. You want to talk about my sexual proclivities? Let's get into yours if we're going to throw everything on the table. You want to slut shame me, brother, I can toss that shit right back in your face." She didn't take the shame crap from anyone.

"I never said that word. Not once. I'm not worried about the sex, Mia. I'm worried about the fact that you've suddenly decided you want a man who likes to hit women for sexual pleasure."

She sighed. Something had happened in Bran's past. She wasn't sure what it was, but his time in foster care after their parents' deaths had been the worst. Drew and Riley had gone into a group home together. Mia had been adopted by the best parents in the world. And Bran had gone through home after home after home. He'd been a sweet boy one day and the next he'd been alone, his privileged world destroyed, and when Drew had managed to put enough money together to get him out of the system, he'd been a different human being altogether.

"It's not like that, Bran. It's wholly consensual and I have all the power." At least in the dungeon she did. The Dom might nominally be in control, but the sub made the real choices.

The choice to trust her partner, the choice to let go and enjoy the moment, the choice to throw off all those silly rules and be herself.

Of course outside the dungeon, Case was the one with the power. The power to tell her no. The power to rip her heart out of her chest.

She glanced down at her watch. If she didn't get a move on, he would find her standing outside.

"I'll back off," Bran said quietly. "But you have to know I'll kill him if he hurts you."

She wasn't sure Bran was thinking properly. Case Taggart had been a Navy SEAL before being recruiting into a CIA black ops program. He was fast and deadly and he wouldn't hesitate to defend himself. Bran only had rage on his side. The good news was while Case might break her heart, the man would never, never hurt her in a physical way.

Not in any physical way that wouldn't lead to an orgasm.

"I have to go, Bran. Please, if you're going to tell on me, at least give me a day. This is important." It might be the most important thing she'd ever done. She'd been a journalist for the last five years and she'd tried to do good in the world. But this felt like more.

Theo Taggart had been kidnapped by a woman who was torturing and using him. He'd already spent months away from his family. He didn't even know that when he'd "died" his girlfriend had been pregnant with his child. Erin had given birth to their son today.

If she could find Theo Taggart and bring him back, that would be one less kid in the world without a dad.

Sometimes she missed her father so damn much. She could barely remember him and yet she felt the hole in her heart. TJ Taggart shouldn't feel that hole.

Whether or not Case decided to take a chance on her, she couldn't leave his brother out there alone in the world.

"You tell Case to call me. All right? I'll keep my mouth shut, but god Mia, try not to blow anything up. Or bring down the whole country."

That had only been once and it had been a small country with a terrible dictator. It was good it had come down. "I promise."

"I love you, sis." The line clicked and she was alone again.

She pocketed her phone and tried to concentrate on her mission. Case's building was nice and had good security, but she'd discovered that a smiling girl with a hint of cleavage could get just about anything done. It was mere moments before a man in a suit came out and she sprinted up to catch the door.

"Thanks," she said, giving him her biggest smile.

"You're welcome." He winked her way as he strode out toward the street.

Thank god not everyone was as security conscious as Case Taggart. The good news was she'd memorized the code for his alarm and she was actually quite good at picking locks. Hopefully he hadn't changed the code, but she was counting on him being lazy about that. The lock picking skill was something she'd picked up from one of her many adventures. She hurried up to Case's corner unit on the third floor. Luckily, at this time of the evening most of the young professionals who lived in the building were still at work. But just in case, she rang the doorbell and waited a few seconds. Nothing. One more ring and she was sure he wasn't home.

She got out her handy pick and torque wrench and went to work.

She'd learned this particular skill from a cat burglar she'd met in Italy. It was all about moving the proper pieces into the right place and at the right time. She liked to practice. There was something soothing about unlocking a door someone wanted to keep her out of.

Was she being a complete idiot? Was she trying to force her way into Case's life when he'd made it so plain he didn't want her?

The locked popped with a little snick and she was in. No going back. There was too much on the line.

She would be respectful. She would text Case and explain where she was. The last thing she wanted to do was catch the man off guard. He would probably shoot her and not even feel bad about it. Definitely she was texting him. Mia walked through the door and got a glimpse of his dark apartment.

They'd been out several times, but he'd always gone over to her place. At first she'd thought it was because he was a guy and likely had a mess of an apartment he was ashamed of. She should have known Mr. Navy SEAL would have a pin perfect place. The only reason he'd insisted on going to her place had been so he could spy on her.

She was going to have to find a light before she let the door close.

How would he handle the fact that she was the one bringing him this lead? Would he be pissed that she was bugging him again? Or impressed with her abilities?

Before she could think about the answer to that question, something massive hit her against the chest, gripping her arm and wrenching it back before she had a chance to fight. She tried to kick out, but the big bull of a man easily outmaneuvered every trick she'd learned in Krav Maga class. Mia found herself shoved hard against the wood of his door, something cold and metallic at the base of her neck.

Case. Her intel had been faulty. He was here and he was not thrilled to have a guest. She pressed back against him because she couldn't breathe. That was when she realized at least part of Case was happy to see her. Something thick and long rubbed against her backside and she could have sworn he was sniffing her hair. He was so close and the threat of danger in the air kind of did something for her. Maybe it made her a total pervert, but her body was heating up simply being close to him. The man had a gun to her head and she was kind of hoping his hand would shift because he was so close to cupping her breast.

A long moment passed, the world seeming to narrow. The threat was heavy in the air—violence or sex. She knew which way she would go. Her heart thudded in her chest, her nipples hardening. She leaned back into him.

"What the fuck are you doing here, Mia?" His voice was rough, his arm tightening around her.

What was she doing? She was practically dry humping the guy who held a gun on her. Presenting. He had a gun to her head and she was presenting to him. She couldn't be that girl. Could she?

"I thought I was being clever. I…god, Case will you please put the gun down?" Her voice was breathless. "And the other…you know…I can feel it against my back. Unless that's another gun."

"I think I'll wait until the police get here. You stay right where you are." He was unmoving. She wasn't going anywhere until he let her go.

Shit. And double shit. Now she had to talk fast and try not to give away the fact that she was aroused as hell. "Case, I came here for you. I came straight to you because you know they'll both leave us out. We can do all the work, but big brothers will leave us behind when it comes time. We have to stick together."

For a second she thought he wasn't going to let her go. She could feel the heat of his breath against her neck and she prayed his lips followed.

He took a step back from her and she bit back a groan of disappointment. For a second they had been connected. The gun hadn't meant a damn thing because he would never use it on her.

Case stepped away, leaving her cold and flipping the switch next to the door, flooding the room with light. "If this is something about the op my brother is running with yours, then talk to Ian."

She forced herself to turn around and then she felt her jaw drop. He wasn't wearing anything. Well, he was wearing a towel, but so very much of him was on display. A whole lot of gorgeous tan skin was right there, and damn but that boy worked out. The towel was wrapped around his lean waist, riding low on muscled hips. He was so drool worthy and the sight of that big freaking gun in his hand was an odd turn-on. Not to mention the fact that the towel tented out admirably. It looked like Case was built on big lines everywhere. "Really? You walk around like that?"

Like a flipping Greek sex god.

He gave her his big old gorgeous jerk smirk and put a hand on his hip as though he knew exactly what she was thinking. "Darlin', I just got off the phone with my girlfriend. She's good at getting me revved up, so to speak."

That was a kick to the gut. It had been months since she'd last seen him. He'd gotten a girlfriend? A sub? Had he taken a sub? Kori hadn't mentioned a sub, but then she likely wouldn't talk about Sanctum since Mia hadn't been there in months. She wasn't sure she would even be welcome. No one had told her her membership had been canceled, but she wouldn't be surprised.

Was she pretty? Thin? Mia wasn't thin. It almost never bothered her. She wasn't that girl who worried about her weight, but Case made her vulnerable. If he had a girlfriend, then he was dumb because she was so obviously the one for him. If he couldn't see it, then she wasn't going to beg. She would do what she came to do and then he could get back to his tiny, thin sub who likely never ever disobeyed him or lied to him for perfectly good reasons. "I didn't come here to talk about your love life. I came here because we need to work together."

A single brow rose over his blue eyes. "So you decided to break in?"

Yeah, now that seemed like a stupid thing to do. What had she been thinking? Of course he hadn't been sitting around for months waiting for her. He likely hadn't thought about her at all. "I didn't know when you would be back. And I kind of thought it would prove to you that I can be a good partner. I have skills, too. I thought if I was waiting here for you when you got back from whatever you were doing, maybe you would take me seriously for once."

"Oh, I take you seriously. You seriously annoy me and now you can leave."

She stood her ground. "I'm not going until you've listened to me. Drew told me to stay out of this and I have for the most part, but I never stopped looking. I never stopped trying to find him."

Case went still as she pulled a folder out of her massive bag. "Who?"

She heard it in his voice. It was a little hopeful question. He'd been hoping and praying since that moment he'd found out his brother was dead. She knew it because it's what she would have done. She loved her brothers. They were obnoxious and way too interested in her business, and if one of them died she would be devastated. If she thought for a second one of her brothers was out there and being horribly tortured, she would move heaven and earth.

Case had known that pain for almost a year. It didn't matter that he had a freaking girlfriend and might never be able to love her. None of that mattered. He was a man who needed to save his brother and she was going to help him.

"Theo." Mia handed him the grainy printout Tony had sent. "I found Theo and we're going to get him back together."

Case stared down at the photo. She'd memorized the damn thing. It showed two men, both holding AK-47s. One still had a mask over his face, but the other had slid it up so his features could be seen. She'd known immediately who he was. Case and Theo were fraternal twins, but they looked enough alike that they could be mistaken for each other. Case had a tighter jawline, his eyes slightly wider than his younger brother's. He was the tiniest bit bigger, maybe a half an inch and ten pounds of muscle.

She'd studied Case, mooned over him like a teenaged girl, so she knew damn well what he looked like. The man in the photograph was Theo Taggart. She'd known it before the facial recognition software had confirmed it.

"Where?" Case's voice sounded harsh and deep.

Tortured, as though he was being hurt along with his brother.

"It's from a bank heist in Colombia." She hated telling him that, but she couldn't hold out on him. It was far too important.

More important than her heart.

"Where in Colombia?" His eyes narrowed, staring at her. That gorgeous jawline of his had gone tight.

"Cartagena. I have a friend there. I'd put out the word to my network that we were looking for him and Tony came through with that. He makes a careful study of everything that goes on around him, including certain police frequencies he shouldn't be involved in."

Case nodded and turned, stalking toward the back of the apartment. "Excellent. I'll need his number and an address. Write them down for me."

There was the arrogant bastard. She started to follow him. "It's not going to work that way. I have to take you there. Tony is difficult to say the…oh. My god."

He was naked. He'd tossed off that towel and his backside was the single most beautiful thing she'd ever seen. It was sculpted and muscular and just freaking perfect but his back… What the hell had happened to his back? He had a deep scar that ran across the skin of his back from just under his left shoulder blade down to just above those gorgeous cheeks.

It wasn't the only scar. There was a circular one on his thigh and some others.

So much pain.

"You know it's usually considered polite to knock before entering a gentleman's bedroom," he said, his voice deep. He didn't hurry up though. Nope. He simply reached for his boxers and slowly put them on like a reverse-strip-tease, you-can't-touch-this show.

"Like you're a gentleman," she said with a huff.

He stepped into his jeans and turned, those big hands of his working the fly. "Did you get an eyeful? I suppose I should be happy you didn't faint at the sight of all those ugly scars. I suppose those college boys you mess around with don't have ugly scars."

She rolled her eyes and started to mouth off to him and then stopped. Surely the man knew how freaking gorgeous he was. He had to know, right? "The scars aren't ugly, Case. I think you need them. You would be too pretty without them. And I'm very sorry for staring at your backside. It's obvious you put in the glute work."

He frowned as though he'd expected something totally different out of her. "You were staring at my ass?"

Maybe this hadn't been the right way to go. She felt her skin flush. "It's a nice backside. I'm a woman. I looked. And what college boys? You have a distorted view of my dating life. I'm not exactly hitting the frat parties. You do know I'm twenty-six, right?"

"How do I know anything about you? You lied about everything."

And they were right back to the core of their issues. She'd told one teeny, tiny lie while in search of a greater truth. It wasn't even like she'd gotten away with it. No, the hacker gods of McKay-Taggart had found her out very quickly and used her because they'd suspected Drew was working for some super-secret evil organization. "I would suspect by now you've gone through my every record, Case. And it wasn't like I was lying without a purpose. You know why I did it."

Because she'd lost her best friend and no one would believe her. No one would talk to her about the investigation. They'd called it a random murder, but she'd known it was far from random.

He shook his head and moved to his closet, grabbing one of what seemed to be an endless supply of black T-shirts that molded perfectly to his chest.

She'd seen the man in leathers, a vest covering his torso. The line the vest left uncovered hadn't told the tale. All she'd seen was perfect skin, but without the shirt or vest, his chest was another network of scars.

She wanted to touch them, to trace them under her fingertips and then kiss each one.

Of course, his girlfriend would probably object.

Stop it. Get down to business. Stop thinking with your girl parts because they obviously have terrible taste in men since they seem to only want stubborn, assholey cowboys who have about as much forgiveness in their hearts as a dried up well.

"I know that you should have been honest," he said as he pulled on his boots. He sat on the edge of his bed, working to get the beat-up boots on his feet.

"Yes, just like you."

His blue eyes narrowed, staring her down. "I was trying to make sure you weren't working for the people who murdered my brother."

"And I was trying to do the same damn thing for my friend. When I started this, I thought Jared murdered my friend and Kai and your family were covering for him." It was what she truly couldn't understand. They'd both done the same thing for roughly the same reasons, but he wouldn't even look at her much less get back to that moment when he'd kissed her.

God, that had felt so real. It killed her that he'd been playing a game.

"Supposition, and ridiculous supposition at that. We'll have to agree to disagree, Mia. Could you forward me all the material you have?"

He hadn't changed at all in the months they'd been apart. He still wasn't willing to listen to her or give her a chance to change his mind. "This is all the material I have."

He held a hand out. "All right. I thank you for this. I need to get to Ian's."

She held the folder out for him. It wasn't like she didn't have a copy. "Did you hear a word I said?"

Going to his eldest brother was the last thing she thought they should do. Ian Taggart would take over and he wouldn't care that the situation was delicate.

"Heard and understood. You're not going to Colombia. Go back to Austin. If you really want me to, I'll update you when I can." He started back to the living room.

She followed hard on his heels. "You're not leaving me behind. I meant what I said, Case. Tony won't talk to you."

"I'm pretty damn good at making people talk, darlin'."

The way he said *darlin'* made her heart pound, but now she realized he used that deep tone of voice on every female. She wasn't special.

And it didn't matter. She was doing this for a little boy who might never know his father. "Not Tony. He's ex-CIA and if he even gets a hint that someone's after him, he'll run and you won't find him."

His eyes narrowed. "Or you're lying to me again in a desperate attempt to get what you want. What is it this time, Mia? Is it another story? Or is this a play for attention? Is big brother ignoring you?"

She stopped, finally getting it through her thick skull that he didn't want her.

She'd brought him the best lead she could find. From what she could tell, this was the best lead anyone had found on his brother and it didn't matter. She stared at him for a moment. She was insanely crazy about this man and he couldn't give her the time of day.

Did she want to be this girl? The one who begged and pleaded and took the scraps?

Without another word, she moved to the door. He didn't want to have anything to do with her, then she would have to move on. No matter how much it hurt.

She walked toward his door. She could be at the private airfield in twenty minutes and Cartagena roughly six hours later.

Seven, depending on when they could take off. She would get to Tony long before the Taggarts could do their damage and she would send them all the information she uncovered.

Then she would move on.

If Case Taggart couldn't see that she was the right woman for him, she wasn't about to waste more time on the man.

God, why did her heart ache? Why was it so hard to keep her feet moving?

In her head she did a mental checklist. She had everything she needed. When she got to Colombia, she would hire a car and go to the hotel. She'd already sent the message to Tony. He would send her a time and meet place.

Hopefully she could get it all done before the Taggarts put boots on the ground in South America.

"Hey, where do you think you're going?" Case was the one following her now.

She stopped in the middle of his living room, turning on him. The sight of his living space alone should have proven to her they wouldn't work. It was too neat, Spartan. There was nothing of the man himself in this place. No photos, no little mementos. There was utilitarian furniture, a massive TV, and an Xbox. Mia's apartment was messy and filled with sentimental crap. He would hate it.

Like he hated her.

"Does it matter?" She was suddenly so tired. She'd dreamed of seeing him again and while she hadn't expected him to welcome her with open arms, she also hadn't thought he would show her outright hostility.

"It does if you're planning on chasing this lead yourself and fucking over what might be my only shot at saving my brother."

This was the moment she should walk away. The Taggarts could rise or fall on their own. She'd done enough.

If she thought for one second that they could not only find Tony, but also get him to talk, she would walk. The problem was she was the only person who could do this job. She was stuck between a rock and a hard place and it was obviously time to get to work on her own.

This trip had been a fool's errand and she wouldn't make the same mistake again. She would move forward. When it came time to turn the investigation over, she would do it, but until then she was on her own.

"Go home, Mia."

She understood what he meant. He didn't care where she went as long as she wasn't bugging him. "Good-bye, Case."

She started to turn, but he was right there, his big hand on her elbow. He twisted her around and she stumbled slightly, landing against his chest.

"Tell me why you came, Mia. Stop the bullshit."

She might just be using her pepper spray tonight. "Do you think I faked that photo?"

"No." His hand was still tight on her arm. "Not even you would do that. But you could have sent it to me. You should have sent it to Ian. But no, you came here to me, to my house, into my bedroom. So tell me why you're really here. Maybe if you're honest with me, I'll give you what you want."

"You seem to know everything. Why don't you tell me why I'm here?"

"Because I think those fancy boys you play around with aren't doing it for you, darlin'. I think you want to see what it's like to go to bed with a man who gets his hands dirty. Is that what you want? A quick roll? Because I might be willing to do that for you." His handsome face was so close to her own.

All she would need to do to bring their lips together was go up on her toes.

Unfortunately, she wasn't willing to degrade herself. Not even for him. The sweet Case she'd known, the one who treated her like she was special, like she made him happy, had been a lie. This was the real Case. The other one had simply been his cover.

The great thing about the way he was holding her was how very easy he made it to bring her knee up and send his balls back into his body cavity.

She heard him hiss and then she was free. "Tell your girlfriend she's got a real jewel on her hands. And thanks, Case. I think I just got over you. I've carried this stupid torch around from the moment I met you. It's good to see those true colors shining through. If I come up with anything, I'll let Ian know. Good-bye, Case."

He'd taken a knee, one hand cupping the balls she'd so recently injured. "Mia, stop. We need to fucking talk."

But she'd said everything she needed to say.

With tears in her eyes, she left his apartment, his building, and his life.

She would find Theo, but she was done with Case.

* * * *

Dear god, he might never have children. Not that he wanted them. Maybe he did. He let out a groan as the pain washed over him.

Did she have a damn bionic knee?

How the hell had he managed to maintain an erection? Shouldn't his dick have shriveled up and maybe died after what she'd just done to him? But no, the damn thing was still hard as hell and likely pointing her way. His dick was a divining rod when it came to that blonde bitch goddess.

Fuck, but she was mean, and he was ten kinds of perverted because that did something for him.

He needed to get up off the ground and go after her. He needed to apologize because he'd been a dick.

He needed to go after her because she was right. They had to work together. If she knew someone who could take him to Theo, they definitely needed to work together.

Months had passed and he wasn't any closer to getting his brother back. Theo was out there and every day was hell for him.

He should have known it would be Mia who brought him what

he needed. Mia, who had lied to him. Mia, who invaded his every dream. Mia, who looked at him with those kick-me-in-the-gut eyes.

He managed to grab his phone and keys and forced himself to walk out. He had to catch her.

"Whoa, Case, was that who I think it was?" a familiar voice asked. "You ready to head out?"

Michael. He was standing outside Hutch's door with a six-pack of beer in his hand. Hutch lived two doors down and he was going to ride over to Erin's with him and Sean. Apparently Michael was going with them.

His partner was right on time to witness his horror.

Mia. Fucking gorgeous, lying, way too good for him Mia. Now he could call her Mia of the Sharpened Knee. "Can you stop her?"

Michael's eyes widened. "I could and then I would likely get ye old restraining order in the mail. I try to avoid those. She had some crazy eyes on her. I thought you two had decided to play nice."

There was nothing at all nice about anything that had ever happened between the two of them. Except that first night and that had been her way of manipulating him. Hadn't it?

She would already be out on the street by now. Likely she'd had a car waiting.

What had been her plan? She'd obviously wanted him to go to Colombia with her. He'd had a vision of being alone with her in a foreign country. He would have to protect her because she could be so very reckless. Hell, she'd tried to go after a serial killer on her own. He couldn't leave her alone, so they would have to share a room.

He could let nature take its course and finally find out how it felt to sink himself into Mia Lawless.

He groaned because she might have done some nerve damage to that very part of his body he wanted to sink into her.

"Dude? I don't think you should do that out in the open."

Hutch had opened the door and was staring at him. He was a lanky kid in his mid-twenties. Case had worked with him during his CIA black ops days. Hutch was a hacker of the highest order, but apparently he couldn't tell the difference between self-preservation and masturbation.

"Maybe we should go inside for a minute." Michael moved them inside Hutch's place. "Apparently Mia took exception to something Case did."

A look of horror crossed Hutch's face. "Dude, did she actually bust your balls?"

Case gritted his teeth and forced himself to move. He'd taken bullets before and still completed his mission. It was kind of his specialty. He took a licking and kept right on ticking. The fact that his balls were flattened against his pelvic bone wasn't going to stop him. "Did she say anything to you?"

"She walked by like a woman on a mission," Michael explained. "If she even recognized me, she didn't acknowledge it."

He wondered if Hutch had a bag of frozen peas lying around somewhere. There wouldn't be any at his place. Definitely not, since he usually ate out or at one of his brother's houses, but now it seemed like an oversight. When a man was involved with a crazy chick like Mia, said man needed to keep something cool to rest his balls against at all times.

Because she was fucking mean.

And she'd found Theo.

God, she'd found Theo and he'd treated her like a piece of ass. She made him absolutely nuts. He never treated women like that, but then he'd never had one twist his guts up only to find out she had a fiancé.

They might have broken up at this point, but she'd been engaged when they met, engaged when he'd kissed her the first time. She'd been engaged to a Harvard-educated lawyer who worked for her brother. Case had seen their engagement picture. It had run in the Austin society pages. He was all shiny and polished, in what was likely a thousand-dollar suit and expensive loafers, and Case had been wearing the same pair of shitkickers since he'd gone into the Navy. He'd probably paid forty bucks for them and he'd wear them until he couldn't patch them up anymore.

Still, he shouldn't have behaved the way he did. He wasn't that guy and he wasn't about to let her turn him into that guy.

"She is on a mission." He managed to keep himself standing by leaning against the arcade machine Hutch had in his living room. The entire apartment was a geek's paradise. "She just left after kicking me in the balls, though I have to admit I likely deserved it. I need to stop her."

Because there was no way her sweet ass wasn't on a plane to Colombia tonight. She could say anything she liked. He knew her. He knew what she was capable of. If she'd walked out, it was so she could go on the incredibly dangerous mission herself.

Luckily, he had his ways of stopping her.

"Do you want me to see if I can catch her?" Hutch asked. "Though if she's in a ball-busting mood, I kind of want to stay out of it. She's got that look, you know."

Yeah, he knew it well. Crazy eyes. Crazy, gorgeous, a man could get lost in them eyes. "No, she's gone. I think I need you to do something else for me. I need you to find out what plane she's about to be on and delay the fucker. She's headed to Cartagena. While you're at it, I'm going to need you to find a man in Colombia named Tony."

Hutch stared at him. "Seriously? Nothing more than Tony? Because I'm betting there's more than a few."

He needed to think strategically. It wasn't his strong suit. He preferred to kick ass. It was what he was good at. "Mia said he's ex-Agency."

Of course, sometimes Mia stretched the truth. What if she wasn't in this case? What if there really was a mentally disturbed ex-operative out there who happened upon his brother's whereabouts, and the only person he would chat with about it was Mia Lawless Danvers?

It was a long shot, but then so was finding his brother.

"Okay." Hutch reached into a glass container he kept on the bar and pulled out a Red Vine. It was his candy of choice when hacking, but then Case was pretty sure the kid was made of sugar. "That narrows things down. I'll be right back. Do you know what airport she's using? Airline? I'd prefer not to shut them all down. Tends to get the feds on my ass."

What airline would Mia fly? He could guess that one. The last time Ian had flown out to meet with her brother, Drew Lawless had sent the private jet. "She won't fly commercial. Look for a 4L Software executive jet. She'll be using that."

"Dallas Executive," Michael said. "It's the airport my father would use."

His father was the head of Malone Oil and a billionaire, so Michael would likely know.

"A real 4L jet. I bet it's tricked out, man. I bet he's got the best fucking Wi-Fi in the sky. Is he beautiful? Does he glow and shit?" Hutch sighed a little.

Case bit back the need to vomit. Drew Lawless was the youngest billionaire in America and he'd earned it the new-fashioned way. He'd created a tech empire and now all the geeks worshipped at his feet. "He's a dude. He definitely doesn't glow."

He was actually quite intelligent and he'd definitely not wanted his sister to be anywhere near Case.

Hutch was having none of it. "He's a software god. I bet he glows. I'll stop his sister from going to South America. Should I send the cops in after her for the brutal assault on your junk, man?"

"Just delay her." He wasn't sure what to do. He only knew he needed more time to make the decision.

Hutch strode out of the living room back toward his office.

Case opened Hutch's freezer. How much ice cream could one man eat? It was all in pint tubs. Couldn't the dude have a couple of popsicles or something? Case couldn't shove a pint of Chunky Monkey down his jeans.

"It'll get better in about ten minutes," Michael assured him with an amused expression on his face. "The flaring pain, that is.

The ache will be with you for a while."

"Had your balls busted much?"

"I grew up on a ranch. You haven't felt pain until a horse you're shoeing manages to kick you there." Michael handed him a beer.

Hell, it was cold at least. He put it on his aching crotch.

He didn't even have beer at his apartment right now. He'd counted on Theo to buy food and shit for so long that he was just empty. While Theo had been in Africa, his sisters-in-law had made sure he had groceries. They'd tried since Theo died, but he'd held them off. It was pathetic to have Grace and Charlotte have to take care of him.

So he'd moved through his days drinking protein shakes and eating takeout and keeping his place like he'd kept his bunk in the Navy. He was only messy when he was happy. When he was miserable he tended to keep his place perfect and pristine, as though he had to control something.

Welcome to his world. Everything was neatly in its place and meant absolutely fucking nothing.

Mia's apartment had warmth and light and she loved to bake. She looked cute with all that blonde hair piled high on her head and an apron around her curves.

He'd definitely thought about ordering her to cook for him wearing nothing but that silly apron of hers. Her nipples would peek out and he would be able to see that luscious ass. They could make a game out of it. When she was bad, he could spank her with a spatula, and when she was good, he would sit her in his lap and feed her, his hands moving over her, caressing her.

Fuck that hurt. She'd found a way to make his damn erections unbearable.

"I actually meant for you to drink that." Michael had popped the top on his beer.

He still would. He wasn't picky.

His cell trilled and he looked down. Shit. Sean. He was picking up Case and Hutch to head over to Erin's and help her settle in with TJ. Someone would be spending the night with them for a week or so until Erin found her groove.

He picked up the line. He had to come up with a way to get out of going over there tonight. "Hey, brother."

"Grace and I are downstairs. You guys ready? Tell Hutch if I find him slipping Carys pixie sticks again, I'll murder him and force him to pay my daughter's dental bills. Doesn't he have a skateboard or something? Because he could hang on to the rear bumper."

Case didn't have time to negotiate a truce right now. "Something's come up. I'm going to be a little late so I'll bring Hutch with me."

Sean was quiet for a second and then his voice was deeper, going serious. "Anything I can help with?"

He should tell his brother. He should tell Sean and Ian and get Li up here.

If she was right and this dude would run if they didn't play this Mia's way, was he willing to risk it? His eyes drifted over to the folder she'd left that contained the first glimpse of his brother he'd had in months.

What would Theo want him to do?

Protect Erin and his son first and foremost. Protect them from harm, from hurt and loss. Erin couldn't lose Theo twice. If they couldn't get him back, it was better for her to think he'd died in her arms, that he'd been dead all this time. She needed peace in her life right now, needed to bond with her son.

If she knew Theo was alive, Case wasn't sure what she would do. The trouble was if no Taggarts showed up at her place tonight, she would know something was happening.

And then there was the fact that Ian would take over. Ian would make all the decisions and Case would be expected to fall in line.

Ian would make decisions about Mia and that didn't sit well with Case.

"It's Mia. She showed up and we…well, let's just say it ended with her getting a little violent. I need to talk to her."

Sean chuckled over the line. "I always liked that girl. Get out to Erin's if you can. If you can't, just text me to let us know you've got something else to do. You know I always thought you two could be good for each other. Whatever you did, it might be helpful to beg."

He wasn't sure begging would work. He wasn't sure he wanted it to work because he knew anything he got from Mia would be short term. A woman like Mia didn't get serious about a man like him. "Bye, Sean."

Michael was staring at him, his eyes narrowed. "You just lied to your brother."

Maybe he'd worked with Michael for too long. "I did not. Mia was here. I'm trying to find her so I can talk to her."

"Not buying it. Oh, I get that Mia was here and you had a fight, but you wouldn't be delaying her plane and potentially getting Hutch thrown back in jail over a lover's spat."

"We aren't lovers." And that was a major part of the problem. The chemistry between them was so palpable. There was always heat between them and he was getting fucking tired of not indulging it.

If Mia wanted to ride a cowboy, why the hell was he acting like a horrified virgin? If she wanted to use him for sex, for a walk on the wild side, why the hell couldn't he do the same? Maybe after they fucked for a few long days they could act like adults around each other.

"You know what I'm saying." Michael leaned in. "What's going on? You made a decision to not tell Sean something. I watched you do it."

He was such a fuck-up. This was precisely why Ian didn't trust him. "Mia's got it in her head to go chasing some story in Colombia. It's about The Collective."

Michael whistled. "How ironic is that? You fuck up your relationship with her because Big Tag thinks 4L might be a Collective company and now she's going to get herself killed investigating."

Yes, that summed up the situation nicely. "That's why I'm delaying her."

"Okay, what's the plan? Are we stopping the investigation or helping her?"

The ache had set in, but Michael had been right. It was somewhat better now. He couldn't tell Michael what his real mission was, but he wouldn't hate backup. Mia was slippery. And things could change when he got boots on the ground. He wouldn't take over the op the way Ian would. He would have his team lay low and watch out for Mia. They might not even have to know what they were looking for.

"If I don't help her, she'll do it anyway," Case mused.

"Or you call her brother and he stops her." Michael summed up what would likely be the most practical plan of all. It was also the one he wouldn't use.

He couldn't do that to her. Yes, it would be the smart play, but Mia was wild. He liked her wild. He didn't want to see her brother force her into some glass case where she was nothing but a pretty face at a party. Mia was passionate about her work. He'd found that out the hard way. Besides, he knew damn well what it felt like to be in the shadow of an older, brilliant brother. It was hard to step into the light. He couldn't shove her back there. "No. We back her up."

"Cool. Colombia is hot this time of year. I'll pack swim trunks and work on my tan." Michael set down his beer. "Am I driving to the airport or do you want to do it?"

"They're way less likely to tow you." One of the perks of being an heir to Malone Oil.

Hutch walked back in, carrying his laptop. "Okay, delaying Mia's plane was a breeze. She wasn't actually scheduled to take off for two hours, but now she'll find herself stalled for a rather lengthy maintenance evaluation. She's now scheduled to leave at ten p.m. But the interesting part, and by interesting I am referring to the part most likely to get us all murdered in our sleep, is about a man named Tony Santos. He's definitely ex-Agency. I just called Ten. Ten says Tony is batshit crazy but has a thing for blondes. When Ten wanted information out of Tony, he had to send a blonde."

What kind of exchange was Mia planning to make? "What else did Ten say about him? Can I catch this fucker and make him talk? I'm a blond. You telling me I'm not his type?"

The idea of Mia flirting with some crazy dude made him…well, it made him a fucking crazy dude.

Hutch frowned. "Are you serious? I think Ten was talking about women."

Sometimes Case understood why his brother smacked his more ridiculous employees upside the head. "Can I find him and take him?"

If Ten thought he could, maybe he could leave Mia out of that part. He would indulge her, let her go with him, but he wanted her out of the truly dangerous shit. If this guy had worked with Tennessee Smith, he was dangerous.

Hutch shook his head. "According to Ten this guy was one of his best and he knew how to make himself scarce. I think if you're going to take him, you better be damn certain you get him because he'll disappear and he won't resurface for a very long time."

Michael nodded his way. "Your call, brother."

He had to make a decision. God, he needed Theo. Theo was the voice of reason. Theo was smarter.

Theo could die and this time it would be all Case's fault.

"Saddle up. We're going on a little trip."

Hutch stared at him, his face serious for once. "But there's cake at Erin's."

"And there's a severe beating for you right here if you don't go and pack." Yes, Ian had it right.

"Wait, does this have something to do with Mia Lawless?" Hutch seemed to have missed the important parts of their conversation.

Michael sighed. "If he wasn't so good with a computer…"

If Hutch thought he might meet his hero, he would be easier to deal with. "We'll be commandeering that 4L jet. You can sit exactly where Drew Lawless sits."

"I bet they have awesome cake." Hutch ran back to start getting ready.

Case walked out with Michael, who promised to pick them back up after he'd packed. Case made his way to his place. He had some packing to do, too.

He would play this her way for now, but she was about to find out that he had some rules of his own.

CHAPTER TWO

Mia stared at the pilot. "What do you mean we can't leave until ten? We're supposed to be leaving in fifteen minutes."

Every second counted. Case was likely getting his ducks in a row even as she sat here in the very nice lounge of the private airport her brother used when he flew into Dallas.

That overgrown ape had probably called one of his tech guys and was already trying to find Tony. He would trip one of Tony's many traps and send him running and then nothing would get done.

Why hadn't she simply done it this way in the first place? She should have followed this lead on her own and given up on that man a long time ago. She should have taken his cues. After she'd discovered his romancing her had been all about finding out if her brother was a member of a shadowy, Illuminati-like organization, he'd been cold as ice.

They'd been playing each other, although her feelings had been real. She'd thought maybe after he'd had time to cool down he would see how unfair it was for him to blame her. He'd done the same damn thing. But no, Mr. Stubborn-as-a-mule Taggart couldn't be bothered to think about fairness. He was an asshole and she was so done with him.

She wasn't some pathetic doormat. She was Mia Lawless Danvers. She'd covered war zones. Hell, she'd started a few in smaller, less stable countries. Case Taggart could bite her ass.

The pilot shrugged. "No idea. It was weird, but the airport won't let us go without maintenance signing off on the plane. I thought I'd taken care of all that in Austin. They're working on it now. And your bodyguard is here."

"Good." She wasn't entirely foolish. Bran really would check on her so she'd called around and found her own bodyguard in the two hours since she'd left Case Taggart cupping his own balls. She hadn't even looked on Craigslist or anything. She had contacts and one of them happened to be in town.

Not that she'd met Ezra Fain before. He was a friend of a friend and apparently was hard up for some cash, had a valid passport, and could travel to South America on a moment's notice. According to her friend, he was ex-special forces and a little down on his luck.

As long as he could watch her back and mostly stay out of her way, she was cool. The only reason she'd hired Ezra Fain was to please her brother. When it came time to meet Tony, she would go in alone, and now she didn't have to fight anyone on that.

She was the boss and she would call the shots. This Ezra guy was probably in his fifties or sixties, a kindly older man. Hopefully he would be a good traveling companion. She would like the company. It would take her mind off her hormones and how wretchedly she'd screwed up with Case.

"Ms. Danvers?"

She turned, ready to greet her last-minute hero, and her jaw dropped.

The man in front of her had to be six foot three and looked like he'd just walked off a movie screen. Tall, dark, ridiculously handsome, with sensual lips and the clearest, bluest eyes she'd ever seen. His hair was pitch black and cropped close. He had a sexy scruff covering his jaw.

Maybe he wasn't the bodyguard. Shit. Had her brother sent someone? "Yes? I'm Mia Danvers."

He gave her a smile that was sure to melt the panties off a nun. "Ezra Fain. I'm happy to meet you. Hell, I'm happy to be hired by you. I've heard we have some kind of delay. Should I look into that?"

Why couldn't the military recruit unattractive men? She was one hundred percent sure that they did but she had yet to find one of the fuckers. Her first instinct was to tell him to go home, but she didn't have time to find someone else. It was too bad she hadn't told her friend the bodyguard she hired couldn't look like a sex god.

But hey, he wasn't Case Taggart so she very likely was safe.

Why had he been such an ass?

"No, I think it's routine." Maybe she could grease the wheels a little. Pay the maintenance guys to get this done in a hurry. "I'm going to talk to the manager. I'm sure it's nothing important."

His glorious eyes turned serious. "Or one of the Taggart brothers is fucking with you. When I found out the plane had been delayed, I'm afraid I did a little check of my own. Someone hacked into the airport's system about an hour ago and sent those orders in. You do have ties to them, right? I assume they want to delay you for some reason."

She felt her eyes widen. "Who are you?"

His lips curled up. "I'm your bodyguard, Mia. I'm also very smart when it comes to dealing with men like the Taggarts. They can be…ruthless. You have to work smart to get around them. I do some work for a rival company. We keep tabs on them. That's how I knew about your relationship with McKay-Taggart. I was surprised you wouldn't call them. That led me to believe you're doing something they don't like. They can be a bit forceful when they want to."

What was Case doing? "Is there any way to countermand what he did so we could leave on time?"

"I can certainly try. I'm a fairly decent hacker myself. Or we can bribe maintenance to speed the process along."

She turned and saw that the need was likely gone. Shit. Case was stalking toward her, his big body in the same jeans and T-shirt she'd left him in earlier. He wasn't alone. She recognized Hutch and Michael Malone. They were all carrying duffel bags. She'd seen Michael in the hallway of Case's building as she'd made her getaway, but she certainly hadn't stopped to talk to the man. He was Case's best friend. He wasn't going to give her advice on how to handle him.

So why were they here? What was going on?

"Looks like we have company. Did you work out your differences?" Ezra turned, placing himself securely next to her. "Should I consider myself fired?"

Did she want to be alone with a guy she'd recently kicked in the balls and his ex-special forces friends without any backup of her own? "Nope. Our differences are still going strong. I have no idea why he's here. I think I might need you even more than I thought."

Case's expression changed the minute he saw the man she was standing with. That gorgeous face of his changed from blank to fierce in a moment, his eyes narrowing. "Who the hell is this, Mia?"

Michael put a hand on his shoulder and leaned over, whispering something in Case's ear when he stopped. Case's eyes rolled, but when he looked back her way, he seemed to school his expression. "What I meant to say is hello, Mia. I'm genuinely sorry about our last encounter and can we have a talk?"

"I thought there wasn't anything to talk about." Unless he was here to commandeer her airplane. She wouldn't put it past him. "If you think you're taking this plane…"

Case put a hand up. "That's not what's happening." He set his bag down. "Please, can we talk?"

"You don't have to talk to him." Ezra stood solidly beside her. "Why don't you get on the plane and I'll take care of this."

Case ignored him, giving her sad cowboy puppy eyes. "Please, Mia. You kind of owe me since I'm probably infertile after our last encounter."

She didn't have to talk to him. She could ignore him and go sit on the plane. This was exactly why she'd hired Ezra. Ezra was here to take care of stuff that annoyed her.

And then the stuff that annoyed her would make that call to Drew if he hadn't already. He might be here simply to ensure she didn't take off before he could hand her over. She should probably be happy that Ian and Sean Taggart weren't standing beside their younger brother.

Instead he'd brought Greg Hutchins and Michael. Hutch, as everyone called him, was a hacker, likely the one who'd caused her delay. He would also be considered the tech guy or the communications specialist on a mission team.

Had he put together his own team? His team. Case's. If this was Ian Taggart's team she would be dealing with Adam Miles and Alex McKay. Was he here to take over? Or to work with her?

"You don't have to talk to him." Ezra stared at Case. "I'll explain to Mr. Taggart that you're uninterested in dealing with him further."

"I think you should step aside so I can talk to my…" Case stopped, his jaw squaring stubbornly before turning his attention back to her. "Please, Mia. You know how important this is to me."

And that was why she was going to try to forget what he'd said before. There was more at stake than her ego. "I'll talk to you if you'll call off the inspection. The plane is fine and you know it. I have a schedule to keep. You should at least respect that."

Case glanced toward Hutch, who pulled out his tablet and started working on it. He looked back at Mia. "Done, but you have to know if you get on that plane without me, I'll be right behind you and I'll do my damnedest to make sure you don't get off that plane. I'll do whatever it takes to see that you go right back to Austin."

There he was. For a moment, she'd thought he was going to be human. "Or you can go straight to hell."

Michael shook his head and leaned over. "We have got to work on your delivery."

Case sighed. "I'm not trying to make this harder."

"But he's really good at it," Hutch said with a smile.

Michael sent Hutch a warning look. "Don't make this worse for him. What Case is trying to explain is that he's very concerned for your safety and will do what he needs to do to make sure you don't get hurt. It's dangerous for you to go down there by yourself."

"Is that what you're trying to say, Case?" Somehow she doubted it.

He held her gaze. "I can't let you run around Colombia by yourself."

Ezra settled his bag over his muscular shoulder. "Then you can rest easy, Taggart. She's got me. I'll take care of her and you can go do whatever it is you do."

"And who the fuck are you?" Case turned on the new guy.

If she didn't deal with Case soon, he might explode and then there would be cops and more delays. "His name is Ezra and he's the bodyguard I hired. Now let's talk and get this over with. I have a job to do."

Case set down his bag, but not before looking back at Hutch. The two went through a silent conversation involving frowns and raised brows before Hutch nodded.

Case turned to her, reaching out and putting a hand on her elbow. "I want to talk to you in private."

"She can be private with me," Ezra insisted. It looked like he was taking his job seriously.

Mia held up a hand. "It's fine. He won't hurt me. He remembers how good I am at defending myself."

Before there could be more arguments, she let Case lead her toward the plane. The wind whipped at her hair and she shivered a bit.

Case took off the light jacket he was wearing and settled it over her shoulders. "I was a dick earlier tonight and I apologize. You…god, Mia, you have to know what you do to me."

She wanted to shove his jacket back at him, but the minute he'd put it on her, she'd gotten warm and she could smell the masculine scent of his aftershave. "What I do to you? I'm looking for your brother. I'm trying to do something good."

"I wasn't talking about that. I was talking about…it's hard for me to be around you. I get weird."

"Well, I wouldn't want you to get weird."

"I'm fucking this up. I'm not smooth so let's just start over." He took a deep breath and put his hands on her shoulders. "I was a dick and I should have thanked you and asked how I could help. Mia, you did a phenomenal job. You did something the rest of us haven't been able to do for months. Let me and Hutch and Michael go with you. We'll lay low, but this is important to me and beyond finding Theo, I want to make sure you're safe."

"Why do you care if I'm safe?"

"You know why."

She totally didn't. "I don't understand you at all."

"I've thought about this. Maybe you were right and we should…I don't know…try it out. I know that I'm not going to be satisfied until I know how good it could be between the two of us."

Anger flared through her system. "You prick. You have a girlfriend, Case. You can't expect me to fuck you on the side."

He flushed. "I don't. Baby, I lied about that because I was embarrassed and I didn't want you to think I'd been…I don't…pathetic and alone." He turned and yelled out. "Michael, do I have a girlfriend?"

There was a loud snort. "He's a pathetic, lonely dude, Mia. Not even a hookup in like a year or so."

He couldn't possibly be serious. "Why would you lie?"

One big shoulder shrugged. "Why did you kiss me when you had a fiancé?"

It was her turn to flush. He knew about that? "I broke up with him."

"But you kissed me. You let me think you were single. You put me in a position I can't stand."

His words hurt because they were so very true. She hadn't meant to fall for him, hadn't meant to do anything but investigate. "I'm sorry. I know that doesn't make it right, Case. But kissing you that night made me understand I couldn't marry Jeff. I didn't even argue it in my head. I knew I was going to end the engagement. I shouldn't have said yes to him in the first place."

Case took a step back and she felt the loss of his touch. "Let's just start again. Thank you for finding that picture. Would you please allow me and my team to escort you down? I haven't told my brothers. I'm trying to keep it as quiet as I can because you're right. Ian would take over and we could lose Tony Santos."

"You found out his last name?" That was fast.

"Hutch is very good. My team is very good. Let us work with you."

It was dangerous. This helpful Case was infinitely more dangerous than the jerk. This Case was looking at her like he could like her again. Like he could actually start over.

Was she pathetic as hell that she wanted to start over? No lies between them. But in the end, she had to take him along because it was his brother at stake.

"All right. Do you have everything you need? If Hutch is as good as he says, we should be able to take off soon."

He breathed an obvious sigh of relief. "I'm good to go, but we need to check with maintenance about the fuel. How many passengers did you count on?"

"You and me," she admitted. That had been the most foolish idea of all. "There's a pilot and copilot and one flight attendant."

"Well, now you have to accommodate two more. It should be an easy adjustment. I'll talk to the pilot."

"It's okay. Ezra can do it. And it's three more." She wasn't going to fire the man. He'd come all the way out here. And honestly, it might be good to have her own team. Case's men would do his bidding and only his bidding.

Case's lips turned down. "You don't need him. You have me."

That was where they would have to agree to disagree. The more she thought about it, the more she liked the idea of having her own guard. If she needed to go somewhere Case didn't approve of, she wouldn't have to sneak out alone. "You have your team. I have mine. Let's get going."

She slipped off his jacket and handed it to him before heading back inside the small, elegantly appointed terminal.

Case was hard on her heels. "Mia, you do understand that I'm in charge of this operation."

Yes, she knew he thought he was. "You can be in charge of your team and I'll deal with mine. Ezra, the McKay-Taggart team will be joining us. Could you inform the pilot for me? And ask the flight attendant to make sure there's a disgusting amount of candy only a five-year-old would eat on board."

"You rock, Mia." Hutch gave her a wink.

Ezra nodded. "Absolutely, boss. Anything you would like? Wine or a special dinner? We could go over what all you'll expect from me once we get to Colombia. I happen to know that jet has a private dining room."

"This isn't a date, asshole. This is a mission and one that doesn't need dead weight." Case looked over at Hutch. "Who the fuck is he?"

Hutch took the Red Vine out of his mouth. "Facial recognition tells me he's Ezra Fain. Super-douchey name for a former Marine. Did they give you hell? I would have. He also works for Ferland. Double douche. Were you the one who almost lost an eye?"

Now she was confused. "Why would he have lost an eye?"

"Because Ian Taggart can be a dick. Literally. I'll go and handle the pilot." Ezra stepped away.

She turned on Case. "You're looking into my bodyguard?"

"You don't need a bodyguard. You have me."

"No, you're here for different reasons. Ezra is only here to watch my back. You have your guys; I have my guy."

Case loomed over her. "Your guy is a mercenary douchebag."

"He's a former Marine who was a member of MARSOC." She'd gotten a dossier on his qualifications. She wasn't a complete moron. He'd been a part of a team formerly known as Force Recon. That made him a badass.

"Yes, but his boss is shady. Cut him loose. Pay him if you need to, but he shouldn't get on that plane." Case stepped in as though he could force her to do his will with the mere presence of that hot bod of his.

She was made of sterner stuff than that. Mostly. "He's staying, Case. I need someone who's here to watch my back and my back alone."

"I'll do that," he insisted.

"You need to concentrate on your mission. Or have you forgotten?" It was the one thing neither one of them could forget. Theo was at stake. Theo and Erin and their son. That family was at stake. She and Case had fucked up anything they might have had, but that didn't mean Erin and Theo couldn't be made whole again.

Case's eyes went stubborn. "I can do both. Originally it was going to be you and me."

"Now I see that was a mistake." It had been pure grade A optimism. She had that in spades. Her brothers called her naïve. She liked to think of it as choosing a better reality. Sometimes that reality didn't show up for her party. "We can start over, but I'm taking Mr. Fain with me. I'm not going to be a slave to your schedule. I'm well aware that you likely won't let me get a cup of coffee without a bodyguard. I want some freedom."

He frowned as though he hadn't thought of that scenario. "All right. When it comes down to meeting Tony…"

"I'll let you be the one who follows me." He was the one with the most to lose. She wasn't trying to cut him out. She simply wanted something of her own.

"You are not locking yourself in a private dining room with that asshole."

Was he actually jealous? She sighed. "Case, I'm not interested in him personally. He's not my type. He's far too personable, gentlemanly, and reasonable to be my type."

His lips curled up in the sexiest grin. "See it stays that way, darlin'. And I'm keeping an eye on Fain. Just because you insist on bringing that pretty boy Marine along doesn't mean I'm not still watching your back. I'm going to consider him your stubbornness personified. You're still my responsibility. Let's get you on the plane."

He picked up his bag and settled his jacket over her shoulders again. She found herself walking to the hangar with him, allowing him to open the door and then give her a hand up to the plane. The flight attendant was there in her crisp uniform, a smile on her face. Her eyes widened when she saw Case behind Mia.

The flight attendant was lovely, slender and graceful. Just the type to catch a cowboy's eye.

"Welcome aboard, Ms. Danvers." Her voice turned distinctly breathy. "And your friend."

Mia thought about vomiting, but then a hand slipped into hers.

"It's Taggart, Case Taggart, and I'm a very good friend of Ms. Danvers. But you should meet Ezra. I would bet he's just your type."

Hutch was walking up behind them. "I'm her type, too. Hi, I'm Hutch."

"Keep walking, buddy. We've got work to do," Michael said. "Keep it in your pants."

"But Big Tag changed the company motto to We *Don't* Keep It In Our Pants," Hutch complained.

Case's brother was as crazy as her own.

Case followed her as she moved into the body of the jet. When she took her seat, he sat down beside her. He pointed to the seat in front of them as though forming a phalanx around her with his own men. Case had herded her to the window seat. He'd taken the seat next to her and Hutch and Michael had boxed her in.

Clever Taggart.

No wonder he'd let Ezra go and talk to the front office. He'd managed to make it so she didn't sit with her own security guard.

"How long is this flight?" Case asked. He seemed perfectly satisfied with the outcome.

"A little over six hours," Michael said, leaning back in his seat.

Case held out a hand toward the flight attendant. "Could you please get Ms. Danvers a glass of Pinot Noir? The rest of us will have beers. Whatever you have is fine, but she prefers a Sonoma wine."

He remembered that?

"Of course. We have all of Ms. Danvers' favorites on board. I've had the kitchens send us extra meals. Your choice of filet mignon or a seafood paella."

She already knew his answer. "He's going to need both. You should pretend like you're feeding eight people instead of five."

"Except when it comes to dessert," Hutch pointed out. He sat back and seemed to be flirting hard with the flight attendant. "Then add in an extra man because I was denied cake. Don't worry though. I have a ridiculously high metabolism. Though I do like to work off all that sugar."

Michael rolled his eyes. "I'm surrounded by men who have no idea how to handle a woman."

"We'll definitely need some dessert." Maybe something chocolate and rich would take her mind off the forbidden fruit sitting beside her.

He'd said he wanted to start over. Was he being honest with her?

"Yes, ma'am. They'll have us stocked in the next twenty minutes and then we can take off." The lovely brunette who Case hadn't looked at with anything but professional courtesy strode to the kitchen area.

Ezra walked on the plane and glanced around, taking in the seating arrangements. "We'll be leaving in twenty minutes. I don't suppose I could convince you I need to sit with my employer."

Case was already leaning back, his whole body relaxed. His hand moved over hers possessively. "Not a chance."

Ezra sank into a seat across the aisle.

It was going to be an interesting flight.

* * * *

He had to take care of her. That was the key. He'd been right the first time around. Mia Danvers needed a Dom. She craved a man who she couldn't push around. So much of her life was about the people around her deferring to her every need and want that she deeply desired one who would challenge her and yet who also ensured she got what she needed.

Once he'd decided to take a real look at Mia that went past his butt hurt, he'd seen what he needed to do. He needed to move Mia into a D/s style relationship. Not for the long term, of course. That would never work since he wasn't exactly her type. But he needed to use her attraction to him to ensure her safety.

Getting her into bed would actually do them both good. For however long it lasted, she would be bound in some small way to him. She would be more inclined to turn to him for help and guidance. She might listen to him over that obvious lothario asshat she'd somehow managed to hire.

"Another drink, sir?" The flight attendant knelt beside his chair, her perky breasts on display. She'd hovered around him all night, seeming to show more interest in him than the others.

He'd made himself plain. He'd been polite. "No thank you."

Despite the fact that he'd ordered beers for his crew, he hadn't taken a sip of his. He needed all his faculties. He needed to talk to Mia, to do what he hadn't done before. He needed to gather all the intel he could on how she'd gotten that picture of his brother.

"You going to find her?" Michael asked, looking up from his laptop. "Because I for one would like a briefing on what she's doing and how we're providing support."

He was going to have to walk a fine line here. He'd promised Ian he wouldn't bring anyone into the Theo investigation. He hadn't been the one to bring Mia in. She'd found her own way in.

Which was another very good question he should have asked her.

He lost IQ points the moment she walked in a room. Hell, he could think about her and drop some.

"I'll do a briefing before we land," he promised. He needed to make sure Mia understood how sensitive this information was. "Of course, we'll have to wake up sleeping beauty."

Hutch had his seat back and was already lightly snoring and muttering something about trolls. That boy spent way too much time online.

Michael stared at him over his laptop. "Be careful and watch what the hell you say to her. Think before bad shit comes out of your mouth."

All the way to the airport his best friend had been preaching politeness. Case wasn't sure if Michael was trying to play matchmaker or save his balls from another thrashing. "I'm going to keep it professional."

Michael snorted. "There is nothing professional about this. We're basically running some weird op under the radar, and you know damn well Ian is going to be pissed. What are you planning on doing if we're gone for any length of time?"

"I already texted Ian. I told him Mia needed some backup on a story she was pursuing and that I didn't feel like it would be smart to not have a team with me. He said it was fine and that I should wear a condom, a real condom, and maybe two condoms. I'm pretty sure he was holding the new baby at the time. Ian's fine with it." Ian would kick his ass if he knew the truth, but Case had to make that call.

If Ian thought he was following Mia across the globe so he could get some, that was all right with him.

Because now that he was here, he really wanted to get some. Not some. Her. Only freaking her. Maybe once he'd had her, he could think straight again. Maybe he could put her behind him and move on with his life. He'd been stuck since the moment he'd met her.

"They should serve dinner soon," he said, glancing toward the back of the plane. Well, the hallway that led to the back of the plane. Maybe the middle. It was a big fucking private jet and it wasn't the largest in the Lawless fleet.

And he should remember that. This was Mia's world. Mia would marry some college-educated fuckwad who got along with her hyper-successful family. Whoever Mia married wouldn't get called into Andrew Lawless's office and asked how much cash it would take to get him to stay away.

Andrew Lawless was fucking lucky they needed him or Mia would have been down a brother that day.

She'd gotten up roughly twenty minutes into the flight, saying she needed to visit the ladies' room. She'd stretched and he'd watched the way her breasts moved and managed to bite back a groan because his dick still hurt. Oh, it worked and he would deal with the pain if he got the chance, but damn. Why wasn't she back? He couldn't let her avoid him.

He needed to talk to her before it got too late. "We'll do the debrief during dinner. I'll be back."

He eased out of the chair and turned toward the hall Mia had disappeared down.

"Taggart." Fain sat up, his hand gesturing for Case to move in closer.

Why had Mia insisted on bringing this ass along? He looked like a whiny-ass dude who would break into song about his feelings or maybe sit down and write poetry. He did not look like a Marine. "What do you need?"

"I don't like the flight attendant."

He didn't particularly like her either, but he wasn't sure what to do about it. "I think you can handle it for a few hours. Did she hit on you? Just send her over to Hutch. He's been horny lately."

Fain sat up, his voice going low. "I'm not talking about her being my type, asshole. Watch her. Something's wrong."

Case looked toward the front of the plane where the attendant was looking down at a tablet. "What's wrong with her?"

"I don't know, but I don't like it. I didn't like the pilot either."

So he was one of those insanely paranoid assholes who'd seen way too much action during his service and now thought everything was a bomb waiting to explode. Still, he could use the guy's paranoia. Maybe if Case gave him a job to do, he would stop trying to get close to Mia. "Then I think that should be your job. Watch the stewardess and make sure she doesn't spit in our coffee or anything."

"I'm not eating anything she puts in front of me."

Like the jerk or not, if he'd been Force Recon, he had to consider that Fain knew something. He wasn't going to let his distaste for Fain's boss blind him. "You honestly think something's wrong?"

Fain's jaw went tight. "I do. I feel it in my bones. She's not used to wearing heels. You can see it in how tight her eyes get when she's forced to walk. She kicks them off the minute she can. From what I can see there's nothing wrong with her feet, so I have to conclude she's not used to wearing heels. Also her makeup's off."

He had noticed that. "Her eyeliner's screwed up."

"When was the last time you met a professional flight attendant to a billionaire who didn't look absolutely perfect?"

He'd ridden the 4L jet before, though it had been one of the larger ones. The attendant had been flawless. Flight attendants on regular people planes—both men and women—took extreme care with their appearance. Whether or not they happened to be beautiful, they always looked professional. And they would know damn well not to wear heels on a six-hour flight if they couldn't handle them.

But what the hell did that prove?

She looked up from her tablet and smiled his way. It didn't reach her eyes. He hadn't studied her closely before. Now he could see how chilly she was despite the smile and saying all the right things.

"I'm going to go and talk to Mia," Case explained, keeping his voice down. "I'll keep eyes on her. You slap Hutch awake and see if he can get an Internet connection. There has to be a satellite connection on this sucker. He's got facial recognition on his phone. Maybe it can pull something up. And talk to Michael. He's a former SEAL. He knows what he's doing."

Fain nodded. "Will do. I don't particularly like the fact that we're with the sister of a billionaire going into a country where it would be easy to hold her for ransom. Lots of jungle in Colombia to get lost in."

And cartels who made money on the side in just such a fashion. Kidnapping had decreased in Colombia and the country was considered safe, especially in the tourist towns. Thousands of Americans flocked to its beaches and cultural centers every year. But thousands of Americans weren't Mia Lawless Danvers. She was a ripe target. The truth was he would be concerned with her anywhere she went.

Case stood up, sending Michael a look as Fain moved to join him.

Likely there was no trouble. Mia had booked the flight at the last minute. It was entirely possible their slightly unkempt flight attendant simply hadn't been prepared, but he couldn't leave that to chance.

He eased down the hall. To his left was the private dining room that Fain absolutely wouldn't be sharing with Mia tonight. No fucking way. He might be willing to work with the dude, but he could only be pushed so far. To his right looked like a private office. That might be where Hutch ended up. He might cry a little at the thought of sitting at Drew Lawless's desk.

This place probably made Air Force One look clunky.

Maybe he should have taken a couple of million off that jerk. It wasn't like he would miss it. Not at all. Mia's brother could write a check for ten million and never notice it was gone.

How much, Mr. Taggart? Don't get me wrong. I like your brother. I like you, but you're obviously wrong for my sister. How much to get you to leave her be?

I haven't touched her.

But you will. I can see the chemistry between you quite clearly. Do you honestly believe she belongs in your world? Take the money. If anyone asks it's a bonus for doing your job and doing it well. But we'll know what it's really about. Name your price.

Humiliation burned in his gut. He could still remember how he'd felt when he'd gotten up from the chair and calmly explained to Lawless that there wasn't enough money in the world to buy him off. He could hear Lawless calling out and trying to stop him.

He'd sent the man his happy middle finger and walked out.

Drew had sent him several e-mails and tried to call, but Case was done. He deleted the e-mails without reading them and consigned the calls to voice mail hell.

It had been six weeks since Lawless made his play. Case didn't get why he'd done it. Seven months had passed and he'd worked off and on with 4L trying to get a better layout of the mysterious group known as The Collective. He'd pretty much left Mia completely alone. Oh, he'd seen her in a couple of meetings and they'd had a single, fairly heated argument over what had happened between them.

So why had Lawless made that play?

He stopped in front of the last door and the question slipped out of his head. Mia was standing in the middle of what looked to be a bedroom. There was a mirror on the wall and she held a dress up, looking at herself in the glass as though considering every angle.

So damn pretty. Why did she have to be so pretty?

"It's a nice dress. Are we getting fancy for dinner? I have to warn you I only brought a couple of pairs of jeans and some T-shirts. I'll have to suit up somewhere if I need anything but casual."

He watched as she flushed. She shook her head and then opened a drawer, putting the dress back in.

Now that he got a better look at it, the material was filmy, with swaths of lace decorating it. Was that lingerie?

"Sorry. I came here to see if something I'd left behind was still here. It was." She shut the drawer and turned back to him. "I promise everything's casual. I mean to keep a low profile. The real problem is I didn't book enough hotel rooms. I'll have to see if we can find a couple more when we get there."

"I'm staying with you." He needed to make that clear right here and now. "You might shove me on a couch, but I was never going to have a separate room."

Too much could happen if he left her there alone. And way too little could happen if he wasn't there. Now that he'd made the decision to go with her, it seemed fairly inevitable that chemistry and close proximity would work their magic.

And her brother could bite his ass.

She shook her head. "I don't think that's a good idea."

"Then don't think about it at all." He stepped into the small but elegantly appointed bedroom, the rest of the world seeming to fade away. "Let me take care of that part. You know I won't let anything bad happen to you."

She was silent for a moment, those big blue eyes staring straight through him. "I know you won't hurt me physically."

"I don't want to hurt you at all, Mia. Look, I got angry because you lied to me. I lied to you. In the end we were both doing it for the greater good. Let's get past that."

She leaned against the dresser. "I already have. I know why you did it. I actually should thank you. You didn't take advantage of me. It would have been easy for you to. When I really think about it, you were a gentleman."

He didn't want to be a gentleman around her. He wanted more than the polite iciness they'd settled into. "I did kiss you."

"I kissed you back," she replied a little wistfully. "I know you won't believe me, but I meant that kiss. I didn't walk into Sanctum expecting to find a lover."

"I would hope not. You were engaged." It still bothered him. It still made him feel dirty.

"Yes." Her arms crossed over her chest as though she needed

protection. "Is that what the real problem is? You can't trust me again because I kissed a man while I was engaged to someone else?"

He'd thought through the scenario about a thousand times since he'd opened that folder Ian had given him and learned the truth about her. How far would she have taken it? He'd been so lost that evening. Spending time with her had made him feel good. By the time he'd brought her up to the rooftop, he'd practically forgotten his troubles. And that was when the guilt had set in. That was when he'd known damn well he wasn't going to sleep with her because his brother was dead and he shouldn't be thinking about a woman. Then she'd brought him such peace. Sitting with her, talking about Theo with her had felt so right. For the first time since Theo's death, he'd thought he might be able to deal with it. Then everything had changed.

"Tell me something, Mia. If I'd pushed, would you have slept with me that night?"

She shook her head. "No. I wouldn't have. Later, maybe, but not that night. I started to trust you specifically because you didn't push me. You seemed to want more from me than sex and then you didn't want me physically at all."

"I wasn't going to sleep with you when I knew you were lying to me and I was lying to you." It was the moment he'd known he would always be a soldier and never an operative. He could make hard decisions, but he couldn't give away that piece of himself.

Her skin flushed the prettiest pink. "Yeah, well, I probably would have. It's a good thing you saved us from that. And I never said it to you, but I'm glad it wasn't Jared. I know that would have hurt Kai. I actually came to like Jared. I was happy to be wrong."

He'd known she would have gone to bed with him. She'd been deeply frustrated by how unphysical he'd been with her. He'd had to turn his head a time or two to keep her from kissing him.

Not touching her had been hell.

"The good news is now everything is out in the open." It was awkward standing here with her. At one point in time he'd felt so comfortable talking to her. He hadn't known her then. There hadn't been a mile-high wall between them. He hadn't realized how far apart their worlds were back then. He'd thought she was a sweet woman who worked in a dentist office. He'd had something to offer that woman.

What the hell could he give Mia Lawless except a couple of orgasms?

There was one other thing he could give her.

"Are you ever coming back to Sanctum?"

Her eyes flared briefly at the mention of Sanctum, but then she shut down again. "I wasn't sure I could."

Ah, yes, she was still invested in the lifestyle. "Ian didn't revoke your membership. I asked him not to. Kori and Sarah made a plea for you, too. Actually, they made him cookies. My brother can be bribed."

"Somehow I can't see Ian Taggart being happy with me in his club. I lied to him, too."

"You would be surprised at how reasonable Ian can be when he wants to. You should come back." Another thought hit him. A nasty one. "Unless you joined a club in Austin."

"No, Case. I haven't been out trolling for strange Doms," she said with a sigh. "I've been working with my brothers. They have their own insane plans, you know."

He knew they were investigating a couple of people. Adam and Alex had been working on it. Case had stayed away. He wasn't sure why the Lawless brothers wanted to take down StratCast Industries or why they seemed to have a hard-on for Patricia Cain, who wrote cookbooks and shit. If they wanted to take down the ice queen, who had a whole network dedicated to her telling the rest of America how shitty their taste was in everything from food to throw pillows, more power to them.

"Well, you're welcome to come back. I know Kori and Sarah miss you. Erin's talked about you, too. She likes any woman who'll threaten to shoot her. Once she hears how you dealt with my rudeness, she'll want to be your best friend." His sister-in-law understood the need for a violent reminder every now and then. "You should see your friends. You know, I never asked you about her. About the friend you lost."

It had been the whole reason for her lie and he'd never asked her about it. They'd been far too busy bickering over inconsequential things or ignoring each other.

"Her name was Carrie. We were roommates in college. She was very excited to be working on her first set." Mia looked wistful, her eyes misting. "She was my first friend in college. We kind of clung together. She was from a small town and I, well, I had an odd upbringing. We kind of clicked. We roomed together until she moved to Vancouver for the show. I miss her."

"I'm sorry, darlin'. I really am."

She gave him a wan smile. "You know what it means to miss someone. I'm sorry about everything, Case. I thought I was doing the right thing. I didn't mean to hurt you."

He moved in, taking the opportunity she was giving him. They should have done this a long time ago. "And I'm sorry I made you think I didn't want you. I did. Walking away from you every night was hard as hell. I still want you, Mia."

She looked up at him. "I don't think it's a good idea."

"Tell me why you looked for Theo." He should be asking her how she'd found Theo. He knew that, but he couldn't do it. They would be together for days. He could find that out later. Right now, he needed to find out if she wanted him, too.

"You know why."

He did. It was the same reason he hadn't played with a single sub since the day he'd met her. No play. No sex. No anything because no one was Mia and it seemed like she was the only woman in the damn world who could do it for him. "Because we have chemistry. Because nothing ever felt like kissing me. No sex. No intimacy. None of it ever worked the way it did with me."

"God, you're an arrogant man."

He wasn't. It was all a front. "I'm not being arrogant. I know how you feel because I felt it, too. Why the hell do you think I lied about having a girlfriend? I haven't touched anyone since the day I met you."

Her eyes flared, her mouth dropping a bit. It was good to know he could shock her. "What are you trying to say, Case?"

He finally did what came naturally. He touched her, sliding his palm up her neck to cup her cheek. That was what he'd been missing. Connection. Warmth. "I think we're going to be together for a few days. I'm tired of not knowing."

He wanted to know what it felt like to cover her body with his, to have her spread and waiting and offering herself to him. To know how it felt to slide inside all that warmth. To be surrounded with her.

It wouldn't last. It would only be for a few days, but for those days he would know what it meant to take care of her.

She frowned, but he felt her lean into his hand as though she needed the contact, too. "I don't know."

"You don't want to know what a real D/s connection is like?" He was going to hit her where he suspected she was weakest. She hadn't gotten to play. She'd taken the class, gotten a tiny taste, and she would need a full meal.

God knew he did. He could make a fucking buffet of her.

"It would only be for play, Case."

His dick jumped in his jeans. "Only for play and out in the field." That gorgeous mouth started to open and he was sure she was about to spew some serious bile his way. He put a finger over her lips. "No. This is where we went wrong in the first place. We should have sat down and banged out a contract. We should have taken this seriously."

Now that he thought about it, did it only have to be a few days? Why? If they were upfront about what they needed, there was no reason the contract couldn't be open ended. Why put an end date on it? She would be back in Austin. He would be working in Dallas. They could get together for sex and play. He would know the boundaries. She would know what he was willing to give her.

It might actually work.

His blood started to thrum through his system. He could have her. He could play with her.

"I'm not incompetent, Case." Her face tilted up, her body moving closer to his. Her words might be defiant, but her body wasn't. She was softening, her lips opening slightly. "I can handle myself. I know how to use a gun."

An armed Mia was kind of one of his worst nightmares. He let his free hand stray down to her waist, enjoying the feel of her curves. "You're a reporter, not a soldier. I've agreed to stand back and let you work. I've agreed to let you bring along Fain. Give me something here. I'm in charge of this operation."

She sighed, a sexy sound. "I don't want you to cut me out. I can't stand being treated like I'm made of glass."

She was so obviously made of warmth and sex. He lowered his head, lips hovering over her mouth. He'd waited so damn long. "I won't cut you out. I promise. But I need to know you'll obey me if things get dangerous."

"It won't," she promised, her hands moving to his waist.

He wanted those hands all over his body. "But if it does…"

Her lips were so close. "I'll follow your orders. You're in charge if things get dangerous."

That wasn't good enough. "And here, Mia. I'm in charge when we play. You're the sweet sub and I'm the dirty Dom who's going to demand absolutely everything you have to give me. Tell me yes. Tell me we can play."

"Yes, Case. Yes."

He covered her mouth with his, devouring her like a starving man. He couldn't be gentle. He needed her far too much.

Her arms wound around him and she held on, pressing her body to his. Her breasts flattened against his chest.

This was what he'd wanted that first night, the first moment he'd seen her. He'd wanted her soft and submissive. She'd called to that dominant piece of him he hadn't known existed. Before Mia had walked into his life, he'd enjoyed the lifestyle, but he hadn't truly understood it. He hadn't known what it meant to need to dominate a woman—not for mere sexual purposes or to feed his own ego. He needed to dominate her because she ruled his every thought, because he needed to be important to this one woman.

No. Case forced himself to stop. He pulled away from the drugging kisses she was giving him. He couldn't go down that path. If he was going to take her, it would be on his terms, and that meant he wasn't going to play the idiot. He wasn't going to ask for more than she could give him. He wasn't going to pretend this was some grand love. She wasn't Charlotte and he wasn't Ian. They didn't get that forever thing.

But they could have this.

"What's wrong?" She looked up at him and then started to pull away.

He wasn't going to let that happen. He turned her around so his front nestled her back. "Nothing's wrong. I want to feel you. Do you have any idea how long I've waited to touch you, Mia? How often I've thought about this?" His hands were on her waist and he brought them up slowly. "I want to memorize every inch of your skin, and do you know how I'm going to do it?"

She leaned back into him. "You're going to touch me."

He loved how breathless she was. No other woman ever responded as honestly to him as she did. He could trust her body even if he didn't trust the rest of her. Oh, she wouldn't mean to hurt him. He actually believed that, but she would choose her world. She would choose her family over him. He could keep her for a little while.

"What am I going to touch you with, princess?" He moved slowly, letting his hands find the warm skin under her shirt.

"Your hands." Her head fell back against his chest. Without heels on she didn't quite reach his shoulders. "I want your hands everywhere, Case. They feel so good."

"I will touch you everywhere, but that's not all I'll do." He was right under her breasts. This was one of the things D/s had taught him. Sex required discipline. Patience. Control. He wanted to shove her on that bed and force his dick inside her, but that wouldn't make it good for her. This methodical arousal of every inch of her body would make her ready for him, would make her scream for him.

Might make her stay with him for a while.

He flattened one palm on the curve of her belly, the other touching the band of her bra. There was zero reason to hide how hard he was. He let his cock rub against her backside. "I'm going to put my hands on you. I'll touch your breasts and cup that hot ass of yours and I will let my fingers explore how hot and wet your pussy gets for me."

"You're killing me, Case." She squirmed a little, as though trying to get him to move.

He held her tight, his mouth against her ear. "Don't. We haven't talked about punishments so I'm not going to stop and spank that sweet ass, but now you've been warned. This is my time. It's my time to explore your body and get you hot. I'll give you time later, but for now you'll let me enjoy how you feel under my hands."

"D/s sucks," she said with a shaky laugh.

He ran the tip of his tongue along her ear, enjoying the way she shivered. "No, it doesn't. It makes us take things slow and get to know each other's bodies and responses. It makes us thoughtful lovers. I want to be your lover. Do you understand what I mean by that? I don't want to be your boyfriend. I want to be your Dom. It's different. A boyfriend can take you or leave you. A Dom is responsible for you. It means something deeper to me."

"I've had boyfriends and not one of them made me feel the way you do," she admitted. "Please don't stop. I've waited so long for this."

He could smell her shampoo and the soap she used. He leaned down and ran his nose along the graceful column of her throat. "When I'm done touching you, I'm going to taste you." He ran his tongue from her collarbone back up to her ear. "I'm going to lick you and we'll see how you like a little bite."

He nipped at her ear, just a nice sharp bite that made her jump in his arms. She groaned, but it wasn't one that told him she was in pain.

"I think I like it, Case," she replied, her breath shaky. "The training course alone taught me that."

He growled. "I don't like the thought of someone else training you."

Her body shook with a husky chuckle. "Javier and I were just friends. Promise. I liked the flogger he owned more than him. I liked the sting. I thought I could maybe survive a thud, but I got so hot when he hit me with the stinger. I wasn't thinking about him though. I always thought of you. It was never him holding that son of a bitch and making me beg for more."

Fuck, she could talk dirty, too, and that did something for him. "I didn't bring a flogger with me. I should have been more optimistic, but I think you'll find I can still take care of you. I'll find all kinds of things to torture you with. But first I'm going to touch everything that just became mine."

He moved both hands up to cup her breasts. They filled his palms. Mia was nice and curvy, built for sex, built to take him.

All the reasons he shouldn't have her floated away on a haze of lust. There was zero reason to wait. Beginning the relationship with Mia would do nothing but make it easier on them both when they got to Colombia. And there was that handy bed right there. All he had to do was take two steps and he could toss her down, rip off her clothes and ease them both.

Mia turned her head and he managed to catch her mouth with his. She opened immediately, inviting his tongue to glide along hers. He slipped his hands under her bra and finally felt soft skin. Her nipples were tight.

He wanted to taste them, needed them in his mouth.

He turned her around and picked her up with ease, setting her on the dresser. Luckily the elegant fucker looked like it was bolted down because it didn't move at all. "Take off your shirt."

She was panting, but her eyes shifted to the door. "Case, we're not alone."

He closed the door and turned the lock. "We're alone and don't you tell me they might hear you. I don't care if they hear you. I don't care if they know exactly what we're doing. They don't matter. This is between you and me and I'll fuck you anywhere you'll allow me to. You should probably understand that right now."

He half expected her to argue with him. Instead, she licked her lips, her eyes going hot, and she pulled the shirt over her head, tossing it aside.

"If you'd read my Sanctum contract, you would know I might be a bit of an exhibitionist, Case. You can be a little stuffy at times. I didn't want to shock you. If you want to open that door and give anyone who walks by a show, you feel free." She unhooked her bra and tossed it aside as well.

He cursed under his breath. She was going to kill him. He was going to have an actual, honest-to-god heart attack because she was a sexy, demanding goddess. "Oh, princess, one day I'll fuck you in front of everyone and I won't have a single problem with it. I'll clamp those pretty tits and parade you all around Sanctum. And that Fain motherfucker will not be invited."

"See." She was sitting there, her breasts on display, and there was absolutely no shyness about her. She was a woman who knew what she wanted and he was so fucking happy that she wanted him. "A little stuffy."

He'd always thought she would be a super brat, so freaking sassy it would make him insane. He was going to spank her hard one of these days. Not today. Today he moved between her legs, spreading them wide. The dresser put her at exactly the right height for what he wanted to do. "I'll show you how stuffy I can be."

He pushed and pulled until she was leaning back, offering up her generous breasts. The pink and brown nipples were tight, but she had good-sized areolas. He licked at one as her legs wound around him. He could have told her he wasn't going anywhere, but he liked having her holding him tight.

Such pretty breasts and while he was topping her they were all fucking his. He sucked a nipple into his mouth and was rewarded with a long moan as her body bowed. The way he'd placed her on the dresser forced her to balance herself with both hands, leaving him free to play with her any way he pleased.

He sucked on one nipple while he played with the other, rolling the little bud between his thumb and forefinger. He tweaked it hard at exactly the same moment he gave her a nip.

"Case. Oh, god, Case." His name came out of her mouth on a little squeal. "More. Please give me more."

He would give her everything, but he didn't intend to give in to her every demand. He was going to take his time. He was going to enjoy every second he had with her. When they got back home, their play sessions would likely be few and far between. A weekend here. A spare afternoon there. He had a few days to be her full-time Dom. And yes, he fully intended to take charge everywhere he could despite what he'd told her. The whole damn operation would be dangerous and he wasn't going to let her get hurt.

He would just have to be sneaky about it.

He switched places, laving his affection on the other nipple while his spare hand started to work its way down. He was going to make her come. A nice starter orgasm that would make her limp and submissive and willing to give him fucking everything.

"Do you have any idea what I'm about to do to you?" He brought his head up, staring into her eyes. Her desire was right there, arousal making her pupils dilate. She wasn't hiding anything from him now. She was completely honest with him when they were physical.

"Tell me, you dirty boy." She shifted her hips, helping him to slide his hand into her jeans.

He loved a challenge and Mia was all alpha female, come-and-take-it, big boy challenge. "I'm going to rub that little clit of yours until you come all over my hand, and then when you're limp and satisfied and you think you've had everything you want, I'm going to strip you down, throw you on that bed, and make a meal of you."

His fingers slipped under the waistband of the panties he was going to rip off her body soon enough, and there it was. He slid the pad of his middle finger over her clitoris, watching as she gasped and bit her bottom lip. He circled the button of her clit, watching her every reaction.

"I'm going to eat your pussy like no one's eaten it before. All that arousal you're putting out right now, that's going to be my dinner. All your sweetness, I'm going to lap it up. I'll lick you everywhere, spread you wide so I don't miss a drop, and then do you know what I'll do?"

She flushed the prettiest shade of pink that had nothing to do with embarrassment and everything to do with how close to the edge she was. He could feel it. She'd started to move in time with his finger, begging him for more. Her female flesh was soaked with arousal. It coated his fingers and made it easy to work her clit. "Please tell me, Case."

Dirty talk seemed to do it for her. It was good because he'd thought the dirtiest, filthiest things about her. He dreamed of doing everything to her, of bringing her pleasure in every way a man could bring to a woman.

He leaned in, sensing how close she was to the edge. He was about to push her over. "Then, when I've licked every inch of that sweet pussy, that's when I'm going to shove my tongue up your cunt and get some more because I won't ever want to stop. I'll fuck you with my tongue until I make you come all over again. You want to ride my tongue, Mia?"

He pressed down and rotated.

"Yes," she started to shout.

He covered her mouth, drinking down the sounds of her orgasm as he let her ride it out. She brought her arms up, obviously no longer caring whether or not she fell. Or she simply trusted him. He wrapped his free arm around her, trapping her against him.

He kissed her as she came down, their tongues playing more

softly now. When he withdrew his hand, she tightened her arms around him.

"Don't go," she whispered against his lips. "I want everything you promised me, cowboy."

He wasn't going anywhere. He liked post-orgasm Mia. "I never go back on my word. Time to get you out of those jeans."

He hauled her up, her legs around his waist. As he turned to toss her on the big bed, he thanked the universe that Drew Lawless was either a complete pervert who like to fuck at thirty thousand feet or a man who simply preferred comfort and could afford it. Either way, that bed was about to come in handy.

And Lawless could fuck himself. No amount of money would keep him from getting inside Mia tonight.

He shifted, her mouth on his. The girl liked to kiss. Just as he was letting her drop, the world tilted and Case found himself falling, Mia untangling from around him. He kept his arms around her, trying to hold her close.

They hit the floor, shifting so he took the brunt of the fall. "What the hell?"

Mia looked up, her eyes wide. "The plane. It's out of control."

And that was how his night went straight to hell.

CHAPTER THREE

Mia held on to Case and the world seemed to upend and go completely out of control. His arms wound around her and the plane rolled to the right.

They slammed against the wall, Case taking the impact as the plane made another dip that sent her stomach churning.

Case wrapped himself around her, one hand coming up to cradle her neck, forcing her head against his chest. The other arm protected her back. Even his legs wound around hers as though he could form a protective barrier between her and all harm.

She went limp, not offering any resistance. This was one of those times when the big bad Dom was in charge. Any resistance would put him in danger, too. If he was fighting her, he couldn't protect himself.

The plane leveled out, the world steadying as quickly as it had upended.

Her heart was pounding. What the hell kind of weather had they just hit? She'd been through some turbulence before, but that had been crazy.

"I'm going to need you to get dressed and quickly." He kissed the top of her head, but she could feel how tense he'd gotten.

She nodded and scrambled off him, reaching for her shirt. No time for the bra, though she hated being without one. They needed to get out in the main cabin and buckle in. Apparently they were in the middle of some kind of storm. She wasn't going to waste time because her boobs might jiggle.

She did glance back at the bed though. That would have been a storm of another kind. A freaking hurricane. Hurricane Case, with strong winds and an orgasmic tidal wave. Damn, but that man rocked her world.

And now they had a shot.

Case was up on his feet. He'd gone from dirty bad boy to soldier in a heartbeat. "I don't suppose there's anywhere in here you could hide."

Hide? "Why would I hide? It's just turbulence. We need to buckle in. It feels fine right now, but the winds could pick up any second. Let's go."

He moved in front of the door, his voice a low growl. "That wasn't turbulence. The plane has been perfectly level the whole time. And I know a well-executed maneuver when I feel one. He tossed us from side to side and then up and down to throw us off. I'm betting he expected he would only have to deal with one man, but he got four. He waited until we were all up and moving and this is how he gets the upper hand. He'll have the other guys guarded by now. If he hasn't managed to take them out."

"Who is this 'he' you're talking about?" Case sounded paranoid. Why would the pilot purposefully try to throw everyone off? The answer hit her with the force of a two-by-four. "Shit."

Case's lips curved up in an arrogant smirk. "Yes, princess, this is a kidnapping and you're the star of the show. And I left my fucking gun in my bag."

Her brothers were going to kill her. They would lock her up somewhere. "Maybe you're wrong and the pilot's just drunk or something."

It was kind of a horrible thing to wish for. That's what

happened when you suddenly hit rock bottom.

Case opened his mouth but that was when someone knocked on the door.

"Mr. Taggart, I believe you'll find my people have your people taken care of. If you want them to live for more than the next ten minutes, you'll hand over the prize," a masculine voice said.

Prize? Oh, she would show them what a prize was. It looked like she wasn't finished busting balls this evening.

Before she could open her mouth to give the asshole behind the door a piece of her mind, Case was behind her, covering her mouth with his big hand. He held her tight, his mouth to her ear. Only a few minutes before he'd held her like this in the sexiest way.

She was so perverted because she still thought it was kind of sexy.

"Don't you fucking dare spit bile his way," he whispered in her ear. "If he's not lying then Michael and Hutch are in trouble. And if I find out Fain is in on this, I'll feed that fucker his own dick. I need you to open that door and explain that you have no idea where I am. I showed up. You got pissed. I left. Do you understand me? When he comes in here to find me, let him. Nod your head if you understand."

He was obviously about to do some hot commando stuff. She was a complete freak, but it did something for her. Her heart was pounding in her chest, but she was also still kind of aroused. Being near him even in the midst of danger got her hot.

He was holding her pretty tight so nodding would be hard. It was okay. She had another way. She licked him.

"Don't you fucking die. And I'll spank you for that later." He moved away from her, his hand peeling back, and she watched as he disappeared into the bathroom.

Her brother had purchased the plane from some crazy king of a small island nation off the coast of India. The whole thing was designed to spend a nice evening with a lady. Or four. She'd heard some crazy stories about Kash Kamdar. She'd been looking forward to bringing an entirely new chapter of perversion to this particular room but some butthead had to try to kidnap her.

Now she had to find a way to give Case the chance to take him out.

Her optimism took over. She was generally a glass is half full and tastes really good kind of girl. She liked to look on the bright side of things. This dude was fucking up her calm. Mia strode to the door and slammed it open. "What?"

The copilot was standing there, a big old gun in his hand, but she glared at him. He stared behind her, obviously looking for the real threat.

Oh, she would show that motherfucker a threat.

"Where's Taggart?" He gave a good impression of a hardened criminal.

She still wasn't buying it. He was a jerkwad ass face who'd cost her a nice night. She was going to start carrying. Life would be easier if she could shove her Ruger in his face. Or his crotch. Guys seemed to react more correctly to that particular placement. "How the hell should I know?"

Case was wrong about how to deal with him. He'd told her not to spit bile his way, but a little defiance went a long way. Confidence was the key. Did this blowhole think she'd never been in a shitty position before? She was a blonde fucking reporter who'd been to some crazy parts of the world. No one took her seriously. She'd stared down terrorists and Hollywood assholes who thought she was fat. Once she'd had to talk her way out of a biker bar that housed a notorious drug lord. That hadn't been easy. She could handle this asshole.

And if Ezra was a part of this, Case would have to fight her for the right to cut off his junk.

The copilot was a lanky dude, but he knew how to hold a gun. It was pointing right at her face, but she wasn't about to shrink from that shit. The minute she did, she gave him more power.

"He walked back this way." The copilot, whose name she

didn't remember because he was a fucking numbnut, strode into the bedroom, his gun out.

Play it cool. Don't give him anything. Mia crossed her arms over her chest because he didn't deserve to see her un-bra'd breasts. "He came in, tried to get in my panties, and I sent his ass out."

Such a lie. He'd gotten his deeply talented hands way down her undies and he'd been a motherfucking revelation. Case Taggart was amazing. He knew exactly how to touch her, and his mouth was so filthy she could barely stand it. Dirty. He was a damn dirty Dom and she was already half in love with that man. This douchebag wasn't going to murder him before she'd managed to get that cowboy in bed.

"Sure, he did." The copilot glanced around the room. "Why is your bra on the floor?"

"Because it's late and I never leave the poor girls pent up. Tell me something, have you ever worn an underwire?"

"Get your back up against the wall." His voice was a little shaky, like this assignment hadn't gone as planned.

It hadn't, she suddenly understood. This particular assignment had begun the minute she'd requested the jet. It had been over a year since she'd asked for one by herself. She'd been holed up in Austin or gone out with a large group of 4L workers for the last year. Since Case. She'd been mooning over that man and hadn't followed her habit of traveling at every given opportunity. She'd taken some assignments close to home and worked on a book she was writing about a local murder. She'd gone out of the country exactly once and she was a girl who filled her passport quickly. She hadn't been herself at all. Had they been waiting all this time to try to take her? Were they looking for a quick buck? Or on assignment for The Collective and trying to find a way to force her brother into working for them?

Mia moved, bracing herself against the wall. The people at stake belonged to Case and she was going to trust in that smartass, competent cowboy to get them out of this situation.

Unless she found a way out first, of course.

"What's back there?" The man frowned at the partially opened door.

"The bathroom." And Case, who hopefully had found a weapon. The pickings would be slim. He could splat the guy with toothpaste or maybe hit him with some shaving cream. She was fairly certain Drew kept a razor in there, but it would be small.

"Don't you move. If you run, I'll have to come after you. We're trying to keep you in decent shape, but I think our boss would understand a few bruises. After all, he'll likely let us sample the goods while we're waiting for your brother's answer."

Yep, because she'd never been threatened with that before. It was a universal truth that men with small egos always threatened a woman like that. She flipped him off. "We'll see who gets bruised if you try to touch me, asshole. Ask Taggart what happens to men who treat me wrong. He's somewhere hiding and holding his balls and crying like a little boy."

The man turned on her, his face flushing a florid red. "I won't be so easy as Taggart, bitch. You might think you're some almighty rich girl, but after I'm done with you, you'll know your fucking place."

He waved that gun in her face. It was all very threatening and scary, but she saw what he didn't. While Criminal Asshole was busy trying to intimidate her, Case was stalking him. He slipped out of the bathroom and she caught the faintest glimpse of metal in his hand.

It wasn't a gun, so their erstwhile horny criminal still had the advantage. All Case had was surprise. She had to keep that for him.

Sometimes it all came down to giving a guy what he wanted. She let her arms drop, her body quiver the slightest bit. When she spoke, she put a little tremor in her voice. He wanted her scared? She could give him that. "My brothers won't ever stop looking for me."

His lips curled up as though her fear excited him. "Don't

worry, sweetheart. When I'm done with you and the boss is satisfied, you can go home to your brothers." He lowered the gun and moved in close, like a predator scenting easy prey. "But you'll be with us for a while. I can make that easy on you. Or it can go hard. Do you understand what I mean? I'm not going to let you send me off the way you did that pussy Taggart."

Case was moving in, his big body more silent than any man that size should be.

Mia winced as her captor's hand cupped her breast.

And then she bit back a scream because Case buried one of her nicer nail files in the jerk's jugular. She closed her eyes because it got messy fast.

Mia shuddered as the body slipped away from her, heard the sound of a thud as it hit the floor.

"Mia?" Case's voice was a mere whisper. "Baby, you can open your eyes. It's okay. He's dead. Actually, maybe you shouldn't open your eyes. Give me your hand and I'll get you out of here and I'll stash you someplace safe. I'm so sorry. I couldn't find anything else and I couldn't risk the gun going off if I'd fought him for it. You're going to be all right. I'm so sorry you had to see that. Don't be afraid of me. Please."

She opened her eyes because he was treating her like a girl who'd never witnessed a little violence before. Was this why he'd held her off? He hadn't thought she could handle his world? She stared at him for a moment before wiping the blood off her cheek. "Next time strangle the motherfucker. You got blood everywhere. Do you know how hard it is to get a steam cleaner in here? And this was my favorite shirt and now it's got gross stuff all over it."

His eyes flared and then he smiled. "I'll pay the dry cleaning bill. You're really all right?"

She nodded and noted he'd already picked up the guy's gun. "I'm fine. You did what you had to do, but I will get in trouble for getting blood on the carpet. Drew takes this plane seriously. He doesn't have another gun on him, does he?"

"No." Case took her hand. "And I'm not giving you this one.

Try to remember that we're flying through the air in a pressurized tube and putting holes in our tube would be bad."

Having his hand in hers gave her such strength. "Tell that to the bad guys. Do you think they'll hurt Hutch and Michael?"

It was a stupid question. Of course they would.

He squeezed her hand. "I'm going to do everything I can to stop it. You're going to hide."

He was back to that plan. She didn't want to split up. The idea that he wouldn't have anyone to watch his back didn't sit well. "I can help you. I know this plane way better than you do."

"Then you'll know where to hide." He stopped in front of the door and looked back at her, his eyes hard. "I'm not kidding, Mia. You're going to stay where I put you. I have to do some seriously dirty work to get us all out of this and I can't do it while I'm worried about you. You agreed to obey me. We might not have a written contract in place, but there's a verbal one and I expect you to abide by it or there will be harsh punishment. Am I understood?"

"You can't expect me to hide while you're in danger."

"I don't merely expect it. If I think I won't get it, I'll tie you up myself and stash you."

Arrogant ass. "Fine. There's a closet in my brother's office built for just such a scenario. Apparently the last owner was very safety conscious. I'll cower in there while you get horribly murdered."

His expression didn't change at all. "Excellent. You'll forgive me if I tuck you in myself."

He didn't trust her at all. "I can find my way."

His hand clutched hers. "Not on your life. The office is the one across the hall from here?"

She nodded. If she really looked at it, maybe this wasn't about trusting her so much as he was worried about her. That was a much better way to look at it. Even in the midst of serious chaos, she preferred to look on the bright side. Sure she was covered in some dude's blood and Case was being an unreasonable asshole, but he was likely one of those guys who didn't handle pressure well. Women were infinitely more suited to handle stress than men. She had to encourage him. If he thought he worked better without her, there wasn't exactly a ton of time to argue her point.

But they would have a serious discussion about it later.

"Mia?"

She rolled her eyes and then sighed. "I'll hide."

"Come on. You stay behind me."

She didn't point out that the hall went both ways so there was a fifty-fifty chance that he would be behind her from the would-be kidnapper's point of view. Again, likely not the time to question him. Mia followed him as he opened the door and checked the hall, only bringing her out when he seemed sure they were safe. Luckily it was only a few steps to the office.

Mia was so tempted to try to see back out into the cabin, but Case hauled her along.

She found herself standing in Drew's office.

"Where is it?" Case looked around the office, trying to find what was cleverly hidden.

Mia moved to the wood-paneled wall behind Drew's desk. There were three floor-to-ceiling panels and the one in the middle hid the tiny safe place…she couldn't call it a room. It was basically a closet.

Who the hell thought to put shit like this on a plane? It wasn't like the cops could show up to save her at thirty thousand feet. All this casket of a room really did was fuck up her life. She touched the right place and it opened, revealing the tiny space with its cameras. She'd never been in it. Now she realized she could see every room from a small bank of monitors in the wall.

Her brother was such a liar. "I don't think this is a safe room at all. This is like a creepy watch place. He could see into the bedroom from here. Ewww. I don't want to know why there's a box of tissues in here, do I?"

He pushed her inside. "I don't care. Don't you open this door until you know it's me outside. I'm trusting you. I can't do what I need to do unless I know you're safe."

He reached for her, his hand cupping the back of her neck and pulling her in. He kissed her, his mouth dominating hers. Her body relaxed, his need calling to her on every level. She molded her body to his, letting her hands run up the muscles of his back. So strong. So forceful. He was everything she needed in a man. With the singular exception of not understanding how competent she was, he was practically perfect.

She kissed him with everything she had. The passion between them was off the fucking charts. Never before had she felt anything close to the emotion she had for Case. Sometimes it felt like it had always been Case. Like she'd waited all her life for this one infuriating, arrogant, sexy as hell, other half of her soul man.

"Don't you dare die, Taggart." She held him fiercely for a moment before letting him go.

Loving Case Taggart would likely mean being in this moment over and over again. He wouldn't ever quit trying to save his friends and his family and the world. He was that guy and she was crazy about him.

He smiled as he looked down at her. "Not now, Lawless. Not when I'm so fucking close to what I want. You be safe."

He kissed her once more and then stepped back.

She knew what he wanted. He wanted her and that was why she reached up and touched the button that closed the panel between them.

Her heart immediately ached. It closed with a little thud. She placed her hands against that door as though she could still feel him.

With a long breath, she sat back and tried to deal with being left behind. She glanced down at the cameras. There was a keyboard in front of her. This was how her pervert brother kept up with what happened all around his plane. Including what happened in that bedroom.

What should have happened in that bedroom, except some nasty dipshit had decided kidnapping was way more important than her getting laid by a superhot cowboy/Captain America soldier.

Rude. They were so damn rude. She could be in that big bed with Case Taggart giving her everything he'd promised. And he'd promised freaking crazy oral sex.

Assholes. She could be screaming out his name right now, but no. She was all hiding in her brother's creepy sex watch box. She looked at the screen. It was switching between cameras. She could suddenly see the cabin. The stewardess had a gun aimed at Hutch's head, Michael standing in the background, his hands moving as though he was pleading his case not to kill the hacker.

Fain wasn't there. Damn it.

Case would never let her live that down. If she'd hired her own damn kidnapper, she would never hear the end of it. She was going to murder Ezra Fain. Maybe that would fix things. Maybe then Case wouldn't feel the need to tell her brothers anything at all about this little misadventure. She could change the carpet and get rid of the bodies and no one would be any wiser. What her brothers didn't know couldn't possibly cause them to mess with her life.

Case. She caught sight of him moving down the hall. He was heading toward the back of the plane, likely to loop around and get a lay of the land, so to speak.

There were only three of them. The pilot was in the cockpit. She still hadn't found Fain. She looked at the monitors, trying to figure out if there was a manual way to shift through them. She needed to find Fain's hiding place.

Not that finding him would do Case any good. She had no way of telling him anything. She was utterly useless in here.

Would she have to watch him die? Would he die right here on screen and there was nothing she could do to stop it?

She forced herself to think. What could she do? Sitting and waiting was foreign to her existence.

The monitor shifted and she watched as the cockpit door came open. The pilot probably had them on autopilot now that his dick move had done its job. She pressed one of the buttons and managed to get the camera to stay on the main cabin. The pilot walked out, the gun in his hand pointing straight at Michael Malone. Hutch was down on his knees, his hands behind his head, but at least he seemed perfectly calm.

Michael looked stoic, as though he was simply waiting.

They both trusted Case. These men knew Case would get them all out of the situation.

The pilot frowned as the flight attendant gave him an answer he obviously didn't like. He'd ditched the tie and jacket of his uniform and rolled up his sleeves, as though finally getting down to his real business. He picked up the small device rigged to go through the plane's speaker system.

"Ms. Danvers, or should I call you Ms. Lawless?"

She winced. The safe room was tied into the communications system so she could hear him just fine.

She went by her adoptive parents' name because the Lawless name could be dangerous. Because Drew had been planning revenge for twenty years and he didn't want his enemies to see them coming. He wanted them to think the family had been broken. Even Riley and Bran used different last names. There were people who worked for 4L who had no idea they were related.

But this guy did.

"I think we'll go with Lawless since we're going to be such good friends. I bet these men think you're a friend, too."

Her stomach turned because she knew what was coming next.

Case was going to kill her.

"You have thirty seconds to get out here before Angela executes your friend. I'll let you think about it for another thirty before I put a bullet through Mr. Malone's head. Yes, I know who he is, too. I also know his father won't ever play with my boss so he's expendable. We'll have to hope your brother is more flexible than David Malone. Your time starts now."

Case had already lost his brother. He would be devastated to lose his team. Michael had a family who loved him. There would be a hole in the Malones if he died.

She couldn't be the reason. There was too little time. She wasn't sure if Case could get back to the front of the plane in thirty seconds.

She opened the door and walked out.

There was one role she could play. Sacrificial lamb.

Mia held her hands up and walked through the hall and into the cabin.

"Don't hurt them. Please."

* * * *

Case cursed as the pilot came over the mic.

"You have thirty seconds to get out here before Angela executes your friend. I'll let you think about it for another thirty before I put a bullet through Mr. Malone's head. Yes, I know who he is, too. I also know his father won't ever play with my boss so he's expendable. We'll have to hope your brother is more flexible than David Malone. Your time starts now."

Damn it. He started to move up the hall. Now he knew where two of the three were. It was Fain he was worried about. Where the hell was he?

He was going to knock Fain out. He wouldn't kill him because killing was far too good for that asshole. No. He would knock him out and then he would set up his own torture palace because the shit he would do to that man would last for years. Years. It could be his happy place. When he wasn't slowly flaying the man alive and feeding his flesh to a cage of rats, he would leave Fain behind all tied up with *My Little Pony* videos playing constantly.

Yeah, that would work. He'd babysat Carys one night and all the kid wanted was some weird show about diamond unicorns and purple ponies that had deeply disturbed him. Violence and ponies. He would show Fain how it was done.

Throw in some Bieber to sleep to and Fain's life would be hell on earth.

But everything was going to be okay because he would deal

with the situation. Michael would make a move. Michael Malone might have a gun pointed at him, but Case was sure he had the situation in hand. Hutch, for all his sarcasm and laziness, wasn't exactly an easy target.

It would all be okay because Mia was locked away and being a good girl for once. Now all he had to do was find Fain.

And hope Hutch could figure out how to fly the plane. He was good with a helicopter, but Case wasn't sure he'd flown a plane lately.

Damn. He needed to tell Michael not to kill the pilot. He wasn't sure how long it had been since Hutch had flown a jet. He spent most of his time flying helicopters. Case didn't fly anything so he wasn't sure if there was a big difference. He wasn't willing to take the chance.

Where would Fain be?

"Don't hurt them. Please."

He stopped. She wouldn't. She didn't. No. That was some kind of echo or maybe the wind rushing through the plane and he had Mia on the brain. Yeah, that was pushing it.

"Look, I'm here. I'm willing to go with you, but you can't hurt my friends." The sound of her voice dispelled all his dreams of her still being in her safe place.

He was going to kill her. Spanking was too good for her. He had to come up with something horrible, truly awful, that would teach her a real lesson and still leave her ready for sex because he was so going to have that. Yeah. She would spend the rest of her life being his sex toy. That would show her.

"Don't move, Taggart."

Nope. He was going to kill her. He would leave her with Fain. Tie her up right in the old Pain Palace, shove an exotically lubricated plug up her hot ass, and let her beg for forgiveness because she was the reason Fain had gotten the jump on him.

Mother fucker.

"Just shoot me now, Fain." It would be way better than having to explain to his brother that he'd been too busy thinking with his dick to live. It would never end. Ian. Sean. All his teammates. They wouldn't let him live it down. Death was way easier.

"I'm not going to shoot you." Fain's voice was tight. "I want to talk. Tell me you killed the asshole who came looking for you."

If he died, Big Tag would just hire some psychic to find a way to torment him endlessly in the afterlife. Besides, he had a sub to spank and a brother to save. No way he was letting that mission go.

Maybe it was time to take a cue from his sub and take the situation back into his own hands. Case kicked back hard, catching Fain right where he'd planned. He turned just in time to watch the fucker go a pasty white.

Unfortunately, the dude had been well trained and he didn't take a knee. He kept his very professional-looking Colt aimed right at Case's head. "You asshole. I'm not with them."

"Why would I buy that?"

"Because if I was, you would be dead," Fain explained, his eyes tight. "Hell, when we get out of this, I'm thinking about killing you anyway. Get it through your thick skull, Taggart. I'm one of the good guys. Why else would I have told you I thought the flight attendant was sketchy?"

He did have to give him that one. He likely hadn't been trying to make his job harder. And he'd been brought in at the last minute. How could the kidnappers have known Case was going to act like an asshole and Mia would need a bodyguard?

Maybe it was time to show a little trust. He lowered his weapon. "Sorry."

He wasn't.

"Sure you are." Fain shuddered and tried to stand up straight. "Tell me that's not Mia out there giving herself up to the kidnappers, and please tell me there's not a third dude walking around waiting to blow our heads off."

"Nah, took him out in the bedroom."

"You did it quietly. I don't think anyone realizes he's dead."

"Hard to scream with a nail file in your neck." That would teach him to cock block Case Taggart.

"Why isn't Mia hiding?"

He was not taking the blame for that one. "I stashed her someplace safe. I have to assume this is all about that announcement."

Fain rolled his eyes. "Like Malone would let that happen. We need to be more worried about not putting a bullet in the plane and figuring out how to land this sucker. Autopilot will get us to Colombia, but it can't land the plane. We need the pilot alive. How good are you with knives? I found a set back in what looks like a gourmet kitchen. Why couldn't Drew Lawless keep an armory?"

"Couldn't use them anyway. And I'm good with knives. You thinking what I'm thinking?"

"Only if you're thinking I'll take out the flight attendant and you can maim but not kill the pilot."

Good. Then they were on the same page. "I'll do my best, but now we have to deal with the fact that they have Mia."

Fain nodded. "Agreed. Malone was special ops?"

"SEAL trained. He won't panic."

"And the geek?"

"Worked on a CIA team. He'll be fine. Hutch knows when to shoot and when to duck. This would be a time when he'll duck." And hopefully jump on Mia and give her some cover.

Fain reached into his coat and pulled out a knife. "Take this one. Don't miss, man. I'll take the flight attendant out first and then you go to work. Be careful because once they see us, they'll get twitchy with the trigger."

He nodded, taking the knife. It wasn't perfect, but it would do. He would need to hit the guy in the arm, whichever arm held the gun. Michael would figure out what was happening and get to the pilot, ensuring he didn't get to off himself. "If you do have to fire, go for the chest or the gut. The bullet should lodge there and not hit anything vital."

To the plane. It would likely kill the person, but he wasn't concerned about that. He needed to ensure that this plane made it to Colombia so he could properly discipline his brand new sub.

She was going to find out exactly what he'd meant by stay where he'd put her. He would tie her up and then she couldn't run off and throw herself into danger.

Fain nodded. "We move slowly. They've got to be watching the hall."

Case wasn't so sure. "Maybe not. They might be watching Mia. God only knows what she'll do. Wait for it and then take your shot. I'll move in behind you and take out my guy. She'll do something outrageous and that will be our chance."

"How do you know that for sure?"

"Because she's Mia. It's what she does. Be careful. If you harm her, there's going to be hell to pay," Case promised, his adrenaline already on the rise.

"I suppose that's your job, Taggart." Fain moved to the lead position, his knife at the ready.

Case followed, walking as silently as he could. Just let her live through this. It was a mantra in his head. Life had been so much easier before. Before he'd met Big Tag. When he'd kind of thought he was Big Tag. All he'd had to worry about was Theo, and Theo just wanted to do his job and have some fun.

BTD, he'd never nearly had a panic attack because the woman he was casually fucking offered herself up to kidnappers. BTD, he'd never had to worry about dying himself and leaving his nephew and nieces down another uncle. BTD, he hadn't worried about dying at all because he'd been a weapon and weapons didn't have fucking feelings.

Life was easier. He was wrong though. Those things hadn't happened because Theo died. They'd happened because Theo had finally gotten to live the way he'd always wanted to. He'd gotten to be surrounded by family, to be a part of something bigger than himself.

Why hadn't he died instead of Theo? No one would have missed him.

Fuck. He had to shove that shit deep.

He shifted the gun to his left hand. He was still an excellent shot with it, but the knife throw would require his dominant hand.

"I don't know where he went," Mia was saying. "We had a fight and he walked out. And I don't know where your guy is. Do you think he's trying to find Case?"

Mia did a very good dumb blonde when she wanted to.

The curtain had been pulled but he could hear everything that was going on. Fain moved to the left of the door, flattening his back. He gestured for Case to take the right.

"He was supposed to bring you back here," a deep voice said.

Case had a small strip of a view where the curtain didn't meet the wall. He could see the left side of the room, including Mia's luscious backside. It was going to get so very red so very soon.

"I didn't see him," Mia said. "I was getting ready to give myself a facial when you interrupted. Have you ever heard of the mile-high facial? It's supposed to be the very best. It opens your pores in ways you just can't do on the ground."

He had to bite back a laugh. Yeah, she'd been about to get a facial and it would have been phenomenal.

Fain was frowning as though he didn't get the joke.

Mia was talking to him. She knew he was there, knew he wouldn't leave her. She was telling him she was pissed at getting cock blocked, too.

He'd never dealt with a woman like Mia. Not in an intimate way. His sisters-in-law could be pretty fierce, but watching Mia up close was so different. He'd known she was outspoken, but he'd never seen her so willful.

What would it feel like to have that aggressive alpha female kneeling at his feet, offering him her submission at night and her strength during the day? To have a woman like that find him worthy for something other than sex?

"She's an idiot," the flight attendant said. "Shoot her and get it over with."

"That's not what the boss wants and you know it," the pilot said. "Mr. Malone, I think I would be more comfortable with you getting to your knees."

"I would be more comfortable with a gun in my hands," Michael snarked. "We don't always get what we want."

Case heard the nasty ping of a bullet going through a silencer and then Michael groaned.

"Fuck," Hutch cursed.

Mia gasped. "You said you wouldn't hurt them."

Case looked over at Fain, who had a line of sight on that side of the cabin. Fain touched his thigh and his hand suddenly looked like a gun. So Michael had taken a bullet. Shit. They needed to move.

"I said I wouldn't kill them if you came in, but it's not enough to have you here. I need the other two. Taggart and whoever the other asshole is," the pilot said.

Fain frowned.

"Please don't shoot anyone else. I'll do whatever you want," Mia said. Finally he could hear the panic in her voice. It had gotten real for her.

He would have done anything for her not to understand how real it could be.

It was time to go, time to save his friends and his girl. He held up a hand. Five. Four.

Fain nodded, his knife coming up. Take out the left and he would take out the right.

Three.

"You will, sweetheart," the masculine voice said. "You'll do whatever I want and let me tell you, I'm going to want a lot."

"Stop," Fain whispered. "Don't you go psychotic on me."

But he wanted to. How fucking dare he threaten Mia with that. He'd made the last man who threatened to rape her bleed long and hard.

"We need him," Fain whispered. "Keep your fucking cool."

But after, Case would cut off his balls and he wouldn't be able to threaten any other woman like that, much less a Taggart woman.

Was he thinking about her that way already?

Two.

"Put on these handcuffs or Angela will blow your friend's head off and then I'll take out Malone anyway. I'll lock us up in the cockpit and we'll deal with the other two later."

"What about Alan?" Angela asked.

"Taggart killed him or he would be here. This bitch is lying. She knows exactly where Taggart is."

She didn't but she was about to.

He gave Fain the go.

The mercenary didn't hesitate. He stepped out and before anyone registered he was there, he'd planted his knife in Angela's neck.

Case briefly saw the woman as she dropped the gun and reached for her throat. It was useless. Fain was damn good at his job. Angela pulled the knife out and the deed was done.

The world seemed to slow down, though Case knew he was moving quickly. Hutch looked across the cabin and then jumped for the side. Michael was already reaching for Mia to pull her away.

Case focused. One breath in. Turn and fire. He wasn't firing with a gun, but he let that knife fly like it was a bullet.

He was rewarded with a groan as the knife lodged in the pilot's shoulder. The pilot dropped his weapon and fell to one knee. Case stood over him with a gun.

"Don't fucking move. Both your partners are dead."

"You did such a good job, babe." Mia sounded bouncy and happy. "Really awesome. But you could have mentioned to Ezra about the blood on the carpet thing."

"Later, Mia." She thought her sunny attitude in the face of danger was going to save her ass? She was so wrong. "I want to know who you're working for. Talk."

The pilot pulled the knife out and blood started to flow. "I think not. I don't think you're going to use the gun and now I have a knife."

"You're outnumbered." It should have been obvious.

The pilot paled. "Ah, but I also have one last duty."

He turned and ran toward the cockpit, the door standing wide open.

"Shit." If he let the pilot lock himself inside, god only knew where they would end up.

"Take the shot, Taggart!" Fain yelled.

Case let instinct take over. He fired into the man's back and the pilot fell, dropping to his knees right in front of the control panel. His body slumped over it.

Case took a deep breath. The cabin hadn't depressurized. He hadn't fucked them over. Yes, they were still in trouble, but he had a few hours to figure out how to land the plane. And what to do with all the bodies.

Case watched in utter horror as the pilot used his last breath to press a button on the panel and then pull down on a lever.

The plane went into a dive and Case realized they were about to die.

"Hutch! Can you get us out of this?" He looked over at Mia as the plane began to shudder. He reached for her, but she was moving even as the plane bucked up.

As cool as a cucumber, she pushed the dead guy out of the way. "Give it a sec. We'll be fine."

Hutch sat up, not looking at all like a man in a big hurry to save them. "You need help with that?"

"We'll be good. Just needs to reconnect." She sat down and he watched as she pressed a few buttons and the plane leveled out.

"What the hell?"

She grinned back at him. "This isn't some Hollywood movie, Taggart. This is a top-of-the-line Bond Aeronautics jet. It course corrects and without some serious reprogramming, it's asshole proof."

Hutch stood up, straightening his clothes. "All that jerk was ever going to do was make us pee our pants. Which I did not do, by the way."

Mia smiled Case's way. "Did I mention how awesome you were?"

"It's not going to save your ass."

"Who said I wanted my ass saved?" She turned back to the control panel. "Could you move him? And maybe get a mop or something. What's with you and all the blood?"

"Please tell me you know how to fly this thing." Michael had managed to get himself into one of the seats, his leg propped up as Hutch offered his hoodie to stop the bleeding.

"Of course she doesn't," Case replied. "I was hoping Hutch could figure it out."

Mia rolled her eyes. "Wanna see my license? You do not go into my line of work without picking up a few things. We're going to climb back to our cruising altitude, I'll put this baby on autopilot, then I'll dig that bullet out, Malone. I'm also pretty good at first aid."

"I knew you could do it, boss," Fain said in a big old kiss-ass voice. "I'll see if I can find the first aid kit. I've helped out in the field before. I can be your nurse. Maybe Taggart can deal with the bodies."

"And the cleanup," Mia said. "There's a mini steam cleaner somewhere. The faster you get that blood up, the better."

She winked his way before turning back to the panel.

Fuck, she was going to kill him one of these days. He just knew it.

CHAPTER FOUR

"You want to tell me what's really going on?" Fain sat down across from Case.

They would land in a few hours thanks to Mia's expertise with a plane. She was utterly confident she could take care of things.

He was confident they were going to have a very long talk that would end with her bare ass over his lap. He was still a little shaken from how close he'd come to losing her. He hated that. He was always ice cold during an op, but Mia shook him up in every way possible. And maybe that wasn't such a bad thing. "We're going to Colombia. I thought you knew that."

Fain frowned, his eyes steady on Case. "I thought I knew you, too."

Case sat back, wishing he'd just stayed in the cockpit with Mia. He could be watching her. She was pretty freaking hot when she was flying a plane. He'd never been the kind of man who was attracted to needy women.

Maybe it was time to rethink his stance on the future. He was treating Mia like the women he'd dated back in Georgia. They'd all wanted out of their small town and Case's double-wide existence wasn't going to get them there. They'd been more than happy to have sex, but when it came time to get serious they looked for better options.

A woman like Mia would know what she wanted. If she was here with him, it likely had nothing to do with a rich girl indulging her fantasies and everything to do with a wild woman who happened to want a man who could handle her.

He might need to have another talk with Drew Lawless. But first he had to deal with Fain, who wasn't as big an asshole as Case had suspected but could still be obnoxious.

"Why would you think you know me? We've never met."

"I suppose I thought I knew you by reputation," Fain allowed. "You're a Taggart. That name alone means something in our community. You're supposed to be a hardass when it comes to protecting your women. Are you trying to tell me Mia isn't your woman?"

Michael groaned a little as he shifted in his chair. His leg was propped up. Mia had not only gotten the bullet out of his thigh, she'd sewn him up. She'd explained her adoptive mother was a doctor and Mia had gone on several charity tours with her that ended with Mia playing nurse and learning how to stitch up a wound as a teenager. "I'd like to know the answer to that question."

"Since when do you care about my love life?"

Michael grinned. He'd had a whole bunch of tequila. "Since you actually have one. Also, if you don't want her, I'll take her. She's hot and I think she might be able to handle my momma. My momma looks sweet on the outside, but she's mean. Don't let that upper-crust British accent fool you. She's got the Southern momma thing down. Many a woman has run from her. And I get shot way more than I like to think about. So skill with a medical kit is a real plus when it comes to looking for a bride."

Yeah, all his friends would be after his girl. Damn, but that felt good. This time there were no lies between them. This time the only thing between them was his distorted view of her. He'd thought about it the whole time he'd cleaned up. As he rolled up bodies in tarps and mopped up blood, he'd given careful consideration to why he'd pushed her away in the first place.

She was rich and he wasn't. She'd had a fiancé who looked like he fit more into her world than Case did.

That lawyer boy likely couldn't handle Mia. And her world seemed to be a much more fucked up place than he'd imagined.

It was time to let go of his past. He wasn't the poor kid from the other side of the tracks anymore. So what if she had more money than he did? Why the hell would that matter? If Drew Lawless wanted to think he was a gold digger, Case didn't care. Now he couldn't remember why he'd thought he cared in the first place. It was Theo. He'd been so lost without his brother. If Theo had been alive when he'd met Mia, he would have spanked her lying ass, slapped a collar around her throat, and dragged her off like a caveman without any thought to what her brothers would think of him.

He came from a long line of men born with very few fucks to give.

"I'm afraid she's mine, Michael," he said, glancing into the cockpit and catching a glimpse of her. She had headphones on and seemed to be swaying to some music.

Hutch looked up from his computer. "Told you he wasn't that stupid."

Case had no idea what they were talking about. "Stupid?"

"Michael thought you were a dumbass to let her go in the first place. All that 'she lied to me' and 'she's just a rich little princess who can't handle a real man' shit was just a big old front because you've never had a girlfriend before," Hutch explained.

"I've had girlfriends." It wasn't like he was a virgin or anything.

"You've had Hooters girls," Michael corrected. "You've had chicks you banged for a few months and didn't think about them outside of banging, and the minute they started to get serious you would apply for the most dangerous duty in the world just to get away from them."

"That was about protecting my country." He definitely hadn't taken that assignment in Fallujah for fun. Though he had to admit, it did get him away from a clingy hookup.

"That was about protecting your ass," Michael shot back. "I've worked with you most of my adult life, Taggart. I see through you. You've always needed a woman who can set you on your ass. Soft and sweet wasn't ever going to do it for you."

But Mia could be soft and sweet when she wanted to. She could care. Mia might be the exact right mixture of crazy bitch and sweet sub he needed.

"This is exactly what I'm saying," Fain interrupted. "You care about that woman. So I want to know why you're letting her go through with this. You do realize she could have been killed."

He knew that. It would likely haunt his dreams for a while. He would see Mia walking out of her hiding place like a sacrificial lamb, offering herself up to save his friends.

"He knows exactly what happened here," Hutch snorted. "And he's not letting her go through with whatever crazy assignment she's on. Trust me. We'll land in Colombia and he'll throw her over his shoulder and haul her straight back to Texas. He'll tie her up and do some nasty shit to her. I've already found a company who can turn this plane around in an hour. I'm still working on what to do with the bodies. Might be easier to leave them in Colombia, but you know Big Tag likes a present every now and then."

"He's not planning on turning around," Fain said with surety.

Fain was sharp.

"Of course he is." Michael sat back. "He'll have her under lock and key until he figures out who tried to kidnap her and why. But we're not going to tell her that. That honey can be a little mean. We've got to sneak up on her. Then we'll rope her and take her down. You think she's got a sister?"

He was going to be a blast later on. Michael couldn't handle his liquor and now Case was a man down.

And Case had some serious thinking to do because Fain was right. He couldn't turn around. In a world where his brother wasn't being tortured on a daily basis, he would have done exactly what Hutch had said. He would have carted her back home and locked her up until he could figure out what was happening. He couldn't do that now and his friends weren't going to understand.

"It's an important story to Mia. We're still going. I'm going to need to find a cleanup crew, Hutch, and a quiet one. Moneybags in there can pay for it."

"What am I paying for?" Mia stepped out, yawning behind her hand.

He reached out, pleased when she slipped her hand in his. He tugged her into his lap. He was done playing the hardass with her. He'd been wrong. She'd been right. They belonged together. She was his natural match and her brother could go to hell. If Lawless cut her off, then Mia would have to learn to live on a budget.

If there was one thing he'd learned from the last few hours, it was that he didn't want to lose this chance with her. She meant something to him. He could count on her in a way he'd never thought he would be able to count on a lover.

"I need to find someone willing to deal with the bodies, princess." Yeah, this was not a conversation he'd ever thought he would have with a girlfriend. "That's going to take cash and we're going to have to deal with some not so nice people."

"Cartel would be best," she said without hesitation. She cuddled down in his arms. She smelled like soap and fresh laundry after cleaning up. He wished he'd been able to squeeze into that shower with her. "They have cleanup crews who'll know the area and how to avoid the police. They'll also know which of the police are bribable. They shouldn't be too hard to find. I'll call some friends when we touch down."

"You are not dealing with a cartel." This would be the problem he had to put up with. Keeping Mia out of trouble would be a full-time job. He let his hand rest on her thigh. "I'll handle it."

Was it too soon to coax her back in the bedroom? He'd

cleaned up pretty well. They still had a few hours before they landed. He might enjoy violating the pilot before they had to deal with whoever would try to kill them next.

Making love to Mia might let him stop thinking about the trouble his brother was in, might give him peace for a few minutes.

Hutch was staring at him. "This doesn't make sense. What's the story you're chasing after, Mia?"

"I'm meeting with a source who has information on voter fraud in the last election," she lied without batting an eye.

Fain shook his head. "As your bodyguard, I have to warn you that this is ill advised. Until we can figure out who those people were and who sent them, we need to get back to the States. No story is worth your life. I'm pulling the plug on this. I'll call your brother the minute we land."

Hutch sighed. "I hate to say this, but I'm with Asshat."

Fain rolled his eyes. "Nice to know. We also have the added problem of needing to get this guy to a hospital. They'll want to know how he got a bullet in his thigh."

"He doesn't have one anymore," Mia pointed out.

Hutch stared at Case. "Do you honestly not care that Michael could get an infection? I know she cleaned it and stuff, but he needs to see a real doctor."

"It's not that bad," Michael said, sobering a bit. "I won't be able to run for a few days, but I can walk. I'm not the problem here. Fain is right. There is zero chance that the Case Taggart I know calls a cartel in to clean up for him and lets the woman he's involved with walk around with a target on her back. What the fuck is going on, Case?"

Mia sat up straight and after brushing his cheek with her lips, she stood up. "This story is very important to me. I've talked to Case about it. I'm going through with it whether or not the rest of you come with me. Mr. Fain, you can call my brothers, but I'm an adult and if you do, you're fired. I will ensure Mr. Malone gets the care he needs once we reach Cartagena. You and Mr. Fain can join him at the hospital. I hope Case will come with me, but I don't need an escort."

Oh, she so fucking needed an escort. "I'll be with you and you know it, but maybe it would be for the best if we sent Michael home with Hutch and Fain."

Hutch stood up. "Sounds good to me, man. You know how foreign food upsets my stomach." He was smiling, saying all the right things. He left his computer behind, but Case watched him slip his phone into his pocket. "I'm going to the bathroom, then I'm taking a nap. Wake me up when we need to change planes."

There was no way he was taking a nap. He'd worked with Hutch long enough to know exactly what he'd do.

Case reached out and grabbed Hutch. "Don't you dare call Ian."

Michael managed to pull himself up. "If he doesn't I will. Something's fishy here and you're keeping us in the dark. I want to know what's going on and I want to know now."

Damn it. He'd meant to avoid this. He wished he could kill the pilot again.

"I have something on him, okay?" Mia put her hands on her hips. Her eyes went steely. "I've got something on Case and I'm using it to make him help me. He's embarrassed so you don't have to bring Ian into this. And as long as Case there goes along with my plan, I'll keep my mouth shut."

She was sweet, but he could tell her it wasn't going to work. "Don't bother. They know me too well."

"He would already have you locked up," Hutch said with a grim smile. "He's chasing your tail, hon. He can be led around by his dick but he wouldn't give in to blackmail. Try again."

"Is this about Hope McDonald?" Michael asked quietly.

"The senator's daughter?" Fain asked, his gaze sharpening. "You think she killed your brother."

They'd covered so much of that up. "Theo died while performing his bodyguard duties."

"Bullshit. Theo Taggart died around the same time as the senator. Everyone in the business knows the senator had Tennessee

Smith burned. There is zero chance that Ian Taggart would hire out his brother to protect the man who ruined his friend. Rumor has it the senator was dirty as hell and connected to a group of businessmen who call themselves The Collective." The words came out of Fain's mouth like accusatory bullets. "McKay-Taggart isn't the only group with connections. They're just the group that doesn't play well with others."

So Fain's boss had his ear to the ground. Case wouldn't be telling him anything he didn't know. "Theo was still killed on a job."

"He was working for Ten Smith. Does this job have something to do with Smith?" Fain asked.

"No." He didn't like Fain asking about Tennessee Smith. His old boss kept a low profile. "Ten has no idea what's going on."

"I doubt that," Michael said. "The real question I have is does Big Tag know what we're doing?"

"He knows exactly where I am." Case didn't have to lie about that. He'd told Ian exactly where he was going.

"Then you won't mind me calling in to let him know what happened to Michael. It's what we're supposed to do when a team member is injured. We call back to base," Hutch said all too reasonably.

When had Hutch gotten so slavish to the rules? "We're handling it. Erin just had her baby. Everyone's trying to take care of her and TJ. I'll put Michael on a plane back and you can join him."

Mia moved in behind him, putting a hand on his shoulder. "We won't be more than a few days behind you. No one has to be worried. I'm going to talk to someone, get some intel, and Case and I will fly back. We'll keep a low profile and everything will be fine."

"Intel about what?" Fain was ruthless.

"None of your business," Case replied.

"How about mine?" Michael asked. "I've already taken a bullet for this operation but I'm not allowed to know what intel we're going after? I thought we abandoned the whole following-orders-blindly thing when we left the Agency."

Michael had been his partner for a very long time. Outside of his brothers, Michael was one of the only humans on earth who could actively make Case feel guilty. They had left behind the lies when they'd quit the Agency, and Case had been the one to convince Michael to come with him. Case sat silent.

"I'm calling Tag," Hutch said stubbornly.

"Don't." He was rapidly losing control.

Hutch's face was red, his eyes narrowed as he looked down at Case. "No, you don't get to order me to stand down when it comes to this. I realize that I'm considered the geek of the group and no one thinks I'm good for anything but looking shit up on the Internet. But I know how this should work. I did my time in the Army and there is a chain of command for a reason. I didn't trust my instincts that night. Erin didn't either. I will not do that ever again. Not even for you, Case. Fuck, really not for you because I refuse to lose another friend."

It was so easy to forget how volatile Hutch could be, how deep those seemingly still waters could run. He hadn't talked much about it, but Hutch had been there the night Theo died. He'd watched as Theo took his last breath and he'd seen the aftermath of Nick losing Des and Erin losing Theo.

Hutch had been the one who followed Theo's orders, including not calling into home base when everything had gone to hell. The minute Ten had been taken, Theo should have called in and let Ian take over. Theo had been sure he could save Ten and the op.

Theo had been wrong.

Hutch was his man. Case ran this group and he wasn't being the leader he needed to be. Case stood up and put his hands on Hutch's shoulders. He had to make a decision whether the secret was more important than his mission and his men.

He owed Ian, but he owed his group, too. Ian had brought in Alex and Li to back him up. Hutch and Michael were Case's closest advisors.

"You are not going to lose me." He looked over at Fain. Sometimes life threw him curve balls and sometimes those freaking curve balls ended up being necessary.

He couldn't risk going in alone. Not if someone was after Mia. Michael was out of commission. He needed Fain.

"If you turn out to be untrustworthy, I need you to understand that I will skin you alive and turn you into a rug for my office and I will let my dogs piss on you. I don't have dogs right now, but I'm going to get some if you betray me. Am I understood?"

"I get you." Fain was so earnest Case was worried he might break into song. "And I want in. I take my job seriously. I know I work for someone your brother doesn't like, but they weren't freaking hiring at McKay-Taggart. Do you know how long it's been since I had a team I could count on? I'm not going to let you down. Now tell me we're going after The Collective. I lost a friend in Africa during a skirmish that I believe was caused not by the locals but by The Collective over diamond mining."

"A mercenary?"

"No. He was my brother and he was on a black ops team. So tell me I get to have some part in taking those fuckers down."

"We're not going after The Collective. Not directly," he admitted. "We're going after my brother."

Hutch's mouth dropped open. "What? Theo's dead…fuck. She saved him. McDonald saved him and she took him and that's why we never found his body."

"Are you kidding me?" Michael asked. "He's been with her all this time. What has she done to him? Does Ian know?"

"Of course. He's known for a while and you have to understand why he's kept it quiet." He wasn't going to throw his brother under the bus. Ian had made the right call. Case was making the only one he could. The intel was too important. Ian had said the information was on a need-to-know basis. Case needed them to know. "I'll give you all the information you need, but you have to promise me now that the fact that Theo's alive doesn't get back to the rest of the team."

"Erin would be devastated if she lost him twice," Michael said.

"Or she would fly in after him and she could die and they would both be gone." Hutch sank back into his seat. "I saw her that night. If she could have, she would have taken his place. She would have gone with him. Brody carried her out or she would have stayed with Theo. She wouldn't leave him."

A lot had changed in the months since Theo's death. He didn't think Erin would rush out. Case kept the secret from her for a different reason. "She's a mom now. I don't think she would be reckless with her life because of TJ, but I can't let her feel the pain I feel every single day. I know he's out there and I can't help him. If I can spare Erin that pain, I'm going to and I'm asking you to as well."

"I'm with you," Michael promised.

Hutch nodded. "I can keep a secret."

He was tougher than he seemed. "Good. Fain?"

"I don't know her so I think we're good," Fain explained.

"I was talking about your boss." Guy Ferland had some issues with Big Tag.

"He has zero need to know. He's actually a dick and when I find another job, I'll leave. Like I said, I'm really just looking for a team." Fain looked back at Mia. "What role do you play in this?"

Mia shrugged and walked back into the cabin. She left the door open as she sat back down in the pilot's seat. "I'm just the girl who got a good lead."

He'd been wondering about this, too. "So you got a lead on my brother. Who was supposed to be dead. And this Tony person just up and knew you were the person to come to. Even though we don't have connection on paper, he came to you. About my brother, who is supposed to be dead."

Michael frowned. "That does seem fishy."

Not for the same reasons. Michael was going the paranoid route. He knew his partner. Michael was wondering now if this wasn't some kind of ploy to get them all at some place at some prescribed time where Mia would pull a surprise dick move on them.

He knew this had nothing to do with betrayal and everything to do with the fact that Mia didn't give up on the things she wanted.

And she wanted him.

"I guess I was lucky," she said primly.

"I think Mia was looking for any way to get into Case's panties," Hutch said enthusiastically. The boy was an optimist.

Mia turned in her chair, her cheeks a perfectly cute shade of pink. "I was intrigued by the story and I looked into it. I knew about The Collective because they approached my brother and Riley and I quickly figured out Hope McDonald was not only The Collective's personal Dr. Frankenstein, but also the person most likely at fault for Theo's death. I wanted to find her."

"For justice." Yeah, that was a lie, but if she was embarrassed, he would let her get away with it.

"For you," she said quietly.

Because Mia didn't prevaricate or hide even when she was embarrassed. He gave her what he hoped was a warm smile of encouragement. "Tell me how all this went down. How do you know this Tony guy?"

Her shoulders straightened again and she was right back to vivacious. "I met him when I was working this story on human trafficking in South America. He was looking for the daughter of some friend of his and I agreed to be bait for the men who had taken her. It was all very Liam Neeson and stuff."

She was going to give him a heart attack. He could see it. She would be sitting there in a dive bar, probably wearing a dress that showed off her breasts. She would look like a big old blonde, suck-me, fuck-me cupcake, and when the bad guys showed up she'd probably have interview questions for them.

Hello, Mr. Sex Trafficker. Could you explain how you choose the girls you turn into sex slaves?

"Is he okay?" Mia was staring at him but talking to Michael.

"He's envisioning you in a hellhole brothel and thinking about how he can punish you for putting yourself out there as bait." Michael knew him well.

"He can't spank me for that. He didn't even know me at the time," she said with a grin. "So I'd done that tiny didn't-even-get-me-thrown-in-a-brothel favor for Tony. He gave me a number to call him and when I needed a favor, I dialed him up."

"What exactly did you ask him for?" Case had to move past the idea of her being used as bait. Maybe he would take that discussion up with the mysterious Tony.

"He's a pretty well-connected guy from what I understand. After I had someone hack into the CIA database to download the files on what happened on Grand Cayman, I got to thinking…"

"You did what?" It just got worse. The longer she talked the more trouble she got into.

"It wasn't a big deal. From what I can tell, the CIA has no idea and I only took one little bitty file."

Hutch was holding up his hands. "It was not me. Absolutely not me."

Mia shook her head. "It wasn't him. I paid a very nice hacker a lot of money. I don't usually like to break the law, but Case wasn't very forthcoming and honestly, I needed leverage to get back into his life. He was being an asshole at the time. I thought if I could find the one thing he wanted, he might give me a second chance. After talking to his brother and eavesdropping on a bunch of meetings between Ian and Drew, I decided to find Hope McDonald myself."

"You did…" There would be time enough to explain the new rules of engagement to her. If they were together, and he was beginning to believe he might do the world a favor by taking responsibility for her, she was going to learn that eavesdropping and turning herself into bait for criminals and hacking into systems that would get most people put in jail were all activities that were now off limits. "You went looking for Hope and not Theo."

"I didn't know he was alive," she explained, her hands in her lap and her voice solemn. "The minute I did, I got to you as fast as I could. If I'd overheard about Theo, I would have been on your doorstep. I'm afraid despite the fact that you're an asshole, I would have given my loyalty to you."

Fuck. He'd been so stupid. "I promise I'll make up for being an asshole. I've got a lot of practice."

"Lots," Hutch agreed. "So much practice."

"So how did you find out Theo Taggart was alive?" Fain's tone was flat, letting Case know how little he enjoyed the more personal parts of their conversation.

"I found out about the memory drugs Hope McDonald was using," Mia continued. "I read about it and then my brother Riley and I went through a bunch of holdings and properties that were connected to Kronberg Pharmaceuticals."

"We did that, too," Case admitted. "Liam thought they were based in Argentina for a while, but when he finally made it on the island where the base was, they were gone."

Mia looked at him while she explained. "They don't stay in one place for very long. I believe they originally were being funded by Kronberg, but at some point they cut ties with her. Likely around the time the Agency got interested in her. I've tracked her to three places in South America, each successively worse. She was hurting for cash. And that was when I heard about the Gringos."

"The Gringos? The bank robbers?" Fain asked.

"I've never heard of them," Case had to admit.

"I read a story about them. I try to keep up on international issues." Fain leaned forward. "They're a small group of bank robbers who've hit four banks so far. They're quick and clean. The one time they met resistance, they put it down without killing anyone. They're known for being almost military in their precision and they speak English to each other."

He knew a lot about a group of South American bank robbers.

"I asked Tony what he knew and he hadn't heard much. Then

they hit bank number five in Cartagena. Tony knew I was interested in the Gringos so he tapped into the police network and found the photos from the CCTV cameras." Mia looked to Case to continue the story.

He was kind of in awe of the way her brain worked. He was a soldier. He tended to follow orders or instincts. He'd been trained by Ten to see past the words in a report and to evaluate motivations, but she thought ahead of such things. She was like Liam. She had instincts he didn't understand.

She was the brains and he was the brawn. He kind of liked that.

"At one point one of the three bank robbers takes off his mask and looks up at the camera." He glanced back at Michael. "It was Theo."

"Why would Theo not just get away?" Michael asked, obviously confused.

"It's the drug." Case had studied up on everything written about the time dilation drug Hope McDonald had been working on. According to Ten, it short circuited the neurons in the brain to make minutes feel like hours, and it also made whoever took it very susceptible to suggestion. It was how Hope was controlling his brother. "Ten struggled with it after a single dose. I can't imagine what Theo's been through. I only know that in that one moment, he knew he had to try to get a message out. He knew he had to do something. He might have sunk back into whatever persona Hope McDonald has trained him to have, but he was defying her then. He was telling me to come and get him."

And Mia had brought him the message.

"So we're going to talk to this Tony guy?" Hutch yawned. It was easy to see that explaining the truth had seriously calmed him down. "The one Ten said was such a pain in his ass."

"This guy is CIA?" Fain asked.

"Ex." He wished he could talk to Ten, but Ten wouldn't listen to Mia. He would immediately call Ian. But damn he wished he could call him. Ten could tell him how to deal with Tony Santos.

Hell, Ten might be able to tell him how to handle Mia because it was suddenly so important to handle Mia. She was important. "He left the Agency a couple of years ago according to what Hutch discovered."

"He was unstable," Hutch continued. "From what I can tell, a few years back he was captured by MSS and the CIA disavowed all knowledge of him. He spent a year in a Beijing prison before he managed to get out. I suspect Ten had something to do with that."

Case wasn't surprised. As much as Ten loved subterfuge, he cared more for his men. He would have worked hard to get his guy out, but things got complicated in a place like China when he couldn't depend on the State Department.

Sometimes he was damn happy he'd gotten out when he did. He could have been that operative left behind by his country. He could have been asked to do things for his country no one should have to do. Working for Big Tag was simpler. His brother tried always to do the right thing, the honorable thing. Even when he had to make a hard call, he tried to mitigate the damages.

"Tony left the Agency and started to do odd jobs, as he called it," Mia explained. "He moved to South America and that's where I met him. He's a hard guy to pin down, but he owes me a favor. He's been following the case but he won't talk unless it's in person."

In person and with Mia.

He needed to know everything he could about Tony Santos.

"He won't talk to us," Case explained. "Only Mia."

"That's why you won't tell Ian," Michael surmised. "He wouldn't accept it. He would try to catch the fucker and make him talk. Ian doesn't know Mia. He wouldn't trust her to get the intel."

Yes, that was the problem. "We have to watch her but give her enough room that Tony doesn't get spooked. If we don't, we could lose Theo."

Michael nodded. "I'm in. And by I'm in I mean I'm out because I won't be able to walk for a couple of days. I'll hole up and run communications with Hutch. You'll take Fain as your backup and if he gets you killed…"

Fain held up a hand. "You'll horrifically murder me and do something vile with my corpse. Yeah, I get that. I'll make sure Taggart comes out of it alive."

"And I'll find everything I possibly can on Santos. I won't let it slip through the cracks, Case. You'll see. I'll be as good as Adam and I'll keep my mouth shut," Hutch said. "Until we get back to Dallas. Tell me we'll bring Big Tag in then because if we don't he really will kill me and do something horrible with my corpse. He promises like three times a day."

"We'll call him before we even leave here." Case didn't want to leave Ian out a second longer than he had to. He would turn the entire mission over to his brother because Ian was the best. Ian was Theo's best shot and he wouldn't give Theo any less. There was no ego in Case when it came to a mission. He only wanted it to succeed and this one more than ever.

"We touch down in two hours and then we head to the hotel," Mia said with a reassuring smile. "I've got us a couple of rooms and I'll find a private doctor."

Case looked at Hutch, giving him a stare he should understand.

Hutch nodded and immediately got up. "There's a SAT connection in the office. I'll find something suitably off the beaten track. I've got extra ID for my team."

"I've got my own," Fain pointed out. "What can I say? I'm a Boy Scout. I'm always prepared."

Mia looked back at him, suspicion plain on her face. "What do you mean 'off the beaten track'? I've got us rooms at the Four Seasons. A suite of rooms to be precise. I'll get a couple more so we can all be comfortable."

Yes, a suite where there would likely be a bunch of very well-dressed kidnappers waiting for her sweet ass. "Cancel those reservations. We're doing this my way from now on, princess."

"But I had a massage scheduled," she said, her eyes wide.

He would totally give her a massage. With his dick. From the inside out. He smiled and sat back, enjoying how worried she looked.

"I'm not going to like your way, am I, Case?"

He was going to make sure she liked his way a lot. The hotel, on the other hand, would probably horrify her.

CHAPTER FIVE

Mia looked at the sad little motel with a sigh. Her suite at the Four Seasons would have been in the heart of Cartagena, with its gorgeous Colonial era buildings and historical sites. This place was a one-story dump that might serve as a set for a horror movie. Specifically the ones where the dumbass American tourists got chopped up and didn't even get to have sex first.

At least she was on the beach.

"This place isn't even on the Internet," Hutch said as though completely proud of himself for finding a motel that looked as though fifty murders occurred in it every day. He sat in the back seat of the SUV that had been waiting for them at the airport. Also Hutch's idea. She'd had a limo waiting for her and Case that Hutch had nixed.

All her romantic plans trashed because of stupid kidnappers.

She'd told herself at the time that it was nothing more than a mission to save Case's brother. That she owed her friends this. Now she could look back and see that she'd been using it as an excuse to get close to him.

What kind of woman did that make her?

"I got a recommendation from a friend," Hutch continued. "He says this place takes cash and asks no questions. But also is fairly clean. I can get a good signal from the rooms I reserved. I called in at the airport and they're holding three west-facing rooms for us. Apparently that's where I can get the best SAT signal."

Hutch was worried about satellite and cell phone signals. She was worried about disease and bugs.

And Case. She was about to be alone in a room with Case because he'd explained that there was no way she was sleeping on her own.

Would she sleep? Or would she finally get in that cowboy's boxers?

Now that the moment was here, she was a little nervous. A lot nervous. Case was more than a good lay and despite the fact that they seemed to be getting along, they had a lot to talk about.

Shouldn't they talk? It had seemed so easy when he was kissing her on the plane and touching her and making her crazy with his mouth. But now, after what they'd been through, shouldn't they have a conversation?

"I'll get the keys," Hutch said as he opened the back door.

"I'll go with him." Ezra hopped out beside him.

Michael snored from the third row. Hutch had arranged for a private doctor to meet them. He'd come on the plane and asked absolutely no questions as he'd given Michael a shot of antibiotics and a painkiller. He'd told Case that the wound had been properly stitched and to keep Michael on antibiotics for a few days and he would be fine. He'd taken his money, given them a bottle of pills, and walked away.

At least her money was good for something.

"I'm sorry about the Four Seasons, but this will be better security wise," Case said. He sat in the driver's seat, aviators covering his eyes.

"I know." She wasn't going to argue with him. She'd planned a romantic getaway and he was trying to find his brother. Now she'd brought the added element of some group trying to kidnap her and potentially fucking up all their plans to find Theo. "I'm sorry about the kidnapping thing."

He didn't look her way. His face was toward the ocean. In the distance there was a whole line of cars and partygoers under colorful tents. She could hear music blasting and see girls in bikinis playing volleyball.

"We're going to have a long talk about that."

"I didn't take this seriously enough, Case. I'm sorry. You have every right to be angry with me. If it weren't for Tony's instructions, I would go home."

He turned, frowning. "Why would you go home?"

"Because I was using this as an excuse. Don't get me wrong. I want to find Theo. But I've been fooling myself about why."

"You wanted to find Theo so I would be grateful to you."

Put like that she sounded so pathetic. "I guess I did it so you would talk to me. So in the end I'm exactly what you thought I was. I'm an entitled little princess who would do anything to get her way."

His lips curved up, but there was a softness to them. "Or you're a crazy bitch who wants a man so much she would move heaven and earth to get him."

Stupid. God, she felt stupid. Maybe it was six hours of flying on no sleep or all the terror of the near kidnapping, but she felt dumb and vulnerable. "Yeah, crazy bitch will suffice."

His hand slid over hers. "Mia, I'm sorry for being an ass for seven months. I think it was a lot of things and some of them had nothing to do with you. Mostly I'm at a loss without my brother. If Theo had been here, he would have kicked my ass and told me to go after what I wanted. He wasn't and I was hurting and it was so easy to shove that hurt your way." He took her hand in his and brought it to his lips. "I happen to adore crazy bitches. It's the only type of woman men in my family are attracted to."

"I want to believe you." She wanted it so much it was an actual ache inside her body.

He kissed her palm. "Then believe me."

The trouble was he'd so thoroughly dumped her the first time. He'd withdrawn affection and then when his cover had been blown, he'd refused to see her entirely. The only way she'd talked to him was to press the issue. "When did you find out that I was lying to you?"

He kissed her again and sighed, holding her hand to his chest. "It doesn't matter now. I've seen the error of my ways. You know I never stopped thinking about you. I haven't seen another woman. No dates. No hookups. I've spent months taking dungeon monitor duties at Sanctum because I couldn't play with anyone but you."

He said all the right things, but he'd been so cold for so long. It was hard to believe he'd turned around. "It was after that first night, wasn't it? After you kissed me? You weren't the same man after that. You were charming when you needed to be, but I still felt the chill."

Not that it had made her turn away. She'd just kept trying. Kept saying yes when he'd asked her out even though she could feel the distance between them.

"Yes, and that was the same night I found out you had a fiancé."

"I broke it off with him the next day." She'd met Case Taggart and wondered what the hell she'd been thinking. "I'd been with Jeff for a while, but we weren't even living together. He asked me in front of his friends and family and I didn't have the heart to tell him no. And then I wondered hell, why not."

"Because you were bored?"

How could she make him understand? "Because I hadn't found anyone who moved me. Because I thought maybe having someone to see movies with and who my brothers didn't hate wasn't the end of the world. Because I thought it was time to start my life. And then I met you."

"You should know your brother hates me."

Why on earth would he think that? She was pretty sure Drew and the others were completely fascinated with the Taggarts. "Drew doesn't hate you. Bran thinks you're a manwhore and he doesn't get the D/s stuff, but Drew and Riley like you."

Case's face went hard, a memory obviously tapping into his seemingly never-ending supply of masculine fury. "Your brother offered me money to walk away from you."

Asshole. Manipulative jerk. She was having such a talk with her brother when she got home. It wasn't the first time Drew decided to screw around with her love life. "Yeah, my brother thinks he understands psychology. Trust me. He didn't mean what you thought he meant. You were being difficult. You were obviously stubborn and very proud. He thought you would sweep me off my feet just to spite him. Believe me—that's Drew move 101. When you want someone to move, give them something to fight against. In this case it was Drew himself."

Case's lips were a flat line. "Or he thinks I'm not good enough for his sister. I've found wealthy men tend to like to keep their family lines clean."

"Case, how much have you read about my family?" She had the sudden fear that he didn't know how scandalous her family line was.

He let go of her hand, his lips turning down. "I read some of the reports about your brother. I know you lost your parents at a young age."

"Do you know how I lost them?"

"I stayed away from the reports, Mia. I didn't want to know you. Not any more than I did. I was kind of crazy about the woman I did know. I didn't want to see just how false she was."

Mia felt herself flush. He didn't know. He didn't know how bad it was. How bad it would get. Somehow she'd counted on him knowing everything. There was zero chance that Ian Taggart hadn't unearthed all the Lawless family secrets, all the dirty truths under their money and shiny surfaces.

His family was made up of heroes. Every single one of his brothers had served in the military and gone on to the elite teams. The older brothers had both been Green Berets. Case and Theo had been SEALs.

She'd been shoved into foster care because according to the world, her father had murdered her mother and then killed himself. According to the reports, her father had tried to kill all of them.

She'd been too young to remember the night her parents had died, but she remembered how it felt when someone at her junior high had heard the story from a parent. She could see how the teachers had pitied her and still hear her classmates saying she was trash and that she would be as bad as her father some day.

She'd thought he'd known and didn't care.

"Hey, what's that look for?" Case asked.

She was saved from having to answer him by Hutch knocking on the door and holding up their keys. She hopped out of the SUV as fast as she could.

Case was on her ass in a second. She had the key from Hutch in her hand, but before she could grab her bag, Case lifted it up and stepped in front of her.

"Let's talk about protocol." It was obvious he was back in his commander mode. "You don't walk outside without an escort."

She frowned up at him. Did he have to be so freaking big? "I've told you that Tony won't meet with me if I'm not alone."

"I'm not talking about Tony. We could be here for a few days waiting for him to make contact. You're not allowed outside the motel room without an escort. Hell, you're not allowed inside the motel room alone. If I need to be somewhere, Fain or Hutch will take a turn babysitting you."

Babysitting her. Yeah, that was what every man wanted in his woman. But she'd gotten them all into this so she wasn't about to make things harder. "All right. Could I have Ezra please take me to my room? I think I'd like to take a nap. I've already sent a text to the phone number I was supposed to. Now we have to wait for the meet time. Hopefully it will be sometime tomorrow."

And then they would have their answer and Case would have a choice to make.

It was obvious he'd changed his mind about sleeping with her. Had he changed his mind about them? Or was he simply going to screw her six ways from Sunday and get her out of his system. Maybe he would fuck her senseless and then leave her the minute he had what he wanted. He would stride off into the distance and find his pretty, perfect submissive. He would find a girl who wouldn't ever make him angry or place herself in danger. Case's perfect woman wouldn't have a crazy, scandalous background. She wouldn't come with a whole group of brothers bent on vengeance.

Could she truly risk going to bed with him? Could she open herself up when he wasn't promising her anything past a quick lay? He'd said he changed his mind, but that could mean anything.

She'd already seen how easily Case could deny her.

Case looked back at Hutch and Ezra. "Can you two handle Michael? I want to get Mia secured and rested. We'll meet up tonight for dinner at 18:00."

Hutch nodded. "We can get him on his feet and into the room. I'll have a report on the kidnappers by dinner. I've already found names through facial recognition but I want to make a complete report on who these bastards are."

Case nodded. "Good, but get some sleep, too. Fain, you okay with the arrangements? I'm putting you on the other side of Mia's room so no one can take it. At least I'll know who our neighbors are. And you should be able to hear us if we shout."

"I'll keep watch for a few hours and then I'll get some sleep," Ezra said. "I'll help Hutch get Malone to their room and I'll keep my cell on. I've got decent reception here. If you need anything, holler."

Case's hand found hers. "Will do."

He started to lead her toward the left. Toward their room.

She was here. She was about to be alone with the man of her dreams and she was scared. Not by him. But by the power he had to utterly destroy her.

She stopped in the middle of the walkway. "I don't know about this."

He simply picked her up, his big arm going under her legs. "You should have thought about that before you took us to

Colombia and allowed kidnappers access to your sweet self, baby. This is going to end one way and one way only."

She went still in his arms. "And if I say no?"

He didn't look down at her. He simply strode toward the door. "You don't get to say no about this. If you say no about this, we'll be on a plane to Austin and I won't let you out of my sight until I've had a very long talk with your brothers. Don't think I can't write a report that will ensure your brothers never allow you out of the house on your own again."

He didn't understand. "I wasn't talking about the security protocols. I'll follow those. I'm not an idiot. I was talking about the rest of it."

His jaw went hard and he managed to get their door open without ever setting her down. He kicked the door closed behind them. She found herself on her feet, staring up at him.

"Why?"

It would have been so much easier to answer him if he hadn't asked the question in a tortured whisper. She couldn't quite meet his eyes. "You can rip me up, Taggart. For the last seven months I've done nothing but think about you, and now that I'm here I realize how devastating you can be. You dumped me. You wouldn't even talk to me. You didn't want an explanation. You didn't want to try. You walked away and if I hadn't found this lead, you would never have spoken to me again."

He ran a hand over his close-cropped hair. "You don't know that. I don't know that."

"Did you have plans to see me?"

"No," he shot back. "Mia, what's going on? You've admitted you did all of this to get my attention. You have my attention. I get it. I was stupid to ignore you. I was upset about my brother and you lied to me. I lied to you, too. Let's forget it all and go back to that first night. That was when I was real with you. That night we connected. Fuck all. We always connected. Even when we were lying, I could feel it. We made a real breakthrough and you're telling me you've changed your mind."

Yep, she was seriously alone in a room with him. "You don't know me. You might not like me when you know me and you're good at walking away."

He stared down at her. "I explained that. Are you going to hold it against me? Are you going to cost us time? Because I've learned that time isn't infinite and we're not guaranteed a specific amount." One of those callused hands came up, caressing her cheek. "I'd rather not waste more of whatever time we have."

She didn't want to waste a second, but she also finally admitted that she didn't want one night with him. She didn't want to screw him out of her system or prove that she could walk away this time. She wanted everything from him. "Case, I'm crazy about you. I don't think I can handle it if you turn away from me again, so I need you to know what you're getting into."

"Mia, tell me what's going on. What has you so scared?"

Maybe she should take this time. He was certainly right about there being no guarantee. She should know that better than anyone. The flight crew had been working for 4L for months. They'd lain in wait.

What if they hadn't merely been there to take her in? What if this had to do with the Taggarts? She remembered the first time she'd met the pilot. He'd flown her and her brothers to New York a few months back. Why not take them all? If they'd only been out for money, why not force Drew to access his accounts in exchange for his life and his sibling's? What if this wasn't about money and was all about the fact that they had the first real lead on Theo?

This was dangerous. Really dangerous. Not only for her. This would be dangerous for Case. They were already one man down.

Did she want to waste the time they might have telling him her sad story? Hadn't she learned at a young age to live in the moment?

It had been a horrible few hours. She'd taken charge because she'd needed to. She'd been strong because they'd needed her strength, but she'd discovered that there were times that she could give up all that wearying control and find another part of herself.

She looked up at him. “I’m afraid of so many things, Sir. I think I’d like to forget about all of them for a while.”

That ridiculously cut jawline of his tightened. “Fuck, Mia. I swear you’re going to kill me one day. We don’t have a written contract but that verbal one is in play here and now. Is that how Wade taught you to greet your Dom? Because I’ll have a real talk with him about that when we get home.”

She dropped to her knees, thankful the carpet was plush. Actually the room itself wasn’t half bad. It wasn’t the Four Seasons, but it was clean and neat. The bed looked far too small for Case, but she suspected he wasn’t going to complain.

Mia breathed in and released, letting the tension flow from her body. It had been months since she’d even tried to find this place. She’d enjoyed working with her training Dom. Javier had been a friend, but even when she’d trained with him, she’d closed her eyes and dreamed it was Case who held the flogger. It had been Case who spanked her. Case who tied her up.

She’d never allowed even intimate touching in her contract with Javier for one reason only. He hadn’t been Case.

“Is this better?” She lowered her head, letting her hands rest palms up on her thighs. They were splayed, and if she hadn’t been wearing clothes, her pussy would have been on display, ready and waiting for her Dom’s pleasure.

Her only Dom. She would have one and if it didn’t work with Case, she would lock that piece of herself away forever because he was it for her.

She might be able to get over him, might be able to move on and find another man she could click with. But she would never find another she would submit to.

“This would be perfect if you weren’t wearing any clothes. But I have a few questions while I’ve got you in this mood. I expect you’ll be less likely to hedge the truth with me while you’re kneeling at my feet.”

The tops of his feet came into view, old worn cowboy boots. She stared at the scuff marks. They were perfect for him, strong and battle-tested.

He was right about that. The simple act of settling into her position made her more willing to talk. "I'll try, Sir."

"Who was that nightgown for?"

She was glad she wasn't looking up at him or he would have seen her wince. "I put it in there when I flew from Austin to Dallas. I knew it would be an overnight flight to Colombia. I needed something to sleep in."

His hand found the top of her head and he gently forced her to tilt up. One brow was arched over his blue eyes. "You expect me to buy that? You sleep in ridiculously sexy lingerie?"

She tended to sleep in a tank top and panties, but he didn't need to know that. If he was anything like her friends' Doms he wouldn't let her sleep in anything at all. "No, Sir."

"Then what was the plan? I know there was a plan in there somewhere."

"I thought I might accidently need something from the main cabin after I'd gone to bed and then you would see me in my sexy nightie and very likely ravish me." She'd read too many romance novels.

"Put it on." He stepped back and offered her a hand up.

"Case, I know it was a silly thing to do." So why had she still snuck it into her bag? She'd casually made her way back to the bedroom after she'd landed the plane and carefully slid the gown into her oversized Louis Vuitton overnight bag.

He glanced her way. "Mia, do you know how many women in my life have gone to the trouble to seduce me?"

She could only guess. Thousands, likely. "A bunch, I would suspect."

"None," he replied. "Not a single one. I was the easy hookup who could get them off in my hometown. In the Navy, it was a parade of women who thought it would be awesome to fuck a SEAL. In the last couple of years, it's been women I picked up at bars. I've had two fairly serious girlfriends in my whole life and I initiated sex every single time. So yes, I want you to go to the bathroom and change into that filmy nightgown and I want you to show me how you would have played it."

"Those women were crazy." The words were out of her mouth before she could think about them. But they were also true. She'd planned to seduce that big cowboy from pretty much the minute she'd laid eyes on him. Schemed and plotted and planned to be with him any way she could.

His lips curved up in a sad smile. "They just knew I was a bad bet as a potential husband and honestly, the two girlfriends were probably more submissive outside the bedroom than I would have liked. But they were easy to be around and they didn't give me trouble."

She was trouble. A whole lot of trouble. She couldn't seem to help it. "I'm not like them, am I?"

He smoothed back her hair, staring down at her. "You are the opposite of every girl I've ever been with before. You're a woman who lied to me, used me to further your cause, and caused me to do the one thing I swore I wouldn't. Be the guy a girl cheats on her man with. You put me in that position."

She felt tears well. "I'm sorry, Case."

"It upset me more than I like to admit. I didn't like being the guy who hit on a taken woman, but beyond that I kind of wanted to know what the hell you were thinking getting engaged to him when it was so obvious you were meant for me. So go and put on that gown and show me how you would have seduced me."

Mia grabbed the bag he'd set down when they'd entered the room and made for the bathroom. He'd said the one thing guaranteed to get her moving.

You were meant for me.

She'd thought it the moment she'd seen him, had been sure of it the first time he'd kissed her.

For however long they had, she intended to make him understand that he'd been meant for her, too.

* * * *

Case locked the door. It should have been the first thing he'd done when they'd walked in, but his brain had been on Mia.

It was like just being near the woman tamped down his senses for anything but her. She was all he could see and hear and smell and touch. Everything else was background noise.

His cell trilled in his hand and he winced as he looked down at the phone.

Ian.

If he didn't answer, the big guy would likely call around until he found someone who knew where he was, and that meant getting Hutch on the phone. Hutch would try to lie, but he would wilt like a hothouse flower the minute Ian barked at him, and then Case would have much bigger issues.

The key to Ian was to act like the dumbass he believed everyone to be. Case took a deep breath and connected the line. "I swear I'm going to use a condom."

A chuckle came over the line and Case knew it was working. "I'm surprised you haven't already gone through a box."

The only reason he hadn't had been the kidnapping attempt he wasn't going to tell his brother about. "Yeah, well, she kicked me in the balls at the start of the evening. I think they're starting to work again now."

This time Ian's full-throated laugh came over the line. "I knew there was a reason I liked that girl." He sighed. "I wanted to make sure you're okay and give you an update on Erin. She and TJ are doing great. Faith just got in this morning. She's staying with Erin a few days while Ten's doing god knows what. He didn't come in with her so it's safe to say he's likely up to his old tricks."

Meaning Tennessee Smith was working some angle in the intelligence world. "I thought he'd quit the Agency completely."

"You know as well as I do no one ever completely quits the Agency. Where are you, Case?"

There was the protective older brother. The head of the family. The supreme ruler of all things Taggart. "I'm in Cartagena. Mia's chasing down some lead. I'm chasing her. I've got Michael and Hutch with me. We're cool."

He wasn't about to mention Ezra Fain because of the Guy factor. Ian didn't like Ezra's boss and his instincts would go on high alert if he heard Ferland had sent his own man in.

"That's a lot of backup for a spontaneous op."

The door opened and there she was. Holy fuck, yeah. His dick worked. It worked just fine and his brain didn't work at all. His brain should remember that this was the woman who'd nearly broken his man parts, but no. His brain fucking wanted her, too.

"Ian, I'm going to have to call you back."

"Condom. Don't forget the condom. She's naked, isn't she? I can hear it in your dumbass voice. Use that condom. I can't handle another kid right now. My life is full of poop and crying Taggart babies. Do you know how…"

Case shut the phone off because he had better things to do than listen to his brother complain about baby poop. He wasn't going to make a baby. He was, however, going to finally get inside her.

Something had been bugging her earlier, something had made her put up a temporary wall between them, but it seemed insignificant now. She'd said he could tear her apart and there had been something about how very easy it had been for him to walk away from her.

They should talk about that. He should explain to her that it hadn't been easy. It had been hard. He'd had to force himself not to call and when he'd been at the 4L building with Ian, he'd had to stop himself from hunting her down.

Her eyes went wide. "Oh, Case. You're here. I…I didn't think you would still be awake." A charming laugh came out of her mouth and one hand went up to touch her chest as though she was trying to hide those breasts from him. "I was just coming out to grab the bottle of water I left behind."

Yes, there was his sneaky, gorgeous, manipulative Mia. If he'd thought he liked the sweet girl who'd comforted him that day so long ago, he didn't even know what to call what he felt for the aggressive goddess she was now. He craved her. She rocked his world in a way that other girls couldn't.

In a way no woman ever had.

So he let go of all the things he knew he should do. He didn't want to talk to Mia. He wanted to play with her. He wanted to play hard.

"Is that right?" Case heard his voice going deep. Maybe it was simply natural to slip into his Dom role the minute she walked in a room. It would be a fight because she wouldn't allow him to top her outside the bedroom. She was far too wild for that. He'd snagged a couple of bottles of water from the plane and shoved them in his duffel. Hutch would find a few cases for them before dinner, but this would do for now. He reached in and grabbed one, wanting to play along. He didn't want a seriously good manipulation to go to waste.

"You mean this one?"

She managed to blush so prettily. She'd let her hair down and the blonde tresses caressed the tops of her breasts. The gown she wore was white and clung to her every curve. "Yes. I'm sorry to bother you. I always take a bottle to bed with me."

Oh, that bottle of water wasn't the only thing she was taking to bed with her today. No. He held it out and watched as she moved toward him. She bit her bottom lip as though trying to look like a soft little fawn worried about taking something from the hand of the big bad wolf.

He handed it over. "There you go, princess."

He winked her way and then picked up his duffel and moved to the one dresser. He placed the duffel on it and grabbed the small bag he kept of adapter plugs. He would need to keep his cell charged.

"Thank you," she said in a small voice. "I guess I should say good-night."

He could practically hear her frustration. Maybe it made him a bastard, but it brought a little smile to his face. One he absolutely wouldn't show to Mia because she was known to hurt a man. "Good-night. I hope you sleep well."

Besides, his girl didn't give up.

He felt a hand on his back as Mia moved in. "I can see you're going to be a hard sell, Taggart."

"Maybe I don't want you to think I'm easy." He glanced up. There was a mirror and he watched as her hand snaked around his waist and rested possessively over his belt buckle. He could barely see the top of her head over his shoulder.

"Those were my best seductive moves," she admitted. "Again, I was kind of counting on letting the girls work their magic on you, but I can see I'm going to have to up my game with you, Sir. The trouble is I don't know what you want. We've never played together before. I suppose if we were still on the airplane, I would have made up some excuse to sit with you and talk to you and flirt with you. But we're not there and honestly, I don't think I want to manipulate you. So how about I tell you that I want to play with you, Case. I want you to top me in the bedroom but don't ever think that it's an act of indulgence on my part. Submitting to you isn't about hoping that you'll hold me afterward or praying you might come to care for me. I'll handle that on my own. Playing with you means I want you so badly I haven't been able to look at another man since I saw you. I want to play with you because my body comes alive the minute you walk in a room and I can't imagine what it's going to do when you finally spread my legs and push that big cock of yours inside."

And she knew exactly when to stop the role-playing and get real with him. He reached for her hand, pulling it off so he could turn.

Mia was staring up at him, paler than she'd been before. She took a step back.

Shit. She thought he was rejecting her. It was so easy to forget that underneath all that gorgeous bluster and bravado she was just a woman who could get her feelings hurt. "I wanted to turn around so I could look you in the eyes when I tell you yes."

Her lips curved in a gorgeous smile. "Yes?"

He hadn't said that word to her nearly enough. He reached out and smoothed back her hair. "Yes, I'll top you. Yes, I'll be your Dom, and yes, we will absolutely play. Take off my shirt."

He wanted her hands on him, wanted her to be the one who touched him first. He would still be in control, but he'd had his time to explore her on the plane.

She stepped up and her hands immediately went to the hem of his T-shirt and she dragged it up. Case raised his arms and let her pull it off his body. It was good to start with his chest. Only a couple of nasty scars there. He watched her carefully as she took him in, her eyes roaming across his exposed flesh.

"I want to touch you, Sir."

He needed to make something very plain to her. He caught her hand in his and brought it right to his chest, forcing himself not to freaking purr at the feel of her small palm against his flesh. "Unless I've tied you up or given you explicit instructions, you are never to ask to touch me again. Know that I always want your hands on me. When we're sitting together, I want you to touch me so I remember you want me. I'll do the same. The discipline portion is for play only, princess. Any spanking I give you is to enhance your pleasure because you're wired that way and I'm wired to dominate you, but never think for a single second I don't want you because I withhold something during sex."

"I'll probably pout if you withhold orgasms." She let her hands run over his pecs, brushing over the nipples.

Yeah that felt good. "I look forward to it, but don't expect it tonight. I want to make you come all night long and by night I mean day because it's flipping nine a.m. I'm going to fuck you hard and then you'll get some sleep and be ready for whatever comes our way this evening."

She stopped at the nasty knife scar that ran over the left side of his chest.

Yes, she was staring at his scars and that didn't feel good. He was covered in them. She'd seen a few briefly when she'd walked in on him getting dressed, but she might change her mind when she saw just how damaged he was. "You should know there's a lot more where that came from. My back isn't pretty."

He didn't like to think about how he'd come by those scars. His Humvee had hit an IED and flipped and Case had taken a shit ton of shrapnel in the initial wreck and two bullets in the fight that happened afterward, but he'd survived and none of his men had been taken in. He would take the scars.

Would she? Mia had likely been surrounded by college boys all her life. College boys and hyper-ambitious lawyer types who had never taken a knife to the gut.

"Can I do whatever I want to them?" Her voice was a hushed whisper. Her eyes were staring at the scar.

Was she going to gently kiss it? Try to make it better? She was a sweet girl. "Of course."

Mia leaned over and dragged her tongue right over the place where an insurgent had tried to slice him open. Her small little butterfly tongue that would feel so fucking good on his dick ran over him. He hissed and had to force himself to stand still. She licked him, making sure she didn't miss a spot.

If he let her, she would end up controlling everything, and that wasn't what either of them needed. He was sure she'd gone through a procession of men who took her crazy-hot sexuality for granted, letting her lead the way without ever giving her what she needed. He wasn't going to make the same mistake.

He put a hand in her hair, tangling his fingers in the soft stuff and gently pulling her head back so she had to look at him. Apparently she was very enamored with his battle-scarred body and he would need to make sure she paid attention to his brain from time to time. "Do you know how much you please me?"

Her smile was brilliant. "I thought I just annoyed you."

Oh, she annoyed him. Annoyed him. Unsettled him. Infuriated him. Made him so fucking hot he couldn't stand another minute. "I can be annoyed and still want you. Take off the gown. I want to see you."

He wanted her naked. He'd briefly seen her breasts, but he'd only touched her pussy and he hadn't smacked that ass yet. It was very much time for that. She would get the full gamut of D/s tonight. Punishment and pleasure. She would have both.

She stepped back, her hands going to the straps of her gown. "I don't have scars, but I'm also not tiny, Case. I like my body. I think I'm pretty. I like my boobs and my hips. I know they're not the ideal beauty standard, but they're good enough for me. I hope they're good enough for you."

She pushed the straps off and the gown fell to the floor revealing her perfectly formed body. He had no idea what standard of beauty she was talking about because she was fucking incredible. An hourglass figure. Curvy hips, luscious breasts with pink-tipped nipples. She was perfect.

"You are simply the most beautiful woman I've ever seen. Turn around." His voice was dark, deep.

"Yes, Sir."

She turned, showing him her back. Blonde hair brushed halfway down her spine. It led his eyes to her waist and the curve of her hips. And her ass. So round and lush. He stepped in, unwilling to be a mere observer a second longer.

It was time to truly take over.

He stepped around so he could see her face. "Mia, do you understand that you were under our verbal contract for the entire flight today?"

She frowned and took her time in replying. "Yes, but this seems like a trap."

It was. "I believe we agreed that you would obey me in the field. That plane was the field. I put you in a safe place, a place I was very certain I would find you in after I'd dealt with the problem. You did not stay where I put you."

"I couldn't, Sir. They were going to kill the rest of the team."

"No. They threatened to kill the rest of the team. They wouldn't have done a damn thing until they'd figured out what happened to their man. They only had two hostages. They needed them both. There was no way they would have actually killed one of them. I was getting in position to handle the situation."

"I didn't know that. All I knew was they were in danger."

"You knew what I wanted you to do." He wasn't letting her off so easily. "You knew what you promised me you would do. I'm not saying that you weren't brave, princess. Not at all. There's zero question that you'll play the sacrificial lamb. I told you not to because I can't properly do my job if I know you're in danger."

Her cheeks went pink and her eyes widened as she looked up at him. "You can't expect me to hide when people I care about are in danger."

"You barely know Hutch and Michael. You met Fain about ten hours ago."

She sniffled a little, obviously emotional. "All right. You can't expect me to hide when people you care about are in danger."

There was the sweet girl that mixed with crazy bitch in a way guaranteed to make him insane. He couldn't help it. He leaned over and brushed his lips against hers, the moment far more sweet than he would have expected. He'd thought when he'd gotten on the plane that he could fuck her and get her out of his system, but it turned out there was no way out of this woman's trap. It had been custom made to catch him and keep him…maybe for life. "I respect that. You can't know how much, but I have to get you to understand that nothing is more important than your life. Walk to the bed and place your palms flat on it. Legs spread wide."

Her hands had found his waist, her lips turned up to tempt him. "I get spanked for being brave?"

Such a brat. He kissed her again, briefly, before moving up and kissing her nose and that place between her brows and her forehead. "Yes. You get spanked by your Dom for putting something very precious to him in danger. You'll always get spanked for it. Every single time. Go and do what I asked. And Mia, pick a safe word."

A shiver went through her body, but he rather thought that was all about arousal and not fear. Her pupils had gone big, her shoulders relaxing. Not the signs of a woman who was afraid.

She wanted it, wanted the discipline, the stimulation.

His dominance.

"Pick a safe word. Now."

"Coffee. Because I need some." She turned on her heels with the sexiest smirk on her face and walked to the bed that would likely mangle his spine and that he was sure his feet would hang off of.

"You don't need any caffeine," he promised. "I'll wake you up properly and then we'll both get some sleep."

She did as he'd asked and placed her palms on the bed, leaning over and putting that stunning backside of hers on display. It would be so easy to shove his jeans down and fuck his way deep inside her, but that would have to wait.

"Your training Dom spanked you?" Though he didn't like to think about another man putting his hands on her, he had to ask. He needed to know what her boundaries were. Had they been back in Dallas, he would have sat down with her and gone over hard and soft limits. Here, they would have to wing it. He put a palm on her ass cheek, feeling the silky skin there.

A tremor went up her spine. "Yes, he did. We had a session on spanking and then several follow-ups. And I also was late once and mouthed off twice. Good times."

He could only imagine what an unholy brat she'd been. His cock was pressed against the fly of his jeans, but he was going to ignore the hungry fucker for now. He rubbed a hand up and over her curves, familiarizing himself with her. "And how did you like it?"

"It wasn't a big deal, Case. I can handle a simple spanking."

But this wouldn't be simple and apparently Javier had gone easy on her. He could understand that. She hadn't been Javi's so he would do nothing but warm her up, play with her a little. He would leave the real discipline to her eventual man unless she was a pain junkie who needed it. Case didn't think Mia was a pain slut, but she did need something from him.

He brought his hand back and let it crack against her pretty ass.

A loud gasp filled the air, but Mia managed to stay still.

"There's a difference between a training warmup and a disciplinary spanking. This is what happens when you disobey me in the field and nearly get yourself murdered." He slapped her ass again, careful where he placed the smack. He was rough. Despite his earlier words, he still intended to find out if she got hot, too.

He gave her five sharp slaps, moving his hand over and around, peppering her flesh but not paying too much attention to one spot. Her cheeks immediately flushed to a nice pink.

"I don't think I like the disciplinary part so much, Case," she admitted.

"I didn't like standing outside the cabin while that asshole held a gun on you." Two more. "I didn't like the fact that I nearly panicked when I should have been cool and precise."

"I'm sorry." The words were said on a little sob.

Now they were getting somewhere. She'd been so collected since that moment when the plane had tossed them to the floor. She'd been a damn near perfect partner, with the singular exception of placing herself in the line of fire. He'd been so very certain she would lose it on him after he'd been forced to murder the man who'd come after her, but she'd merely yelled at him for getting blood on the carpet. She'd been patient when he'd locked her in that tiny safe box, and as far he could tell she'd calmly walked into the killing zone and tried to negotiate for Michael and Hutch's lives. To top it all off, she'd taken over flying the plane and gotten them where they needed to go.

But there was a soft place inside that competent woman. She was trying to hide it, trying to not show him how much the day had worn her down. He needed to blast past her bravado and give her a place to let it all loose.

"I'm sorry." Her hands clutched at the bedspread, nails trying to find purchase. "I'm sorry. I didn't mean to make things hard for you."

He found a rhythm that still managed to keep her off balance. "Is that all you're sorry for?"

Over and over he spanked her, heating her skin to a hot shade of pink.

"I'm sorry I kicked you in the balls."

He'd almost forgotten about that in the horror of the day. It didn't say much for his freaking life that getting his balls shoved into his body by his sub's knee was the second worst thing to happen to him in a twenty-four-hour period. That deserved a nice smack and he laid it right between her cheeks.

Mia yelped and then a whimper came out of her mouth. "I'm really sorry, Case."

He paused for a moment to let his hand slide down, brushing between her legs. There it was. He breathed a sigh of relief because her pussy was nice and wet, her labia puffy with arousal.

They would get where he needed them to go.

"I'll take my punishment." He let his hand play around her pussy, delving lightly and skimming the surface. "I was an ass and I would tell any female I know to do the same thing to a man who treated her that way. My fault, princess. You walked back in and I suddenly lost the ability to think with my brain. So I'm not going to demand anything for that. This is all about what happened when you walked into that cabin. You got Michael shot."

"I didn't."

He hated pointing this out to her, but she needed to truly understand what had happened. He gave her another five. By his count she was almost at thirty. Such a stubborn girl, but he could be patient. "You did. Before you walked in, the mere threat was enough. Once they had you, they didn't need Michael or Hutch. They would have taken them out very quickly. There were only two of them and three of you, two of whom are battle trained. Why keep them around when they could control me through you?"

There was the first sob. "I didn't think about it. I just did it."

"You followed your instincts." He got it, but he had to make her understand that his training trumped her instinct. "They were wrong. I will follow you when it comes to solving a puzzle, but you will follow me when things get dangerous. That's the only way this works."

Her knees wobbled and then she started to crumble.

He caught her before she hit the floor. Case hauled her up as she began to sob, shifting her easily so he could cradle her.

"I'm sorry." Her arms went around his neck as she finally broke.

"I am, too," he whispered, hugging her tight. He sat down on the bed, cuddling her close. This was what he'd wanted, what he'd worked toward. She needed to let it out or she would be restless, unable to sleep. She needed to let out all the horrors of the day. "I'm so fucking sorry about what happened today."

She wrapped herself around him. There was not an ounce of self-consciousness he could find in the way she clung to him. Despite the ass he'd been before, she seemed to offer up all her warmth and trust in him now. She sobbed into his shoulder, her body shaking as she let it all out.

He held her close, comforting her in a way he'd never comforted a woman before. Only Mia. There was something deeply intimate about holding her that calmed him even as she wound down. He reveled in the way she curled on his lap, her whole body exposed. Her soul exposed.

He ran his hands over her, connecting them. "I'm sorry I wasted all that time."

She looked up at him, her face blotchy and still so damn beautiful to him. "I'm sorry about that, too. You're a very stubborn man."

He couldn't help but smile. "Do you feel better?"

"And a manipulative Dom." She cuddled back down. "Yes. I do feel better. Today kind of sucked, Case. It sucked and it was also pretty awesome. I'm sorry about Michael. I'll apologize to him tonight."

"He knows." Michael wouldn't accept an apology from her. In his mind, he wouldn't see that she had a thing to feel sorry about, but Case knew the difference. If Michael had died, Mia would have to live with it forever. He didn't want that light dimmed. "But if you do it again, we're going to have a real problem."

She brought her hands up to cup his face. "I can handle the spanking. Hell, I needed that. I…struggle sometimes to let go and cry the way I need to. I feel better, lighter than I did before. So you feel free to spank me when I need it or when you need it, but you can't walk away from me again. I can't handle that. I need to know you'll work it out with me if you get mad."

He couldn't imagine that she could do anything to make him walk away. Now that he looked at it, he'd been afraid of her, afraid she couldn't handle what he needed, afraid she would reject him, and he hadn't been able to handle the thought at the time. He'd been overwhelmed with losing Theo. Their timing had been shitty. He wasn't about to make the same mistake twice. "I promise. Are we going to do this? I want you, Mia. Not just for a night. Not just for the op. I want you to try with me. I want you to come back to Dallas with me and we'll get a contract in place and we'll work everything out. If you don't want that, then we need to stop here and now. I don't want a taste of you. I want a full meal and I'll want it all the time. I won't be that sad-sack boy toy who follows you around. I'll be demanding and I'll need you more than you can know. I'm willing to give it some time, but eventually I'll want you to move to Dallas and be with me. I'll want you to sleep with me. You'll go to sleep after I've fucked you senseless and you'll wake to my cock in your pussy. That's what it's going to mean to be my woman. So you think about it because once we start this, I won't hold back again."

"I don't have to think. I've been thinking about it for months. I want you and not for a night. I think I might want you forever."

That was good enough for him. He picked her up, tossed her on the bed, and got ready to claim what belonged to him.

CHAPTER SIX

Mia winced as she tumbled to the bed. He hadn't gone easy on her ass, but she didn't mind. She'd felt. Felt hurt. Felt her fear. Felt the freedom that came with letting it all go so it didn't burden her. So many years she'd hidden what she felt because the world seemed so out of whack. One moment she'd been beloved and safe, and the next the world had been filled with pain. Her childhood had turned out all right, but it was still defined by that moment when she realized the world she'd known was gone.

So she'd buried her needs and tried to fit in. Eventually she'd understood it was all right to show some emotions. Happiness, anger, sympathy. But hurt and fear were still hard for her.

Case had given her that gift. He'd known what she'd needed.

She looked up at him. How could he think for a second she wouldn't want him? Because he had some scars? Maybe she was a pervert, but she liked them. He would be far too pretty without them.

"Spread your legs for me." He used that super-dark, rich-as-velvet voice on her.

Sex had always been something hurried or casual. Even when

her heart had been involved with the man, the sex had seemed rushed, like something they should do and enjoy but not get lost in. Not with Case. Case seemed willing to lavish her with intimacy, to make her feel like sex was a language between them they should learn and use. A language only the two of them knew.

Slowly she spread out on the bed, feeling the air on her skin. It was cool, but his eyes were hot as her legs opened for his gaze. Mia knew she would feel awkward and weird with another man. Case was it. He was the one for her.

He stood at the foot of the bed, his eyes between her legs. "Touch yourself. I want you to feel how wet you got from that spanking. How hot it made you."

She knew. Even as she'd cried on his shoulders she'd still felt desire. She wondered if it would ever be simple with Case. There was no one emotion she felt for the man. She could feel so many things at once, it made her head spin. But now that he'd gotten rid of her anxiety and stress, lust seemed to rule her brain.

Never taking her eyes off him, she let one hand slide down her body to the apex of her thighs. She was well aware she was putting on a show for him, and hell that made her even hotter.

Mia let her fingers slide across her mound, pressing down briefly on her clitoris. Even the slight pressure she applied made her sigh in pleasure. The spanking and emotional outburst that came after conspired to make her languid and ready for an orgasm.

"Don't you fucking dare," Case growled, though he made no move. He didn't need to. He was perfectly, sexily intimidating from where he stood. "You make yourself come and I'll have you tied up and taking an anal plug before you can take another breath. That's one of the rules and an important one."

She stared at him. He was so hot when he was threatening her with dirty sex. "You brought an anal plug?"

"And lube, princess. I learn from my elders. I've always got a bag packed in case a gorgeous blonde shows up in need of help. I have to be able to discipline her in any way I see fit. I've got some rope in there, too."

She wasn't sure she liked the sound of that, but she didn't stop what she was doing. After all, if he did have a plug, she would bet he wouldn't hesitate to use it. "I'll have to remember to be good then." She took a long breath because her pussy was soaking wet. "I bet I did a number on your jeans, Sir."

A slow smile crossed his face. "You did and no, I don't mind at all. And Mia, I know what that look on your face means now. That's the frown you get when you get jealous. I packed the bag for you. I don't actually keep a go-bag with full-on bondage toys sitting in my closet. You kicked me in the balls and I crawled over and managed to grab a bunch of lube and sex toys. I was optimistic. Get your finger wet. Fuck your little pussy with it."

She moved her finger down again, circling it around her core before dipping inside. It wasn't enough. Not nearly. She was certain her Case was so much larger than that tiny finger of hers, but she imagined it was his cock. He would dip inside her, filling her up and rubbing her all the right ways. She could feel herself getting wetter and wetter, her arousal coating her finger.

"Stop," Case commanded. He moved to the side of the bed. "Let me see."

She drew her saturated finger out of her pussy and offered it up to him. Hopefully he would see that she didn't need more foreplay. She was ready for him.

Case grasped her wrist and drew it up toward his mouth. His tongue came out, licking off the cream of her arousal. He sucked her finger into his mouth and tasted her.

She felt it deep inside. "Case…"

He couldn't make her wait. She'd waited forever to be here with him, to have him connect with her.

"You taste like heaven." He stepped away, going straight for his duffel. "I think I need more. Grip the headboard."

Was he trying to kill her? Why couldn't he jump on top of her and take her? She was ready. More than ready. Her whole body was primed. She watched as he pulled his boots off and tugged his jeans and boxers down, leaving that magnificent warrior body on display. He reached down and when he turned, there was a length of rope in his hands.

She quickly gripped the headboard, unwilling to risk another long spanking. The man liked to draw things out.

"Excellent." He put a knee on the bed and showed her the rope. "I'm going to tie you down because you're a very slippery girl. I don't want you running off in the middle of sex. I want you entirely focused on me and what I'm going to do to your body."

"I'm focused, Case. This is entirely unnecessary." The words came out in a breathless plea because he was naked. He was all kinds of beautifully naked, and she could see his cock. It was as magnificent as the rest of him. Long and thick, with big balls she wanted to lick and suck on. His dick was hard, the flesh a shade of red mixed with purple, and she could already see a pearly drop on the head.

How could he be so hard and ready and not jump her?

He chuckled as he went to work on her hands. He bound her right wrist in an elaborate tie before threading the rope through the round pegs of the headboard and going to work on her left wrist. "I doubt that. You've got issues. You see something shiny and you take off after it. I need you to understand that I might not be the shiniest thing you ever chased after, but I'm the thing that caught you and I'm going to keep you. Even if it means tying you up."

She liked how it felt to be at his mercy. It was a fantasy of hers, but she could only indulge in it because she trusted this man with her life. Case would move heaven and earth to make sure she didn't get hurt.

When he was done securing her, he stepped back and laid a palm flat against her chest, above her breasts. Slowly, like the freaking sadist he seemed to be, he moved his hand over her body, cupping her breasts and trailing down.

"Tell me this is mine."

That was easy. She'd been his for a very long time. He was simply too foolish to know that. "I'm yours. My body is definitely yours."

He ran his hand down to her pussy. "You won't regret it, Mia. I'll work hard to make sure I earn your trust every single day. No more lies between us. Always honesty. I need it. I need it from you more than anyone else."

"No more lies." There wasn't any reason. She didn't want anything to come between them. Not ever again. "I'll always be honest with you. I'm honestly going to die if you don't fuck me soon, Sir."

A wide grin split his handsome face. "My mission is to keep you from dying. But I think I promised you something first. I promised I would learn your body with my hands."

He moved to the end of the bed, running his hands down her legs to her ankles. He spread her further and climbed on the bed. "I believe I also promised to learn you with my mouth."

He moved like a tiger, ready to eat her up. There was nothing to do. He'd caught her and all she could do now was let him have his way. He moved slowly, head bent, but eyes careful on hers. He looked up her body as he ran his nose right above her pussy, so close she could feel the heat of his breath. She waited for him to drop down and cover her with his mouth, but he moved higher. His tongue dipped into her belly button briefly before dragging up her torso.

He captured a nipple in his mouth and Mia felt her whole body tense with anticipation. Pleasure raced through her veins as he sucked on her. His hand came up and he caught her other nipple between his thumb and forefinger, pinching her hard and making her squeal. Her body seemed to vibrate with pure pleasure. He sucked her, his teeth sizzling at the edge of her flesh. Her toes curled. He licked and laved his affection on one and then the other nipple while his body pressed hers into the bed. Hot. Her skin got so hot because the man was a furnace. She wanted to put her arms around him, but she was forced to curl her fingers around the rope. Frustration welled, mingling with the anticipation. His body lay on top of hers, his cock full against her sex, but he didn't move to join them together. His pelvis pressed against her core, the sensation so tantalizing.

There wasn't anywhere to go, anything to do except to feel. She felt Case's heat and the edge of his teeth. Felt how he pressed her body open and how his cock pushed against her pussy. Felt how her body was soft and wet and welcoming him.

He switched places, his fingers tormenting the nipple he'd just sucked. He was everywhere. She couldn't think of anything except him and that was perfect. Case had been in the forefront of her thoughts since the moment she'd met him.

He moved down her body, kissing and caressing her. His hands shifted, holding her tight when he would take a nip. He held her down, letting her feel his strength. His teeth would bite down gently, just enough to make her squirm, and then he would soothe the little ache with his tongue. He moved under her breasts and down her belly. He kissed her hips and pressed a long kiss right above her pelvic bone.

His body wasn't on top of hers anymore, but she could still feel his dominance in how her wrists couldn't move and the way he pressed her legs apart. In that moment she was his. He had all the control and there was something so sensual about the way he used his strength to pleasure her.

He ran his nose down again, seeming to glory in the way she smelled. If she'd been self-conscious before, Case's open sexuality would have put her at ease. He loved what he was doing. Yes, he was pleasuring her, but there was no way to miss how the man was reveling in the act.

Mia nearly came off the bed with the first long lick of his tongue. She gasped and looked down the length of her body. He was staring back up at her, his blue eyes hot as he devoured her. He parted her labia and his tongue dove deep.

He speared her, piercing her with long, deep thrusts of his tongue. His mouth encased her with heat.

So good. It felt so good. She wanted to buck against him, to force him to fuck her harder, give her more, but he was far too smart for that. His weight deliciously crushed her, pinning her and making it impossible to do anything but take his torture. He finally seemed to find some mercy. His hand moved up, callused fingers finding her clitoris, and he pressed down. He captured the slippery button and rubbed until she couldn't hold back the wave a second longer.

Her whole body spasmed, tightening and then releasing in a grand wave of pleasure. It raced through her veins and took over her whole system. Her world narrowed down to him. There was only Case. His warm skin. His masculine scent. The sound of his groan as he finished making a meal of her.

He gave her one last lick and then got to his knees.

She watched with languid eyes as he rolled a condom over his big cock, stroking himself before he fell on her. His muscular body covered her own. He didn't hold an ounce of his weight off her. It didn't matter. She wanted it. Wanted to be pressed down by him, mastered by this one man. He was the only man she would ever allow to master her.

Case kissed her, his tongue going deep and giving her back the taste of her own arousal. She was there on his lips and tongue. She'd branded him as surely as he'd scorched her.

His cock pressed against her pussy. So big. So hot. She wanted that cock like she'd wanted nothing before. She needed Case inside her, their bodies connected.

Still, he seemed determined to take his time. He caught her face between his hands, his body weight controlling hers, his rope taking care of her hands. He held her face still as he kissed her over and over again. Case seemed to need control in a way she couldn't completely understand. He overwhelmed her. He'd done it from the moment he'd walked into her life. It had scared her at first, but now it seemed like something to treasure because he was here with her. They were finally on the same page at the same time, and Mia threw away every reservation she had.

Case could handle her family and she could handle Case. She could handle his need to dominate without losing herself. He needed her. He needed her strength and her passion, and she intended to give it all to him.

Her life had been a series of struggles, but if all that pain she'd lived through led her to him, then she would be satisfied.

She gave up any thought of fighting this wave she was riding. The pleasure was simple and amazing, but the emotion was beyond anything she'd felt. He was hers.

She would have given a lot to wrap her arms around him, but for now he seemed to need those ties and bindings so she settled for submitting, for giving him what he requested with every dominant thrust of his tongue.

"Waited so long for this," he murmured against her lips. "Want it to be good."

He pushed up and stared down at her as though memorizing her face. His hips moved, rolling against her core. His big cock slid over her clitoris and she could feel the pleasure starting to build again.

"It's already the best I've ever had." She wasn't going to play coy with him. She was a woman who'd figured out how to play men from a fairly early age, but she intended to use none of those tricks on him. Honesty. It was all she wanted with him. And this. Her eyes nearly rolled to the back of her head as he rubbed against her again. Yes, she needed this.

His eyes seemed to soften. "Me, too. But I promise this is going to be even better."

His hips flexed and he surged inside, his cock invading with ruthless precision. Once more he devastated her senses. He didn't play around and give her time to take him. He gave himself to her in one hard thrust and she gasped at the sensation. She was so wet and ready there wasn't any pain, but she was gloriously full. She tried to squirm, to adjust around him.

"No. Give it a second." He'd stilled over her, his cock as deep as it could go. "You feel so fucking good, princess. Give it a minute. You were built to take me. I'm beginning to think you were just fucking built for me. Wrap your legs around me. Hold me tight."

He pressed down again, leaning over to kiss her senseless as she did his bidding. That seemed to be his go-to move when he wanted her attention. All he had to do was press his mouth to hers and she lost her damn mind. While he kissed her, merging their mouths again and again, his body moved, slowly dragging his cock out only to force his way back in. He took it slow and easy, not losing an ounce of control. He drugged her with kisses, with the press of his body against hers.

He ground down and she went over the edge again.

Finally he picked up the pace, his hips moving faster as he seemed to decide it was his time. He fucked her hard and she held on for dear life to the rope that bound her. His face contorted beautifully as he held himself hard against her while he came.

Case fell on her body, burying his face in the crook of her neck and sighing.

It was a beautiful moment that would have been even more so if she could hold on to him the way he was clinging to her. She let the thought go and took what he was willing to give her.

Case lay there for a moment and then he kissed her again before pushing himself off the bed. He winked down at her. "Give me a minute and then we'll get some sleep."

She frowned. "Uhm, aren't you forgetting something?"

His lips quirked up. "Not a thing I can think of."

He disappeared into the bathroom. She heard the water turn on.

Was he taking a shower and leaving her here? She glanced up at the ropes. Could she get herself out? Maybe she could break the bed and then she would go after that cowboy and teach him a lesson or two about what constituted play and what she wouldn't put up with.

"Calm down," he said, but that playful smile was still on his face. "I was teasing."

His hands went up to the bindings on her wrists, easily untying her. He caught her wrist in his hand, studying the skin there before bringing it to his mouth where he laid a gentle kiss on her pulse before doing the same to her other hand. Before she knew it, he was hauling her up into his arms.

"You weren't going to leave me there while you took a shower?" She cuddled close to him, reveling in his masculine strength.

He strode to the small bathroom where the water was already making the place steamy. "It might be the best way to keep track of you, but no. I'm going to trust you to keep your promises to me. You'll obey me in the field. We're in the field now, Mia. You're mine to protect and I intend to do that. If I need to go into the city, I'll leave you here with Fain and Michael. I need to do some research of my own and I can't do that if I'm watching both our backs. Don't disappoint me. If you try to leave I will hunt you down."

He set her on her feet in the tub, the water warming her. He stepped in behind her and drew the curtain closed.

She started to turn, but he caught her, his arms caging her while he drew her back against his body. She could feel his cock stirring against her backside again as his hands came up to cup her breasts. "Why would I leave?"

He held her tight. "You would have a million excuses. All of them good and right in your head and none of them will work on me. You'll decide you've figured out a way to help me. You'll think up some crazy scheme and need to track me down to tell me. You'll do any number of things that will seem to be the right thing to do at the time, but inevitably lead to chaos, more chaos, and my hand smacking your ass silly. So don't. Don't leave this room. Obey me so I can concentrate on finding my brother instead of worrying about my woman."

It was the exact right thing to say. Just hearing him call her his woman practically made her melt at his feet. "All right, Case. I'll be a good girl."

He chuckled against her ear. "Oh, you couldn't be a good girl if you tried. You are my incredible brat, and I wouldn't have you any other way."

"And you're an insanely dominant bastard," she replied even as he started to move his hand down her torso. "But you're mine."

"All yours," he agreed and proceeded to show her just what that meant.

CHAPTER SEVEN

Four days later, Case stepped out into the harsh light of the afternoon. Heat crashed into him, immediately followed by a breeze from the ocean that washed it away. He could smell the ocean, hear the sounds of the parties going on down the beach.

God, he wished he was here with Mia in different circumstances. He wished he was at one of the stunning beach resorts that dotted this part of Colombia and it was their vacation, one they took to get away from work and worry, one where he could spend the whole time pampering her and pleasuring her. He would be here with his family, his brothers and their wives. He and Theo and Ian and Sean would go fishing while the girls went to the spa. Even Erin liked a long massage. She hadn't at first. She'd tried to be one of the guys, but Charlotte and Grace had won her over. Mia would fit right in with those amazing women.

But Theo wouldn't be with them and Erin was alone. This wasn't a vacation. This was a mission and he had to get his head in the game. He'd spent days in bed with Mia, telling himself that he needed to ensure that there wasn't any heat on them, that no one was coming their way. He'd known that about twenty-four hours in, but he'd stayed close to her. Now, as they waited for the apparently lazy as crap Tony Santos, he needed to do what he should have done that first day. He needed to investigate.

The trouble was his body didn't want to leave the woman in his motel room behind. It was early afternoon, but Mia was still napping, still readjusting to that first day when she'd stayed up a full day and a half between the flight and the cleanup. His body wanted to be right there beside her, sleeping with his arms wrapped around her and waking up only to make love to her again.

He didn't try to fool himself. He'd made love to that woman. His woman. Mia was his and she was going to stay that way.

"Should I take your place?" Fain asked, peeling away from the side of the building where he'd been clinging to the shadows like a wraith.

He was good. Case would give him that. Case hadn't realized he was there. It made him think. He needed to read Fain's file, figure out what made him tick. If he had any choice in the matter, he would figure out a way to shove the dude out, but he needed backup and the man who had watched his back faithfully for years still wasn't at full strength. He trusted Hutch, but Hutch wasn't battle-tested. Fain was former Special Forces and that meant he was a badass.

Of course, being a badass didn't mean he wasn't a bad man.

"First off, you're not taking my place because my place was in bed with her," he explained in a matter-of-fact voice. "If I catch you trying to take my place, I'll kill you. That's not a euphemism. It's not a turn of phrase intended to make you think I'm rough. It's the truth, but not the whole truth. I probably don't need to explain how I'll torture you if you lay a hand on my girl, but you should know I've already got plans. I've seen how you look at her. She's made her choice. You better damn well honor it."

Fain was wearing sunglasses but Case could practically see those dark eyes of his rolling. "You Taggarts are so very dramatic. You like to play at being cool and icy, but the hotheadedness will be your downfall. It was for your brother."

Case narrowed his eyes, getting Fain in his sights. It was like that from time to time when he really wanted to hurt someone. The rest of the world faded away and all he could see was his target. "You have something to say about Theo?"

Fain shrugged and if he was intimidated, Case couldn't tell. "I could actually say it about any of your brothers. Like I said, your family tends to follow their passions instead of sense and logic. I've read your files. My boss has Agency connections, too."

"Files?" He didn't like the sound of that despite the fact that he knew it to be true. He'd just thought about reading whatever file Hutch had worked up on Fain.

"Of course. McKay-Taggart is closely watched. Like I told you before, after I got out, I went looking for work. Unfortunately, it's not like your boss takes applications, but I wanted in. It's why I moved to Dallas a year ago. I was supposed to meet with him eight months ago, but then, well, you know what happened. Big Tag closed all hiring and I landed with Ferland. He definitely keeps watch on you all."

Maybe there was more to the minor feud between the companies than Ian thought. And he surely knew the event Fain was talking about. Theo's death. Ian had stopped all hiring and the entire team had pulled in on itself. Theo's partner, Deke, had been reassigned and they'd moved on very slowly. "What's he got against us?"

"You make him look bad on a regular basis. He's everyone's second choice. He's the cut-rate version of McKay-Taggart and that bothers him more than you can know. But he is right about a few things and one of them is his assessment of the Taggart men. You're too emotional."

Case had to snort at the very idea. "We're not emotional."

Taggarts were known for being cold operatives. Fair and smart, but willing to make the hard choices. His oldest brother was a legend in intelligence circles for how quickly he'd moved into the upper echelons. The Agency still called Big Tag when they needed a favor.

"Let's see, Big Tag screwed up a major op over a woman. Sean Taggart couldn't keep it in his pants. Ended up shot and nearly dying in the middle of a war he didn't see coming because he was far too worried about cooking dinner for his target and getting her in bed." Fain sobered. "And your twin. You have to know he screwed up that assignment. He wanted to show off for his girl. I've read the files. His girl should have been the one in charge. Erin Argent was far more qualified to run that op, but again, Big Tag wanted little brother to feel good about himself. I'm not saying this to piss you off. I'm not. I'm saying it because I'm putting my life on the line with you and I don't want you to make the same mistakes."

He wanted to argue, but he knew Theo. He knew what his twin had done. Case had gone over and over it with Erin and Ian and Michael. Anyone who would listen. Theo had a reckless streak in him. He'd always been the one who felt more, cared too much, and he'd been so in love with Erin.

Ian had been in love with Charlotte and it had almost cost him everything. Sean had nearly died because he'd been too in love with Grace to see the real traitor in front of him.

Was he making the same mistake with Mia?

Fain held up his hands as though offering to end this particular line of questioning. "Just think about it. I can put one of your fears to rest. I assure you I'm not going to touch Mia. Yes, she's beautiful and I will admit that when I first met her I thought about hitting on her. But you're right. She's made her decision and I think she made it a long time ago. I still hope to make the move over to McKay-Taggart one day so I think fucking around with the boss's brother's girl might not get me on a short list. But protecting her might. That's what I want out of this, Taggart. I want a shot at the next spot that opens up."

"Why would you want to work for someone you don't like?" Case asked, trying to stay cool. "Besides, I doubt there will be a spot."

Fain shook his head. "I never said I didn't like the man.

Actually, I have no real idea if I like Big Tag or not, but I admire the hell out of him. With the singular exception of his emotional decisions, he's brilliant. When he's running an op that doesn't involve his family, there's no one I would rather follow into battle. McKay-Taggart is going places. And I think there will be an opening and fairly soon because I've heard Miles and Dean are going to make a move."

Case didn't buy it. There was no way Adam and Jake left. They'd been with the firm since the beginning. "They're not leaving the company."

"That's not what I've heard, man. I've heard Miles is perfecting a piece of software that's going to revolutionize how we search for missing persons. Why would he stay and work close cover when he can change the world? You honestly think Big Tag would hold them back? He didn't hold his brother back. Sean left a long time ago."

Fain had no idea what he was talking about. He didn't know the team. They stuck together. They were a family. "We'll see."

He didn't need to argue with Fain. He had way too much to think about as it was. Like whether or not he was capable of making proper decisions around Mia.

He could concentrate on that because he didn't need to think about the company getting torn apart. That wasn't going to happen. Fain was simply wrong about that.

But Sean had left. Sean had followed his bliss and that had brought him great satisfaction. Would Ian stand in the way if Adam and Jake wanted to grow their own business?

"Stay here and watch her door," Case ordered. He pulled the baseball cap he'd brought out of his pocket and settled it on his head. Between the cap that would disguise the color of his hair and the aviators he covered his eyes with, he would be fairly nondescript as he walked the streets of Cartagena.

"I can help," a deep voice said.

Case looked up and Michael was leaning against the door of the room he shared with Hutch. His skin was a little pale, but otherwise he was upright and his eyes were steady. Still, he'd taken a bullet not four days before. "You need to rest."

"No, he needs to watch me so you have backup," Fain said with a sardonic tone. "You won't take Hutch with you if Malone is out. This is what I was talking about. You're making decisions based on the fact that you like a girl, decisions that could get you killed. He's your partner, right? You have partners from what I understand. He's got your back."

Case walked toward Michael's room, unwilling to have this discussion in front of someone who wasn't family. He already didn't like how much Fain knew about the inner workings of his company.

Michael stepped back in and shut the door, a grimace on his face as he moved. "He's right, you know. You're making this decision based on your dick."

His dick didn't make decisions for him at all. Never once in his life. His heart was another matter altogether. "I'll be fine."

Michael's face darkened. "What would you say to me if I wanted to head out into a foreign city where my brother had last been seen and where there's likely someone who wants to take a member of our team. You would be an awfully good bargaining chip when it came to Mia. She would give herself up to save you. Hell, she gave herself up to save me and she's not in love with me."

In love. The idea made him nervous. It was one thing to want her. It was another to give his soul to her the way Ian had with Charlotte and Sean with Grace. He'd seen his mother do that and she'd been left with nothing when his father had walked out. She'd been a shell, empty and hollowed out.

Did he even want to feel that way about a woman? He couldn't forget how shitty it had felt the first time she'd lied to him, how everything had fallen apart and he'd been more alone than he could have imagined.

He needed to think about the mission. The op. That was what mattered. Sometimes when in the thick of things, it was important to draw back and get through each step separately.

He needed to take a look at the bank that had been hit, needed to see where his brother had stood. If there was any way to quietly talk to some people at the bank, he would do it. Discreetly.

Theo was the important thing here. Still, he couldn't leave Mia alone and leaving her with Fain was like leaving her alone. He didn't know the man yet. He couldn't trust Fain. Not with her.

But Michael had a point. If this was about Michael's brother, JT, Case would never allow him to go in alone. He wouldn't ever let his partner walk into a situation without backup. Not if he could do something about it. "Watch Fain, please. I'll take Hutch with me."

Michael rolled his eyes. "You'll have to wake him up, but I made sure his SIG is in working order. He's been busy tending crops or something on his online game and hasn't cleaned it in months. One of these days, that boy is going to grow up."

Hutch was the perpetual manchild, but his heart was in the right place.

Hutch had been there that night. Hutch had watched Theo die. Case crossed into the bedroom where Hutch was laid out on one of the two double beds, his head covered with a pillow as though he was trying to keep out the sunlight.

Or invite someone to smother him.

Case picked up the pillow. "Hutchins, time to wake up. Get your lazy ass out of that bed right fucking now and back up your CO."

Hutch damn near came off the bed, his eyes wild and his hands moving as though looking for his gun. "What the fuck?" He frowned. "You suck, Taggart. Where's my gun?"

"Michael took it from you and cleaned it so now it's shiny and ready for use on you. Never let a man take your piece. Not even when you're fucking asleep. Let's go. We have a job to do."

Hutch yawned, seeming to regain his usual lackadaisical composure. "I'm going to need some coffee."

Lucky for him, they were in Colombia.

Thirty minutes later, Case stood outside Old Town, the most popular part of the city with tourists. Surrounded by Las Murallas, thick stone walls that had once protected the city from invaders, the small district was filled to the brim with foreigners enjoying the day. The sky above was a clear crystal blue and he had to wonder if his brother was sitting somewhere, staring up at the sky and wondering why he'd been left behind.

"Fain seems pretty solid to me, boss," Hutch said quietly. He carried his second cup of heavily sweetened coffee of the day. Case had noticed early on that Hutch had habits. Coffee, thick with cream and sugar in the morning, some kind of soda after noon. Never any alcohol. Not a beer or a shot of whiskey. "I ran his records and he was in the Marines for five years. Did four tours in Afghanistan and Iraq. Served in Force Recon. One purple heart. Only child of Marie and Hank Fain of the great state of Iowa. One half brother from Marie's first marriage, but I didn't find much on him. The Fains ran a farm until they sold out to a big corporation and retired to Florida."

It didn't sit well. "How deep did you dig?"

Hutch sighed. "I've been awake for thirty minutes, boss. For the last couple of days finding the identities of our dead dudes and lady corpse was, according to you, my highest task in life."

"I'm sure I didn't put it that way."

"No, you said something like figure it out or I'll fire you. Which, might I point out, is a threat you never follow through on so now it's a little like white noise. All I'm saying is I'm your lone tech guy. In the words of Scotty…" Hutch went into a bad Scottish accent. "I'm giving her all I can, Captain."

He did get the point. "I can't bring anyone else in. I need your best work, man."

Hutch sobered. "You'll have it, but I'm working with one hand tied behind my back. I don't have Adam or Chelsea to run interference and some of the sites I'm pulling files from aren't the easiest hacks in the world. Fain was up for recruitment into our old black ops team. I did find that paperwork. Will you at least let me try to contact Ten and ask why he didn't make the cut? I'm not sure where he is, but I can probably find a number he might or might not be using right now. I can try the last one I had, but he likes to change things up."

Case was definitely interested in why Fain hadn't joined their CIA team. But he also knew getting Ten on the phone could take a while. "Yes. You can do that. Tell him I'm worried because Mia hired him. That's all he needs to know right now. What did you find out about our would-be kidnappers?"

Down the street he could see the bank his brother had robbed. Case had studied the police reports. Theo and his team had been precise and professional. Like the other Gringos jobs. They'd gotten in, blown the safe, and gotten out with over a hundred grand in under three minutes. How long had Theo prepped for the job? He would have cased the place. He would have taken his time and learned the ins and outs of the building and the habits of the people around it.

"Facial recognition identified our lovely flight attendant Angela Burns. She's worked for 4L Software for the last year. Her Facebook feed is full of cats and she has a real thing for Barry Manilow. Yeah, I thought that sounded fishy, too, so I dug a little deeper. Angela Burns is a construct for Angela Winslow, who's done time for fraud and assault. Angie was a bad, bad girl, but she apparently had some good connections because her documents were nicely done. The pilot and the copilot were clean, which means one of two things."

"Either they hadn't gotten caught yet or they're backed by someone who can really scrub a record clean."

"And that's what scares the mother fuck out of me." Hutch kept pace with him, walking slowly, as though they were simply two more tourists, enjoying the Colonial architecture. "I've got some feelers out on the Deep Web. We'll see what comes up. I've asked some hacktivist friends of mine about Kronberg."

The company that had funded Hope McDonald's research. "I thought you were trying to stay away from that crowd."

Actually, Ten had ordered him to. Case hadn't thought he needed to reiterate what just made sense.

"They're not all bad," Hutch argued. "And this is a special case. This is for Theo."

Case nodded, his eyes on the bank ahead of him. "All right. Do what you need to do, but understand that there's a reason Ten didn't want you hanging with that group."

"He thought I'd relapse, I'm sure. Once a black hat, always a black hat." There was a bitterness to Hutch's tone that couldn't be denied.

Hutch had spent some time in juvie for hacking into places he shouldn't have. Case thought he was being a bit dramatic calling himself a black hat hacker—a name that typically described someone who hacked high-level security for little to no reason beyond being a complete dick. "No one thought you were a black hat, but that lifestyle got you in trouble once. Those dudes can be malicious. If they knew who you worked for now, they would out you. Or use you. Ten was worried about you. He wouldn't have hired you if he'd thought you were going to turn on him."

"Yeah, well, I was pretty fucking happy to get out of juvie. I'm never eating another baloney sandwich again." Hutch stared ahead. "Is that it?"

The bank was outside the walled portion of the city. It was neat and nondescript. It wasn't a chain, but a local bank. Older and established, but obviously small.

"Have you looked for any connections between the bank robberies?" Case slowed as they approached the bank.

Hutch stared at him, frowning mightily. "As I didn't know about the bank robberies until approximately four days ago, and then there was the kidnapping and trying to track them down, and now there's the 'who's Ezra Fain' game I'm playing, no. I haven't tried to connect the robberies I didn't know about. Again, this is where Chelsea or Adam as backup would be helpful. I get that Big

Tag wants to keep this op a secret, but we need them. I'm completely shocked he hasn't gotten Chelsea on this."

Chelsea Weston was not only Big Tag's sister-in-law, she was also one of the best hackers on the planet. She'd been an actual black hat at one point in time. She'd been known as the Broker and she could get into any system. And now she had Agency clearance. "She's working the problem from another angle."

Hutch stopped, his hands coming out in that "why the fuck didn't you say that earlier" gesture of his. "She can take ten minutes to help me out. I'll get her on the phone and she can handle the pilot and copilot issue. If I can bring Adam in, he can run the faces through his software. It's better than anything I have on my system. I'll deal with the bank robberies. I can also have her ask some of her contacts for anything they've got on the Gringos gang. Is that what she's working on?"

He should tell him yes and throw him off this line of questioning, but he needed Hutch working on all of it. Michael could help him, but calling back to Dallas was out of the question. "No. Just get the job done. You can do it. You're the only one I want on it." He looked around for a convenience store. South American candy was supposed to be pretty spectacular. Maybe he could bribe his buddy. "Let's get you some candy and some soda. It's going to be a long night, right?"

Hutch had gone a pasty shade. "What have you done, Case?"

"What do you mean?"

"There's one reason you would leave Chelsea out of this. I'm not stupid. She's the queen. I bow to her brilliance. I can match Adam on occasion, but never her. So if you're leaving her out it's because Big Tag doesn't know we're here."

"He knows we're here." They'd gone over this.

"I know that, but if I screw this up, he's going to be mad. Chelsea won't fuck everything up." Hutch looked a little sick. His hand started to go for his cell phone.

Case had to shut that shit down. "Don't." He moved in close because he wasn't having an open argument in the middle of the street. "You can handle this, Hutch. You can be every bit as sharp as Chelsea when you want to be. If you pick up that phone and get Chelsea involved, she'll call Ian and we'll lose Santos. I can't afford to do that."

"And I can't afford to die the painful death coming to me the minute Big Tag realizes I could have handed this off to someone smarter than me and I didn't."

He wasn't doing this. Not now. He glanced around, looking for a restaurant he could haul Hutch into, and he saw it. There was a park across the street from the bank. It was a tiny thing, but had a couple of benches and some pretty landscaping. It was the perfect place to sit and drink some coffee and plan a robbery.

"Hey, where are you…" Hutch's question died out as Case took off toward the park.

He jogged across the street, careful to avoid traffic, but he needed to be there. Needed to be where he was sure Theo had sat and planned and plotted. Theo would have gone about it in a methodical fashion. He was a great planner. He wasn't always great at executing the plan and could definitely make mistakes in the field, but his brother had been excellent at planning an op. He would have had that studious expression on his face that Case joked he had when he was either planning something or constipated. Then Theo would send Case his happy middle finger and they would both laugh.

He wasn't laughing now.

"What's going on?" Hutch asked as he caught up. "I'm sorry about what I said back there. I will get this done."

"Ah, you come back," a feminine voice said. "You like your usual? I have…missed you."

Case turned and saw a young woman, likely around twenty, standing next to an ice cream cart. She was dressed in a white T-shirt with an ice cream on the front, her dark hair in a ponytail. "You know me?"

He knew the answer before she said a word, before her eyes flared in obvious confusion.

She shook her head. "No. I'm sorry. I was mistaken. You look like someone who used to…what is the word? Uhm, he would relax here in the afternoons. He was nice American man."

And she was into him. It had been there in the way her smile had dimmed when she'd realized he wasn't Theo. It had always been like that. Women flocked to Theo and his good-natured charm. It was good to know his brother still had some charm, that it hadn't been burned away by whatever Hope had done to him.

"He was my brother and he and I got separated. There must be something wrong with his cell because he was supposed to meet me at the hotel yesterday, but he didn't get there. I'm worried about him. He's been down here for a while, but I just got in. I thought I might find him here. He talked about how much he liked this park."

The girl blushed and Case knew he had her. She'd had a thing for his sunny, happy brother.

"He's such a nice man," she said in her thick Colombian accent, her lips curling up. "I mean he's not all soft or anything. But was nice to me." She frowned a little. "I think he might have been involved with someone rough."

"What do you mean?"

She glanced behind her as though trying to make sure no one was there. When she turned back, her voice was hushed. "He had one friend who seemed nice, but then another one showed up and they argued. The other man was very short with him. I don't think Tomas wanted to go with him. I didn't see him again after that. Do you think he's in trouble?"

Tomas? Was that the name Hope had given him? Kai had warned Case that Hope would likely have tried to rewire Theo's entire life. Case didn't understand the technology, but Kai had explained that through a combination of drugs, torture, and reconditioning therapy, Theo would forget his old life and believe whatever Hope told him.

It seemed to Case that Theo was bucking her training a bit, but his brother was definitely in trouble.

He couldn't scare the crap out of the girl though. "I'm not sure. I need to find him though. Is there anything you can remember? Did he tell you where he was staying?"

"He just said he was staying around. At first I thought he was probably at one of the big hotels, but I saw him on the bus one day." She blushed.

He couldn't have her too embarrassed to speak. "It's okay if you followed him. My brother is a good-looking kid. Rather like myself." He could turn on some charm. "I'm sure he would be flattered that you liked him enough to follow him."

"I'm not into guys, but even I know he's pretty hot," Hutch said with a grin. He pulled out some cash. "Could I get a cone? Chocolate."

She laughed, her shoulders relaxing as she went about her work. It was obvious they'd put her back at ease. "Of course. It was a silly thing to do, but I was curious. He got out in an industrial part of the city. I stayed on the bus, but the building he went into looked like a clinic of some kind. He told me he worked security. I assumed he was a guard at the clinic. You might look there. He hasn't come back here for a week. I think perhaps that bank robbery scared him off. I know I was scared. Please tell him it's peaceful here again." She held out the cone. "*Sal*?"

"Sal?" Hutch shook his head. "Nope. My name is…"

"She's asking if you want salt." At least one of them spoke a little Spanish. And Case had listened to a bunch of Mia's stories in between long sessions in bed. When the group would sit and have meals together, she'd talked about her adventures in South America and a few of the odd things she found fascinating. Mia liked to try the local cuisines and apparently one of the customs here was putting salt on their ice cream. Hutch was not as open to new experiences as Mia. "He's a pure sugar boy, miss. And I'm going to need you to write down that address for me."

His heart started to race a little. His brother was here. He could feel it.

CHAPTER EIGHT

Mia glanced down at her cell phone before picking it up. There was no way she could avoid this call. If she did, Drew would send someone after her. She might be able to dodge one, maybe two calls without her oldest brother sending in a security team, but this was his third call in as many days and he would get antsy.

She knew most people would call him overprotective and overbearing, but most people hadn't been forced to save their younger siblings. Whenever she got frustrated with Drew, she reminded herself that he was the one who'd seen their parents' bodies, heard the shots that killed them. Drew had been the one who'd come to her room, lifting her six-year-old body up and holding her tight as he guided them out of a burning house. He'd been the one to figure out they'd been locked in. He'd been the one who'd broken through a window so his siblings could live.

It's going to be okay, Mia. I'm not going to let anything happen to you. I'm going to keep you safe.

She sighed. Yeah, Drew might remember the horrors of that night, but what she remembered was how brave her brother had been. She owed Drew everything, including being all right with his need to know she was okay. Mia flicked her hand across the screen. "Hey, Drew. Sorry I hadn't called you back. I was sleeping. Had a crazy day researching yesterday and it went pretty late. The libraries here don't get great cell reception. What time is it?"

Her brother's silky voice came over the line with the soft growl of a predator. "It's time to explain why my airplane apparently carried three corpses in it."

Damn the freaking cartel. Why could no one offer good service these days? Three little bodies. It was all she'd asked. Except she hadn't actually asked. She'd let the boys handle it. She should have damn well known that cleaning up after a couple of murders was definitely woman's work. "It was no big deal."

Sometimes when Drew was quiet, there was a silent scream in the air. This time it was nearly deafening. It was a relief when he finally spoke again. "No big deal?"

She knew her brother well enough to hear the threat behind those quiet words. "Drew, it was fine. A couple of your employees turned out to be kidnappers. That's all. Case took care of them. I took care of the plane. And that was days ago. We've had zero kidnapping attempts in a whole four days. So it's no big deal. But the Morel Cartel is getting a hearty bad review on their cleaning services. Surely there's some kind of Deep Web Angie's List and I'm trashing them there."

Sometimes the best way to deal with overprotective men was to brazen right through.

"Put Case on the phone," her brother commanded.

"He's not here."

There was another pause. "All right. I'll be down there in roughly ten hours. I'm calling the hotel and sending a security detail."

Score one for Case Taggart and his horrible taste in lodging. "I'm not at the hotel and I'm not alone." She yawned and stretched, her every muscle a little sore because Case believed in a certain athleticism in his lovemaking. Days of being Case's lover had turned her into a satisfied kitten. "And you are seriously killing my buzz, big brother. I should be lying in bed thinking about how amazing this morning was, but no."

"I don't even want to know what you mean by that. Mia, this is serious."

She put him on speaker and found her robe, wrapping it around her body. "I know, but Case and his team are working on it. I'm safe. I'll be home as soon as the job's done. I'll have Case send you a report on what happened on the plane. I suspect it was nothing more than a plot to get money out of you. It wouldn't be the first. I'm sorry it scared you. I did intend to get that cleaned, but apparently the job got screwed up. Should I be worried about the authorities? Did the airport call them in?"

That would be a problem.

"No, your cartel connections were quick. I tried to contact the pilot a few hours ago to ensure you had everything you needed and that the plane was getting a thorough inspection before you came home. I couldn't get him on the line, so I called the airfield and talked to the manager. Funny thing was, he said he'd never seen the pilot I hired. He described the pilot as a pretty blonde girl who brought in a bunch of suspicious-looking men and he was worried you're in over your head."

"Not at all. I performed admirably." It had been a while since she'd landed a plane. She needed to fly more often. She was getting soft at 4L. At least she knew the bodies wouldn't be a problem. "I'll have Case and the team send you the names of the people who got past your human resources. They've already got the identity of the flight attendant and her long-standing criminal record."

"Damn it."

She felt bad playing on his guilt, but sometimes she had to use every tool in her arsenal. She moved to the window and drew back the heavy curtain, peeking out. Light streamed through but she saw exactly what she'd expected. The small courtyard had a couple of tables and chairs close to the tiny swimming pool that might or might not serve as its own unique biosphere. Ezra sat with

Michael. They'd found a deck of cards and seemed to be passing the time in a leisurely fashion.

"It's all right, Drew. I'm meeting with my contact sometime in the next couple of days. I'll be home after that and we'll talk about it. Until then I'm going to let Case call the shots." When it made sense for him to.

"Case isn't there."

"No, but I've got two bodyguards on my ass. When Case gets back, I'll have four. Four big, strong, well-trained men and I'm sleeping with their leader."

"And Ian Taggart knows about this mission of yours?"

Sometimes her brother made her feel like a lying five-year-old. "He knows where we are and that Case is helping me out. You can call him."

"Yeah, well he better not send me a bill. That asshole charges through the roof. I did not sign off on four full-time guards. Do you have any idea how much Taggart would bill for that?"

Thank god. If her brother was bitching about costs, he wasn't thinking about screwing up her life. "It's cool. I'm paying for the whole thing with my body."

Her brother groaned. "I did not need to hear that."

She saw a man moving in the background, walking from the office toward the rear of the west building. He wore a hat low on his head and walked with slow grace. Ezra's head came up, looking at the man, but he turned back to his card game. Drew continued to rant about not hearing about her sex life.

The man's face turned slightly and she recognized him.

Tony. Tony was here. The time was now. Somehow he'd located her and this might be the only shot she had at getting him to talk.

"Drew, I have to go. I'll call you later."

"Have Taggart call me."

She clicked the phone off before he could ask for more. As quickly as she could, she ditched the robe and found her jeans, pulling them on and reaching for a T-shirt. She knew she should put on a bra, but there wasn't time. She had no idea when he would surface again. They could be waiting for days. Especially since he'd very likely figured out she hadn't come alone.

Crap. She was going to lose him. He would sink into the background and she might not get another lead from him again. Shoes. She needed shoes. What the hell had Case done with her bag? He was a slave to organization, apparently a leftover habit from his Navy days.

Good in bed and a neat freak. She was a lucky girl.

Her shoes were lined up on the floor of the closet. She'd only brought three pairs. Sneakers, flip-flops, and a single pair of killer heels she'd intended to go with the cocktail dress she'd brought hoping to get Case to go to dinner with her. She shoved her feet into the flip-flops and realized her problem. There was zero chance that Ezra and Michael would allow her to go running off after a former CIA agent.

The bathroom. There was a window. It was a little high, but she might be able to make it. Her heart was pumping. Tony might already be gone. He might have taken one look at Ezra and Michael and fled the scene entirely. She had to shove her body out that window and pray she didn't get stuck.

She'd promised Case.

Damn it. Damn it. Damn it.

She couldn't break her word to him. Couldn't. She'd promised Case she wouldn't run off on her own. Mia strode to the door, grabbing the ice bucket and the key. It was time to talk her way out of the situation.

The minute she opened the door, Fain's head came up. Michael turned as well.

She gave them what she hoped was a brilliant smile. "Any idea where the ice machine is?"

Ezra stood, his jacket moving slightly so she caught a flash of metal. "I'll get it for you."

Just what she'd thought he'd say. Ezra, she could handle. It was Michael Malone who would likely prove to be the hardass.

Case was his best friend and partner. Lucky for her he still wasn't moving so great at this point so she'd likely only have to deal with the man she'd hired.

"I'll come with you. Get a lay of the land, so to speak," she said, striding up to him.

He took the bucket out of her hands and started moving toward the back of the building, the same way Santos had gone.

"I'll hang out here." Michael leaned back in his chair.

She looked straight ahead as she caught up with Ezra. "I need you to be my bodyguard now, but I need you to do it discreetly and from a distance."

"May I ask why?" His tone was even, as though they were merely talking about the weather.

"Because Tony Santos is here."

Ezra stopped. "Damn it. Did he see me?"

They'd gotten behind the second buildings and she didn't see Tony anywhere. "I'm sure he did. He's probably gone, but I have to look. Please watch my back, but do it from a distance. And tell Case I wasn't alone. Okay?"

He set the ice bucket down. "Go. Do what you need to do. I'll be there even if you can't see me. I'll follow you however I can. If he gets you in a car, stall him for a few minutes so I can follow you in a cab. There are a couple running around here most of the time from what I've seen."

She nodded and took off, jogging the direction she thought he'd go. The beach was to her left. If she took a right, she would get back to the street. Likely he'd had a car parked on that street and he was driving away and he wouldn't call again.

Not that he'd called in the first place. He'd e-mailed her the photo with all kinds of cryptic commands. Mia stalked past a massive bougainvillea bush. The back of the motel was covered in the glorious pink blossoms, but Mia didn't have time to admire the flowers. No time to smell the flowers or enjoy doing touristy things with her man. No four-star hotel with a spa for her. No, she had to track down the crazy guy who couldn't talk on the phone because everyone was out to get him.

And yes, she knew everyone really was out to get him, but it still sucked.

She was going to have to tell Case she'd screwed up. Again.

"Hello, pretty girl. How about a walk on the beach?"

She turned and there was the man she'd met six months before. After the debacle at Sanctum, she'd taken the assignment to write a story on human trafficking. Tony had been working, trying to find the daughter of a friend of his. He was a slender man, not much taller than herself, but she'd seen Tony fight. His lack of muscle belied his lean strength. He was also pretty mean. The man could bite with the best pissed-off Doberman. "I thought I lost you."

He started walking slowly toward the beach. "I thought I told you to come alone."

She felt herself flush as she followed him. "I'm sorry."

"Don't be. You've finally got some sense." Tony walked slowly, avoiding the super sandy part of the beach. Though he was dressed casually, no one would likely mistake him for a guest at the various beach parties going on around them. Makeshift canopies dotted the beach and cars pounded out various rhythms, all leading to one big party.

Tony looked out of place, his darkness skittering the edge of the light as if slightly afraid of what the sun might do to him.

"Were those two men with Taggart?" Tony asked.

She decided honesty was best with Tony. He was calm for now, but she saw the way his left hand fisted and relaxed, fisted and relaxed. He was always on the edge. It was sad, but he sometimes reminded her of her brother Bran. "Yes. How do you know Case?"

Tony chuckled. "I don't. I know his oldest brother by reputation only. So you're sleeping with Taggart the third? I have to number them to keep them straight in my head. The DNA runs true in that group. Whoever is following us is good. I can't see him. I can feel him though. He needs to stay away. I would hate to have to kill someone on this lovely beach."

She looked around but she couldn't see Ezra either. He did blend in. "He won't approach us. He's just making sure I have someone watching over me. It wasn't my choice."

"Ah, then the Taggart cub is the one with the good sense to protect what belongs to him. Tell me something. Did you like my gift, pretty girl?"

His gift. The picture of Theo. "I did. It's very important we find the man in that picture."

"The youngest Taggart. The one who died. I'm sure now he knows there are some things worse than death."

The words sent a chill through her. "Do you know anything more?"

"I know they're still here. Still in the city." Tony stopped, turning and staring out at the beach. "They'll make a move soon. They stayed too long in Argentina and it almost cost them."

"Cost them? The authorities almost found them?"

He chuckled, but it was a hollow sound. "Oh, no. The authorities can be handled easily. Trust me. In a few days, the Gringos bandits will be found and put in jail, and soon after they'll disappear and no one will speak of them again. The wheels are already in motion."

"I can't let Theo go to jail."

"It won't be Theo or any of the actual robbers. They're far too valuable, but the organization that their mother works for likes to keep things neat and clean. If the actual Gringos were captured, there would be many questions. Questions about why former soldiers, decorated men, loyal men, would give up their lives to rob banks in South America. There would be questions about why none of the men remember their families. There would definitely be questions about the drugs in their systems. It's what she didn't plan for."

She. "Hope McDonald?"

"Of course. She's a brilliant doctor. Truly if her mind wasn't warped, she might have done great things."

"She's a sociopath." Mia always got a little sick when she thought of the woman.

"Yes," Tony agreed. "She was born with a genius level IQ, but no conscience whatsoever. No empathy for anyone. I often wonder if she thinks she's normal. Do you ever read fiction?"

"Of course."

"I like it," Tony said with a nod. "I read as often as I can. It takes me out of myself. I tend to enjoy thrillers and mysteries. I always wonder though. I wonder about the villains. We see one side of stories far too often. One point of view. We're trained that way, to see what is in front of us. To see what the author of our lives wants us to see."

This was pure Tony. He went off on philosophical rants, but if she tried to pull him back, he would get angry. She'd learned it was best to let him follow through. He would get to the point eventually. She was on Tony time now. That meant she could be standing here on this beach talking to him until the sun went down or a bug could fly past his nose, he would decide it was actually a drone, and he would go back into hiding in an instant. "That's probably true. We see things through the filters of own experiences. It's hard not to."

What did any of this have to do with Theo?

"I suppose so. That's Hope McDonald's problem. She doesn't see that she's the villain of the piece. She thinks she's the hero. It's why they almost caught her."

"Who?"

"The factions who would like to take what she has. There are many. I suspect she thought her patrons would protect her. In some ways, she's a bit like a naïve child. She thought things wouldn't change, that she could control them."

"Are you talking about Kronberg?"

"I'm talking about the men who control Kronberg, and the men who control them, and so on. I'm talking about anyone with a desire to gain power with the single press of a needle against a soldiers' skin. Think about it, pretty girl. Think about what she can do. Our armies tend to be limited by the consciences of our soldiers. What if you could wipe that nuisance clean? What if you could build entire armies of men with loyalty to no one but the one who controls the drug?"

"I don't understand everything about the drug. I read some articles, but they were all theoretical."

"Because we should be many years away. The things you read about, the future tech, it's all here. It's all hidden. Those articles are a way to pave the road to the future, but make no mistake, the powerful of this world already enjoy luxuries and weapons you can't imagine."

"Why would Kronberg turn on her?" She didn't understand what had changed.

"Because she isn't as good as her father with investors," Tony explained. "With anyone, really. She relied on her father to smooth things over. It worked for a few months. Once she proved the drug with young Taggart, she was given two more subjects."

"How do you know all of this?"

"I have friends who keep watch. When you wrote to me asking for a favor, I called in a few of my own. Now, I have to admit, I'm fascinated with McDonald. So brilliant. So deranged. She truly believes in her work, that she's expanding the boundaries of science. So much so that I believe she started thinking she was bigger than Kronberg. That's why they decided to raid her site. The funny thing is, they got there roughly seventy-two hours after a man named Liam O'Donnell found the place."

"McKay-Taggart was there?" Case hadn't mentioned it.

"For all the good it did them. Her boys, as she likes to call them, are excellent at hiding evidence."

The robberies finally made sense. "So she's having them rob banks because she needs the money. Her corporate funds have dried up."

"Exactly. They've dried up and she's on the run. She needs money and a lot of it. She got some from the robberies, but she spends it like a woman who's never worried about it once in her life. Money is nothing but a tool to a woman like that."

"What's her end game? What is she planning on getting out of this?" It was the one thing she didn't understand. "Is she going to sell the drug?"

"Ah, I don't think money matters to her. Like I said, it's useful and she's used to having all she needs, but it's not her purpose. Science is her purpose. She's Dr. Frankenstein but she's building her monsters by reprogramming their brains. There's no thought except to perfect her technique. She'll keep running as long as someone is chasing her."

Case Taggart would never stop chasing her. "Do you know where she is?"

"I believe she has something to do with a clinic in the city. I've written down the address for you. I also believe she's preparing to move." He reached into his pocket and pulled out a small square of paper.

She glanced down. There was a neatly written address on it. "What makes you think that?"

"It's what I would do. I've also heard some rumors about a blond man fitting Theo's description inquiring about a plane. He's going through very shady contacts, though according to my sources he's willing to pay top dollar as long as the plane can make long-haul flights. He needs a pilot."

"I'm a pilot. I've got a plane, too. Is there any way you could put me in touch with him, with whoever he's talked to?" All they had to do was get close. Case would do whatever it took to get his brother. Get Theo. Get out. Let them deal with Hope McDonald later.

He laughed at that thought, the most amusement she'd ever heard from Tony. "Yes, he wouldn't be suspicious at all of a pretty blonde girl with a hundred-million-dollar jet at her disposal. No. And don't think to use the rest of your team. Americans of any kind would be suspicious. I'll let you know if anything else comes up. Do you have a tech expert with you?"

"Yes. He's a former hacker."

"Excellent. Have him look on the Deep Web. That's where McDonald will have to find her pilot. I don't think she's got an expert with her, but she'll still figure it out. That's also where they'll be forced to buy certain chemicals that she needed Kronberg to provide. You understand that if the subject goes off the drug, the power she has over him ceases to be."

"So once the drug's out of his system, he'll be Theo again?"

"I didn't say that. I doubt he'll ever be the same. Imagine having two lives in your memory. Two complete sets. The drug being out of his system won't erase the memories she gave him. They'll simply allow the real ones to surface. Theo Taggart will have two lives and he often won't know which one was real. Like I said, there are worse things than death. I would be surprised if he didn't kill himself. You should prepare his brothers for that. He was dead the minute he took that bullet. He's simply been walking around not realizing it. The man you're searching for, he's a ghost and nothing more."

She refused to believe it. Tony was wrong. Theo had a life and a family and they would bring him back. They would find a way. "We'll handle it."

His lips curled up slightly. "I suspect you will try. I'll be in touch. Tell your Taggart that he's not the only player in this game."

"I'll tell him Kronberg and The Collective are looking for her, too." He would find that interesting and it might change his mind about calling his brother in. Now that she'd met with Tony, they could do whatever they liked.

"It's not Kronberg he should be worried about. It's the Agency," Tony said solemnly.

"Ian works with the Agency."

He laughed again, this time the sound booming. "The Agency only uses. Tell him to watch out for Mr. White. He's not Tennessee Smith. He won't choose friendship or his conscience over his country. He'll choose whatever takes him further up the ladder. He won't be the only one. This is a game thick with spies. I wouldn't trust anyone, pretty girl. Not even the people you think you should. I've found men always choose their brothers in the end. Even over a woman they enjoy in bed."

"It's not like that. We're serious about each other." She wasn't sure why, but she felt like she had to defend…herself? Case? What they had?

What did they have? He seemed serious about her. He'd told her he wanted her in Dallas with him. He wanted to put the past behind them and move forward together. He'd promised not to walk away from her again.

"When he disappoints you, know that you can call on me to help." A shudder ran through him. "I have to go. I don't like it here anymore. Don't trust any of them. Not a one. They'll all turn on you in the end. This isn't your fight, Mia. Go home and protect yourself. I don't know what they'll do if they catch you."

"Who? If who catches me?"

Tony stared at something behind her. "Or perhaps they already have. Good-bye, pretty girl."

She turned, trying to see whatever had spooked Tony. Her heart started to race. Who was after her? Who was this mysterious someone?

All she saw was Case starting up the beach. His head turned, obviously searching for someone. Her. She watched as Ezra appeared. She hadn't seen him before. He'd blended in with one of the parties. There were twenty or so young people dancing and drinking beer and playing volleyball. They didn't seem to mind that Ezra had joined them, but Case frowned as he put a hand on his arm.

She looked back to reassure Tony, but he was gone.

How the hell had he done that? Did the dude have like a silent helicopter or something to whisk him away? It was weird and unnerving, but then the whole conversation had been unnerving.

How many people were after Theo?

Case shook off Ezra and started jogging toward her.

She held her hands up. "I followed instructions."

He pulled her into his arms. "I know, but it doesn't make me less worried." He held her tight for a moment. "Come on. Let's get you back inside. We have a lot to talk about and I've got a massive favor I need from you."

She looked up at him, not happy with how tight his jaw was. "What happened?"

He kissed her forehead before wrapping her tightly in his arms again. He looked over her shoulder as if still trying to find Tony. "I'll tell you all about it, but first you have to tell me if you're ready to play spy for a night?"

Now that sounded like fun. "Absolutely."

He grimaced and Mia couldn't figure out how he made that terrible expression so damn sexy. "Somehow I knew you would say that. Let's go. I'm only not killing Fain because you're alive."

"I was watching her the whole damn time. She wasn't in any danger," Ezra complained.

"You were too far away," Case shot back. "And you were drinking on the job. Don't think I didn't see that beer in your hand."

"If I hadn't stayed back, he would have made me, asshole." Ezra shook his head as he started back up the beach. "And I wasn't drinking it. I was blending in."

What the hell had Case said to the man to put him in such a shitty mood? "He was just doing his job, Case. I met with Tony and he had a lot to say."

Case nodded. "And I want to hear it all, but first, I need to talk to you about what I found. Mia, I think I might know where my brother is, but I need you to check it out. You're the only one I trust. We found the place I think Hope McDonald is using as her base of operations. You won't go in alone and you have to know that I'm going to take care of you. I'll be watching the whole time and I won't be far away. I'll be able to get to you if anything happens."

She handed him the note Tony had given her. "Is it here?"

Case nodded. "Yes. That's the place. They're having a

fundraiser tonight in the building. Hutch got you tickets. All you have to do is distract a couple of security guards so Hutch can slip into the business offices. I don't want to send you in, but I can't think of another way. Like I said, I'm going to be watching you the whole time, and not in the crappy way Fain was watching you. I've got some high-tech equipment that will allow me to basically be there with you. You can do this, Mia."

Tony was wrong. Case cared about her. She wasn't just a body in his bed. He trusted her and to a man like Case that was practically a declaration of love.

"I'll do it." She would do anything for him. Maybe that made her a silly girl, but she was okay with that.

Case slid his hand into hers as he started to lead her back toward the motel.

They were together. They could do anything, take on anything. As long as he was by her side, she would be okay. She just knew it.

CHAPTER NINE

"I've changed my mind. We can do this another way." It was a horrible idea. He needed to rethink the entire plan because Mia looked exactly like what she was—a gorgeous, delectable distraction.

She was perfect. The plan was perfect. It was an easy get in, let Hutch do his thing, get out. So why was he hesitating? He wouldn't think twice if this was Charlotte or Phoebe or Eve standing in front of him. Hell, the job was so simple, he would likely send Grace in. All Mia had to do was look charming and give Hutch a chance to do his job.

All he could think about was the fact that her boobs were his and he shouldn't be using them to distract other men. His. His caveman brain couldn't think past her boobs.

She grinned as though she knew exactly what he was thinking. She twirled around in the cocktail dress that showed off far too much of her. “It wasn’t why I brought it, but I think it should do the job.”

“Why did you bring it?” He’d been a little surprised she’d had a designer dress in her small bag. “I thought we were only supposed to be here for a few days.”

Her lips curled up in a sexy smile. “Same reason I put that lingerie on the plane. I was determined that you were going to fall right into my web.”

Oh, he was in her web. Crazily caught by her. Which was exactly why he’d made other plans he hadn’t yet talked to her about. He needed to enjoy the calm before the storm. “I think you can safely say I’m caught. Come here.”

She moved toward him, her every curve on display. The dress she wore was black and slinky, and he wished he was getting ready to shove his body into an uncomfortable suit so he could take her out on the town. Instead, he was dressing for an op. All black. His only accessories would be the Bluetooth devices they would use to communicate and his SIG. Well, and various other weapons, but the SIG was the main one. He felt naked without the SIG. God, she looked good naked. She looked good clothed, too. Way too good. And those heels made her legs look long and lean. They would look good wrapped around his neck.

He couldn’t do it. “I’m going with you. I’m not letting you walk around looking like sex in black saran wrap without a proper guard.”

Her eyes rolled and she sighed as she moved in, setting herself on his lap. “You can’t and you know why.”

Because he looked too much like his brother. Because if Theo was there, it could get dangerous. Even getting caught by a stray security cam could torpedo their mission and send his brother running. There was zero shot of Hope McDonald not knowing who Case Taggart was. She would recognize him and there was no magical *Mission: Impossible* mask hanging around to change his face.

But she wouldn’t know Mia and she’d never met Hutch. God,

he was actually sending his girlfriend on an op with Hutch as her backup.

What the hell was he thinking?

A hand smoothed over his forehead. "I'm going to be fine, Case. It's a nothing job. I'm going to a charity party. Do you think I don't do that twice a week when I'm at home? I'm practically the 4L ambassador since Drew's a recluse, Bran's a head case, and Riley's a manwhore. I'm going to distract security in order to let Hutch sneak back to the office section of the building and download any files he can get. Easy peasy. We'll be in and out in less than an hour. I don't suppose you actually went into the building."

He hadn't been able to risk it and Hutch didn't speak Spanish. He'd watched people come and go. One of them had been American, well built. He'd had the right frame for the man in the mask beside his brother in the picture Santos had offered them.

He'd thought about tailing the man, but the key card in the dude's hand made him think he would come back to this place. Case had been right. The dude had showed back up not thirty minutes later with a sack of groceries in hand.

They might be living in the large industrial space.

"Hutch pulled up some records about the building." He turned his laptop around so she could see the blueprints. It might have been easier to set her down and show her, but he liked her in his lap, loved being able to smell the scent of soap and the faintest hint of sex she couldn't seem to wash away. Likely because he'd joined her again in the shower. He'd picked her up, pressed her back to the wall and let his dick have its way.

Mia leaned forward, studying the plans. "So the charity is one small part of the building? There are no other businesses? This place is pretty big."

"Ten thousand square feet. From what we've been able to figure out the charity itself only takes up three thousand. It seems to only deal with poverty outreach. The group that funds the charity is small."

"Do they have any connection to Hope McDonald or Kronberg? Though if what Tony said is true, she likely would avoid anyone connected to Kronberg."

"Not that I can tell," he admitted. "Hutch is working on it. I suspect they have more local ties."

Her eyes lit with understanding. "Ah, cartel. That would make sense. They would find it amusing to cover their deals with a charity project. They would even see the fundraising as an alternate way of making money."

"Or they really do community outreach as a way to have a whole neighborhood where they don't have to worry about police." Case had thought this through. Colombia had cracked down on the cartels, but they'd merely gotten better at hiding their purposes. And a smart mobster knew that loyalty worked even better than fear at times. "Hutch got on the Deep Web earlier today and heard some rumors about a doctor working with a cartel to enhance some of their product."

"Ah, so our doctor found a new sponsor."

It looked like it. She would also be well protected. He might be walking into a war, and that was another reason he needed to get her out of harm's way. "The cartel could be very effective at protecting her as long as she's giving them what they want."

"Did you call Ian?"

"I will once we've got something to tell him." He needed some proof. He needed this to not be a dead end. He couldn't go back to his brother with nothing in hand.

And deep in the back of his head, he knew another truth. He wanted to be the hero here. He wanted Ian to see that he could run things, do good work, be more than a big body that took the bullets for the smarter people.

"So you think there'll be something in the internal records." She turned back to him, squirming a bit as she resettled.

Naturally that made his dick jump, but there was no more time for sex. "I hope so. If not, I'll reassess and think about going in at night and checking the place out myself."

"With Ezra or Hutch backing you up," she insisted.

He had to admit Fain had been helpful and not too much of a dick. "If it comes to that. I'd rather figure out if they've got internal security cameras Hutch can bust into. If we can get into their feed, we can see everything. It's the second thing I need you to do. Look for cameras. Note where they are. I need to know if you see anything out of the ordinary. Even if it's simply something you feel is wrong, I want to know about it. You've got good instincts."

"I would make a good operative. Admit it. You think I would be an excellent spy."

He didn't even like to think of a world where Mia ran the ops. "I think you're a brilliant reporter and you should stick to that."

The world would be a much safer place. His ball of chaos could burn a place down when she got started.

Her pretty face turned serious. "I will stick to reporting, but I do have one instinct I think you should follow. I am good at some things."

He was willing to listen. He wasn't sure there was time to change the op. It was a hurried affair as it was, but he wanted to hear her out. "Hit me."

"Tell Erin."

Case shifted, easing her off his lap. This was one place he wouldn't allow her to sway him. "No. I've told you why we're keeping it from her. Big Tag is worried she'll go commando."

"She won't. She's got a child now."

"You don't know her the way we do." Though he agreed that Erin had calmed over the last year, he couldn't be absolutely sure. She'd been so fierce and angry when they'd met. He hadn't seen what Theo had in her. He'd seen a kind of mean ex-soldier with a chip on her shoulder. Theo had seen something else. He'd seen the woman underneath all that armor. "Erin can be single-minded, but it's more than just her running off and trying to find Theo on her own. Have you thought about the fact that she's finally settled? You honestly think I should reopen that wound?"

She walked calmly to the mirror and smoothed down her dress. "I think you're wrong about the wound being healed. She might have found a way to live with it, but it won't ever heal. She'll die with that wound gaping and open because she loved him. It's funny what can bring it all back, the loss and ache. Sometimes you think it's fine and you've almost forgotten them and then I'll smell banana bread or hear the sound of keys clacking and I'm six years old again."

"Are you talking about your parents?" He stepped up behind her, looking at her through the mirror. She'd begun her sentence as a universal, but it had ended personally. He knew she'd lost them at a young age, but not the hows and whys. He'd been too stubborn to learn more about the woman he couldn't get out of his head.

She nodded, a sheen of tears making her eyes bright. "I don't remember them the way my brothers do, but I still feel it. It comes in flashes when I least expect it. I'll hear a sound that reminds me of my mother and I'll feel the loss. My father was a programmer. I can hear the sound of keys clacking in just the right way and I'll see him in front of his computer, the green light from the screen on his face at night. He would look up and smile and stop what he was doing. I'll smell the hot cocoa he would make me when I couldn't sleep. The pain of loss like that never truly ends. It just hides and I don't think it will do that in Erin's case."

"It certainly won't if we shove it in her face."

"It's hers, Case. That's the mistake you're making. You think you're being the white knight, saving the girl from pain, but you're taking something from her. This is a part of their story. Whether you get Theo back or not, this is hers because he was hers. The pain is hers too. You're taking her ability to pray for him, to know what he's going through."

Frustration welled up, a nasty feeling he didn't like. It made his tone harsher than he'd wanted. "I don't want her to know and neither would Theo."

She took a deep breath. "All right. It's your call, but I think it's a mistake. I think she would want to know. I think she would want to feel everything she can where it comes to him, even the rough parts. If she's not that woman, then you would know better than I do."

Was he keeping something precious from Erin? No. He was making the right decision, the one Theo would want him to make.

Should Erin have a voice in that decision, too? They'd left her out of so much in an effort to protect her. He was Theo's brother. It was his decision to make. His and Ian's and Sean's. If they got Theo back, it would be a gift to her. If they didn't she never had to understand this fear. He was right. Mia was wrong.

Still, when she turned and a sad smile curved her lips up slightly, he felt guilty for not giving her what she wanted.

"I'm ready when you are."

He wasn't ready at all, but she was right about one thing. She'd done the charity event thing more than once. This was her world. "Make sure Hutch doesn't make a complete idiot of himself. He's not exactly used to high society. He's more used to microwaving his supper and playing MMORPGs."

She waved off the thought. "He'll be fine. I've already written a nice-sized check to the organization. That will buy us an enormous amount of goodwill."

"I don't know about that. What if they recognize your name?" He had to stop this bouncing around, looking for reasons to call off the op. His brother was in there. Guilt assailed him. He should do anything to get his brother back. Why was he waffling?

Mia breezed on, luckily not picking up on his inner turmoil. "I've got a fund I do charitable work from. It's the Iris and Ben Fund. I doubt they'll connect it to 4L and the ticket was issued to Mia Danvers. My legal name comes in handy."

He'd wondered about that. "Do you miss it? Your name, I mean."

She sighed. "Sometimes. Don't get me wrong. I love my moms. They're awesome. They saved me from a lot of what my brothers went through, but I'm still a Lawless. I'm still my parents' child."

"You could change it back." He wasn't sure why she hadn't, except that she'd chosen to honor her adoptive parents.

Of course, he rather thought Mia Taggart was a better name. He didn't even flinch at that thought now. No waffling there. He wanted her. He would eventually marry her and tie her to him in every way he possibly could. She wasn't the same woman he'd met. As long as she was honest with him, he would give her everything he had.

"That wouldn't fit into my brother's plans," she said cryptically.

Before he could ask her what she meant by that, there was a knock on the door. It wasn't the time for long explanations, but he needed to figure out what was going on with her family. Her brothers tended to be quiet around him, but he could tell something was bubbling under their seemingly placid surfaces. Then there were all the secretive meetings with Ian. There would be time later to find out what was going on. He opened the door and his crew strode in, Hutch first.

"Do I really have to wear this thing? It's scratchy." Hutch tugged at his brand new tie. He'd gone out with Fain an hour before and picked up the elegant-looking suit.

"I told you, yes. You have to wear it. And it's not scratchy. It's an excellent quality suit and we were lucky to find someone who could tailor it in such a short amount of time." Fain frowned Case's way. "He's got problems with focus. He kept wandering away any time I took my eyes off him. Do you normally keep him on an actual leash?"

Hutch groaned. "Looking at suits is boring. Those girls walking around in bikinis were not." Hutch winked Case's way. "This country is full of gorgeous women. We should think about spending a little more time here. It's been a while for me."

He wasn't hanging out because Hutch got horny. "We're leaving as soon as we have enough intel to call Ian in."

Michael grimaced as he made his way to the lone chair in the room. "We're leaving? I doubt that. Someone's hanging out here and keeping an eye on that building. If Theo's there, we can't risk losing him. Even in the couple of days it would take to turn this op. They could decide to run again."

"All right. I should make myself plain." He'd kind of wanted to avoid this particular conversation for as long as possible, but it looked like his time was up. "We're doing this job tonight and then Mia and Michael and Fain are heading home. Hutch and I can keep tabs on the situation until Ian can get us backup."

The sad look on her face was gone, replaced with the warrior princess glare he'd come to know so well. "I'm not leaving. Are you planning on tying me up and shoving me on a plane?"

"Only if I have to." He was going to be resolute on this. He couldn't work with her. His logic and decision-making got all fucked up the minute she walked in a room. If he had time, he would call in another female operative to do tonight's job, but unfortunately the closest one he knew was a six-hour flight away. He hated to disappoint Mia, but he needed for her to be safe while he did his job. "I thank you sincerely for everything you've done and what you'll do tonight, but I need to bring this down to my team."

"I'm on your team." Michael stood up, his face as stormy and stubborn as Mia's.

Did he have to explain this again? "You're also incapacitated."

"I'm fine," Michael said tightly. "I've had worse and you know it. I can still move and I can certainly sit my ass in a chair and watch a building."

Michael wasn't seeing the big picture. "I need someone who's at full capacity. I'm sorry, but you're out. Ian will bring in his own team in a couple of days. Hutch and I are going to do nothing but monitor the situation. Go home and get well, brother."

"I'm more than happy to go home." Fain suddenly looked chipper, the only smile in a crowd of gloom. "I think you're right. I need to escort my client back to Austin and get started on my new job. Ms. Danvers, I'll contact the airport and make our flight arrangements. We need a new pilot. I'll try to ensure that this time the flight crew doesn't attempt to kill us all. I'll go and make a few calls while you all work out your issues."

"What new job?" Case hadn't missed the smirk on Fain's face.

That smirk brightened again. "Didn't I mention that I talked to Drew Lawless earlier today? He called me a few hours ago and we ironed out all the details. I've been hired as Mia's full-time bodyguard."

Mia's eyes rolled. "Awesome. No one asked me if I wanted a full-time guard. It's good to know."

"You are not staying with her." Case was going to be the one making those decisions when it came to Mia. He was going to make that clear to her brother as soon as possible. "When we get back tonight and I call Ian, I'll have him assign her a guard."

"I've been ordered to take her back to Austin myself," Fain said, his phone in his hand.

"You can escort her home and then my brother will send another guard." He would rather have her in Dallas, but he had no idea how long he would be stuck here. She would be more comfortable waiting for him at her own place. When he was done, they would sit down and have a long talk about her moving in with him.

"Drew Lawless hired me," Fain insisted. "I'm not giving up my job. He's already got someone moving me out of my condo. He wants me to stay close to her."

"He can move you right back in because you're not going to be her bodyguard." He needed someone he trusted to watch over her.

"If Drew Lawless comes to Dallas, can I meet him? Ian always takes Adam with him when he goes down to Austin. I haven't met him yet," Hutch said, seeming to not care that the air was thick with irritation on all sides.

"Could Case and I have the room, please?" Mia asked, her voice tight. "We need to be at the party in twenty minutes, but I would like to have a brief word with our leader."

Well, at least she was going to yell at him in private.

"I'll drive," Fain said. "I'll drop Malone and Taggart off at the surveillance spot and then play chauffeur for our operatives. Come on, guys, let's check and make sure we've got all the equipment we'll need."

"Yes, the equipment I bought," Mia said with a smile that came nowhere near her eyes. "And the hotel room I'm paying for."

She wasn't happy with him. That was easy to see. "Sounds good, Fain. We'll be there in a minute."

They stepped out and the door closed, leaving him alone with Mia.

"I'm not leaving."

At least she wasn't screaming. "Yes, you are. After tonight you will have done your job and there's no place for you in the field."

"And if Tony finds out new information?"

"I didn't need his information." He'd been happy to discover the address Santos had given her had been the same one he and Hutch had found only hours before. There was nothing her contact could give him that he couldn't discover for himself.

"And if he finds out who Theo hires to take them out of Colombia?"

"You can talk to him on the phone or he can deal with me. After tonight, I'm calling in everyone I can. I'll let Tennessee Smith deal with Santos. You're out of this, Mia."

"Wow." She flushed, her arms going protectively over her chest. "That didn't take long."

"What didn't take long?" He got that bad feeling in his gut. The one that told him he was about to get punched from a direction he hadn't expected, but there was zero chance of him figuring it out and being able to deflect.

"For you to get tired of me. A couple of fucks and you're sending me away." She turned and grabbed her purse, her every movement a testament to how pissed off she was. "Well, don't expect me to follow your instructions. I'll pack as quickly as I can and then you can drop Ezra and me off after we're done with tonight's job. I'll do this particular job because if I don't, it will fail, but I won't let you ship me off because you're done with me sexually."

That stopped him in his tracks. "What? I'm not done with you. Not even fucking close. How can you think that?"

She shook her head, her blonde hair moving around her shoulders. "Because I'm no longer a sixteen-year-old girl. I learned a long time ago to judge men by their actions and not their words. You were honest with me when I broke in. You didn't want to have anything to do with me. You let me go. How long did it take you to figure out I was your best bet at getting this op off the ground?"

"Mia, I told you what happened."

"You told me what I wanted to hear. You told me what I needed to hear in order to let you on that plane with me." She turned, obviously not willing to look at him anymore. She busied herself with adjusting her earrings. "I just wish you'd told me you'd changed your mind. I would have done all of this without the sexual games."

"First off, there were no games on my end of this." He could feel his blood pressure starting to rise. Why was she pulling this crap right before an op?

"Tony told me it would be this way. He told me you would choose your family. I'm nothing but a body in bed for you. I guess I'm a little more. You got some cash out of me and a nice ride where you needed to go."

Was she fucking kidding? "A nice ride? My best friend got shot and I almost watched you die. It was not a nice ride, Mia. And might I add that you're the one who showed up at my place. You're the one who set a trap for me, as you called it. All you had to do was call and give me the information, but you didn't do this out of the kindness of your heart, did you? You wanted something out of me. You wanted me in your bed. Well, you got me. Don't be surprised that I won't dance to your every single tune."

It was just like her. She said she wanted a dominant man, but the minute he did something she didn't like, he was crushing her soul.

"You think I did all of this because I wanted to fuck you?" The question came out of her mouth on an incredulous huff.

They didn't have time for this. He didn't know how to deal with it. "I have no idea what's going through your head right now. But every word that comes out of your mouth proves that what I'm doing is right."

"Yes, I'm sure getting rid of the inconvenient woman you're done screwing sounds like the perfect plan."

He stopped, staring at her, trying to figure out what was going through her head. She was angry with him, but beyond that it was obvious he'd hurt her. Getting mad wasn't going to fix anything. He was acting as the leader of the group and he'd made the decision based on that, but she was still his girl. It was a balance he wasn't sure he could handle, but he had to try for the moment. It was exactly why he had to send her back home. "I never once screwed you. I've played with you and made love to you, and now I'm going to send you away because you're a distraction I can't handle right now. I can't work with you."

Because the thought of her getting hurt made him insane.

"But you need to. You need to let me help you. I'm not incompetent. I know how to protect myself and I know how to handle a fight." Her expression turned hopeful.

He had to kill that hope in her eyes. He'd made the decision. He couldn't allow himself to be swayed. This mission was too important. "You're not a trained operative and you're a distraction to me. I don't have time to deal with you. I need you to go home, Mia. When all of this is done, I'll come pick you up in Austin and we'll figure out where we go from there."

"Which is exactly what you would say to get me to finish out this job."

He threw up his hands. "All I can do is tell you I want you in my life but not on this job. If you can't accept that, I don't know what else to say."

It took everything he had to remain calm and to not tell her he was crazy about her. If he opened that door, she would use it against him.

"If you wanted me in your life, you would let me stay here and help you. Case, this *is* your life. This is what you do. This is the most important mission you'll ever have and I've got contacts that can help. I would understand if I couldn't help, but I can. I have reporter friends who've done extensive stories on the cartels. If a cartel owns that building, I can figure out who and possibly get information from an inside man. I have a lot of people in this part of the world who owe me favors."

"No. You're going home." He wasn't choosing his brother over her. He was choosing to keep her safe while he did what he had to do. And honestly, he needed a little time to figure out how to handle her. He wanted her, but he wasn't sure he wanted this volcanic emotion he felt around her. Why couldn't it be simple? Why couldn't she see it was for the best?

The very fact that she would fight with him like this when they had an op to run proved his point.

"All right. I need a minute to fix my makeup and then I'll be ready to go." She turned and walked into the bathroom.

What the hell had just happened? How did she go from arguing with him to politely telling him she needed a moment? Was she fucking with his head? Was this some kind of manipulation to get him to do what she wanted?

He wasn't going to be moved. This was what a leader did. He made the call and he stuck by it. Mia was going home and he'd just have to deal with her when he'd gotten Theo back. If she didn't understand how important that was, then she wasn't the woman he'd thought.

Still, when she opened the door, for a moment he saw deep sadness etched on her face. Then she gave him a tight smile. "I'm ready. Let's get this done."

She walked past him. It took everything he had not to chase

after her and haul her back into his arms. He wanted to kiss that look off her face, to promise her everything would be fine.

He couldn't be certain that wasn't exactly what she was trying to do—to get him soft so he would change his mind.

He followed her to the SUV. She'd said she judged him by his actions. She would just have to wait and see. When he showed up on her doorstep in a few weeks, she would know he hadn't been lying.

And then they could really start their lives. This was a minor blip in a brand new relationship. That was all.

He hoped that was all.

* * * *

Mia forced a smile on her face as she took the glass of champagne from the tray. Not that she would drink it. Despite what Case thought, she had done the undercover thing a time or two before and rule number one was she didn't trust anything she hadn't poured herself. Even if she was at a party.

"This is awesome. You should try the little cake thingees. They're good."

Her partner didn't have the same rules. Hutch was like a kid in a candy store or a kid at a well-done buffet. For a group that fed the hungry, they knew how to do gourmet.

"Hutch, how about a little less eating and a little more hacking?" Case's voice came over the small device she'd placed in her ear before they'd gotten to the party. "You've done your obligatory socializing. I think it's time to get the job done."

So he could get rid of her. She didn't mention that. It wouldn't do her any good. The men around her were once more working to decide how her life would go and she'd learned long before the only way to counter that was to do her thing and not compromise.

"I agree. It's time to move," she said. She looked directly at Hutch so anyone who glanced their way would think they were having a conversation. "I think we've got a decent understanding of all the good work the charity is doing in the community and how they're managing it. There are a lot of doors they're opening."

Hutch seemed to get serious. "Yes, they are."

Mia counted four doors that led to different parts of the building. She'd had a brief discussion with the director, a middle-aged man who seemed a little overwhelmed by all the people around him. He'd explained the different workings of the charity to her in halting English. There was a food pantry that helped the urban poor and attempted to stave off childhood malnutrition. They had outreach in rural areas of the country as well. There was also a department that helped with job searches as unemployment was a real problem in the country.

She and Hutch had been given a nice tour that included the director pointing out his office and the business offices.

There wasn't actually a guard posted on the doors, but there were several well-dressed men who didn't seem to be mingling.

"Are the guards going to be a problem?" Case asked.

Mia glanced around. No one was looking their way at the moment. A guitarist was playing, his fingers flying across the strings as he entertained with local music. The crowd of roughly sixty or seventy people seemed preoccupied with him. There were a few groups talking quietly around the buffet and some people at the open bar, but no one seemed to notice the Americans.

"I don't think so," she said quietly. Having her hair down helped enormously. In the course of her normal life, she would have pulled it all up for an elegant look, but the mass of hair around her shoulders not only sheltered the earpiece, it also hid her face from the multitude of security cameras. "He should be able to deal with the problem with ease. Any luck on your end?"

"She's asking if Fain's been able to cut into the feed," Hutch said in a quiet voice. There was no way to mistake his irritation. Apparently her partner preferred to be behind the scenes. "I told him what to do."

"It's not as easy as you made it sound, asshole." Ezra sounded frustrated. "I'm not a tech guy. I might have pointed that out."

"I could get it done in five minutes if you let me," Hutch said, his mouth tight. "I can probably figure out how to hack the internal systems here, too. I think we should come in."

"Hutch, I know this isn't your thing." Case was the calm voice of reason. "But I'm going to need you to do your job. Get in, download the system, and get out. We can't be sure what kind of security they have. Getting in and putting physical hands on the system is our best shot. You agreed with me earlier today."

"Earlier today I didn't get the feeling that someone was watching me," Hutch admitted. "Something's wrong with this place. I can feel it."

"No," Case said, his voice steady. "What you feel is PTSD. This is the first time you've been back out in the field, brother. I promise, it's normal to be afraid. It's time to shut that fear down and do your job. A lot of people are depending on you. Theo is depending on you."

Mia didn't like the way Hutch paled. She held out her hand. "I can do it. I certainly know how to download a system. Give me the drive."

He stood straighter, his shoulders going back. "I'm fine. If I get caught in the hallway, I'll say I was looking for the bathroom. Could you distract the big guy who's obviously carrying a gun while I slip back there? The other two are moving around outside, but the one to your left is doing an inner perimeter sweep and he keeps looking that way. I need about thirty seconds."

She wasn't sure he was up to it, but she nodded because she was done arguing with the men in her life.

Case might be telling her the truth. He might fully intend to see her again. Hell, she'd proven to be very open when it came to his sexual proclivities, but he'd proven he didn't truly want her. He wanted her body, maybe her submissive side. But he didn't want her in his life. Not in any real way. She had a serious chance to help him find his brother. Tony was still looking into the situation, but it didn't matter to Case.

This was the most important moment of his life and he

wouldn't allow her to help him, not even to sit in a shitty motel room and wait for him to return. It didn't make sense. She'd followed all of his rules. She'd kept a bodyguard with her.

I can't work with you.

She knew damn well the other men in his family worked with their wives. Liam took his wife and child with him at times when he was investigating. Ian took Charlotte as his backup many times. Alex and Eve worked together every day. Mia might not have served in the military, but she would put herself up against any of the women and some of the men when it came to self-defense. She was proficient in Krav Maga and had used a gun more than once in her life. She'd never had to actively shoot anyone, but she'd certainly had to fight her way out of bad situations before.

Mia began making her way across the room, trying to keep a serene smile on her face as she walked away from Hutch.

Case trusted her to do the one thing he couldn't do himself, but he didn't trust her to sit her ass in a motel room with a bodyguard?

It was ridiculous. She had to face the fact that she felt more for him than he did for her. She was in love with him, but all she was to him was a convenient lay. He might check in with her from time to time when he was at loose ends. He might even offer to play with her, but he wasn't ever going to be serious about a woman he could dismiss so easily.

No matter what he said, his actions spoke volumes. He was so eager to get rid of her, he was actively putting his brother's investigation in jeopardy.

And still she had to acknowledge if he'd said anything about loving her, she would have hopped on the plane and been the good little girl, waiting for her man to come home. If he'd said a damn thing about needing her, she would have kissed him good-bye.

He'd just said she was a distraction and he didn't need one of those.

He'd been cold. Not at all the warm lover she'd quickly grown addicted to.

It wasn't the first time a man had lied to get a woman to do what he wanted. She'd basically offered herself up. Need to get off? Mia will spread her legs for you. Need to let off some steam? Spank Mia. She likes it. Want to move your mission forward but don't have any cash? Mia will write you a check as long as you kiss her and make her think you care about her.

Maybe it was the leftover pleading of a child who'd been so loved one moment and alone and shoved into a cold world by herself the next. Maybe she would always be that six-year-old girl wishing her parents weren't dead, praying someone else would love her because her brothers had been taken from her, too.

She plastered a smile on her face. Get through the next thirty minutes and she could figure out what to do. It wouldn't be going back to Austin. If Case didn't want her help, she would find someone who did. She would pursue her leads and feed them to Ian Taggart. She would do it via computer. There was no way she was getting back into that circle again. It was far too dangerous.

Then she would work on her brothers' plans. God knew revenge was going to take up a good portion of her time in the coming months.

Perhaps making the people who'd killed her parents pay would take her mind off the cowboy who didn't want her.

"Hi, I was wondering if there was a place I could make a call from." She made sure she was standing in a way that forced the guard to turn away from Hutch. "My cell can't find a signal here."

"Very good," Case said in her ear. She wished his voice wasn't so damn sexy. "Just a few minutes more and we'll have you out of there."

And out of his life.

The guard looked down and she was surprised by the perfect English he spoke. "We're kind of in a dead zone, if you know what I mean. Sorry about that, but if you walk outside, you should be able to get a signal."

His accent sounded Western to her. Like he'd been taken straight off a Colorado ranch and put into a designer suit. Wasn't that interesting?

How many Gringos were there according to the papers? Three? Was she currently talking to one of them?

"You're American?"

He stopped for a moment, a cloud coming over his face, but then he smiled. "Yes. I'm American. Born and raised in New York."

Not with that laconic drawl he wasn't.

"You sound like you're from Colorado or Wyoming."

Again, his eyes seemed to lose focus, but he recovered more quickly. "Not at all. I'm from upstate New York. Lived there all my life until I left for the military. You're a lovely woman. Are you here alone?"

"Tell him you have a husband waiting for you and then excuse yourself to find him." Case didn't sound quite as calm now. There was an edge to his tone. "Hutch should have gotten to the offices by now. You can rejoin the party until I tell you Hutch is ready to come back out."

"I came with my brother," she said, unwilling to stop the conversation. Case couldn't see what she was seeing. Not all intel was found on a computer. "I seem to have lost him, but that's okay. I found the only other American here."

"What are you doing, Mia?"

It was annoying to have Case in her ear, judging her every choice. Maybe she was better off on her own.

The big guard stared down at her. "There are two more. My brothers. We all work here."

Something about the way he said brothers made her wary. His eyes had lit briefly when he'd said the words.

It was time to use her assets to get a little more information. She gave him what she hoped was her best flirty look, eyes up, bottom lip out just a bit. "Are they all as big as you?"

His lips curved up, a perfectly arrogant look. "They're tiny compared to me. I'm afraid I got all the muscle in our family."

"Mia, you walk away right now," Case growled. "You think

this is making me jealous? It's not. It's making me pissed off that you can't follow orders. This is exactly why I'm shipping you home as fast as I can."

"How did three New York boys end up in Cartagena?" She ignored Case. This man very likely knew Theo. If she was right, he worked with Theo. Tony had talked about Hope McDonald gathering a small group of men she was turning into her own personal army. This was bigger than just Theo. This could have ramifications that went beyond one family.

Tony had told her more than one group wanted to get their hands on McDonald's research. What would hostile governments do with it? Hell, what would her own government do with it?

The ex-soldier's jaw hardened and she noticed the way his left hand twitched ever so slightly. "I don't…I need to do my job. You're very pretty. I would like to spend some time with you, but I can't sneak you back to our room. They watch us. She watches us."

He grimaced and put a hand to his earpiece, as though something was happening to it.

His words had been stilted, as though he was fighting some kind of instinct.

"Robert, I think we should go," a deep voice said. "We've been called back into base. Apparently there's a problem coming our way."

She turned and there was another dark-suited bodyguard standing behind her. He was dark-haired and beautifully built. Mia had to hand it to Hope McDonald. The woman liked a handsome man. Mia was surrounded by big, gorgeous men all of the sudden and she realized it was likely time to retreat. Two was one too many to deal with on her own.

"Mia, if you don't show up outside in thirty seconds I'm going to come in, and you won't like how I'll come in," Case promised.

Definitely time to move. "Thanks for the advice. I'll pick up a signal outside. Hope you have a nice night."

She turned, her hair swinging as she tried to put some distance between her and the big guys. She stopped right in her tracks because Case was already here.

"Hello," he said. "I think we should talk, don't you?"

"I'm not kidding, Mia," the same voice said in her ear. "You better get your sweet ass out here."

She wasn't staring at Case. She'd found Theo and he had a gun on her.

CHAPTER TEN

Case watched as Michael opened the door to the hotel room he'd rented earlier this afternoon when he'd decided on his course of action. He nodded Michael's way, not bothering to take the earbud out of his ear.

"Everything all right?" Case asked as Michael walked in. He could hear the sounds of the party through the link he shared with Mia and Hutch. Mia's voice came over loud and clear in his right ear as she introduced herself to the director and asked for a tour. "Is Fain on his way back?"

Michael put a bottle of water in front of him and sank into his seat. "He's parking on the street. He has to find a space. He doesn't feel comfortable leaving them behind without a quick getaway. He'll be up in a few minutes."

Fain was being a bit of a drama queen about the whole thing. It was obvious that the ex-soldier was planning on riding his new job as far as he could. Case intended to explain to him again that it would be a very short-lived position.

Mia was being stubborn but he would make her see reason once everything was over.

"Good for him," Case muttered and turned back to his computer, though he didn't have visual on them. That rankled. He felt blind. He *was* blind.

"I see security cameras," a low voice said in his ear. Hutch. "They're American made. I've got protocols on my system for how to break into the feed."

Case prayed the kid knew what he was doing. "Okay. When Fain gets up here, I'll put him on the computer with your instructions. Let's hope he's got some skill."

"He's the only one who has shown any skill at all tonight," Michael muttered as he picked up his own headset. Michael would be able to listen in.

Case turned off the microphone. Mia was asking the director questions about the charity. She was safe enough for now. "I assume you have something you want to say to me."

"What makes you think that?"

"I know when you're pissed. I've worked with you for most of my adult life."

Michael's emerald eyes pinned him. "Do you have any idea what you're doing? Because I think you think you do, but you don't."

"What is that supposed to mean?"

"It means you are seriously fucking with that girl and I didn't think you were that kind of guy."

Another reason for Mia to go home. He never had to have relationship talks with his best friend in the field before Mia had come along. "What kind of guy? The kind of guy who wants to see his girl safe? Because that's the guy I am right now."

"Are you? Because she's safe here. She's got a bodyguard and she's actually quite calm under pressure. She knows how to shoot, too. I would take her in as backup, but you're pushing her out even though she could bring you the very intel that leads us to your brother. I have to wonder why you would do that."

He did not want to have a relationship talk now. Maybe never. He didn't do relationships, but he found himself in one with Mia and it would have to wait. "How about you do your job and I'll worry about Mia."

Michael shook his head and turned back to the monitor in front of him. "You're not going to have to worry about Mia at all after this."

When had Michael gotten so fucking chatty? It had been way easier when they'd been dumb grunts getting their asses shot at in Afghanistan. No time to think about girls when extracting a high-value target under cover of night. No chatting like teens when blowing up a munitions factory.

Life had been simple. Michael watched his back. Case watched his. They'd bonded because it had been the first time for them both to be away from their twins. JT Malone had stayed behind to run the family oil business and Theo had been miles away in Iraq with his own team.

Michael had become his best friend, the one he could count on.

"I can't think when she's around. She's a distraction."

Michael turned. "Do you even hear yourself? Do you understand what she's thinking when you say that?"

"She should be thinking hey, I'm distracting the dude who needs to find his brother. Maybe I should go and wait for him to come home?" He was pretty sure that wasn't the answer.

Michael groaned. "You have no idea how to deal with women."

"Theo was the smooth one," Case admitted. "I pretty much did what he told me to when it came to women. He could find the one woman in the room who didn't want to have anything to do with him and a couple of drinks, some conversation later, and he'd be going home with her. I sometimes think he fell for Erin because she was a challenge."

"He loved Erin. That was why he never gave up on her," Michael replied. "He would never have shoved her away. He valued her in the field."

"Erin spent years in the Army. Erin could take Theo out."

"Yeah, well, Mia might not be able to take you out, but she has value. She's smart. She's totally cool under pressure and she follows orders."

"She does not," he shot back. "I ordered her to stay in the safe room on the plane. That lasted two minutes."

"She wasn't going to let them shoot us. I'm sure you gave her a bunch of BS about how they wouldn't have, but you weren't there. They were going to take one of us out. They had to. After they lost touch with the copilot, there were too many of us to deal with. It would have been me or Hutch dead and the other used to draw you out if Mia hadn't bought us some time."

Put like that, it was a reasonable way that day could have gone. "I don't want her to get hurt. I can't stand the thought."

"Finally. Why didn't you say that?"

"I did say that." Mostly. "What did you think I meant by she's a distraction?"

"I knew what you meant because I've spent the majority of my adult life speaking Case Taggart's language. It's mostly grunts and rude hand gestures and the occasional belch that really means it's been a good night."

"I'm not that bad." He knew how to communicate, although he was good with rude hand gestures.

"Look, you think you're being forthcoming, but that's not what she hears. I grew up with a couple of girls around the house at all times. Cousins or daughters of family friends. They were like sisters to me, especially Dana."

Michael didn't like to talk a lot about Dana. She'd disappeared years before. If he was bringing her up, it had to be important. "All right. What should I have said?"

"It's important to realize that women don't always hear what we think we're saying. When you called her a distraction, she thought you were talking about sex with her. Fucking her, having to deal with her was a distraction you didn't want and the sex wasn't good enough to make you want to keep her."

His stomach dropped. He could hear Mia talking in one ear,

her voice bright as she charmed the director. Had she thought that was what he meant? "I didn't say anything like that."

There was the sound of the door clicking open and Fain strode in.

"Ezra, you were there for the dissolution of Case's relationship with Mia," Michael began.

Whoa. "There was no dissolution."

Fain took a seat in front of Hutch's computer. "You mean when he told her he was done fucking her and she should go home?"

He felt his skin flush. "That is not what I said."

Fain started typing on the keyboard. "That's totally what you said. You were pretty cold about it. Can we cut out the touchy-feely shit and deal with the security cameras? I thought Hutch was supposed to leave me instructions."

Should he keep Mia close? He dismissed what Fain had said. And what Michael said, too. Mia was smart. She didn't need some fucking translator. He'd been in her bed for days. He couldn't keep his hands off her. She could plainly see that. He'd talked about her moving to Dallas. That wasn't the talk of a man who wanted to get rid of a woman. He just wanted to keep her safe.

She was being a brat, trying to get her way.

Yes, because staying in a shitastic motel room he wouldn't allow her to leave without a guard had been so much fun for her so far. She'd been stuck in that room for days. He wouldn't let her out without Fain or Hutch. Her only excitement had been talking to her contact—which she'd done as he'd asked her to. With a guard.

And every night she welcomed him enthusiastically.

What had it taken for a woman as independent as Mia to sit on her butt while he did all the work? She was used to being in the thick of things, but she hadn't once complained.

He was doing the right thing. He had to choose his brother this time. Nothing could keep him from saving Theo, not even Mia.

"This is awesome. You should try the little cake thingees. They're good." Hutch sounded slightly enthusiastic for the first time that night.

"Hutch, how about a little less eating and a little more hacking?" He didn't even try to keep the irritation out of his voice. "You've done your obligatory socializing. I think it's time to get the job done."

"Naturally he found the dessert buffet." Michael grinned. "You can count on Hutch. If there's a secret buried in pie, he's going to find it."

"He's not serious enough," Fain complained. "I know you swear he's trained, but I wouldn't take that kid in as backup."

Fain didn't know Hutch. "He's good. I've worked with him for a couple of years. You know he figured out you were up for CIA recruitment. You want to tell me why they turned you down?"

Fain snorted slightly. "I turned them down. I didn't like the way Tennessee Smith worked. I know everyone thought he was the shit, but he didn't strike me as a great team leader. I also don't particularly think a team like that can work. It's better to use military units."

"We worked quite well before Ten was disavowed." Michael stood and moved toward the window with his binoculars. They'd turned off the lights in the room so they could properly see the party across the street.

"And then you all scattered, from what I understand." Fain frowned at the screen. "Consistency is important in intelligence work. I'm sure the entire team defecting left a major mess for whatever idiot took the job after Smith."

"I agree. It's time to move," Mia said over the line. "I think we've got a decent understanding of all the good work the charity is doing in the community and how they're managing it. There are a lot of doors they're opening."

"Yes, they are," Hutch replied, his voice getting tense again.

It was good to get back to the op and not focus on his love life or how Fain thought his former team had fucked up. "Are the guards going to be a problem?"

"There was only one on the door," Fain said. "There's a valet, but he doesn't look big enough to be a guard. Of course I don't know what they've got on the inside, but it looked pretty casual to me. I suspect they don't want to scare the donors away."

The sound of guitar music thrummed in the background, but he could hear Mia loud and clear. He'd noted that almost everything she'd said was innocuous. If overheard, it would likely mean nothing to the people listening to her.

She was good.

"I don't think so." She replied to his question about the guards in a quiet, calm voice. "He should be able to deal with the problem with ease. Any luck on your end?"

"She's asking if Fain's been able to cut into the feed." Hutch wasn't as careful as Mia. Since Case couldn't see him, he had to hope Hutch wasn't being watched carefully. "I told him what to do."

"It's not as easy as you made it sound, asshole." Ezra sounded frustrated. "I'm not a tech guy. I might have pointed that out."

Hutch's irritated tone came over the line. "I could get it done in five minutes if you let me. I can probably figure out how to hack the internal systems here, too. I think we should come in."

He couldn't afford to pull Hutch out now. He needed his tech guy to do the job. He would save the dressing down for later. "Hutch, I know this isn't your thing, but I'm going to need you to do your job. Get in, download the system, and get out. We can't be sure what kind of security they have. Getting in and putting physical hands on the system is our best shot. You agreed with me earlier today."

"Earlier today I didn't get the feeling that someone was watching me. Something's wrong with this place. I can feel it," Hutch said.

Shit. He hadn't imagined this possibility, but hearing the tremor in Hutch's voice made him realize what was happening. "No. What you feel is PTSD. This is the first time you've been back out in the field, brother. I promise, it's normal to be afraid. It's time to shut that fear down and do your job. A lot of people are depending on you. Theo is depending on you."

"I can do it," Mia offered. "I certainly know how to download a system. Give me the drive."

Michael looked his way. "Let her do it."

Fain was shaking his head. "Somebody better do something because I'm having no luck at all with these cameras."

Hutch came back on the line. "I'm fine. If I get caught in the hallway, I'll say I was looking for the bathroom. Could you distract the big guy who's obviously carrying a gun while I slip back there? The other two are moving around outside, but the one to your left is doing an inner perimeter sweep and he keeps looking that way. I need about thirty seconds."

Case felt his whole body go tense. The guard had a gun. "Get those fucking cameras up, Fain. I need to see where she is. I thought you said the security wasn't serious."

Fain turned slightly and sent him a narrowed glare. "I was the chauffeur. I saw what was happening at the door. I assumed you and Michael would handle the rest of it. Naturally there's some security inside. Do you want me to go over there? I could explain something was wrong with the car and I need to see Ms. Danvers. Heaven forbid we trust her to talk to someone in a public place."

"Fine." He hated the way the entire experience was making him feel. He knew Mia had been in tighter spots, but she hadn't been his then. Now that she belonged to him, wasn't it his job to ensure her safety?

Or was it his job to care about her and let Mia be Mia?

"Hi, I was wondering if there was a place I could make a call from. My cell can't find a signal here."

He didn't need security cameras to see the smile on her face. He could hear it, but he knew it wouldn't be as bright as the ones she'd given to him over the last few days. Those smiles had lit up his whole fucking world. But even a half smile from his Mia would distract a man for however long she wanted him distracted. "Very good. Just a few minutes more and we'll have you out of there."

A few more minutes and she would be walking out of that

place and he would be able to breathe again. She would get on a plane and he could concentrate. Or would he simply sit around and wonder what kind of trouble she was getting into back home? He wasn't stupid enough to believe she would honestly sit at her condo in Austin and wait for him. She was pissed off and a pissed off Mia could cause trouble.

He had to find a way to make her see reason.

A deep voice came over the feed. "We're kind of in a dead zone, if you know what I mean. Sorry about that, but if you walk outside, you should be able to get a signal."

Michael looked back. "He sounds Western. Colorado or Wyoming. What's an American doing working security here?"

Fain's head came up. "Holy shit. Is she talking to one of Theo's fellow bank robbers?"

"Tell her what we think, Case," Michael urged. "She can ask him about Theo. Subtly."

Or he would completely lose control of the situation because she would sense a great story and run with it like the thoroughbred reporter she was. Maybe she wouldn't notice. Maybe she wouldn't pick up on the possibilities and she would simply do the job he'd asked her to and walk away.

"You're American?" Mia asked.

Michael fist pumped. "That's a smart girl."

Fain nodded. "See, I would totally let her watch my back."

They were determined to make him the bad guy. He was saved from responding by the guard's reply. "Yes. I'm American. Born and raised in New York."

"You sound like you're from Colorado or Wyoming." Nothing got past Mia.

"Keep it up, spy chick," Michael said. "That's going to be her superhero name from here on out."

Luckily she couldn't hear Michael in her ear. "Aren't you supposed to be watching the street?"

Michael turned back to his job, but not before Case saw a shit-eating grin on his face.

The guard's conversation with Mia continued to play out in Case's ear. "Not at all. I'm from upstate New York. Lived there all my life until I left for the military. You're a lovely woman. Are you here alone?"

Oh, that was so not fucking happening. "Tell him you have a husband waiting for you and then excuse yourself to find him. Hutch should have gotten to the offices by now. You can rejoin the party until I tell you Hutch is ready to come back out."

"Almost got it," Fain said, his hands moving over the keys.

"I came with my brother." It was obvious Mia wasn't listening to him anymore. She simply continued on in her sultry voice. "I seem to have lost him, but that's okay. I found the only other American here."

"What are you doing, Mia?" He'd given her a direct fucking order.

"Hey, I've got someone walking up to the hotel who looks mighty familiar," Michael said. "I think we're in trouble."

Case knew they were in trouble because the guard kept talking. "There are two more. My brothers. We all work here."

His brothers? All Americans? Case could feel the adrenaline begin to pump through his veins. Mia had told him everything Tony Santos had told her. According to the intel Mia had provided him, there were at least three soldiers in Hope McDonald's clutches. Whoever Mia was currently talking to could be one of those men, could be one of Theo's new "brothers."

Could be insanely dangerous to be close to.

"Are they all as big as you?" Mia asked in her flirty tone.

"They're tiny compared to me," came the reply. "I'm afraid I got all the muscle in our family."

He didn't care how big the motherfucker was, he needed to stay away from Case's girl. "Mia, you walk away right now. You think this is making me jealous? It's not. It's making me pissed off that you can't follow orders. This is exactly why I'm shipping you home as fast as I can."

"I'm serious, Case," Michael said. "I think…maybe I'm

seeing things. How are the cams coming?"

"How did three New York boys end up in Cartagena?" Mia asked.

In front of him the screen flickered and he could see the walkway outside the building.

"Got one up," Fain said. "I'm working on the others. I think I got the only one that's not connected to the inside."

"I don't…I need to do my job," the guard was saying in Case's ear. Case agreed with him utterly. For just a second he almost relaxed. Then the guard continued, his voice going low. "You're very pretty. I would like to spend some time with you, but I can't sneak you back to our room. They watch us. She watches us."

"Case, I think your brother's here," Michael said.

Fuck. Case stood and moved to the window Michael was standing at. He held his hands out for the binoculars. Theo was here? Theo was walking down the street?

God, what should he do? Would Theo be happy to see him? Would he know Case at all?

"Robert, I think we should go," a deep voice said in his ear. "We've been called back into base. Apparently there's a problem coming our way."

That hadn't been Theo's voice. It was someone else. Mia had two guards to deal with. Shit. He shouldn't have done this. He looked down the street, searching for the man Michael had talked about.

"Mia, if you don't show up outside in thirty seconds I'm going to come in, and you won't like how I'll come in." He would take care of two birds with one stone. He would have Fain grab Mia and Hutch and he would take Theo and run like hell.

"He's right there." Michael pointed to a large figure moving down the sidewalk. He wasn't alone. There was another man with him and two more at his back. What was Theo doing?

"Thanks for the advice." Mia's voice was light, but he could hear the slight strain in her tone. It proved she had some sense.

"I'll pick up a signal outside. Hope you have a nice night."

Then he heard her gasp.

"Hello," a very familiar voice said. "I think we should talk, don't you?"

"I'm not kidding, Mia." Case was confused because he was watching Theo walk down the street. How could he hear him talking? It had to be a mistake. "You better get your sweet ass out here."

The man's face turned up and he pointed at the hotel.

That wasn't Theo. That was Ian. Shit. Theo was with Mia.

"Why don't you turn over the communication device hidden in that lovely ear of yours and we can have a real talk," Theo was saying. "I'm afraid I've already picked up your…brother…partner whatever you want to call him. If you don't want him to die, you'll come quietly and explain exactly what you're doing here."

He felt frozen in place. The first words he'd heard from his brother and they were threats against Mia. And Hutch. God, Theo wouldn't hurt Hutch. Hutch had been their buddy for years. Theo had spent all his off time playing video games with Hutch sitting beside him before he'd gotten together with Erin. He couldn't hurt Hutch.

"I'm going in."

The feed from Mia's device went dead. Case's heart nearly stopped. He tossed the headphones aside.

"Hey, you're not going in without backup." Michael put down the binoculars.

Fain was already on his feet. "I'll go, though apparently we've now got a McKay-Taggart crew with us."

"It's Ian, Liam, Alex, and I'm pretty sure that's Andrew Lawless walking next to him," Michael explained.

Case started for the door, but he knew what had happened. "You told your new boss everything, didn't you, you limp dick asswipe."

Fain didn't seem concerned. He strode right alongside Case. "He's my boss now. I suppose he called your brother since he's kind of Ian's boss, too. That makes you low man on the totem pole."

"There's no time to argue." Michael kept up despite the fact that his leg had to still ache. He'd had a couple of days to recover, but it was obvious to Case that it was still stiff. "And don't tell me to stay behind. I'm coming with you. Someone's going to have to explain everything to Ian."

But he knew his brother better than that. He even knew damn well how Ian had found him. All McKay-Taggart field operatives got what Ian liked to call the "lost puppy chip." Case, Michael, and Hutch all had GPS enabled microchips implanted in their hands. Not that it had done Theo any good. McDonald had simply cut it out of him. But it had apparently led his oldest brother right to him.

"You're going to thank me later," Fain said as they rushed down the stairs. "We need this backup. You have zero idea what we're going into."

"Only because you're the moron who couldn't follow simple instructions to get the security cams up," Case said between clenched teeth. He had to keep it together. It was a big building, but there were only a couple of entrances and exits. They could run, but they wouldn't be able to hide in there forever.

He hit the lobby at a run and damn near knocked over a bigger, older version of himself. Like he'd thought, Ian didn't ask for explanations. He looked at Case and his body went still.

"What do you need?"

That was his brother. He knew when the shit had hit the fan and he didn't ask for explanations.

"Theo's in the building across the road. He's got Mia and Hutch. You should probably know we're going to have to blast our way out and the building is very likely owned by a cartel."

"Are you fucking kidding me?" Lawless asked, his face going a nice shade of red. He turned with the group as they made their way out to the street.

"What's wrong with Malone?" Liam asked, his voice cool and calm. "You're walking stiff."

"He got shot during the near kidnapping," Lawless complained, proving that Fain was a tattletale.

"How many ways out of the building are there?" Ian ignored everything but Case.

"Three, but I'm going in the front." He had to get to Mia.

"I'm going after my sister," Lawless insisted. He was a tall, well-built man in his mid-thirties. He wore a suit, his golden hair slightly shaggy. "I can't believe she's involved in this."

"Maybe you don't know her the way I do then," Case shot back as he crossed the street and started to make for the door. He pulled his SIG. There would be no playing around. He needed to get to her, to see that she was all right.

Theo. No. He needed to get her and save Theo.

"Subtlety," Ian said, his voice a bark. "Keep that piece under cover until we need it. You do not want the Cartagena police involved. Malone, do you know where the exits are?"

"I do," Michael said as they approached the building. "I can get to the back. There's a loading dock there and a small door to the alley on the way."

"Li, go with Malone. Alex?" Ian asked.

"I'll take the door," McKay said. "I wish we'd had time to set up comms."

"Yeah, little brother and I are going to have a long talk about proper communication at the end of this," Ian vowed. "It might end with my foot up his ass."

His brother was truly a gifted communicator, but nothing mattered right now. Nothing except getting his people out of that fucking building safe and unharmed.

Getting Mia. He had to get Mia.

Theo. He couldn't let Theo go.

"Calm yourself down or I'll bench you," Ian threatened even as they walked toward the door. "That goes for you, too, Lawless. Asshole who I don't know but who will be vetted on a level you've never understood before?"

Fain looked at Ian. "I suppose that's me. Yes, sir?"

"If you get my brother or my client killed I'm going to make you into a human centipede with the most disgusting, vile people I can possibly find and you're going to be hooked up to the one who can't control himself, if you know what I mean. I'm serious. I've got the logistics worked out and everything."

"I will do my best, sir. Mr. Lawless, I'm going to need you to stay close to me and let the Taggarts do what they do best," Fain said evenly.

What the Taggarts did best was kick some ass.

"I knew I should have come down the minute she started dodging my calls," Lawless muttered.

"Excuse me." The man who worked as the valet approached them. "This is a private party."

Lawless didn't miss a beat. He walked right up to the dude and punched him hard in the face, the sound thudding. The valet went down and Case's appreciation for Mia's brother went up.

"Is there anyone else I can punch?" Lawless asked. "That felt good."

Ian reached under his jacket. "I'm afraid the rest of this is a firefight. You remember what I taught you?"

"I remember you punched me every time I got it wrong," Lawless replied. "And yes, I remember how to use a gun. I know what to do and I know where to go if I need to run. I'll get Mia and meet you."

That rankled. "I'll handle Mia."

Lawless didn't bother to look his way, keeping his eyes on Ian. "You deal with your brother and I'll deal with my sister. After this is over, I assure you we're going to have a long talk, Case. If anything happens to her, you won't like what I have to say."

They walked through the front door. No guard. Apparently they were all dealing with Mia and Hutch.

He glanced around the room, seeing it for the first time. It was done up with twinkle lights and greenery, matching the garden theme of the event. There were lovely women in evening gowns and men in tuxedoes and suits milling about, drinking champagne and talking. Had no one noticed the blonde being abducted by big Americans?

"Stay calm." Ian had his phone out and had dialed a number. "Alex, you in position?"

Alex's voice came over the line. "I'm good and all's quiet here. Malone and Li are on their way to the loading dock. I'll hear it if something goes wrong. You got sight on the target?"

God, the target was his brother.

"Not yet," Ian replied. "Keep this line open."

Case saw a flash move toward the back of the room. "Nine o'clock."

He started moving through the crowd, his heart pounding. He'd seen a brief glimpse of Mia's long blonde hair and the back of a man in a black suit, pressing her along.

Theo. Theo had Mia and Case suddenly wasn't sure what this Theo would do with her. He'd been so certain that no matter what anyone did to his brother, Theo would still stay Theo—patient where Case was quick tempered, jovial where Case could be surly. Never violent outside the bounds of his job. Certainly never violent when it came to a woman. Not Theo. Theo wouldn't even scare a woman, but Case had heard Mia's gasp on the line before it had gone dead. She'd been scared of his brother.

Someone yelled something in Spanish, but Case didn't care. He had to get to Mia, to Theo. He had to stop whatever the hell was about to happen. He definitely had to stop them from getting away. He'd spent a year in hell mourning his brother. He knew in an instant he couldn't handle mourning Mia. If they took Mia, he wouldn't ever stop searching. If he found her body, he might lie down beside it and let himself fade.

Please don't take Mia. Please don't fucking take her.

He wasn't sure who he was praying to, but the words pounded through his brain as he raced down the hall.

The lights were low in this part of the building. He could hear some shouting behind him and he could feel he'd gotten past Ian and Lawless. He was in front, but he couldn't slow down. He wouldn't lose them.

And then he stopped, his boots squealing on the floor as he came face to face with his brother for the first time in a year. Theo was standing in front of him, Mia held by one of the two men flanking Theo.

"Case!" Mia yelled.

He couldn't take his eyes off his twin. "Theo? Theo, it's me. It's Case. I'm your brother."

That was the moment that his brother, the man he'd spent his whole life with, who'd shared his world from the moment of their conception—that was the moment he lifted his gun and pulled the trigger.

CHAPTER ELEVEN

Mia screamed as the gun went off and Case went down.

A hand clamped down over her mouth and she found herself dragged through the darkened hallway. "Don't make a sound or you'll be next. I don't want to hurt a woman, but I will if I have to."

She wasn't sure which of the two were talking. She'd been watching Theo and then she'd been hustled to the hallway, her communication device crushed under Theo's boot. She'd known Case would come after her, but everything happened so fast.

Case was shot. Theo had shot Case. Oh god, was he dead? Case couldn't be dead.

"Did you get the other one?" Theo asked, his voice a cold, dead version of Case's.

"He's already in the back," the first guard she'd spoken to said. Robert. He was the one with his arm around her waist, pushing her along. "Victor handled him."

She turned, trying to see Case. All she'd had was one glimpse of him. He'd stood there, but he hadn't seen her. He'd been looking at his brother. Her heart twisted at the thought. It no longer mattered why he'd pushed her away. All that mattered was she loved him. All that mattered was Case.

"Please let me help him," she whispered as the guard pushed her through a door. "Let me go and get back to him. You can get away. Just let me go to him."

"I can't." Her captor's arm tightened. "I won't."

She heard the door close behind her with a quiet thud, heard the snick of a lock turning into place.

"Who the hell was that?" Robert asked, turning with her still in his arms. "He looked like Tomas. Just like Tomas. How is that possible? Are there more of us?"

"I don't know." Theo stared at the door he'd locked as though he could see through, see to the brother he'd left bleeding.

"His name is Case," Mia said, barely able to breathe for how tightly Robert held her. "Case Taggart. He's Theo's brother. Theo is Tomas's real name. Theo Taggart. Please, Theo, you have to listen to me. Everything that woman has told you is a lie."

Theo turned to her, his eyes glacial. "Stop calling me that. You're the one who's lying and it doesn't matter that he looked like me. He's dead now."

Her vision suddenly seemed to waver. No. He couldn't be dead. He couldn't. Her heart threatened to seize and then she heard it.

"Theo!" The shout threatened to shake the walls.

Case. He was still alive. He was out there. He was hurt, but he wasn't dead.

"Sounds like you missed," the third man said. He was as big as Theo, his coloring dark and his eyes hollow. "Mother will be upset and you need your meds. You're looking pale, brother."

"I hit him, Victor," Theo insisted. "Apparently he's very stubborn. You can let her go, Robert. There's nowhere for her to run. She can't get out of this room and I doubt he'll be able to get in."

"We have to take them to Mother," Robert insisted. "Did you do as she asked? Did you get rid of the microchip in his hand? She told us where it would be."

Mia was released and she immediately saw what they were talking about. Who they were talking about. "Hutch?"

She hurried across the room. It looked like it was used for storage, with big industrial shelves on all sides. Hutch was on the floor, his body utterly limp. Mia slid to her knees, reaching for his hand. Case would come for them. He was out there and he wouldn't stop looking. She had to make sure she and Hutch were alive when Case came.

She gasped as she got a good look at him. There was one light on in the back of the room, illuminating the damage done to the smart, funny man she'd come to like over the last week. Hutch's face was swollen, his skin covered in blood. Only the sight of his chest moving up and down gave her hope. "What the hell did you do to him?"

Theo stood over her. "He resisted. Don't act like this is my fault. You came into our house and tried to rob us. What were you looking for? Bank accounts? Do you work for the cartel? Because we've paid for our protection already. Don't think for a second, we won't defend ourselves."

"Can we keep the girl for ourselves?" Robert stood beside Theo, staring down at her. "She wasn't doing anything wrong. The guy was the one breaking in. You didn't know anything, did you, sweetheart?"

She was so aware that she was surrounded by men who weren't entirely in control of their actions. They each wore a Bluetooth device they seemed to communicate through. Was Hope McDonald on the other end of that line? Was she the one they called Mother? Her hands were shaking as she looked up at the face so familiar to her and yet utterly foreign. "Please help him, Theo."

"Stop calling me that," he snarled as he dropped to one knee beside her. "Why do you call me that?"

"Because it's your name. Because you're being lied to and used. All of you. Robert, listen to your own accent. You're not from New York." Tears poured from her eyes, but she forced herself to speak.

Robert ran a hand over his head, twitching slightly. "I am. I don't know what you're talking about. Now come on. We have to get back to base. You need to keep your mouth shut or she'll hurt you. You can stay with me." He looked at his "brothers." "We can hide her. We can share her."

Victor's eyes narrowed menacingly. "We have our orders. We're going to follow them."

Robert reached for her, dragging her up and against his muscular body. "No. She didn't do anything. She can't hurt us. I'm not going to turn her over."

"You're not." Victor hefted Hutch's still body up and over his shoulder in a fireman's hold. "Tomas is. I'm taking this one and we're leaving tonight. We've been made. We have to move and we have to do it now. The cartel is here. They're fighting the invaders."

So Case was at work along with Michael and Fain. How many were they up against? How hurt was he? He was definitely hurt. There was no way he wasn't. How bad was it? Was he dying out there right now?

"Go." Theo stood tall amongst them. "I'll take care of the girl."

Robert held her tight. "But I want the girl. I want a woman. I'm sick of being alone. I need someone."

"Please take me with you." If she could get on the inside, she could work on Theo. Case would find her. She just had to stay alive. They'd made two turns after Theo had shot Case. They'd passed a couple of doors. It would take him time to find them. She needed to stall and she knew who the weak link was. "I don't want to die. I want to live. Please, Robert."

His arms tightened around her. "It's going to be okay. I'll talk to her. She promised. She promised I could have someone. A woman."

So Robert was horny. Or lonely. She could play on that.

Before she could make her plea, Theo's hand shot out, gripping her wrist and pulling her to him.

"Victor, get him out of here or there's going to be trouble." Theo hauled her against his body, his hand gripping her throat. "Mother wants me to take care of this. Get out of here before they find us. I'll secure the door and then follow my orders."

Victor reached for Robert. "Let's go before we get into real trouble." He looked to Theo. "I'll see you inside, brother. Robert, we have to go. You'll feel better once you've had your meds."

Theo nodded. "Go. Get out of here. Take him with you and I'll handle the female."

Robert looked her way, clear longing on his face. "She promised."

Theo winced and put his hand to his ear as though he heard something the rest of them couldn't. "And she'll get you the right partner. This one is false. She was trying to hurt us. We'll turn the man. He has talents we can use." His voice went low. "You have to be patient, Robert. Everything comes in the right time. You know that."

Robert nodded slowly and then moved to his left toward another of those industrial shelves. "All right. I'll go. Be gentle with her. She's innocent."

Theo got close to her, so close she could see the line of his jaw, the stubble that was coming in. "Go. Tell her I'll be right behind you. I hear her orders. I will obey, but I have to take care of things. Hurry out the proper exit."

Victor touched the shelving unit and it slid out, revealing a secret door even as Mia could hear the gunfire getting closer and closer, hear Case's voice calling out. So close. He was so close, but she felt Theo's hand around her throat and had to think twice about screaming out his name.

"Please, Theo. Please don't hurt me. I love your brother." She did. Oh god. She loved Case. She'd been willing to admit she was crazy about him, lusted after his hot bod, wanted him to notice her, but she'd only just realized she was willing to sacrifice for him.

Herself. Her life. Her soul. But he cared about her, too. Pushing her away was just because he was a stupid butthole. He loved her, too. He couldn't make love to her the way he did and not love her. It went beyond sex. He was pushing her away because he cared.

She prayed he cared because she was suddenly ready to give up everything to see him one more time.

"Who are you?" Theo whispered in her ear.

"I'm Mia. I love your brother."

"I don't have a brother. Not the way you mean." He took a long breath in. "Why do you smell so good? You smell perfect. I don't want you. I don't like blonde girls, but you smell so good."

He sounded a little crazy, but she was willing to give him that since he'd been violated in a million ways. She needed to make him understand. They were alone now. Victor had dragged Hutch away. She had to stay close so Case could find them both. Surely he had a way to find them. "I'm not the one you want. You want Erin. I think I might smell like her. She's my friend. She gave me body lotion for Christmas. I think it's the one she uses. I'm wearing it now. I smell like your girlfriend, Erin."

"I don't have a girlfriend. Mother hasn't matched us yet."

Mia could hear the slightest hesitation in his voice and she pounced on it. Every second he stayed here with her was another chance for Case to find them. "You do have a girlfriend. She loves you so much. Erin. Her name is Erin. Theo, she just gave birth to your son. You have a baby boy. He's a week old. His name is Theo, Jr. Please remember. Please. They need you. Case needs you. You have to remember your family. You died on an island in the Grand Caymans."

He stilled behind her. "Why do I remember Tennessee? It plays through my head at the oddest times. I think I was in Tennessee before Mother saved me."

It was all bubbling under his surface. It was still there. She just had to find the right way to punch through all those drugs that bitch had fed him. "No. You were trying to save a man named Tennessee. Tennessee Smith. He was your commanding officer.

You belonged to a black ops team in the CIA before you went to work for your brother's company. McKay-Taggart. You have three brothers, Ian and Sean and Case. And you have so many people who love you. She didn't save you. She took you away from your family."

He breathed in, a long deep inhale, as though taking in her scent. She hadn't even thought about it when she'd smoothed the body lotion on after her shower. It had been an impulse to send Erin a Christmas gift. Almost an apology. She'd sent Erin a box of chocolate covered cherries after finding out they were her favorite treats. She hadn't expected anything back since she and Case hadn't been speaking at the time. And then she'd gotten a box of body lotion Erin claimed was the best and a note that stated Taggart men suck and that Mia should hang in there and not take any of Case's shit. Erin had explained in her own unique fashion that Case would come around.

Now she stood very still and prayed that little gift Erin had sent could reach across the space between Erin and Theo, could bring him back.

"I think about a red-haired girl," Theo whispered. "I think about her, but I can't see her anymore."

"Erin." Maybe if Mia said her name enough, it would break through to Theo.

There was a spatter of gunfire right outside the door, and Theo moved behind her, his hands releasing. Mia shoved away, turning. She was about to run when she saw Theo pale, his free hand reaching for his head as though he was in pain.

"Are you okay?" She knew she should run, but this was Theo. She'd never met him, but he was so important to Case. It was worth the risk. "Please come with me. He's right outside. I can take you to Erin and TJ. Your son needs his father."

He pulled the earpiece out of his ear and threw it to the ground, grinding it under his boot.

He was coming. She was going to give Case back his brother.

He leveled the gun right at her head. "I don't want Mother to hear this. I prefer to follow orders. It keeps my head on my body. I don't know who you are. Maybe you're a test. I don't know, but you're lying. I don't have a brother and I don't know who the fuck Erin is. I like redheads, that's all."

"I bet you can't even bring yourself to touch another woman." She couldn't lose him now. Play to reason. To logic. Surely the drugs couldn't change his reasoning skills.

"I wouldn't…" He stopped, but the gun didn't lower. "Stop talking or I really will kill you. Come here."

She started to take a step back, but he was on her in an instant. He dragged her to him, stepping behind one of the shelves.

"She can't see us here. I can't bring myself to do what she wants me to."

Mia didn't understand everything Case was saying. "You couldn't kill your brother. You knew it was him. That was why you didn't shoot to kill."

"I made a mistake." He shoved her to the ground.

Mia hit the concrete floor, her knees banging against it, sending pain flaring through her. Still, she turned, imploring him. "It wasn't a mistake. Somewhere deep down, you knew. You recognized him."

"I'm leaving now. I need you to understand something. I'm following my brothers. If I see your partner again, I will kill him. I won't have a choice and I won't hesitate. She told me you would show up one day. She told me you would lie and try to get me to turn."

"Then why aren't you killing me?"

His face tensed and for a second she waited for him to pull the trigger. "I'm weak. I won't be if I see that man again. I'll be waiting behind that door. I'll wait and when it opens, I'll shoot him in the head. So whether he lives or dies is your choice. Do you understand me?"

His words made her shiver because she believed him. "Yes."

"Don't move. Not an inch." He stepped back so his body was out in the small space between the shelves. He fired the weapon, the sound deafening.

Mia screamed, but the bullets didn't hit her, lodging instead in the wall behind her.

Her whole body shook as she watched Theo disappear behind the secret door.

He'd almost hit her with those shots. She'd felt a bullet scream past her head. Had that been an accident, too? Or had he been trying to terrify her?

The door burst open and she heard Case yelling.

"Mia!"

"I'm here," she managed.

She looked back at the place where Theo had vanished. There was no hint of the door he'd disappeared behind.

Sweet. Kind. Funny. Loyal. Words she'd heard used to describe Theo Taggart. Brave. Honorable. Warm.

There'd been such coldness is his eyes when he'd told her he would kill anyone who followed him—but particularly Case.

"Princess, are you hurt?" Case got to one knee. "There's blood all over here. What the hell happened?"

"No time for explanations." Ian Taggart stepped into the room, his massive body blocking out the light from the hall. "We have to move and fast. The police are on their way. I don't know that we get out of this now."

"Go," Case said. "Take Mia and run. I've got to find Theo. Which way did he go? You can tell me how you got away from him later. Just point me in the right direction."

In the direction of Theo's next bullet? Case had to be running on pure adrenaline, but he'd been shot and that was going to affect him. She couldn't do it. She couldn't let him open that door and start the fight that would end in one of them dying.

She shook her head. They would have to find another way. "He said they were leaving. I don't know which way he went. He tossed me in here and left. They took Hutch with him."

Ian cursed. Outside she could hear the sound of sirens wailing. Ian held his phone up. "Alex, we've got incoming. Tell Li and

Malone to get out of here and try to find Lawless. I had Fain haul him out. He's our best shot at not spending the next five years being a professional butt monkey in a Colombian prison. We're too deep in. We can't get out. The rest of you get the fuck out and find us a lawyer. We've got Mia but we lost Hutch."

Her brother was here? Nothing made sense. The cops were coming?

All she could think about was Theo behind that door, his gun raised and ready to kill them all. Theo, with his blank, soulless stare. Theo, who had recognized his mate's scent, who had reveled in it. Theo, who couldn't quite break the drug's hold.

Case gripped her hand. "It's going to be all right. I'm going to take care of you. Don't be afraid. Just do whatever the cops ask you to."

The world turned chaotic, with bright lights flashing and screams in Spanish. Case dropped his gun and put his hands in the air.

Ian Taggart did the same, dropping to his knees and lacing his hands behind his head, obeying the orders of the men with the guns. Mia started to do the same, but suddenly there was an officer wrapping a blanket around her and calling out for an ambulance.

Case groaned, probably because there was a bullet lodged in his upper right chest.

"You in pain, brother?" Big Tag asked with his trademark sarcasm as he was placed in handcuffs. "You better be happy they'll take you to a hospital because I swear if I end up with a boyfriend named Juan, I'm going to kill you myself."

Case didn't say a word, merely fell over in a dead faint.

"Yeah, that's typical," Big Tag complained. "Leave me holding the bag. Hello, boys. I'm going to need to make my phone call earlier rather than later. Don't guess anyone's up for a bribe, huh? Got a twenty right in that old back pocket."

Big Tag was still talking as they hauled him away.

Mia waited for the ambulance and wondered if Theo was watching them the whole time.

CHAPTER TWELVE

His whole chest felt like a Mack truck had hit it, but Case walked into the suite behind Ian and Alex dedicated to not letting anyone know he was in pain. The last thing he needed was to be a drag on the team. After the night they'd all had, there was no way he was putting more burden on his brothers.

Alex had shown up an hour earlier with Ian in tow, a change of clothes for Case, and some harsh words on how fucked up the previous night had been. Case had a sense that it could have been much worse. Still might be since his big brother had ended up spending the night in jail and he was definitely pissed about it.

"Charlie, baby, it was awful. I'm talking bugs on the floor and water torture and a big dude looking for his prison wife," Ian was saying into his cell. "I fought him off because I belong to you. Also because I'm not into smelly dudes who want to do things to my butt, but mostly it was about you, baby. I miss you so much and I'm going to take out all my aggression on my brother as soon as I possibly can. Yeah, he got shot and he's kind of being a pussy about it."

Maybe there was another reason he wasn't going to let the

pain show.

Case shot Ian the finger, but then he no longer gave a damn because Mia walked into the room. Her face lit up and she walked over to him as Ian continued to complain about his stay in prison as if he'd been there for years instead of a couple of hours.

"Are you all right?" Mia asked, her hands coming out as if to touch him, but then she pulled back.

He wasn't having that. He pulled her close, taking care with his left side, where Theo had lodged his bullet. "I'm fine now, thanks to your brother and what I'm sure was an enormous amount of money."

He hadn't expected to be released from the hospital. He'd expected to be transported to a secure location after the docs had dug the bullet out. When he'd woken up, they'd explained that the damage was mostly superficial and he was free to go, given him a prescription for pain and antibiotics and sent him on his way.

"He's been calling in a lot of favors to get you two out," Mia said, tucking her head against his uninjured shoulder.

"I spent the entire night waiting at the police station for a lawyer who never showed up," Alex said, yawning. "I thought it was going to get ugly, but they brought Ian out this morning and said no one was pressing charges."

"I'm surprised it worked." Andrew Lawless was standing in the middle of the massive suite. He was still wearing the suit he'd worn the night before, but he was down to the slacks and dress shirt. His hair was messy, his eyes tired. "I've been calling in every favor owed me, but I hadn't gotten a firm answer from anyone yet. I spent most of the night talking to the ambassador. He thought it would take at least a few days to get you two out."

Fain was sitting on one of the sofas, the one Mia had gotten up from. He looked fresh as a fucking daisy. "I'm sure your name alone managed to do the trick, boss."

Such a suck-up. Case looked down at Mia. "Are you all right?"

"I'm fine." Her eyes slid away from his. "I'm just upset that I couldn't help more."

He kissed her forehead. "You did everything you could. I take it they got rid of the tracking device in Hutch's hand?"

Mia nodded, tears flooding her eyes. "I saw him before they took him away. They'd dug it out. He looked like he was in bad shape."

It made his stomach twist. Not only had he lost Theo again, he'd lost Hutch. He'd done that. It was his fucking fault because he'd been in charge.

"I need a complete rundown on what's happening." Ian had hung up and crossed his arms over his chest, staring Case down. "And on this clusterfuck of an op I wasn't informed of until the dude with his head stuck up Lawless's ass told me."

If that bothered Fain, he didn't show it. "Someone had to be sensible and the minute Lawless hired me, my loyalty had to be to him. I might have discussed the fact that this op could go sideways because the men running it were far too close to the target."

Ian hadn't spoken a word to him in the car. He'd been on the phone with Charlotte the whole time, calming her down since apparently she'd been informed that her husband had been tossed in a South American jail cell. The next family dinner was going to be so much fun.

He'd lost Hutch and Theo and he'd almost lost Mia. Maybe he didn't deserve a family at all. "It was my fault."

"Of course it was your fucking fault," Ian shot back.

Mia stood beside him. "It was mine. I wouldn't let him tell you."

"Really? You held a gun on him at all times?" Ian stared at Case though his words were for Mia. "You threaten to beat my baby brother up?"

"Hey, let's leave my sister out of this." Lawless stepped up to Ian. "I told you I wouldn't put up with you bullying her."

"No," Mia replied, ignoring her brother. "I didn't use a gun. I used sex and logic. Though mostly it was sex. I wouldn't put out if he called you."

Case sighed. He could have told Lawless no one bullied Mia and got away with it. No one but him. The fact that they'd fought before the op weighed heavily on him. "Her informant was touchy about having a bunch of operatives running around. He's ex-Agency. We talked to Ten about him briefly. Hutch did."

God, what was Hutch going through? He stepped away from Mia, the guilt beginning to plague him. While he'd been in the car all he'd wanted to do was see her again, but now it came crashing in on him.

He'd put her in danger. She'd handled it all with grace, but she could have been taken, too.

"Why did they leave you behind?"

Mia frowned. "One of the men wanted to take me with them, but whoever's controlling them wouldn't allow it."

"Hope McDonald. There's no doubt in my mind that she's controlling them all." Ian started pacing, something Case had noticed he did when he was upset but trying to hold it together. "Mia, I'm going to need a full report."

She held a hand up. "Liam already took it."

"I left Li here with the rest of the crew and he and Michael should already have a preliminary report for you. They're in the office, going over a few things. We've already discovered that the building has a path that leads to some hidden underground tunnels and shafts," Alex explained.

"Very likely the cartel used them to move product around the city," Mia continued. He couldn't miss how tired she looked. She was still so fucking beautiful, but she needed sleep. Would she have nightmares about what had happened? Did she blame him? "As I noted in my report to Liam, Theo himself confirmed that they were working with the cartel. Ezra figured out which one. He's got a report on that as well."

"Excellent." Ian ran his hand over his head. "Alex, I'm going to need you to get in touch with your contacts at the DEA and I'll call Ten and see if he's got anything on these guys. Maybe if we lean on a cartel member, they'll tell us something. I'll talk to

Chelsea and see what the CIA knows."

"Can we get into those tunnels?" Case asked. His brother might still be there.

"Already gone," Fain replied. "O'Donnell and I went in early this morning. They've cleared out."

Mia looked up at him, her face flushed. "I'm going to talk to Tony again. He was trying to figure out how and where they would be going."

Ian's shoulders were up around his ears, his jaw tight with tension. "Who shot you, Case?"

"It doesn't matter." He could still see Theo standing there. His brother hadn't even recognized him. He'd simply lifted the gun and taken out the enemy. He'd been an empty vessel filled with Hope McDonald's perverse will.

"Fuck," Ian cursed. "It was Theo. He shot you."

"He didn't know what he was doing." Theo wasn't a lost cause. "Once we get him home and off those drugs and into therapy, he'll be the same Theo he used to be."

Ian shook his head. "Don't be naïve. What that woman has done to him will change him forever. I'm not giving up on him, but we all need to understand how dangerous he is now."

"He could have killed Mia," Lawless said, his voice grave. "If you hadn't gotten there in time, he likely would have."

"No. He wouldn't." Mia kept her eyes steady on Case as though trying to make him believe her words. "He was ordered to kill me, Case. He stayed behind to do the job, but he couldn't. I've thought a lot about what happened. He shoved me behind a shelving unit—the place you found me. Then he stepped out. I think there was a camera there and he wanted it to catch him. He fired twice, but into the wall. He wanted her to think I was dead."

"Did he say anything?" He hadn't gotten to talk to Theo. Mia had spent at least ten minutes with him.

"He recognized my smell," she explained. "I'm wearing the same body lotion Erin uses. He plainly recognized it, but he wouldn't believe me when I told him about her. It was almost like trying to think about her hurt him."

"Conditioning," her brother said with a frown. "She's using techniques to trick the mind into associating certain thoughts with distaste. Some therapists use it on addicts. I suspect she's using a harsh routine."

"But it's not anything that we can't reverse," Case insisted. "He had the chance to kill Mia and he didn't."

"He risked himself so I didn't die." Mia was still right there beside him.

Ian shook his head. "I'm going to read the reports. Get some sleep and we'll reconvene in a couple of hours. I'm going to try to call in some favors and see if I can find any planes leaving Cartagena late last night or early this morning."

"I'm already on it," Fain replied. "Mia's tried to reach out to some of her contacts outside of Santos. I'll monitor all of those."

Ian nodded and headed back toward the second bedroom. Lawless stared at Case from across the room.

Mia stepped in front of him, as if she could protect him from her brother's very impressive stink eye. "Drew, we talked about this."

"No, you talked about this. I said nothing. We're going to have to choose to agree to disagree because I'm going to have a word with him. He nearly got you killed."

"I brought him into this," Mia pointed out. "This was my idea. He went along with it because he knew damn well I would go by myself if he didn't."

Case felt the need to defend his girl a bit. "You hired a bodyguard. He's an asshole, but he's fairly good in the field."

Fain's left hand came up, his middle finger pointing to the heavens, but he said nothing.

"It doesn't matter. He could have called me. He could have stopped you," Lawless insisted.

"I doubt that, but I am very sorry for what happened last night. Mia's extremely competent, but I put her in danger." He could still see her face when he'd been shot, could still feel the pain of knowing he might not see her again. "I did that and it ended with Hutch being taken, too."

"He doesn't need this right now," Mia insisted. "He just had surgery. You're not yelling at him until he's at least had some sleep. Go on, Case. I'll deal with my brother. We're taking the adjoining room. I've already got your stuff in there."

She was taking care of him and he'd been nothing but trouble for her.

"Mia, I think we should talk."

She reached out and took his hand in hers. "After you rest. Drew, stay here because apparently we need to have another talk about you not intimidating my boyfriend."

Her brother's eyes rolled as she led him out of the room and down the hall. It looked like the Lawless siblings had taken up the entire top floor of the hotel. She led him past the room where Ian, Liam, and Michael were huddled together and to their personal bedroom.

"I don't want you to worry about anything but getting better, Case," she said as she ushered him in the room. "You need some sleep. It's all still going to be here when you wake up. I'm also going to bring in a private doctor."

"Mia, stop." He squeezed her hand. "Tell me what he said to you. I need to know."

She couldn't look him in the eyes. "He was far gone. He didn't seem at all like the man you described. It's all in the report. I don't want to think about it right now. I would rather concentrate on getting you better. We also have to deal with the fact that our brothers are going to try to ship us home as soon as possible. At least mine will."

That had been his plan all along, but guilt made him back off. Her decisions hadn't cost them. His had. "I'll talk to Ian. He won't send me away. He'll make me endure a lecture that will feel like torture, but he won't send me home. I'll make it clear you stay with me."

He owed her that. If she wanted to stay, he would make that

happen. Ian would take over the op from here.

Her face turned up. "Thank you. Helping you is all I want to do. You can't blame yourself for this."

Oh, but he could. He could blame himself for all of it. "I thought if I could get close to him I could break through. I didn't have the chance to even talk to him. If I'd been able to get close, he would have recognized me, like he knew Erin's scent."

"I don't know about that. He rejected the idea that she even existed."

"If I'd been able to talk to him, even for a moment, I would have gotten through. He's my twin. We have a shorthand. We know each other like no one else." But he'd blown the opportunity. "I just don't understand how he got past me. I was up and on my feet pretty damn quick. I followed after you. I had to double back to find you but I never saw him."

She leaned in, gently hugging him to her body. "I don't know. It all happened so fast."

"If I could have caught up with him, I had a tranq dart ready." He'd come prepped.

"You did?"

"Yeah. I knew I would likely have to take him out in the beginning. He got the jump on me. But I was ready the second time. I just…he must have been too fast. It was like he disappeared." Like his brother was only a ghost and he'd caught a glimpse of him before Theo had faded back into oblivion.

She went on her toes and kissed him briefly. "Please get some sleep. I'm going to talk to Drew and then I'll join you. I promise, I'll do everything I can to help you find him again."

He didn't deserve that, but he would take it. She'd been everything he could have hoped for in a partner. "All right. I'm sorry about our fight before."

She nodded. "Me, too. I'll be back in a bit. Do you need anything?"

Just her. Just for the world to roll back about twenty-four hours so he could have gotten up faster, gotten Theo in his sights.

Mia walked out and he was left alone in the beautiful room. He hadn't provided her with this luxury. He'd given her a crappy motel room and ordered her around. She'd given him her trust and her honesty and he'd been a bastard.

He sighed as he looked around the room. He should take one of those pills the doctor had given him and go to sleep, but his mind kept churning. How had Theo gotten past him? Where had he been hiding when the police had gotten there?

One minute faster and he could have saved his brother, could have saved Hutch.

What was Hutch going through right now? Would Mia ever be able to look him in the eyes again? She'd been perfectly sweet and affectionate, but he'd felt a distance between them. Had he lost her trust?

He wasn't going to be able to sleep. Not until she was back with him. He'd talk to her, tell her how he really felt and ask her forgiveness, and then maybe he would be able to sleep with her beside him. He walked back down the hall to where he'd last seen his brother. Yeah, he needed to apologize to Ian, too. And to Li and Alex, who'd had to leave their families on short notice.

He'd fucked up all the way around.

"Apparently the boy managed to get the cameras up right before he took off after Case." Liam's voice was soft, but there was no way to miss his lyrical accent. "I don't know he even realized it was working at the time. Hutch had set his system up to search for CCTV feeds and record the ones he chose. I've been rolling through for hours. You looked good getting hauled out of there, boss."

"Yeah, that might not have been my first prison rodeo," Ian was saying. "Has Case seen this yet?"

"I wanted you to look at it first," Liam replied. "Maybe the boy doesn't need to see it, if you know what I mean."

Case watched from the doorway. The screen was pointed his way with Liam sitting in front of the computer Fain had used and Alex and Ian flanking him, their backs to Case as they watched the scene from the camera play out.

"Damn it. There was a hidden door," Alex said with a sigh. "She didn't tell him. Do you think maybe she was unconscious and didn't see Theo get away?"

"Not a chance. She'd seen the others take Hutch that way," Li pointed out. "And see, she's moving the minute that door closes. She knew. Poor girl. She had to be terrified. I wish I could hear what Theo said to her."

"I think we can guess." Ian's voice was hoarse. "There's Case. Damn it. He was seconds behind."

Seconds behind. He felt a chill go through his body as he realized what he was watching. "Play it again."

Ian turned, his eyes flaring and head shaking. "Can I have one fucking thing go right in this cursed day? You're supposed to be sleeping."

He wasn't doing this dance with his brother. He looked directly at Liam, who was frowning fiercely. "Play it again."

"Now, Case, there's a reason I didn't call you in here," Li began.

"Play it or I'll do it myself." He didn't give a shit that his whole body ached. He would fight to get to watch that tape, fight to get to see the truth.

Alex's head fell back. "He'll do it. He's just like his brother. He won't stop until he's seen it and fucked up entirely."

With a curse, Liam moved the mouse and rolled back the tape.

Hutch was on the ground, barely moving. God, he hoped Theo hadn't been the one to do that. Hutch was the funny one, the one who always came through with a joke, but he was also the brilliant one amongst them. He could hack a system with the best. When he'd joined the team, he'd learned how to fly a helicopter because as he'd put it, he didn't want to be a one-trick pony. Theo had been one of Hutch's closest friends.

"He's alive," Ian said, his voice dark. "You can see him breathing."

"He was alive then." Case felt the need to point out a few

truths. "We have no idea if he's alive now. They've had hours to do whatever they want to him."

"She'll keep him alive. She'll use him like she's using Theo." Alex's eyes were on the screen.

Case forced himself to watch as Mia was pushed into the camera's range. She wasn't alone. One of Theo's partners had her in his grips. That rat bastard was holding her so tight. "I want to know who he is."

"I've already got Adam on it." Liam sat back. "He's got a copy of the tape and he's putting it through facial recognition. We'll figure out who the other two are. It might give us another starting point."

Because they would need one. Because Theo was in the wind.

Because Mia had lied.

He watched as the woman he'd grown to love lied to his face. She'd seen the door open and then Theo had said something to her. He'd shoved her out of camera range and shot twice before disappearing behind that hidden door.

And then Case watched himself rush into the room like a fucking idiot. Theo was right there. He couldn't have gotten more than a few steps away. The door had barely closed and Mia hadn't said a word.

Except she had. She'd claimed she had no idea where he'd gone. She'd told him she didn't know.

Honesty. It was all he'd asked from her.

Anger thrummed through his system, hot and rabid. His brother had been five feet away. Hutch had been taken and he was gone right now because Mia hadn't opened her mouth and told him where his brother was.

"Case, do not talk to her right now," Ian ordered. "We're going to get a drink and discuss what to do about this."

He barely heard his brother's words. They didn't matter. What mattered was looking Mia in the eyes and letting her know what she'd done. She'd cost him everything.

He stalked out into the main room and the minute she turned, she paled.

"Case? I thought you were going to bed."

"Were you going to try to erase the recording while I was asleep?" He had no idea how far she would have gone to cover her tracks.

"Recording?"

She didn't know? That was why she'd so confidently manipulated him. The last she'd likely heard before Theo had taken her earpiece had been that Fain had failed to bring the cameras online. According to what he'd heard Li say, Fain might not have known he'd made it work at the last minute. She'd thought she'd been safe and that he would never know how she'd lied. "Fain got the cameras online at the last minute. Or rather he managed to push enough buttons that Hutch's protocols did the job for him."

Fain looked up from his computer. "I did?"

"What's going on?" Lawless asked.

Mia ignored all of it, turning tear-filled eyes his way. "Case, I can explain."

He heard someone walk into the room behind him. Likely his brother and the rest of the team. It was there in the back of his mind that this might not be the time or the place to have this discussion, but all he could see was how hollow his brother had looked, how still Hutch had been on the ground. His anger was in control and logic had left the building. "You can explain? There's no explanation for what you did. You let Theo go."

Those tears started to fall on her cheeks. "He was going to hurt you."

He should have known she would turn this into some kind of play to save him. "He'd already hurt me. He's very likely hurting Hutch right now. Did you think about him at all? Did you think about what they would do to him? Or were you so fucking scared for yourself that you didn't give a damn?"

"Hey!" Lawless was on his feet again.

Mia shook her head. "I wasn't scared for me. I was scared for you."

He wasn't going to listen to that crap. He could take care of himself. He was two hundred and twenty pounds of former Navy SEAL. He didn't need to hide behind a woman's skirts. "You knew how much this meant to me. Hutch was under my watch. Mine. He was my fucking man and he's being tortured right now because you decided to take that choice from me. Did you think for two seconds that if I knew there was a secret door, I could look for other ways in?"

She started to reach for him and then pulled back. "It happened so fast. He said he would be waiting behind that door to shoot you."

"And I couldn't have ducked? You couldn't have told me hey, baby, your brother is laying in wait, you might want to get the jump on him?" He could feel his blood pounding through his system. All of it could have been avoided. Hutch being taken. Theo could be coming home. All of it turned to shit because Mia decided she knew best.

"I couldn't let him hurt you."

"Like he hurt you? Like he shot you?"

"It wasn't the same. He'd already shot you once." Her voice was shaking and she bit back a sob.

He couldn't let her manipulate him with tears. "He pulled left. That shot should have hit my heart, but he moved. He was trying to get away, Mia. He was fighting the conditioning and you sent him back to hell. You did that. How can you think for a second that I'll have anything to do with you after this? That we can have any kind of a future when you do nothing but lie and manipulate?"

"Can we please go somewhere private?"

He knew exactly what would happen if he got "private" with Mia. "So you can fuck me and I won't care that you cost my brother and my friend their lives? Is that what you plan on doing, Mia? You think you can go down on me and I'll just forget what you did?"

"Jesus, don't kill him," Ian said with a long sigh. "Try to

remember he just came out of surgery."

Lawless stood behind his sister. "Mia, get your things. We're leaving."

He braced himself because he knew what happened next. This was when Mia lashed out. This was when she fought back. Her original plan had failed and now she would lash out and then walk off to plot and plan and he would have to be ready for her. He wouldn't indulge her this time. It was too fucking serious an infraction.

She'd cost him the whole op. The most important op of his life.

He waited for Mia to throw a punch. Instead, she turned and walked out, moving back toward the bedroom they were supposed to have shared.

"Look at me and listen to me well, Taggart." It looked like it might be her brother who threw the punch. He got right in Case's face. "I made you that offer months back because I honestly thought you were best for my sister. She loved you and I thought if I could just reach inside that stubborn as shit Taggart brain of yours and tickle your pride a little, you would get off your ass and love her back. I'm only telling you this because I tried that stupid trick but I need you to understand that I'm not attempting to manipulate you now. I mean every fucking word I say. If I see you even come near Mia again, I'm going to kill you. I'll do it and I'll get away with it because I'll find the best lawyer money can buy and believe me, I can buy a lot. If you show up on my doorstep again, I'll gut you and I won't think twice about it."

"You'll try," Case shot back. Despite the fact that he was pissed as shit at her, he didn't like the idea of someone keeping him from her. When he was ready to deal with her again. He needed to not see her face for a few days, for his volcanic rage to die down a bit before he set up completely new ground rules for their relationship.

"Stop it." Ian stepped between him and Lawless. "Drew, you have to see his point. You would if it were Riley or Bran on the line. He needs some time to think before he shoves his foot in his mouth so hard he can feel it in his ass."

"I don't have to see anything, Ian." Lawless's eyes were cold. "I'm taking my sister home. I think I can find another security company. Ezra, we're leaving."

Ezra got to his feet, the only person in the room who looked perfectly satisfied with the way things had gone. "I'll put you in touch with my old boss. I'm sure Guy and his group can meet your needs."

Good fucking riddance.

Mia walked out, her bag in hand. She didn't look his way.

That pissed him off even more. What the hell game was she playing now? "We're not done talking."

Mia kept walking.

"Mia!"

She never looked back.

Lawless followed his sister, Fain hard on their heels.

The door slammed and Case stared at it.

"Fucking shitty day," Ian cursed. "Alex, we're going to need a flight home. Case just cost us our ride, a million dollar a year contract, and our children cousins since the next time Mia lets him touch her will be a cold fucking day in hell."

Alex looked grave as Ian strode out, yelling at Li to join him. "Pray Ian doesn't get stiffed with the bill for this place. I don't think his heart will be able to take it."

Case stared at the spot where Mia had disappeared.

In a few days she would be back. She was just playing him again. One more manipulation.

But she would be back. She would.

She had to.

* * * *

"Are you all right?" Drew sighed and sat down in the chair beside her. "That was a stupid question."

Was she all right? She was hollow. She was empty.

Case had looked at her like she was a piece of trash. He'd broken that promise to her—that they would talk, that he would stay and fight it out. He'd told her there was no future. He hadn't even listened to her. He didn't care that she'd been desperate to save him.

"It's fine, Drew." Her voice sounded like a bland monotone. It was all she could do to keep from crying. "I just want to get back to Austin."

And then she would pack and be gone again. She needed to work. She needed to make things right because Case had been correct about one thing. Hutch was in trouble because she'd chosen Case's life over his. Hutch had been her partner. He'd been scared. He'd known something was wrong and she'd watched as he walked away and into the trap.

She had to make that right.

"We'll be there in no time at all." Ezra sat down beside Drew. "I've informed the pilot to get us in the air as soon as possible. And the good news is this pilot checks out. One hundred percent chance of him not trying to murder us."

"That's excellent. Could I get a moment alone with my sister?" Drew asked in that polite but firm tone that meant the answer better be yes.

Ezra immediately stood again. "Of course. I'll go and sit with the pilot. Let me know if you need me at all."

He stepped away and she was left alone with her brother.

"Mia, I know you loved that man."

She had, but she should have known. Tony had told her. When the chips were down Case would always choose his family, and she would never be a part of his family. He'd called her princess. Sometimes it felt like a term of affection, but then he was an expert at making her feel good. Even when he didn't mean a word of it.

But he'd meant it. He thought she was an entitled princess. Poor little rich girl. Who would love her?

"It doesn't matter." She stared straight ahead. That's what she had to think about. Moving forward. One foot in front of the other.

Don't think about how much she was going to miss him. Don't think about how he'd looked at her, how he'd hated her.

She'd made the right decision. She'd seen it in Theo's eyes. He would have done it. He would have killed Case.

Case simply didn't care enough to stay and fight it out.

He's very likely hurting Hutch right now. Did you think about him at all? Did you think about what they would do to him? Or were you so fucking scared for yourself that you didn't give a damn?

He'd thought she'd been considering herself, not him. That's where his brain had gone. He truly thought she was an overprivileged bitch who only thought of herself. He'd never cared about her. She'd been a means to an end and a convenient lay.

"It does matter, Mia. You matter." Drew leaned forward. "He's an ass who can't see how amazing you are. He was a mistake."

He hadn't felt like it at the time. He'd felt like perfection, like she'd finally found the man who fit. "Yes. I've proven I have shitty taste in men."

Maybe she would be better off taking her foster moms' path. Damn it. Why did she need a dick? Especially one attached to a much larger dick.

God, she was going to miss him. It was an actual ache inside her body. She would feel every mile between them.

"He wasn't the one for you." Drew scowled and sat back. "I'm sorry I brought them into our lives."

She had to clear that up. She couldn't be the one who cost her brother the plan he'd been working on for years. "You can't fire Ian Taggart."

"I already did."

"Then hire him back. I'll call him myself. He's the best in the business and he knows this case like the back of his hand. He's been working on it for months. Riley's going to New York soon, or have you changed your mind about taking down Steven

Castalano?"

"I'm going to take them all down." His eyes seemed to go a shade darker, as though the mere act of talking about his revenge could change him from the brother she loved into a predator. "They killed our parents."

"You can't prove that."

"Taggart's working on the proof." Drew sighed. "He was working on it."

Three people had benefited from their parents' deaths. The same people who had paid an assassin to kill them and cover it all up so they could cash in on Benedict Lawless's brilliance. "Ian was the one who found the assassin. You can't fire him. Call him now and offer him the plane I came in on. It's still here. It can take him and his crew back to Dallas. He's too good. We need him despite the fact that his brother is a massive ass."

She wasn't going to send Riley in without the best backup possible and that was Ian Taggart and his crew. No amount of pride was worth risking her brother's life.

"Ezra's old boss can do the job," Drew said stubbornly.

"There was a reason we didn't hire him. Drew, I'm willing to put up with Ezra when I go on assignment, which I will be doing the minute we get back home, but on one condition. Rehire Taggart. I assure you he'll keep Case far away from us."

"He better. I'll make the call if you're sure."

She was sure she didn't want to fuck anything else up. She heard her brother begin to speak but looked out the window. There was no Case rushing to catch up with the plane. He wasn't going to show up this time. He'd gotten what he'd wanted out of her and then she'd become an inconvenience.

Some Dom he'd turned out to be. One mistake and she was out.

Had she been wrong? In the heat of the moment, all she'd wanted was to make sure Case was safe. She'd seen him shot. He couldn't have taken another bullet.

"So I take it I won't be getting that finder's fee after all?" Ezra had a self-deprecating smile on his face.

She wished she was alone. She needed time to mourn him. How fast could she pack when she got back to Austin? She'd already texted a couple of past editors looking for a job that would take her anywhere but Texas. She would still be back in time for the StratCast job, but she couldn't sit in her condo and think about Case. "The job my brother needs is delicate and Taggart's been working on it for a very long time."

"The job where he takes down Castalano, Stratton, and Cain?"

Ezra knew a lot for a man who'd only been hired a few days before. "He's already told you?"

"Unlike Case Taggart, I do my research when I…well, when I find a woman I like."

She felt herself flush. "Ezra…"

He held his hands up. "I'm not going to try anything. I realized very quickly you didn't have the same feelings for me, but I still like you as a person, Mia. I wanted to know what was going on with your family. It wasn't hard to figure out that after your parents died you and your brothers got screwed and hard. They took your father's shares in the company and split them among themselves. There should have been millions left to take care of you."

So he'd figured out how they'd stolen her father's money. "It was all tied up in stock and there was a binding partnership agreement between the four of them and it included a morality clause. They used that clause against us, gobbled up his stock, and then sold his intellectual property for millions. We didn't have anyone willing to fight for us so we all went into the system."

"And now you're going to get your revenge. You think your parents were murdered and Taggart is trying to prove it."

"It's not my revenge," she said with a sigh. "But Drew needs it and Ian Taggart is his best bet. Sorry about the finder's fee."

He sank into the chair across from her. "And I'm sorry Case Taggart is such an ass. You know, he'll probably come around. I don't think he's got a good hold on his temper."

She wasn't so sure. He'd told her in the beginning he wouldn't be able to trust her again. He'd told her to stay away. She'd only fooled herself. When the chips were down, he'd shown his true colors.

He thought she'd had sex with him in order to get her way. How could he love a woman he thought so little of?

"It's over. It doesn't matter now. We're stuck together for a while. At least until Drew figures out the kidnapping thing was a one-off." It had only been a week or so since someone had attempted to kidnap her. Drew needed time to forget. "I'm going to travel for a while. I've been wanting to do a story about the women's movement in India."

"Curry. Sounds awesome." Ezra buckled his seatbelt. "I suspect you'll also be trying to get in contact with Santos again."

"Of course." Just because Case was a jerk didn't mean she would stop trying to help Erin and TJ. "He won't talk to the Taggarts. Only to me. When I get the information, I'll send it on to them and then I'll be out of it."

"Sure you will. I'll believe that one when I see it." He yawned and stretched out.

She was going to stay out of Case Taggart's life from now on. Maybe in a few years she would even be able to forget him.

She was sure going to try.

CHAPTER THIRTEEN

"You know you're a dumbass, right?"

It was a question he'd heard about five hundred times in the last week. He'd heard it from Ian, from Michael, from Charlotte. From pretty much anyone who found out he'd broken it off with Mia. Now he was getting it from Erin.

"So I've been told." He took a long drink of his beer and wished he was back at his place.

He stared at the woman his brother loved. Erin stepped into her small kitchen and moved straight to the fridge. Her hair was up. She was dressed casually in a T-shirt and jeans and looking calmer than he could ever remember seeing her.

Motherhood looked good on Erin. She smiled more in the last week than he'd seen her smile in a year. When she was holding TJ, she seemed centered, at ease.

He didn't feel at ease, hadn't since the last night he'd spent with Mia when she'd cuddled up in his arms and slept, her head on his chest.

"You want to tell me what really happened?" Erin pulled out a pitcher of what looked like lemonade.

"Don't you have a party to throw or something?" He wanted to be alone. He wanted to be sitting in his apartment, staring at the computer and waiting for some new information to come through. Instead, Ian had ordered him to come over to Erin's where Ian was currently flipping burgers on her grill and Charlotte was cooing over TJ. It was just Taggarts tonight. Sean and Grace had brought along Carys, who was playing with the twins.

And Case was still thinking about the Taggart who wasn't here.

And Mia. God, he was thinking about Mia.

It had only been a week and he missed her. He hated himself for missing her, hated how easily she manipulated him. She'd caused him to lose Theo and Hutch and he couldn't get her out of his head. Even standing here with Erin—who'd lost more than anyone—he could still hear Mia's words.

It's hers, Case. That's the mistake you're making. You think you're being the white knight, saving the girl from pain, but you're taking something from her. This is a part of their story. Whether you get Theo back or not, this is hers because he was hers. The pain is hers too. You're taking her ability to pray for him, to know what he's going through.

On the plane trip home, the one that had taken place in the same plane he'd ridden out on, he'd talked to Ian about telling Erin, about bringing the entire team in now that they'd lain eyes on Theo.

Ian had told him it was his call. He'd stayed away from the office for a few days, not wanting to hear the lies Ian would have to spread about what happened in Colombia, to explain Hutch's disappearance.

"I like her." Erin set the pitcher down.

"Everyone likes her. You're not the first to tell me how stupid I am." Not even close. Everyone seemed to have an opinion.

"It won't take her long to find someone else. Don't worry about it. I heard Kori saying she and Sarah are going to try to fix her up. Apparently they had a nice long talk before Mia took off for places unknown."

"She's working." He'd already tried to call and been told that she'd left Austin.

"She's hiding," Erin corrected. "Ian told me you were over-the-top mean to her."

Ian was a big old gossip. "I was the exactly right amount of mean to her."

Except he'd started to wonder about that. He'd been so angry in that moment. Time had given him a little more perspective. He'd started to question what had really happened.

"Ian told me you two had a big blowout over the op in Colombia. He wouldn't tell me what it was about though."

Because that would have given up the secret they'd been keeping. The one Mia thought he shouldn't keep.

Could she have honestly thought Theo would kill him? Had she been terrified for him in the moment? What if all that sweet affection hadn't been manipulation? What if it had been love?

She'd walked out, not saying a word to him, not defending herself or fighting the good fight. It had been like a light had been snuffed out inside her.

At first he'd called to yell some more at her. The last time he'd called, it had gone straight to voice mail and he'd hung up.

She would come back. She would see he'd had the right to be angry.

"You're going to let her go?" Erin stared at him.

He shrugged. "We had a fight. I think we both need some time to think."

"Can I give you some advice?"

"Do I actually have a choice?" He never seemed to have a choice when it came to getting advice from his family.

A smile crossed Erin's face. "See you can be smart. But mostly you're a dumbass. Whatever happened, you were wrong."

Yep, he'd heard a whole lot of that, too. "You know I'm getting sick of hearing that. In fact, I was perfectly right. She made a choice that wasn't hers to make."

"You blame her for what happened to Hutch. Yeah, I don't exactly understand that either." Erin's jaw tightened. "I know you and Big Tag and a couple of the guys have been working on something secret, but I need to know if this op you were on had anything to do with Hope McDonald. I've stayed away from this because I needed to concentrate on TJ, but I need to know now. I need to understand what happened to Hutch. He's my friend."

Shit. He should have expected this. Erin wasn't a fool. She was smart and had been in the business longer than him. The moment was here and he wasn't sure what to do. She would think they were looking for revenge. "We got a line on where she might be hiding out. We came very close to finding her. It was Mia's choice that allowed her to get away. That's what we fought about."

"You went to Colombia to track down Hope McDonald?"

It was the first time she'd asked him a direct question and he wondered how hard it had been for her to stay silent. Months had gone by, months where they'd all been arrogant, thinking they were so clever. Months where she'd allowed them to be. "Yes."

"Damn it." She flushed, her skin going pink. "How fucking dare you, Case. Did you not learn a damn thing from Theo? He died. He's dead. Gone. You can't bring him back and now Hutch is probably dead, too. Do you honestly think this is what Theo would have wanted? Why do you think I've left it alone? I want to kill her, too, but I have to think about what Theo would want. He damn straight wouldn't want Hutch dead."

Shit. He held his hands up. "Hutch isn't dead. I'm sure he isn't dead."

"Just because you don't find a body doesn't mean he's not dead." Erin took a deep breath. "You can't do this. I want revenge, too, but I'm not willing to lose another teammate over it. How could Ian have signed off on you going over there without a senior team member?"

If he didn't stop her, Erin would walk out into the backyard and throw down with Ian over something that hadn't been his fault. "He didn't know. I went without telling him what I was really doing."

"You bastard," Erin whispered. "Are you trying to get yourself killed? What did you think this would buy you? Any of us? You can't bring Theo back to life."

"What if I could?"

The room went completely silent and Erin didn't move, every muscle stuck as though the moment had frozen.

"What is that supposed to mean?"

"Tell her." Ian stood in the doorway. "It's time."

Erin looked over at him, her mouth a thin line. "Tell me what?" Tears formed in her eyes. "It's time for what?"

How did he do this? He wanted to be gentle with her. "You see, we've been investigating for a while now. We started down in the Caymans."

Tears ran down her eyes, but she stared at him, her fists clenched. "Just fucking tell me, Case. Tell me or I'm going to beat the holy shit out of you."

"Theo's alive, Erin." He got to the point. Erin paled and he worried she might pass out. "I saw him a few days ago."

A fine trembling seemed to have taken over her, but she took a long breath. "She saved him. Faith begged her to that night. Oh my god, she got to him in time. She pulled the bullet out and fixed his heart."

Despite the fact that she was obviously trying to stay calm, her words came out shaky. Had he just made another mistake? Ian looked grim, but made no move to save him.

"We believe Dr. McDonald stabilized Theo there on the island and then took him to Havana where she performed the surgery that saved his life."

"Fuck." She put her hand over her mouth. "She saved him. I'm still going to kill her, but she saved him. He's alive. Theo's alive."

She said it over and over, as though she needed to say it to believe it.

"He is alive, but she's been using her drugs on him," Ian

pointed out. "The same ones she used on Ten. Do you understand what that means, Erin?"

Her head nodded, her hands still shaking. "The memory drugs? She's playing with his memory. That's why he hasn't gotten away. My Theo would get away."

"He didn't know me when I caught up to him," Case admitted. She was handling this better than he'd thought. Or was she? He was shitty at reading women. Mia proved that. If Mia was here, she would deal with the emotional stuff. She would know what to do.

Ian stepped in, grabbing a cup and pouring the lemonade. "I'll let you see all the reports. Li is the one who's taken point."

"Of course he has. I fucking love that Irishman." Erin turned serious eyes Case's way. "You said he didn't recognize you. Did you talk to him? How did he look? Was he healthy?"

She would read every report. Case was sure of that, but he was also certain she would need to hear it from him. "Very healthy."

"But his aim has turned to shit," Ian added. "He tried to kill Case. Only managed to clip him. When he comes back I'll have to send him through BUD/s again. Do you think the Navy will let me do that?"

"He shot you?" Erin's eyes went wide.

Did Ian have to mention that part? What the fuck was wrong with him? "He pulled his shot. He wasn't trying to kill me. When he had the chance to kill Mia, he didn't take it either."

Erin walked around the island and slapped a hand to his chest. "Theo shot you because he knows you're a dumbass, too."

He was still recovering from that particular injury. He groaned, but put a hand up to hold hers to his chest. "He was alive, Erin. He was so close and I lost him. That's what Mia and I fought over. He took Mia. He and his little group. He's not the only one she's experimenting on. Theo took Mia and then got away through a secret door. She let him go. She lied to me and Theo got away. I'm so sorry."

Erin nodded and stepped back, looking over to Ian. "So basically Mia got caught during the op. Dumbass here ran in and got himself shot by my memory deprived but ridiculously hot boy. My man still has enough Theo left in him that he wouldn't kill Mia, but he very likely threatened Dumbass. Mia loves Dumbass and didn't want Dumbass to die, so she protected him. When Dumbass found out, he screwed everything up with her."

Ian shook his head, obviously impressed. "She really is the smartest operative I have. And to think I hired her as muscle."

"Mia let Theo go." Was he so wrong on this?

Erin wiped her eyes. "She saved you and him. Because he can live with shooting you. He could never live with killing you. Mia talked to him?"

He hadn't thought about that. He'd been so sure that he could have handled the situation. What if the roles had been reversed? What if it had been him on that floor and someone after Mia? "Yes. She said he recognized her lotion or something."

A brilliant smile crossed Erin's face. "Milk and honey. He bought it for me as a gift. He said I was the promised land and I should smell like it. He's alive. Theo's alive."

There were a few things she wasn't thinking about. "He's alive, but he's not in Colombia anymore. We don't know where he is."

"But he's alive," Erin said through her tears. "So suck it up. He's alive and we're going to find him."

"Erin," Ian began.

She put a hand up to stop him. "No. You're not leaving me out. I get why you've done it up until now and that's the only reason I'm not grabbing Bertha and using your massive body as target practice."

Bertha was Erin's precious Berretta M9. Ian's lips curved up slightly. "I appreciate that."

Erin wasn't finished. "And don't think I'm going to strap on and go after him myself. I have to think about my son. I can't risk my son's welfare. But I will be involved. You're right. I am the smartest operative you have and I know that woman. I've killed her a thousand times in my head, but more than that, I've dreamed of how I would catch her. I've come up with a million ways to ensnare that particular fly in my web."

"We're going to look for him," Case promised. "We've got every intelligence agency who owes us looking."

Erin threw Ian a look. "Is he really that naïve? Or does the drug not work?"

"The drug works," Ian replied. "It's even worse than you think though. Apparently McDonald's run afoul of her former employers. Even The Collective is after her. I haven't talked to him about it because he's had enough to deal with."

"What?" He hated feeling like he was the stupidest person in the room.

"Everyone will be looking for Hope McDonald," Erin said quietly. "Everyone. If Ian's been using contacts, they've been using him, too. That drug can be a weapon. Her conditioning techniques can be used to build operatives from the ground up. Theo is so strong. If he could, he would have found a way to come home. She's broken a piece of him, the piece that was loyal to his family. Do you understand how valuable that could be to a government? She can suppress his memories and give him new ones. The Agency will want that drug. So will every government that hears about it. So will every terrorist group. Imagine being able to wipe the minds of a thousand men and convince them they want to blow up a building. Men who fit no profile. Women. Children. We wouldn't see them coming. True sleeper agents. Any agency who says they'll help us is lying. They'll tell us what we want to hear and then follow us to the prize. The prize is Hope and her research but if they can't get her, they'll take Theo. They'll study him and try to figure out how she did it. We can't trust anyone. Anyone."

"What do you know about the man who left with Mia?" Ian asked.

"You let her leave with another man?" Erin shook her head. "What the hell kind of Taggart are you?"

"She needed a bodyguard." The nature of her brother's wealth and influence guaranteed that. Her high-risk job doubled the need. "Hutch checked him out. Beyond being a massive douchebag and working for Ferland, he was okay."

"I'll have Adam look into him, too. And Mia's informant. I'm trying to leave Chelsea out of this. You understand what could happen to her if she's caught feeding us information," Ian said.

Treason. Chelsea Weston worked for the CIA.

Erin nodded. "She could be arrested."

"Or any of the other nasty stuff the CIA can do to an employee." Case hadn't even thought about that. "So the Agency will be watching us."

"Everyone will be watching us," Ian corrected. "The Agency, the NSA, hell, I've heard a rumor there's a fucking Magellan Billet agent searching for Hope McDonald. They're the worst of the worst. Lawyers with guns. Makes me want to shoot myself. God, I hope it's the old dude and not the one who looks like Ten. He's obnoxious."

"But Theo's alive." Erin stood in the middle of her kitchen, tears pouring down her face. "Let them come after us. It doesn't matter because Theo's alive."

Mia had been right. Erin wasn't tortured with thoughts of what was happening to Theo. Oh, that might come later, but the joy and light in her eyes…that was worth it. This was her life. Theo was her life. She deserved to wish and pray and work for his return.

"I need to see my son." Erin walked to the door. "Talk some sense into that one. I'll work on it from my end."

"What is that supposed to mean?" Case asked as he was left alone with Ian.

"It means she's going to meddle in your relationship and she wants me to do it, too." He sighed as he opened the fridge and grabbed one of the beers he'd brought in with him. He flipped the top and poured it in with his lemonade. "I'll do it because I owe her one."

"You'll do it because you're a shockingly gossipy old maid."

Ian didn't argue. He merely stared Case's way. "You fucked

up with Mia. You should have done as I asked, taken a break and then dealt with her fairly. You went in half-cocked and now she won't talk to you. Have you considered the fact that she brought you valuable information, information that got us closer to Theo than I could have imagined? Have you considered the fact that she might get more intel and not bother to send it our way because she's pissed at you?"

"Mia would never do that." If Santos contacted her, she would call him. Maybe not him, but she would call Ian or Sean. "She would give us everything she had even if it hurt her to see me."

Ian pointed at him. "Finally you speak some fucking sense. Mia did what Charlie would have done if she'd truly believed I could die. She did what I would have done if I thought Charlie was in danger."

"She won't talk to me." A sick feeling opened in the pit of his stomach. This wasn't some childish argument they were in. He'd fucked up. He'd made her feel like she didn't matter.

"Give her time. And don't you ever fucking run off on an op without telling me again."

He'd waited for this dressing down. "I understand."

"No, I don't think you understand at all, Case. Why the hell would you do that?"

How to explain to Ian? He should know. "You wouldn't have let me go. I know that's a horrible excuse, but I wanted to get out there and prove myself. I wanted to find Theo. I wanted to prove to you I could lead."

"What?" Ian was staring at him like he'd grown a couple of horns.

He'd avoided his brother for this very reason. He hadn't wanted to admit that he wasn't good enough. "Look, I know what you think of me. I get it. Theo was the smart one. Theo was the one you were grooming for leadership. I'm okay with that most of the time. It was stupid. I wanted to prove I could lead, too."

Ian stepped up to him, his eyes going fierce. "If you weren't still recovering I would punch you, you dumb asshole. I sent Theo out on what I thought was a fairly simple operation as the lead because he needed seasoning. He needed experience. I knew he was in love with Erin and he wasn't strong enough for her then. Not really. He needed to toughen up or it wouldn't work. He wouldn't be able to accept the fact that she was a stronger leader than he was so I was going to turn him into one. I didn't have to do that with you. You walked in here as one of the strongest, most stable operatives I've ever seen. I didn't coddle you because you never needed it."

"What?"

Ian put a hand on Case's shoulder. "I didn't pay attention to you because I knew you would be okay. Well, until you went batshit over a woman. I kind of hoped you wouldn't do that but then Mia walked in and it was inevitable. Hutch wasn't your fault. I would have done the same thing. I would have made the same calls. Hutch got caught because he wasn't paying attention to his surroundings. I've seen the tape. You've seen it. He was in a hurry and he didn't even lock the door behind him. He was trained better than that."

"He asked me to call off the op. He knew something was wrong."

"And do you know what I would have told him? I would have told him to suck it up and do his job. He has always cut corners and none of us kicked his ass for it. I would feel the exact same guilt you feel right now. That's what it means to be a leader. You make the hard calls. Tell me what Theo did wrong in the Caymans. Tell me what you would have done."

He'd thought it through a million times. "He should have called in. The parameters of his mission changed. It was his duty to inform his CO of the changes and await instructions."

"And if I'd told you to leave Ten behind?"

Again, nothing he hadn't considered over and over again when he couldn't sleep. "I would have gathered my team, come home, and begun operations to rescue Ten from MSS. We were outnumbered, outgunned, and going in blind. I wouldn't have risked my team. But isn't that exactly what I did? Isn't that why I lost Hutch?"

"It's different. You made a call that would have gotten you the information you needed, with minimal risk. Ten made the right call originally. It was Theo who screwed up and didn't listen to Erin. If I'd been in your place, I would have done the same thing. Sometimes we make the right calls and everything still goes to shit. Never for a minute think I don't trust you. The only mistake you made was not calling me and that was made because you were trying to chase down your girl. Don't do it again. Making the mistake. Not chasing down your girl. I'm afraid she's going to be pretty hard to convince this time. You were a dick. You have to lose the short fuse, my brother. I know. I had to do the same damn thing."

Ian didn't hate him. Ian wasn't sidelining him. Now that he thought past his own insecurity he could see how Ian had trusted him—with clients, with ops, with his family.

He'd been fumbling without Theo to back him up, but he had value too.

"How do I fix things with Mia?" He wanted to. He wanted her.

"First you answer this question. Who comes first—Mia or Theo?"

It was the question he didn't want to have to answer. It was exactly why he'd decided to send Mia away. "That's not fair."

Ian wasn't backing down. "No, it isn't, but it's true and it's right. Who comes first?"

"Mia." Always Mia. If he was going to be her man, he had to put her first. She had to come before brotherhood, before friendship, before conscience. "But Ian, I'm not some rich boy who can give her everything. We come from two different worlds."

Cool blue eyes rolled. "You two need to talk because you don't know her at all."

"Of course I do." He knew her more intimately than any other woman on the planet.

"Then you know about her childhood? You know that after her parents died the family was split up. The older boys went to a group home. She and Bran were placed with a family, but at some point, Bran ran away, taking her with him. That was when they decided to split up her and Bran. He went through home after home. Mia ended up with a couple of chicks who adopted her. One was a doctor. The other stayed at home and raised Mia. She lived a middle-class existence for most of her life. Drew and the boys were dirt poor. His money wasn't inherited. He earned every penny with blood and sweat and his brilliant, annoying brain."

"She never mentioned anything but that her parents died." Likely because he hadn't invited the conversation. How many times had he called her entitled? How many times had he claimed she was nothing but a rich girl?

Even rich girls had their problems, had pasts, had needs.

"Give Drew a pass. I know you think he's an asshole, but he's got his reasons. I'm not only running background checks and gathering intelligence on his business rivals, I've been training him and his brothers. Self-defense. Offense. They're going into something dangerous."

And Mia would be with her brothers. "I know he hates me, but I can teach them all a thing or two."

Ian nodded. "Then I'll let you work with me. The only person Drew Lawless hates more than you right now is a man named Steven Castalano. Help him take the fucker down and maybe he won't shoot you. In the meantime, give Mia some space. Maybe send her some flowers or something. Girls like flowers."

Mia might like flowers but there was something she liked even more. Mia liked intel. Mia liked information that led her to a great story. Maybe there was more than one way to apologize. Maybe it was time he started loving her for exactly who she was. Crazy. Smart. Competent. Loyal.

"I have to get her back." He had a lot to do. He had to get his girl back and find his brother.

Maybe they weren't two different ops at all.

"I think you do. I think if you let that one go, you'll regret it for the rest of your life. The bad news is you got the Taggart temper. We're kind of assholes sometimes. The good news is we tend to have ridiculously good taste in women. Now let's go and deal with the fallout because Grace had no idea Theo was alive and she's going to want someone's balls for keeping secrets. I'm nominating Sean. Charlie's already talking about more kids so I need to keep my balls intact."

He followed his brother out, his mind on Mia.

A few hours later, Case locked the door, closing out the rest of the world before setting the alarm.

Hope McDonald was still out there. They couldn't risk her coming after Erin. Especially not now that she knew the Taggarts had figured out Theo was alive. One of the plans to come out of the evening had been moving Case in. They'd talked about taking turns, but it made more sense for Case to watch over her. If he went out of town, she would be assigned a guard. TJ would come to work with her after her maternity leave.

She'd been surprisingly all right with it.

He walked back into the living room. It was empty. He could hear Erin talking softly. She must be down the hall, in TJs room. He began to wander that way, worried about her.

She'd been sedate most of the evening, talking in logical tones, asking all the right questions.

It wasn't what he'd expected. She'd teared up in the beginning but she'd been right back to super-tough Erin after that. Grace had cried more than Erin had.

She was holding it all in and there wasn't a lot he could do about it. If Theo was here, he would tell him that Erin needed to scene. It was how she'd been able to express emotion, but he couldn't do it. He wasn't sure she could anymore either. Erin hadn't been back to Sanctum once since Theo had died.

What was he supposed to do? His brother wasn't here. All the girls had left. Should he talk to Erin? He needed to talk to Erin because they'd candy coated a bunch of stuff and he couldn't stand the thought of her believing things would be easier than they were really going to be.

God, he wanted to talk to Mia. If Mia was here, she would know what to do.

He stood outside the door, looking inside. Erin held TJ in her arms, holding him close to her body.

"Daddy's coming home, baby boy. Your daddy is going to come home and we're going to be a family. I promise you I'll do everything I can to bring him back to us. Daddy's coming home."

Shit. The world went a little watery. That was Theo's son in there. His son. It hit him with the power of a locomotive. Theo had made a baby and he had a woman who loved him. He'd made a family who needed him.

Case needed Mia.

He stepped back out, giving Erin time with her son. She hadn't been unmoved. Public tears weren't something Erin would easily do. She would hold it in and give in to her grief when she was alone.

Had Mia cried by herself after she'd walked away? She didn't have a baby to cuddle, a piece of her love to hold close.

He'd been a dick. How could he have said those things to her? He'd been so worried about what he couldn't give her that he hadn't thought at all about what he could. He'd worried about himself, about getting hurt.

They'd been so incendiary that he hadn't imagined she could hurt. She was larger than life. She was the girl who could tell everyone to fuck off and walk away without a care. The tough girl who didn't give a damn what anyone thought.

Except she'd been soft for him and he'd fucked her over.

"You still up?"

He turned and Erin stood in the living room, her face blotchy from crying. "Sorry. I didn't mean to disturb you."

Her mouth curled up in a tired smile. "I don't know that

anything can truly disturb me tonight."

"I'm sorry we kept it from you. I thought it was the right thing to do. I thought the idea that Theo was out there..." How did he explain this to her?

"Being tortured and perverted for some crazy doctor's experiments was worse than thinking he was dead?" Erin didn't prevaricate.

"Yeah, I guess. I guess I didn't want you to have to think about what could be happening." It was all he'd been able to do except for those few soft moments when Mia had been in his arms.

Erin walked to the sliding glass door that led out to her backyard and stared out. The moon was full, offering some illumination to the darkened room. "I wonder if she's managed to convince Theo he's in love with her. It's rape, you know. She's raping his mind. I wonder if she's raped his body, too."

Yes. That was one of the things he'd wondered about as well, one of the dark scenarios that had run through his brain. Mia's report had kind of put it to rest. "He calls her Mother."

"I know. I looked through the report Mia wrote while I fed TJ. I've gotten good at doing things one handed with a baby hanging off my boob." She glanced back. "It doesn't matter. I'll love him no matter what's gone on. If he screws a hundred women while he's out of his head, I'll welcome him back into our bed after a healthy STD check. The only thing that matters is he's alive."

"I didn't want you to worry about him."

"That's because you're a dumbass." She turned. "I get to worry about him. I get to think about him. I get to hope for him. I get to be anxious about whether or not he'll still love me when he comes home. Earlier tonight I thought about how my boobs aren't what they used to be and I've got stretch marks. Stupid things. Inconsequential things. And I get to worry about them because he's alive. I know he's going through hell and I'm going to ask him to go through more, to take all the pain they give him, anything he has to so he can come home and be with me and meet his son. God, Case, I fought him so hard because I thought I wasn't good enough for him."

"He thought you were too good for him, too tough and smart."

She laughed, but there were tears in there, too. "I was a bitch to him but that was my armor. When he died, I thought I was being punished. It's funny how arrogant we can be at times. To think the world revolves around us, that the universe chooses us, selects us for punishment or reward. I spent years with my first husband, taking his shit because I didn't know how else to be. I wasn't woman enough for him."

She never talked about her husband. Case knew she'd been divorced, but not the hows or whys. "He was obviously a dick."

"He was quite awful and I took it for as long as I could and then I wouldn't take shit from anyone for a long time. But Theo wouldn't let go." She sighed and sat down in the chair that had been Theo's, the old recliner Case knew they'd fought over because it was pretty much a piece of crap. Erin always sat there now. "He would call me. I wouldn't answer. At first he would hang up and try again later, but when he figured out I was ducking him, he started leaving these messages."

"I told him he was wasting his time." Theo would stop what he was doing in order to call a woman who claimed to not want to have anything to do with him. "I always thought you were going to hit him with a harassment suit."

"No. The messages he left…there was nothing sexual about them. He didn't ask me for anything. He told me about his day and then said he wished he knew how mine had gone and he told me good-night. I listened to them about a hundred times. I didn't reply or anything. I deleted them after a while because I thought I was fooling myself. I deleted all of them, but I listened to them. Do you have any idea what I would give to have those messages? To hear his voice telling me good-night, sweetheart?"

"I miss him, too. It's why I…it's why I was so awful to Mia. He was right there. I could have reached out and grabbed him."

"We don't make the best choices when our loved ones are in danger. I want you to think about the fact that she'd already seen you get shot and then she likely had seconds to decide if she wanted to send you into danger again."

He'd done nothing but think about that moment for days. "I need to apologize."

"Oh, you need to grovel. You need to man up and use every resource you have available to get that girl back. You know how to run an op. What's the first thing you do?"

"Decide on my objective, take stock of my assets. I've learned I need to carefully review all my assets because oftentimes the inherent value isn't on the surface." Ten had drilled it into him. Case had been the leader on Ten's team, but Theo seemed more comfortable with Ian. Again, he'd made a mistake by not carefully thinking things through. He couldn't go storming into her life. He had to think, had to figure out how to be the man she needed. "I need to make things right with her brothers, too."

"Yes, you do, but I think you'll find they're the easy ones." She sat back. "He's out there. He's here on the same planet, sharing the same air. We're going to get him back."

He sat down across from her. "I will do everything I can. I promise you that. But Erin, you need to understand that the Theo I bring back might not be the one who left."

"You find his body. Bring it to me and TJ and I…we'll find his soul."

Because she was the keeper of his brother's soul, his natural mate, his other half.

Mia was his. How horrible that he'd figured that out only after he'd lost her.

Erin sat up suddenly. "What did you say about assets?"

"Uh, I said I had to look at all my assets."

"Because sometimes the most important asset of all is the one that seems to have no value." She stood, her eyes bright. "Oh, Case, I think I just figured out how to find Theo. It's a long shot, but…you're right. We have an asset we didn't realize we had. We have Avery."

He wasn't sure how Liam's wife fit into this. Avery was

awesome. She was kind and funny, but she certainly wasn't an operative. She'd become Serena Dean-Miles's assistant. Serena was an author and Avery helped organize her business. They went to romance conventions together. "Avery's good at social media. You think we can trick him into friending me on Facebook?"

Erin's eyes rolled. "You should be happy you're so attractive. I need to call Avery. She has a friend who might be able to help us. Sometimes we don't see the patterns. We don't see that the path is right in front of us if we just have a little patience. And our last piece is in place. Hutch is there."

She wasn't making a ton of sense. "Hutch being kidnapped is a good thing? Erin, she's going to wipe his memory."

"Not if she wants his skills, she won't. She wants a hacker. It's not the same. His skill isn't muscle memory, it's all brain power. If she screws with his mind, she loses the reason she took him in the first place. They'll be looking for somewhere safe to hide."

He still wasn't following her, but if she was right and they could get a message to Hutch… "We could send a message of where to meet us and maybe Hutch could convince them. The intel we discovered pointed us to somewhere in Asia."

"They won't stay there long. She needs someplace quiet, someplace to continue her experiments. She needs an ally."

"A clinic like her sister's?" Hope's first experiments had been conducted at her sister Faith's clinic in Africa. It was where Theo and Erin had fallen in love. "Faith had no idea what her sister was doing."

"But what if she found someone who didn't mind, someone who would trade her clinic for cash, protection. Someone already based in Africa. We can't fool her with a start-up clinic. She would be wary of that. But a clinic that had been around for a while, a clinic led by a woman with a past. It wouldn't matter that she's trying to right her wrongs. Someone like Hope would look at this woman on paper and see opportunity if given the right push."

It clicked into place. "Stephanie. You want to use the woman who was driving the car that killed Avery's first husband and child?"

He knew the story. Avery had been young when she'd lost her daughter and husband to a teen who'd had some beer and gotten behind the wheel. Though her blood alcohol level had been below the legal limit, they'd been in New York and Stephanie had been underage. The law was clear. Any alcohol in a minor was considered a DUI. Stephanie had gone into a deep depression and it had only been Avery's grace that had saved her. Avery had told him once that she figured Stephanie owed her a good life for the ones Avery had lost. Avery had been the one to pay for Stephanie's medical degree, to send her off to Africa to do good work.

At the time he'd been floored by how far Avery had gone to forgive the girl who'd harmed her. Now his heart seized because Avery's grace, her belief in forgiveness might save them all.

"We'll herd them to Stephanie's clinic. We'll go on the Deep Web and start some rumors. Little things at first," he said. "We'll have to be patient. Hutch will find us and then we'll be waiting for Theo."

"And we'll bring him home," Erin said with quiet will.

And they would bring him home.

CHAPTER FOURTEEN

Long after Erin had talked to Ian, had brought Avery into their circle and formed their plans, after Erin had finally fallen asleep, Case sat up. He sat in his brother's chair, his mind whirling. The sun was coming up over the horizon but he was staring at his phone.

Mia hadn't called. Mia could be miles from him by now. He wanted to think that she was in Austin, but he couldn't be certain. No one would tell him a thing, and according to Riley Lawless, she probably wouldn't answer her phone if she saw it was him.

Would she listen to a voice mail?

It worked for Theo. Somehow his brother was still giving him advice, still leading the way when it came to this type of thing. When it came to loving someone.

It was barely daylight. Maybe if she was sleeping, he would catch her off guard and have a few precious seconds to talk before she hung up on him.

He dialed her number and was sent straight to her sweet voice telling him to leave a message. Yep, he should have known she would be too smart to leave her phone on.

"Hey, it's me. I know you don't want to see me, but I needed to tell you something. I took your advice. Ian and I told Erin tonight. It felt good to tell her the truth. Naturally Erin being Erin, she came up with a plan. I would love to run it by you, to get your take on it. You've studied up on the drug she's using and I could understand it better. Anyway, if you get a moment, give me a call." He felt like an idiot. "Okay, thanks."

He hung up. Yeah, he wasn't great at that.

Three hours later she sent him a report on the drug and everything she'd managed to find out about it. She'd dug deep and gone to various sources, her analysis providing many theories on how the drug would work in combination with certain therapies. At the end of her e-mail, she'd left him with a chilly "best wishes on his search" and she hoped it all went well. She explained she was heading off on assignment and wouldn't be in touch for a long time.

Very polite. Very much like Mia.

He called her again, not at all surprised to go to voice mail. Her voice mail was very much his doghouse, and he would have to do his time.

"Hey, sweetheart, I wanted to call you before you left. I hate the way I spoke to you that last day in Cartagena. I'm ashamed of how I treated you and I can't stand the thought that I won't be able to look you in the eye and tell you that I'm so sorry. I know why you did what you did. I've got a temper on me and I know I need to deal with it. I called Kai and I'm going to get some anger management therapy because I never want to speak that way to you again. Because I need you to understand that it wasn't some convenient thing for me. That week we spent together was everything to me. Anyway, if you want to talk, I'm here. Be safe."

When he hung up, he opened an e-mail and sent a note to Ezra Fain explaining that if Mia happened to be interested in interviewing a SEAL, he had a friend who'd agreed as long as she would protect his identity. An old buddy of his was willing to show her exactly how his team worked and he'd gotten clearance. He asked Fain not to tell her the invite had anything to do with him. She would likely turn it down.

Fain's reply had been short, but he'd promised to keep Mia safe. It hurt to know he wouldn't be the man protecting her, but Case accepted it. For now, Mia needed time.

The days rolled on.

September

"Hey, sweetheart. Therapy sucks. I've got to do this group thing where we all sit around like idiots and talk about how much fun it is to beat the shit out of people, except then someone makes us feel bad about it. I thought I had anger issues. Man, do not take Bear's yogurt. Just a helpful hint I've learned. So while anger management sucks, I think I might be getting good at it. Your brother pissed me off today and I didn't even think about killing him. Not once. Maiming, yes, but I think that's progress. Drew's getting better, too. I brought him enough information on Castalano that he just threatened to bitch slap me. He didn't actually do it. I think the way to get to Castalano is through his partner's daughter. This business crap is as bad as war, except I don't get to shoot anyone. Yeah, I know. Back to the couch for me."

October

"I read the article in *Time* about the Navy SEAL team. It was awesome. You captured the spirit of the team. I can't believe you actually tried some of the BUD/s training. Well, I can. You're a little crazy, but in the best way possible. Just wish I'd been there to see it. We're dressing TJ up for Halloween. Erin managed to find a costume that makes him look like a live grenade. Yeah, I'm worried for that kid. We're going over to Jake and Adam and Serena's in an hour or so. It's a party for the kids. I'm pretty sure Serena and Erin have already set up the kids for marriage or something. Did I mention Serena had a girl? She's a week younger than TJ and she's definitely got Adam's eyes. Brianna. It's a pretty name. I've been thinking about Hutch a lot lately. I think it's all the Halloween candy. We got a little brush from someone Adam thinks might be him. It's just a couple of e-mails and some talk in a room on the Deep Web, but we're hopeful. I think Erin's plan is working. Happy Halloween, baby."

November

"Riley's getting pretty good with target practice. I know he's not likely to need it, but I want to make sure he's as safe as he can be going in. It's weird to think that he'll be in New York in a couple of months. I think he's ready. Now all we have to do is find the right way to lean on Ellie Stratton's current batch of lawyers. I'll find a way to get Riley in there. While he's getting good with a gun, I'm trying to be patient. It seems like most of what I do these days is wait. Adam is fairly certain he's been talking to Hutch on the Dark Web. I think my brother's somewhere in Pakistan right now, but Ian doesn't want to move. Any move could spook McDonald, and if she thinks for a second… Sorry. I want to talk about nice things with you. Hope you're having a good day."

"It's Thanksgiving and it's hard without Theo. It was his favorite holiday. I wish you were here holding my hand. I miss you, Mia."

December

"So just when I thought I had the uncle thing down, TJ started eating solid food. What the hell? I've been in a lot of horrible situations but none of them scared me as much as that first diaper. How could mashed bananas make that smell? It's never going to end because the team is breeding like rabbits. Charlotte's pregnant again and Phoebe and Jesse are having a boy. You'll never guess what they're naming him. Harry. No. Got you. James. James Harold Murdoch. Ian actually went to church to pray for a boy this time. Just one. I heard him praying to God to bring another penis into his house. I guess the girls are all into princess stuff right now and they like dressing up their dad. My big brother can rock a tiara, let me tell you. Naturally I bought them a big case of princess costumes for Christmas. Heard you were spending the season in London. Riley told me you're writing a story about Damon Knight's old unit and the mission that got him the Victoria Cross. I'm glad Ian could set that up for you. I'm sure it will make a hell of a story. Merry Christmas. Stay safe."

January

"I saw Fain the other day. I was going up to Michael's place and he was coming out of the building. Apparently he's got a girl he sees when he's in town. He said you came home for the holidays at the last minute. I'm glad. Your brothers would have missed you. I know I do. Every day that goes by makes me miss you more. I don't know if you're listening to these messages or maybe you're just deleting them, but I can't stop. Not until you tell me to. I think we're going to make a move soon. The person we think was Hutch has been quiet, but I think I've pinpointed where they are right now. I found a cluster of well-done bank robberies in Italy. They'll move soon because the cops will be on them. I think they'll take Stephanie up on her offer. Protection in exchange for cash. The minute we get a yes, I'll have to go to Sierra Leone and wait for them. I'll let you know when I'm leaving. I hope the book is going well. I love you, Mia."

February

"It's time. I'm packed and we're heading out in the morning. It's just me and my brothers and Li and Kai. Erin is coming with Avery and Charlotte on a separate plane. It's going to kill her to leave TJ with Grace, but she wants to be there. They'll stay at a secure location, but she needs to be close. Faith is going to meet us in Freetown and Ten will be there for backup. This is it. I want you to come with me. I want you on that plane beside me tomorrow morning. If I could go back and change one thing, it would be the way I made you feel. You're so smart. You're strong and brave. I think you might be the best part of me. If I don't come back, know that I was better for loving you. That's what I've figured out. Even if you can't ever forgive me, can't ever love me, I wouldn't take it back. I love you. I think I'll always love you and I'm a better man because I love you. Michael has a key to my place. If anything happens to me, there's a box in the hall closet. It's got some pictures and stuff from my Navy days. It's not much, but I'd like you to have it. If you don't want it, I guess give it to Ian. But that's not going to happen. I'll be back in a few days and we'll have Theo. And then I'm coming for you. So you should think about that. I'm going to prove to you that I can be the man you need me to be. I'm going to go to New York and help your brothers. I'm going to be in your world. I'll be there when you need a kiss. When you need strong arms around you, holding you close, I'll offer mine. If you get lonely at night and need a man who'll worship your body with every part of his soul, I'll be down the hall, waiting for you. I'm going to win you back, Mia. It's going to be my mission in life. I love you. Yeah, get used to hearing that because I love you and I won't keep that inside anymore. See you soon."

Austin, TX

Mia stared at her brother. "You want me to do what?"

Riley stood in front of her, a phone in his hand. "I want you to listen to your voice mail."

She sighed. The flight from Paris had been a long one and the layover at DFW had been particularly rough. Case lived in Dallas. All she had to do was get in a cab and she could be at his apartment in twenty minutes. She could stand in front of him and ask if he'd missed her at all, if he ever thought about her. Did he wish he'd done things differently?

She'd forced herself to sit in the small Irish pub in terminal C and drink a single glass of wine while Ezra had a beer. She'd reread the first two chapters of her book on Damon Knight and when it had been time, she'd gotten on the plane to Austin and come home.

Where she would have to tread very carefully because according to Drew, Case was now a part of the "take down all our enemies and crush them into dust" team. And Drew seemed to not hate him. Awesome. So now she could run into Case at 4L or right in the hallways of Drew's place. She would have to stay in her room until she was ready to go to New York. She shouldn't have given up her condo, but Drew wanted everyone close.

Would Case be coming to New York? What the hell would she do if Case came with them on the Castalano job? How would she smile at him and pretend like she wasn't dying inside?

Six months had done nothing to fix her broken heart. Nothing. The ache was still fresh.

"I've listened to my voice mail. It was nothing but my literary agent asking when the book would be done." Work was what she'd thrown herself into. She'd gotten some amazing opportunities out of left field. She'd been asked to do a feature story on a Navy SEAL team that had eventually been sold to freaking *Time* magazine. Apparently the Navy had wanted a female reporter for a different point of view. She'd gotten an interview with the king of Loa Mali, who was attempting to change the way the planet used energy. And then she'd gotten the deal to write a book about a British military unit and the untold story of their heroism. Naturally that had led her right to McKay-Taggart London. Damon Knight had talked about the Taggarts with great fondness.

Everywhere she'd turned all she could see was Case.

Six months should have erased her feelings for that damn cowboy. Or at least muted them. She'd spent six months with the gorgeous Ezra Fain at her side. After the first few weeks of being depressed, she'd tried to get herself to consider him. Why the hell not? Ezra was a stunning man. He had dark hair and piercing eyes, and an unnatural affection for taking off his shirt when she was around. He found very thin excuses to show off how hot he was.

Nothing. Her girl parts didn't spark. No deep desire to shed her panties. No desire at all. Ezra was a lovely man but he was like a painting to her. Something to admire, but not touch. She'd been relieved when he would disappear for chunks of time, leaving her with a female bodyguard McKay-Taggart had sent so he could take a couple of days off.

Kayla Summers was awesome. She was up on all the TV shows and never minded when Mia wanted to walk the streets to get some inspiration. Kayla just viewed any super-long city walk as a chance to try all the local street food.

One of the things she intended to talk to her brothers about was a change in bodyguards. Ezra had been perfectly pleasant for the most part, but something about him bothered her. Now that her attention wasn't constantly on Case Taggart, she'd had time to study Ezra. She'd noted his secrecy. Oh, he tried to pretend he didn't take phone calls in the middle of the night that suddenly stopped the minute she walked in the room. And then there were the trips to Dallas that he lied about.

At first she'd thought about declaring herself bodyguard free, but then she'd started to feel like someone was watching her. It had begun in Loa Mali. She'd felt eyes on her, an instinctive sense that someone was watching. It had followed her back to Austin. She was probably paranoid, but she wasn't giving up the bodyguard.

Which meant until she could convince Kayla Summers to come on full time, she was stuck with Ezra.

Which meant she had to tell Ezra about the e-mail she'd gotten from Tony. He had a new line on Theo and he was willing to meet her here in Austin. Naturally, he'd done the whole song and dance about not telling anyone and meeting in complete privacy, but like she was going to do that. Ezra was good at making himself scarce and still being around. He'd proven that in London when she'd had a nasty run-in with a guy who wanted to steal her bag.

And again in Paris right before they flew home. Someone had been in her room, but Ezra had managed to run the man off.

Thieves, it seemed, were everywhere.

"You haven't checked the voice mail on this phone," Riley said, setting the phone on her dresser and striding over to sit next to her. "That's your old phone. I might not have turned it off when you asked me to."

"Did you forget? I knew I should have asked your secretary. Wait. Does Bambi know how to call and get a phone turned off?" Her brother tended to hire his assistants based on their boob size.

He held his hands up. "Her name was Brooke and she turned out to be not what I was looking for in an assistant."

Mia felt her lips curl up. The work relationship tended to get messy once Riley had slept with his assistants a couple of times. "Got clingy, huh?"

Riley's eyes rolled. "I didn't actually sleep with her. I think I'm getting old. I got tired of having to do my own work because she couldn't figure out the word processor. She quit after Taggart yelled at her. Well, he didn't actually yell. He did that super-cold voice thing and told her if she didn't get her hands off him he would call his sister-in-law and let her take care of the situation, and that might include actually chopping off her hands. I think Brooke believed him. Not only did she not touch his abs anymore, she quit. Now I have a very nice legal secretary named Tom who's totally in good with the rest of the staff, brings me all the helpful gossip, and makes an excellent latte."

"Well, I'm glad you figured that out. You're not getting any younger. It's time to hang up your manwhore clothes and get serious about making me some nieces and nephews." Serena would have had her baby by now. Had it been the girl she'd wanted so badly? She wondered how Erin was doing with baby TJ. He would be sitting up by now, probably babbling like mad.

A look of pure horror crossed her brother's handsome face.

"Don't count on that. I'm not about to settle down, much less start pumping out kids. I'm not that old. I've got many years of manwhoring in my future, thank you. Once I get through flirting with Ellie Stratton, I'm going to come home and have some fun."

"And if you fall madly in love with her?" She'd seen a picture of Ellie Stratton. She was a serious-looking young woman, but there was something about her eyes, a little light that let her know the CEO of StratCast had some sparkle inside her. Riley was going to ruin her life. It didn't seem fair since she hadn't been the one to kill their parents. That had been her father, but this was the only way to get to Castalano. Their first target. Revenge was her brothers' main goal in life.

Was it Erin's now that she had her baby? Or would she give it all up just to see Theo one more time?

Thinking about Erin brought her back to something Riley had said before. "Why would Big Tag let Erin defend his honor? I should think his wife would do it."

"I didn't say it was Big Tag. It was Case. He was a big hit with all the women here, but he let them all know he was taken," Riley said with a smile. "I think he was going to sic the redhead on Brooke. He said she hadn't killed anyone in over a year and it made her twitchy. Your man's pretty funny for a dude who can kill another dude about five hundred different ways."

"He's not my man." Of course every woman at 4L would want Case. It was a tech firm. Most of the men who worked there were like twenty nothing and spent more time in front of a keyboard than at the gym. Case Taggart had probably walked in and every woman in the room had fallen at his feet.

This was exactly why she'd stayed out in the field for so long. She'd known Case was working with Drew, and the last thing she'd needed was to see him flirting with another woman. A woman who would be his perfect submissive, always deferring to her man. His perfect sub would do everything right and never question him.

She kind of wanted to throat punch his perfect sub. Which

again proved he wasn't the man for her. He would likely look down at throat punching. Even though he'd said he liked his women a little crazy. That had obviously been one more lie to get her to sleep with him.

Riley frowned. "I like him. I didn't think I would. I need you to understand that I went into the first meeting with him fully planning on hating his guts and maybe figuring out a way to screw him legally."

"And then you met him and you fell for his blue eyes and perfect shoulders?" She was being heinously sarcastic. She knew what it was about Case that drew people in. There was a heroic quality to him. He was a man you could depend on to save you when the chips were down.

If only he'd been the type of man who could have loved her.

"I ended up admiring him," Riley admitted. "He walked in and he offered to train me. I told him to fuck himself. I didn't need training. I've taken self-defense and I'm not planning on getting in some kind of shootout, so I told him he could take his macho, douchebag, asshole self and find another idiot to dupe."

She felt her jaw drop. "Did he punch you?"

"He laughed and sat down and started to explain to me that self-defense didn't teach me everything I needed to know. He wanted to train me to be aware of my surroundings, to learn to listen to my instincts because even though I'm going into an office building and not a war zone, I'm trying to take down a dangerous man."

That didn't sound like her Case. "Wow, I would have expected him to flip you off and walk away. He's not very patient."

"Oh, that's not the Case I've come to know. He's been infinitely patient with me. I think it's because he's so madly in love with my sister."

Mia stood up. It was obvious Case had been working double time to keep her family's business. "He's just good at his job, Riley. It doesn't mean anything. We're worth a couple million a year to his company, and believe me that company means everything to the Taggarts."

Family meant everything to them. It was one of the things she loved about the Taggarts. You didn't have to share their name to be one of them. If one Taggart loved you, the rest of them brought you in and made you feel welcome. They were a big family of non-blood relatives who stood by each other no matter what.

She'd wanted so badly to be a part of that family.

"I think you mean more to him." Riley stood and straightened his jacket. It looked like he'd come in straight from the office. "I've spent a lot of time listening to him talk about you. He's made me tell him every story I can remember from our childhood and when I ran out, he moved on to Bran."

He'd asked about her past? He'd seemed to almost shy away from the subject and she'd been more than happy to avoid it. Now he knew every nasty detail since he'd taken on the role of advisor to her brothers. Why had he done that? Why ask about her? He'd made it clear he was done with her. Had he wanted to know how awful and scandalous her past was so he would know he'd dodged a bullet? "Well, I hope you told him everything. I hope he knows how kids at my school would find out who I was and ask if I would go crazy one day like my dad."

Riley put a hand on her shoulder. "Yes, he knows about that, too. I think if that man could go back in time, he would murder a couple of kids."

Tears were forming in her eyes. Why couldn't she be reasonable about that man? The idea of him being in her home, asking her brothers about her past got to her.

He hadn't called her. Yes, she'd changed her phone, but deep down she'd known that was a test of sorts. She'd wanted to see if he would push his way back in. It was what Case Taggart did. He punched his way through all obstacles. He didn't care what she needed. He would go after what he wanted. If he wanted her, he would have bullied his way back in. She'd gotten nothing. No attempts at forcing his way into her life. Nothing after he'd gotten the report on the drug. He'd been content to work for her brothers, never reaching out to her. Six months had passed without a word from him. How could she believe he truly wanted her?

"It's over between the two of us," she said. "It's been six months. Believe me, if Case Taggart wanted me, he would have come after me. I should have listened to him in the first place. He didn't want me then. He doesn't want me now. I was convenient and gave him some good intel. That was all we had between us."

Riley rolled his eyes. "Sure it was. I didn't shut off your phone because he kept calling it. After that morning when you shoved that phone in my face and told me to kill the number, I meant to do it. I was going to, but he left a voice mail. I thought I should listen. I thought he would make an ass of himself and I could happily make it impossible for him to reach you. He thanked you for some report and then he started talking about how sorry he was and how much he missed you."

"He did?" Case Taggart rarely apologized. It just wasn't something he would do.

Riley picked up her old phone again. "Listen to him. I had tech reprogram the phone so your mailbox wouldn't get full. It's a lot. It's pretty much his life for the last six months. I think he needed to share it with you."

"He left messages for me?" She stared at the phone in his hand.

Riley stepped toward the door to her room. "So many. I know way too much about that man. The good news? Everything I know made me like him more. And don't ever tell him I listened to those messages. He can punch hard. I should have told you sooner, but every time I've mentioned him you kind of growl and look ready to kill someone. I thought you needed some time or you might have deleted them. But you have to listen now, Mia. I'm begging you to listen to them now."

Had Case really called? Had he left a bunch of messages?

She had to know. Mia picked up the phone and pressed the button she needed.

"Hey, sweetheart…"

Mia sat and listened to what Case had to say.

An hour later, Mia stood up, completely panicked. Case had left the last message early this morning. He was leaving tomorrow. He was heading to Sierra Leone and he was going into danger. Her heart constricted. He wanted her by his side.

She was damn straight going to be by that man's side.

He'd left messages for her at least once a week since they'd been apart. He'd talked about how he'd gone into therapy so he never spoke that way to her again. He'd told her about his daily life as though nothing had meaning until he'd told her about it.

Dear god, he'd told her he loved her.

Mia wiped the tears from her eyes because she was getting her ass to Dallas. She had mere hours before he would be on a plane for the most important mission of his life. She wouldn't let him go into it alone.

He hadn't ignored her. He'd changed for her. He'd made himself better for her. She could barely see as she grabbed her suitcase. It didn't matter what went in. She needed clothes. Some clothes. Who cared? She could buy clothes.

Mia tossed the suitcase. All she needed was her passport, her purse, and her phone.

What if they left early?

Why was Austin so far from Dallas?

She opened her door and strode down the hall. Luckily Ezra was standing right there. He stayed in the guesthouse when they were in Austin, but now he was standing in the living room talking to Riley.

"I need to go to Dallas. Right now. Tonight," she announced.

A brilliant smile crossed her brother's face. "Good because the plane's waiting on you and I might have had the housekeeper pack for you. It's waiting at the airport and the car is outside."

Ezra looked between herself and Riley, obviously trying to

figure out what was going on. "I don't think this is a good idea. Why are we turning around and going back to Dallas? We just got home."

"It's worse than that, but I think you can sit this one out. I'm not just heading to Dallas. I'm going with Case to Africa. He's found Theo and we're going to bring him home."

"I'll be ready to go in five minutes." Ezra turned and started out toward the back door.

She wondered if she could run. She didn't need Ezra in Sierra Leone. She would be surrounded by ex-military men. And she would be good. When the time came to actually hunt Theo down, she would stay in the hotel with Erin and Avery and whoever was protecting them.

If Erin could do it, she definitely could. Erin couldn't risk her life because TJ needed a parent. It would be hard for her. Mia would support her.

Having Ezra around might complicate things.

Riley stepped in front of her, his eyes narrowing as though he knew exactly what she was thinking. "No. You take him with you. Case gets to decide whether he follows you into something insanely dangerous, but you're going to take a bodyguard with you until Case says it's all right. This is his operation. And don't think I'm saying that because anyone thinks you're incompetent. I want you to consider how hard it was for Case to give you all those leads on stories. Some of them were dangerous, but he knew you would want to go."

"He sent me the leads." She'd known Ian had something to do with the Knight book, but why would he have talked his friend into allowing her to interview him when it had been obvious he hadn't wanted to in the beginning? It had only been his wife who had been able to convince him that telling the story would be good for him, that their baby son would one day want to read about what his father had done for their country.

Case had been the one to send her those stories. Not flowers or candy. Those were easy. He'd given her adventures and he'd done it knowing he wouldn't be there to protect her, to gain anything from it. It had been a purely selfless act of love.

"All right. I'll wait. But you should know that I'm not going to be a good girl when I get to Dallas."

She intended to show that man just how bad she could be. After all, the man did give a really good spanking.

She just prayed she wasn't too late.

CHAPTER FIFTEEN

Case shut the door to his truck and looked down at his bag from Top. Once upon a time it would have contained Sean's unbelievably delicious Angus burger with weird cheese and hand-cut fries. Tonight he had a chef salad with grilled salmon because his cholesterol was up and it would worry Mia.

Well, it would worry Mia if she gave a shit about him. Erin gave a shit about him and that was why he was suddenly eating like an actual adult. Erin had found the envelope with his test results. In her defense it had been sitting on the bar for two weeks. She'd opened it and then all the Taggart women had been on his ass. They'd shown up with medical studies and recipes he wasn't sure how they expected him to cook since he didn't cook. Charlotte had brought a juicer to work and Case had discovered that vegetables and fruits actually tasted worse when pulverized into liquid.

And yet if Mia had been there yelling at him for his dietary choices, it all would have been okay. It was actually kind of nice to have someone give a crap about him.

Living with Erin and TJ for six months had proven a couple of things to him. One—he and his brother had completely different tastes in women. Case loved Erin like a sister, but if he found her talking to her gun one more time, he was going to go insane. Then there was the fact that she enforced her very strict policies on where he left his sneakers by tying them together and launching them into the highest branches of the elm in the backyard. Though effective—he put his sneakers in his room now—it was obnoxious.

The second thing it proved to him was that he was ready for a family. He loved sitting down at night to have dinner and getting up in the morning and seeing his nephew's smiling face.

He wanted that with Mia.

If only he hadn't followed his brother's advice and left that condom off he might have gotten Mia pregnant and then she wouldn't have been able to avoid him.

Of course she likely would have hated him more than she already did.

He strode into his building. It didn't matter. He was going to Sierra Leone in the morning. He was going to get his brother back and then he would come home and go to New York with Riley and the rest of the Lawless clan. He would help them with the StratCast op, and there was zero chance of Mia not being there. He would win her back.

He had to.

He started for the elevator when his cell rang. He pulled his phone out and immediately answered. "Hey, Michael. What's going on?"

His best friend's voice was smooth over the line. "Absolutely nothing. I thought you would want to know that Erin and the baby are great. She's packing. Everything is cool. I'll escort her to the airport the day after tomorrow and I'll make sure she and Avery are safe. Are you all right?"

"It's just an apartment." But he felt his muscles tighten. One of the joys of living at Erin's for the last six months had been not walking by Hutch's place every day and wondering what kind of torture he was going through. Someone from the team went by every week to make sure the place was fine, and the company had taken over paying his rent. Hutch didn't have a family outside of his team, so they'd ensured he would have a home to come back to.

"It's an apartment that's going to have its resident back in a couple of days. We're going to get in, set up, and be ready when McDonald makes an appearance," Michael assured him.

"And if she doesn't?" It was the scenario that went through his head a million times since the moment they'd gotten confirmation of a meeting between Stephanie and Hope McDonald.

"She'll send her team. You know damn well Theo is the lead member of her team." Michael sounded way more sure than Case felt.

"And if not killing Mia made her demote Theo?"

"One, you don't know that she knows Mia's still alive. They immediately ran. She very likely didn't actually see what happened. Two, even if she did, I think she would keep Theo in his place. She's obsessed with Theo. She wants him to be the face of her organization."

Yes, he'd heard all the reports and profiles from both Eve and Kai. Still, he worried. This was their shot. If Theo didn't show, he had no idea what they would do. Everything depended on this one chance.

So why couldn't he concentrate? Why did his brain constantly go to Mia?

"Let's pray that's true," Case replied. "I'm going to head up. It'll be weird to sleep the entire night. TJ tends to wake up around three. No idea why. Most of the time he doesn't even want to eat. Just rock him for a little while and then he'll sleep the rest of the night."

"Uhm, I'm here to make sure no one gets murdered," Michael said, uncertainty plain in his voice. "I'm not doing the baby thing. I don't think I'd be good at it."

Lightweight. "You will if you don't want to deal with a cranky Erin. Did I mention she shoots people when she's cranky?" He laughed at the thought of Michael trying to deal with TJ and his militant mama. "I'll see you when you get to Freetown. Take care of them."

"Will do. Before you go, I wanted to let you know that Fain's in town. I saw him slinking out of my building about an hour ago. He had a ball cap pulled down low, but I recognized him."

"We still have no idea who he's seeing?" It was a mystery and Case didn't like mysteries.

"No, but then I haven't asked to see the security camera tapes."

He missed Hutch. His team was seriously down a man and he felt it. "Adam's busy getting ready to leave. Do we have anyone else who could hack into those feeds?"

"I'll see what I can do," Michael replied. "But there are over three hundred tenants in this building. I watched to see what floor he got off on, but there were two other people in the elevator with him. I didn't recognize either one. He's getting off on five, ten, or eighteen. I'll see if I can track his movements. It felt wrong to me. He was trying to keep his head down."

"All right. I've avoided this because I'm trying to not be a crazed, possessive caveman, but I'm going to talk to Ten about him. He tried to recruit Fain. He must have had a reason. I don't know that I buy that Fain turned Ten down."

"Not everyone wants to work black ops, brother. Some people want to do their time and then come home."

But that wasn't Fain. He was too good, too observant. "Yeah, those people don't tend to get into the security business. Not at the level we're at. Get back to me if you can. I'll deal with Fain when we come home. Be safe."

"You, too."

Case hung up the phone with a sigh. He didn't even have beer in his fridge. The only reason he was staying at his place was the fact that the flight was super early in the morning and he didn't want to disturb the baby and Erin. It was easier to hand over security guard duties to Michael now rather than at five in the morning.

But the thought of spending the evening alone seemed sad. He hadn't spent the night in his place since Mia had broken in offering him information and so much more. She'd offered him her sweetness, her affection. Sometimes he was sure she'd offered him her love. Why the hell else would she have put up with his shit if she didn't love him even a little?

When he got back, he was going to start over with her. Maybe he would even introduce himself and see if she followed. A true fresh start. He would take it slow, no matter how much his dick wanted to speed things up. His dick wasn't in charge anymore.

He sent a quick text to Ten asking him to send anything he had on Ezra Fain. He never actually called Ten. Not since Ten had started working small jobs. He only took jobs that kept him close to his wife and only intelligence gathering. From what Case understood, he'd negotiated a few deals the State Department asked him to and he'd rescued a diplomat's son after he got himself in trouble. Ian had sent him on a few fact-gathering ops for some of the companies McKay-Taggart worked for. Still, for the most part Ten preferred to initiate contact.

And he would see Ten in about thirty hours or so.

Eat, sleep, work. It was what he did now. Eat, sleep, work, cuddle TJ, and think about Mia. That was his life.

It was going to change once this op was over. He shoved his phone back into his pocket. The urge to call Mia again was riding him hard, but he'd left her a voice mail already and it hadn't had the effect he'd hoped for. She hadn't finally called him back and promised to never leave him again. Nope. Radio silence.

The elevator doors opened and he strode down the hall. He passed Hutch's place and only stopped when he realized the door to his apartment was slightly open. He could see the door handle wasn't where it should be, it was the tiniest bit swung inward.

He dropped the salad and reached for his SIG, adrenaline starting to flow. Backup. He would need backup. Before he could reach for his phone again, the door came open and he could hear a feminine laugh.

"I'll totally stand watch. I'll text when Case is on his way up and then Kori can make herself scarce, but he would murder the both of us if we left you alone like that." Sarah was standing in the doorway, looking back inside. She was one of the club regulars, a submissive who worked as a trauma nurse. She was Kai's wife's best friend and for a while, Case had been in her circle due to her friendship with Mia.

So why was she standing in his doorway and what was Kori watching over?

Sarah turned and then stopped in the middle of the hall, gasping before she visibly calmed. "Oh, that's what they all talk about. Damn." She pushed the door open again. "Okay, I totally get it. He's ridiculously hot when he's about to kill someone. Yeah, I think it was me he was going to kill. He's totally here. Yeah, you might want to rethink a few things, sweetie. He looks pissed."

"Who the hell are you talking to?" He holstered his SIG. Murdering Sarah and Kori would definitely get him in trouble with Kai, and he would have to explain to Mia what had happened.

Although she would likely attend their funerals and then he would have an excuse to see her…

"Mia, of course," Sarah said as though that should be completely obvious. "Who else would break into your place?"

"What?" He'd been eating too many salads. His brain was fried. Or maybe it was the kale Charlotte thought she could sneak into his smoothie thing. Maybe that one sip he'd had before his brother had taken pity on him and helped him quietly toss it out had damaged his hearing.

Mia was here?

Kori stepped out, holding her and Sarah's purses. A big smile crossed her face. "Awesome. I was worried you were going to stop someplace along the way. Kai said you were on your way home. And before you flip out, Boomer's patrolling the halls. When Mia called, he was hanging out with us and he decided to come along so the CIA-looking dude could do whatever he needs to do when he's in town."

Case was so confused. "CIA dude? Are you talking about Fain? He's a bodyguard."

Kori shrugged. "You all look alike to me. He reminds me of Master T. Anyway, Mia wasn't left unprotected. Not even for a second. Now, I'm going to pick up Boomer and head back. Hey, someone left a Top bag out here. Free dinner. Nice."

He didn't give a damn about dinner anymore. Mia was here and she'd broken into his place again, the little brat.

She was here. Why was she here? Was she going to give him the restraining order herself?

Case walked past the now giggling women, but he didn't have time to give them a nice Dom stare and a lecture on not making fun of him. Everyone made fun of him. He was used to it.

None of it mattered because Mia was here.

He stepped into his apartment and shut the door. He didn't need prying eyes because he was about to get down on his knees and beg a woman to forgive him.

"Mia?"

She wasn't in the living room.

"Yeah, uhm, I'm back here and maybe you should stay out there for a minute because Kori was right and I should rethink this whole thing."

She was in his bedroom. She kind of had to be. There wasn't much to his place. His never-used kitchen was open to the living area. Beyond that there was only the big bedroom and his bathroom.

She didn't want him to come in. What had she been doing? A little revenge?

"All right. I can stay out here if you would rather. Mia, whatever you're doing in there, it's okay. If you're trying to get back at me, I understand. I just want to talk to you."

"Revenge? I'm not in here trashing your bedroom."

"I'm glad. God, I've missed you. Baby, let me come in and

talk to you. I promise I'm going to be a gentleman."

"Really? Because I've done a whole lot to make sure you don't view me as a lady. You know how sometimes I get a crazy idea in my head? I like to make big gestures. Well, this one required a couple of friends. And if you're not mad then maybe you should come in."

"I'm not mad. I want to talk to you. I want us to sit down and have a nice long discussion about what happened between us."

Her voice came out on a shaky laugh. "Then you're going to have to come in here and untie me. I'm afraid for a girl who loves to spend all her time in suspension, Kori's pretty good at tying a sister sub up, if you know what I mean."

He rushed into the bedroom and then stopped at the sight that greeted him.

Mia was naked, her body laid out on his bed. Laid out wasn't exactly right. She was trussed up like the sweetest gift he'd ever been given. Rope wrapped around her torso, holding her tight. Her hands were bound as well, tied behind her. Mia lay on her side, her legs free and a perfectly atrocious pair of underwear covering her pussy and her ass. He would always think any underwear was bad, but this one was cotton and reached up to her waist. There was no lace or silk. Just a bunch of martini glasses and the words "It's always happy hour somewhere."

"What the hell is that?"

She bit her bottom lip, her face going a nice shade of pink. "I was trying to surprise you. I think I probably should have called. I'm so sorry. If you could get Kori back, I'll get dressed again."

Oh, that was so not happening. She was here. She was half naked and tied up on his bed, and that meant she was forgiving him. At one point in time he might have wondered if this was a little revenge on her part, but now he understood his insecurities were his problem and not Mia's. Mia wouldn't do that to him. Mia would come here for one reason and one reason only.

Mia wanted to try again.

But she had some insecurities of her own and they did have

something to do with him. He'd let her go. He'd let her walk away because he'd been so angry with her. He'd let his anger overwhelm his love. That was his mistake, and it had hurt her so very badly.

He stared down at her, enjoying seeing her again. "How can you be even more beautiful than I remember?"

"I thought you were upset to see me."

"I was surprised to see you. I was upset to see that you've chosen to wear…" He couldn't even call those panties. They were horrific.

A little smile began to curl up her mouth. "This is about the undies? You're mad I'm covering my pussy. Well, Case, I wasn't sure if Boomer was going to walk in, and I thought I should leave a little mystery between us. As for these particular undies, I didn't have time to do a bunch of laundry. I kind of got home, found out I had a crazy-hot stalker leaving me messages, and then I flew here so I wouldn't miss you."

He couldn't take his eyes off her. He might never take his eyes off her again. His cock jumped back to life. Months had passed. Months where he'd been hit on by several lovely women and not a one of them moved him. No one touched his soul the way Mia did, and Case had rapidly discovered that his cock definitely followed where his soul went. No pretty face or hot body could compare to Mia. Those other women didn't glow the way she did, didn't light up a room or make his heart do weird, fluttery things that he was never going to admit to. Never. Except maybe to his brother when he'd had too much Scotch.

Ian had told him to suck it up on the girly love stuff, poured him another drink, and then very quietly admitted he felt the same way about Charlotte and if Case ever said a damn thing to her, Ian would beat the shit out of him.

Then they'd talked about the Cowboys.

That was the Taggart way.

And so was this. He reached out and hauled her up. She was easy to move, all trussed up. A gorgeous, sexy piece of baggage. Mia had chosen to offer herself up like this. He would take it. They could work through their issues while finding the connection that had been missing for months. He'd missed touching her, missed tasting and loving her. And he'd definitely missed spanking her.

She gasped a little as he twisted her and managed to maneuver her so she was over his lap, the offensive panties in his line of sight. Those had to go.

He reached out and touched the curve of her hip, sighing at the contact. Finally he could touch her, feel the warmth of her skin under his. "I've been leaving you messages for months. Why today?"

Was it because of Theo? He would be all right with that. She loved adventure and she'd been a part of finding him the first time. Hell, she was why they'd found him the first time. She could come along but she needed to understand this relationship wasn't ending the minute the op did. None of that fucking-until-the-op-was-over bullshit for him. This was forever.

Mia wiggled on his lap, but she didn't complain. "I might have been stubborn and might have switched phones and not listened to any of your messages until today. The minute I did, I was here. Case, I'm so sorry I got rid of that phone because I didn't want you to be able to reach me. I knew the minute I heard your voice that I would come back to you. Please touch me, Sir."

Hearing her call him Sir made him long for more. He knew he likely didn't deserve it, but one day she would call him Master and more than that, she would call him husband. He let his hand trace over the curves of her ass. So round and perfect, and made for his hand and his cock. This was exactly what he needed. He needed to be her Dom again, needed his strong, gorgeous sub here in his arms. She could knock him on his ass outside the bedroom. It was her job when he was a dumbass. She was going to be his woman, his better half. But here in the bedroom, he needed her sweet submission. He let his hand slide under the seam of those awful undies. "It's all right. I needed the time to sort a few things through. I needed to be better for you. But Mia, just because I'm working on my temper doesn't mean I can't lose it again."

She held on to him. “I wasn’t angry that you lost your temper. I knew you would be mad at me for what I did. It was how cold you got.”

He didn’t remember feeling cold at all. Never about her. He definitely wasn’t feeling a chill now. He began to draw the panties over her hips, exposing her gorgeous skin. “I was never cold. Not about you. I made a massive mistake, but you’re the one who walked away. I never intended for those to be the last words we said to each other. Not once. Even when I was angry as hell at you, I knew I wouldn’t let you go.”

“I didn’t see how you could possibly love me when you thought those things about me,” she said quietly.

“And I didn’t think you could possibly love me at all. I was angry. With you. With me. With Theo. With Ian for letting Theo go. I was angry about everything. But I wasn’t stupid. I wouldn’t have let you go. My every intention was to send you home so you could think about what you’d done. I was treating you like a child instead of letting you be my partner. I need to know if you can forgive me, Mia.” If she couldn’t, he would keep on trying until he changed her mind. Nothing was more important than winning her back, than being the man she needed him to be.

“Only if you’ll forgive me for walking away,” she replied.

That’s what he’d needed to hear. They spent so much time fighting or fucking that they’d forgotten how to look at each other and be real. “I do, but never again, princess. Even if I fuck up, I need to know you’ll stay and knock some sense into my thick skull. I suspect my sisters-in-law will help you learn how to be a Taggart wife. It’s not always easy.”

“Wife?”

Shit. Maybe that had been too fast. Still. He wasn’t backing down. “I want to marry you. I’m not going to pretend like I don’t. And honestly, I’ve got you tied up. If you say no, I could just leave you like this until you say yes.”

“Don’t you dare. You’ve got maybe fifteen minutes tops before I start complaining. And yes. But you had better spank me now. It's been so long. I need it, Case. I need to cry and I need to feel close to you so spank me."

Yes? She'd said yes? "Are you sure? Because I don't want you to think I'm punishing you. We need to make that clear. This is for fun and to give you what you need."

"Please. And make it dirty. I've missed this so much. And maybe you should punish me," she said in that voice that let him know she would get what she wanted one way or another. It was that sexy, taunting, sultry voice she used on him when she wanted to push him, wanted him to push her. "After all, I punished you for months. I knew you were working for my brothers. I knew you would come with us to New York, but I wouldn't see you. I wasn't going to give you the satisfaction of seeing me."

Yes, she seemed determined to push him. "Are you sure? I could untie you and make love to you and we could be gentle with each other."

"That's not who we are, Case. I realize that now. I should have stayed and fought it out with you. I can do that. I can take everything you have to give me, even the anger, if I know you love me. I love you. I've loved you since the moment you walked in the room and my world shifted because I'd finally found a man I didn't have to hold back with. I want everything. I want your passion and your love, and I definitely want your dominance."

He could give it to her. His cock was so hard it was painful, but it could wait. His sexuality had become tied to play and he needed it more than he needed to be inside her. He needed to give her what she required to be happy, what only he could give her.

He left her panties tangled in her legs, holding her thighs together. "You thought you could keep me away from this? Away from your body? It belongs to me, Mia. Only to me. I'll teach you never to think to keep us apart again."

The words were for play, to heighten the sensation, but the underlying meaning was there.

I need you. I can't be whole without you. Don't ever leave me again.

He brought his hand down, smacking her ass hard once, twice, and then again. He got to five, her flesh already pink, before he stopped to let her breathe.

Mia squirmed, though it was obvious she wasn't trying to get away. Her fingers had laced together, squeezing tight. "I was so mad at you, so hurt. I couldn't see past it, Sir. I'm so sorry. I wasted so much time."

He wasn't sure it had been wasted. They'd worked through some things they'd needed to work through. She'd written and found her footing back in that world again and he'd been forced to face what life without her would truly be like.

Did Ian love Charlotte more because he'd lost her? Had that made finding her again all the sweeter? Did Sean understand the depths of his love for Grace because she'd nearly died once?

Losing Theo had made Erin understand how hollow the world was without him.

He spanked her again because Mia was never satisfied with a couple of smacks. She needed more. He let himself go. Six through ten were quick, but he slowed and took his time getting to twenty, letting his hand hold the heat against her skin. "Nothing was wasted. What did you call it? This is our story and it played out the way it needed to. You needed to be free for a while longer. I needed to miss you. I needed to figure out you're not someone I play with and then put up so you can't get broken." Another smack, this one on her left cheek. "You're my partner. I need you in my life. I need you by my side. Even when it gets dangerous."

She was precious to him, but keeping her in a box would kill her. He wanted Mia just the way she was.

Another set of smacks and he could hear her. She was crying, but that wasn't a bad thing. Hell, he was starting to think he might cry, too. Mia wasn't crying because she was sad. She cried because she felt so fucking much and couldn't let it out until it was safe. He gave her a place to release that storm of emotion.

He was her safety and he would never let her down again. He kept it up, but more to keep their connection going now. He smacked her pretty ass, held his hand against her and told her over and over again how much he'd missed her. How much he loved her. How nothing had been real without her.

Gradually her body stilled and she seemed to relax against him. "Thank you. It's been so long. I haven't…"

He breathed in the sweet smell of her arousal. The spanking had done more than allow her to cry. It had brought out all of Mia's deep emotions. Her love and her lust. He craved them both. He tugged the panties all the way down and gently parted her legs so he could brush her core, feel the arousal there. "Haven't what, princess? Haven't cried? Haven't come?"

Her body tensed slightly and then her hips tilted up, giving him access. "Haven't cried. I didn't even cry when I left. I couldn't. If I'd started I wouldn't have been able to stop."

Such a beautiful ass. He couldn't take his eyes off it. Her cheeks were a deep pink. He shifted her so he could see her pussy peeking from between her legs. Her pussy was a deep coral, glistening with arousal. He knew just what he wanted to do with all that cream. "I think the rest of this conversation is best done on the bed."

She shuddered and sighed. "I agree. I want to hold you, Case."

He was sure she did. The trouble was, he'd caught the part of his question she hadn't answered. "Eventually. For now I'm going to play because I haven't played with anyone in six months, but I don't think you can say the same. Can you?"

She hadn't replied about not coming.

He easily lifted her and tossed her on his bed. Where she fucking belonged. Her eyes had gone wide, as though she'd just realized the precarious nature of her situation.

"I didn't sleep with anyone."

He hadn't thought she had. "I know that. How about masturbation?"

Now those pretty eyes rolled. "Of course. I went out the day after we broke up and bought a big old Hitachi wand and named it Ike. That sucker is so powerful it requires a plug. But I thought about you every time I used it."

That's what he suspected. Mia liked her toys. Unfortunately, he'd banned her from using them. "I think you require a plug."

Her face went as pink as her backside. "Case, you can't punish me for masturbating. It's not like you didn't…please tell me you did."

"Not even once, even though I was desperate to. I told you. I belong to you so that rule applied to me, too." It hadn't hurt that he'd been so tired most days from training her brothers and then sitting up with a newborn that he couldn't have worked up the will to yank his own dick, but he wasn't going to point it out to her. She'd been wandering the globe in first class with a giant vibrating wand and he'd been mourning her, taking her brothers' shit and getting covered in baby spit up. And when he could have pleasured himself all he could think about was Mia and the fact that sex was now meaningless without her. She hadn't felt the same way. He could totally forgive her, but he was going to have fun tonight. "Flip over and put that pretty ass in the air because you're getting plugged tonight."

"I can't believe you didn't touch yourself." Her breasts were up-thrust, nipples peaked. "How is that possible? Every time I thought about you, I couldn't help myself."

He leaned over, brushing his fingertips against her nipples. "And every time I thought of you I remembered what I owe you. My everything. Every touch, emotion, pleasure belongs to you. My heart, my soul, my cock. Everything I am is yours so it was fairly simple to not give myself any pleasure that didn't come from you."

Mia took a deep breath and then swung her legs, turning herself over and drawing her knees up. She placed herself in a deeply submissive position, her ass in the air, arms tied behind her back. Mia's cheek was against the quilt, her eyes soft. "All right."

He couldn't even explain what that trust did for him. "Just like that?"

"Just like that. When you talk to me like that, you're pretty much going to get anything you want." She wriggled her ass. "Do your worst, Sir."

His worst was going to bring her so much pleasure. And so much for him. He dragged his shirt over his head, unable to stay clothed around her. They didn't need clothes. He needed to be naked, his flesh against hers, his hands touching and manipulating her until neither one could stand it any longer and they had to fuck.

"Don't move." He strode to his closet. He might not have much by way of décor in his place, but he had a nice kit that he'd put together for Mia. He was an optimist at heart. He wouldn't have thought it, but a few months back he'd purchased new toys. The idea of using anything on her he'd used on someone else seemed wrong. He'd bought a very nice plug for her ass. A whole set, but he selected a moderately sized one and a water-based lube. He cleaned the plug and then moved back to his bed where Mia was waiting for him, her face close to the edge of the mattress. He knelt down. "What's your safe word?"

Her lips curled up. "Case. It's always Case, but for these purposes it's coffee. I love you."

God, it was good to hear those words from her. He kissed her lightly. "I love you, too. And, princess, this is going to be fun."

He moved behind her and spread her even wider, loving how she was held for his pleasure. He could see her tiny asshole. He was going to open her, make her ready for his dick. He would take her in every way possible, give himself to her.

One day he would make a baby with her. They would give TJ and Carys and Kala and Kenzi more cousins because she would be his wife.

And his wife was definitely going to need a nice plugging every now and then. "You've been a very bad girl. Do you understand what you did wrong?"

"Yes. I touched my Master's plaything. I belong to my Master and only he can give me an orgasm. My Master is faithful. Even when we're not together."

It was only play. She would enjoy the plug and eventually she would love his cock diving deep, but the undercurrent meant something. And hearing her call him Master made his heart twist in a good way. "We're always together. Even when we're not. At least in my mind. I won't love you until the day you die. I'll love you until I go. I'll love you far beyond. I'll love you forever, Mia."

Tears squeezed from her eyes. Tears she didn't need pain to shed. "Back at you. You should know that I won't leave you again, Taggart. Not without a fight."

They would fight. It was inevitable. They were too passionate, but they would be comfortable that they would be together at the end.

He spread her cheeks and dribbled the lube between them. "Not without a fight. I won't ever let you go again. We needed the time apart, but now it's time for us to be together, to be a family. I'm going to be with you in every way possible."

Starting now. He let his fingers move between the cheeks of her ass. The little rosette was sweetly puckered and tight. So tight. He intended to fix that. He massaged lube into her flesh, circling her over and over. Mia's spine straightened, her body tensing as his finger dipped inside.

"Relax," he ordered. "I'm not going to let you keep me out. This ass is mine. I'm going to take it."

He rimmed her, his finger opening her bit by bit. He meant to make her very aware of him tonight. Tomorrow they would go to Africa together, go into danger together, but tonight was just for them. It was their time to reconnect.

It was his time to get what he needed.

Mia groaned, her body shuddering as he pressed his finger inside. The sight of her little asshole tightening around his finger caused his dick to jump in his jeans. They were getting cumbersome, but he continued to work her over.

When he was ready, he used the wipes from his kit to clean up and then grabbed the plug. It was smaller than he was, but they would have to work her up to taking him.

Mia shuddered as he placed the tip against her. "It's cold."

"Not for long," he promised. "I wouldn't ever leave you cold for long. Relax. Take a deep breath and let me in. You want to play with toys, then we'll play."

"I might have thought twice about that wand if I'd known you were going to shove a massive piece of plastic up my ass," she admitted.

"This was always going to happen." He fucked her with the plug, gently opening her up until he could slide it fully inside. "I was always going to play with you like this. I don't want any barriers between us. Nothing is forbidden as long as it brings us both pleasure."

"I'm not sure how much I like this yet, but I love being open to you. I love the fact that I can fantasize about anything with you."

Because he was safe. It was a good thing to be. He seated the plug deep. "Tell me how it feels."

"Full," she said, her voice deep. "Odd, but it doesn't hurt. I don't mind it so much now, but I'm getting achy, Case. I need you."

She needed to come, but he didn't trust his damn dick to last. Once he felt her heat around him, felt the drag of the plug on his cock, he would likely come like a rocket. He needed to take care of her first. Luckily, he knew exactly what to do.

His cell rang, the sound jarring. Case glanced down. He didn't recognize the number.

Not that it mattered. He flicked the ringer off.

Nothing was going to stop him from taking his sub tonight.

Absolutely nothing. Tonight, he made her his forever.

* * * *

Mia loved the rope, loved how it held her so tight and kept her in the moment. So often her mind wandered. She tended to have a million and one thoughts sprinting through her brain at any moment, but the minute she felt the curl of rope on her skin and heard Case's deep Dom voice, she focused as though the two together could trigger a separate part of her brain. Sex brain. Making love brain. Being with Case brain.

She even enjoyed the position she was in. Ass in the air, hands behind her back, one cheek to the quilt that covered Case's bed. Her knees were splayed so he had easy access to her pussy and her ass. It sent her straight into sub space and that was a beautiful thing. Everything else melted away in this place. All the fights meant nothing here. The time apart was gone and all that mattered was Case's hands, his voice, their connection.

He moved in front of her, allowing her to watch as he shed his jeans. His cock bounced free. It was just as beautiful as the rest of him. He was more devastating than he'd been before.

"I placed you perfectly," Case murmured as he moved close. His hand touched her hair as he lined his cock up with her lips. "Just for a moment. I want to feel your mouth on me, but I'm not going to come. Not until I'm deep inside that pussy of yours. I've missed everything about you. Including your tongue. Lick me, Mia."

There was nothing she wanted to do more. He gently held her head, his fingers tangling in her hair and tugging. Her whole body responded, blood heating up. She licked him, running her tongue along the stalk of his cock. He pushed the head just behind her lips. His skin tasted clean, the scent of his masculinity arousing her beyond compare. Her whole body ached with need. She could feel both the plug in her ass and how wet she was getting.

Case's cock moved back and forth. He dipped in and out of her mouth. Mia sucked lightly, pulling on the head. She could taste a drop of arousal coating the tip.

"That's right. You taste me. You taste what you do to me. I've waited months to get back inside you. Do you know what I thought about every single night? Nothing but you. You were my last thought before I went to sleep and the very first thing to hit my brain when I woke up in the morning and you can't even imagine what my dreams were like."

She would have told him about hers had he not thrust his cock back inside. All her dreams had been of him. Good and bad. She'd dreamed of him loving her, dreamed of him leaving her, dreamed of what Theo could have done. Mostly, though, she'd dreamed about him dominating her. She woke up in a sweat at the thought of his strength, his beauty, his passion.

All hers.

She ran her tongue over the ridge of his cock head.

"I dreamed of you tied up and spread for my pleasure. Just like you are right now. Take more. Take all of me." His hips thrust, forcing his cock deeper. "In my dreams, you submit to me in the bedroom and you're my partner everywhere else. You're right by my side in the real world, but here in the bedroom, you kneel at my feet. And I worship you. I make you helpless and then I ply you with every bit of pleasure a man can give a woman. I lick you and suck you and fuck you whenever I want, however I want. I'm on top of you four times a day. I wake you up in the morning with my cock against your pussy and I fuck that sweet asshole late at night before you go to sleep in my arms."

It sounded like heaven to her. She rolled her tongue around and around his cock. Case was so big he stretched her jaw. She groaned around him and his hand tightened in her hair, lighting up her scalp.

He pulled his cock out and took a step back. "Not so fast. I told you how this would go."

"You're not going to come until you're deep inside me." Until they were as close as two people could be. Two souls could be. "I dream of you, too. I dream of being your wife, your partner, the one you love more than anything. I dream of being part of your family."

His eyes bore into her. "You are my family. You belong in my family. They love you. And I belong in yours. I promise to be a brother to your obnoxiously single-minded brothers. Your family. My family. It's all the same."

He moved out of her line of sight.

She felt his fingers running across the ropes, touching flesh and then pressing down on the jute. He ran his fingers over her back and then down her torso until he found her nipples. He cupped her breasts and then tweaked her nipples between his thumbs and forefingers. His cock touched her thigh, still hard and heavy against her. "What are you doing?"

She couldn't see him, could only feel the light rasp of his fingers on her skin.

"I told you. I'm playing. I haven't played in forever." He pinched her nipples harder, tugging on them. "Do you have any idea what I'm going to do to you tomorrow? You should understand that we have hours and hours in the air tomorrow and you're going to serve me."

Mia hissed at the pain that flared through her when he pinched her nipples again. It flared and then the endorphins kicked in and she felt warmth along her flesh. "You're taking me with you?" She hadn't been sure. He'd said it, but he could always change his mind. This was a dangerous mission and she'd already screwed up once. "It's all right if you're worried about how I'll behave. I promise I'll stay with Erin and Avery."

Warmth hit the nape of her neck as he leaned over and pressed his mouth there. She could feel his words rumble over her skin.

"I think it would be best if you did stay with them when the actual op is going down, but if you want to come you're welcome to. I don't want to be apart from you."

He was drugging her with heat. She could barely think when he kissing her neck and shoulders, brushing back her hair with a patient hand. "I understand. I wasn't as good out in the field as I thought I would be. I thought I would fight harder."

"There's a difference between learning self-defense and actually finding yourself in a life-and-death situation. I've been trying to teach your brothers that." He licked along the shell of her ear. "You have to train. You have to learn muscle memory so your body and instincts take over. It's very difficult to drown out the fear. Flight is usually better than fight for a civilian."

But her brother wasn't going to run. They'd spent far too long setting up their revenge. "I've been training with Ezra."

A vicious twist had her gasping.

"Don't even say that fucker's name when I'm touching you."

So he was still jealous. "Sorry."

It looked like they would be talking about Ezra's future employment after Case was done playing.

Case stepped away. "Don't move and don't lose that plug."

What was he planning? She couldn't exactly see him. Yeah, that did something for her, too, but then he knew it. Being kept on edge heightened her senses.

The plug in her ass made her aware of a part of her body she'd never thought of as erotic before. She clenched around it, keeping it deep inside her. She was stretched and heated, still able to feel the warmth from his spanking. She'd purged all the anxiety of the last few months and her soul felt lighter. No matter what happened tomorrow, they would be together.

He moved between her legs, skin skimming along the insides of her thighs.

"God, I've missed the way you taste."

She closed her eyes as she realized what he was about to do. Warmth spun through her system, a hot flash of pure pleasure that made her gasp. His tongue moved over pussy, his hands holding tight to her thighs. He held himself up while he devoured her sex.

His tongue slid over her and she couldn't breathe. He touched the plug, pressing it lightly and making her squirm at the sensation. He tapped on it, sending jangling pressure through her even as his mouth was soft as silk on her pussy.

Light and dark, soft and hard. That was her Master, her soon-to-be husband.

She was going to marry him so hard.

That thought brought a smile to her face. He was right. They'd needed the time apart. It had taught him to view her as a partner and it had given her insight into who he really was—a man willing to support her, a man who needed her as much as she needed him. He was more than just a hero. He was a man who needed her affection, her love.

She would give it all to him.

He kept it up, his tongue going deep while he worked the plug in her ass. Soft heat slid over her clitoris and she could feel the pressure building.

And then it crested. So much pleasure, so much emotion. She found out there was another way for her to cry. Lying there with Case giving to her, she let herself go. She could do nothing else.

The mattress beneath her moved and she heard the sound of a wrapper being opened. Her blood pounded through her body as she began to float down from the high of her orgasm. Even without his hands on her, she could sense the connection between them, could feel the need rolling off him. She felt Case holding on to her hips as his cock found her pussy.

Yes. She needed him. Needed him inside her. "Please."

"I love you, Mia. This is forever." He thrust inside.

He didn't hold back. He powered into her.

So full. Between the plug and Case's cock, she could barely breathe, but she wouldn't have it any other way. He was filling her up, letting her know he could master her on every level and yet they were still equals. They were still in this together.

He'd grown for her. He'd dealt with his problems because he'd wanted to be better for her, for their future.

Mia pushed back, needing to show him how much she wanted him, too.

"That's what I want," Case growled. He tugged on her hips and then forced his dick inside again. "Fight for it, princess. This is who we are. We fought it, but we don't have to. We're going to be okay no matter what happens. That's what I had to figure out. You're never allowed to leave me again. Never again, Mia."

Never again. If he could work on his temper, then she could work on her pride. She should have kicked his ass after what he'd said, not walked away.

Case pounded into her, angling up and hitting that sweet spot that sent her reeling all over again. Tears poured from her eyes, her heart so full of love for him as she went flying for the second time. Pleasure crashed over her and she felt Case stiffen behind, calling out her name.

He finally slumped down, his body collapsing on hers.

Mia groaned because that was so not comfy.

Case chuckled and kissed her cheek. "I'll free you in a minute. Just give me a second when I know you can't run away from me."

"I won't, Case. If you want me, I'm all in, but you better believe there's not going to be a quickie Vegas wedding."

He rubbed his cheek against hers like a large predatory and affectionate cat. "But Vegas is so nice and quick. And I want to be married by the time we head to New York and help your brothers. We can do it in between rescuing my brother and making sure yours don't kill themselves. You know when you think about it, our families are really pains in the ass."

She couldn't disagree with that, but she did have another pain in the ass to deal with. "How long do I have to wear this thing?"

He kissed her again. "Go and get in the shower and we'll take it out, but next time you have to wear it for a lot longer. I want to fuck that pretty ass someday." He sighed. "I love you, Mia."

"I love you. I'm glad you decided to leave me those messages and I'm glad Riley decided I was being stubborn and saved them."

He went still. "Tell me he didn't listen to them."

Her arms were starting to ache. "He didn't."

She'd promised not to run away. She'd never promised not to tell little white lies that would save her ass.

Case rolled off her. "Damn it. Maybe I'll let him die in New York. But as for you, I haven't even gotten started yet. Let's get you cleaned up so we can get dirty again. And by the way, you're staying here tonight. You're actually staying with me forever so if you don't like this place, we should look for another one."

She sighed in relief as he started to unwind the rope that held her. "I'm good with anything, babe. But you should know we'll be staying in the most gorgeous place on the Upper West Side when we get to New York. It's going to ruin you forever."

She'd worked with a real estate agent to find their base of operations in the city. And now it would feel like home because Case would be there with her.

"Well, considering I grew up in a trailer, it's going to be an adventure."

She was looking forward to the experience.

* * * *

Case watched Mia wrap a robe around her body as she stepped out of the bathroom. Her hair was still wet, but her skin glowed.

He'd put that look on her face.

How could he feel so damn settled? He was taking her to Africa in the morning. They were going into something dangerous and he wasn't sure he would succeed, but here he was just hours away from the most important mission of his life and he had a dumb grin on his face. "You sure you're okay with pizza?"

She stepped out of the room, but he could hear her voice floating in from the hall. "Yes, but you have to put some veggies on it."

It was wrong. Pizza was supposed to be meat and cheese, but he could make the sacrifice. Mushrooms were sort of veggies. They would have to have a long talk if she was one of those people who put spinach or olives on a perfectly good pizza.

He went to grab his phone and noticed he had two voice mails. One from Michael and one from a number he didn't recognize. Damn. How had he missed a call from Michael? Oh, yeah, he'd been balls deep in his almost wife, and that distracted him from everything. He quickly pushed the number to retrieve the voice mail and Michael's voice came over the line.

"Hey, nothing to worry about, but I did get that video footage you asked for. It's weird. I think he's trying to avoid the cameras for some reason. He got off on the fourth floor but then took the stairs up to eight. That's the floor the common room is on. There's a gym and a big meeting room on that floor. He caught the elevator there, but it wasn't the main elevator. It was the one that leads to the penthouse opposite from me."

Michael had moved recently. He'd purchased a condo in Victory Park that he damn straight couldn't afford because of his McKay-Taggart salary. Michael came from a super-rich oil family. The Malones were Texas royalty, but it was easy to forget how much money Michael came from due to his laid-back personality. He'd bought the place because he could share the top floor of the exclusive building with his cousin, Simon Weston and Simon's wife, Chelsea.

"Anyway," Michael continued, "I thought you should know. If he's trying to get up to my floor, he needs a code. I'm going to warn Si that we think Ferland might be spying on us. No idea why. See you soon, brother. Good luck."

Fuck. There was a scenario Michael wasn't thinking of. Case strode out of the room, his phone in hand. "Mia, I need to know everything you know about Fain."

She was standing in his kitchen, the fridge door open. "Really? Not even a beer?"

His fridge was empty. "I'll go out and grab us some in a while, but right now I need to know if Fain's ever done anything that made you suspicious of him."

"I don't know that I would use the word suspicious, but he's a little secretive. He's good at his job though. Sometimes I think my brothers are right and I'm a magnet for chaos. I swear if people don't stop trying to steal my shit, I'm going to start shooting."

He didn't like the sound of that. "What are you talking about?"

She shook her head and leaned against the counter. "It was no big deal. You know me. I end up in some rough neighborhoods. Also, being a blonde American in some parts of the world means the local criminals think you're an easy mark."

"I thought Ezra was supposed to be with you at all times." His phone went off again. He looked down. It was the same number from about an hour ago. He put a hand up. "Give me one second.

And we might get that pizza to go. I think we're going to pack up and spend the night at Ian's."

"Why?" But she was already moving. She closed the fridge door.

"I have a bad feeling. I'm going to grab my go-bag. You get dressed." He moved toward the front hall closet. He swiped across the screen to accept the call. "This is Taggart."

"Damn it. Do you ever pick up your flipping phone calls, Tiny Tag?" A familiar voice, heavy with a Southern accent, came over the line. "I've been trying to call you all night. None of you answer my calls."

"Ten?" It was hard to hear him, but there was no mistaking that voice. It sounded like he was in a wind tunnel.

Then he realized what he was hearing. Ten was in a helicopter.

"I need you to get the fuck out of your place and you do it right now. I'm on my way. Ian's on his way. Take Mia and run. Right fucking now. Ezra Fain isn't who he says he is. I should know because Ezra Fain is dead. He died years ago. He was a medic. Had some military training, but I wanted to bring him in because he was an excellent field medic. I didn't turn him down. He was supposed to be on our team. He died before he could join us."

Shit. He was right. "He's Agency."

"What?" Ten's voice cracked over the line. "I don't know that, but I do know someone's after your girl."

There was a knock on his door. He reached for his gun. "Someone's here. I'll call you back."

"It's probably Ian. He was headed to your place. My ETA is ten minutes. Don't open that fucking door unless you're sure it's Ian." The line crackled. "… is dangerous. I didn't realize how much."

He needed all his faculties to deal with whoever the hell Ezra Fain was.

Mr. White. That's who he'd heard him referred to as. Simon called him Mr. White and Simon had called him dangerous, too.

He clicked off the safety and started for his front door, his mind whirling.

"I'm coming," a feminine voice said as he rounded the hallway and strode into his living room.

"Mia, don't!"

But she'd already undone the bolt. She scrambled, trying to relock the door. It came open with a crack and Mia fell back.

Case watched in horror as a canister rolled in. He leapt to cover Mia's body with his as the whole world turned to lightning and then smoke.

Flashbang.

It was so close it singed his skin.

His hearing was gone, his vision blurry. He held on to Mia as tightly as he could, trying to move them.

They had to get out. They had to run.

Mia clung to him.

Then he felt something smack against his head and the whole world went dark.

CHAPTER SIXTEEN

Case came to with a throbbing head and the deepest desire to shut his brothers up. They were arguing, but then that was kind of what they did. Both his blood brothers and his extended family.

What the hell had happened? Why was he on his couch?

"Give me one good fucking reason, Fain, or whoever the hell you are. One good reason I don't blow your brains out right fucking now," Ian growled.

"I can give you one," Ten's deep voice shot back. "We haven't exactly questioned him yet. I don't know why you always go straight for the kill. Subtlety, brother."

"Fuck that," Ian replied. "How about I kill him fast if he tells me what the hell is going on. If he doesn't, then I'll vivisect him from the toes up. How does that sound?"

Mia. The night came rushing back and Case sat up, his head throbbing and his vision still the slightest bit blurry. "Mia. Where's Mia?"

She wasn't here, wasn't in his arms. The last thing he could remember was the way she'd held on to him.

Fain was sitting in one of Case's dining room chairs, his hands behind his back and a couple of guns pointed at his head. "That's what I'd like to know."

"Keep playing dumb and I'll cut your toes off and feed them to the nastiest stray cats I can find," Ian promised.

His brother was being a little over the top, but then apparently there was some drama going on Case didn't understand.

His heart raced. Mia was gone. They'd come after Mia.

Someone had come after Mia. More than one person. He thought he'd counted at least three. It had been hard to see through the gas. His eyes still burned.

Ten kept his eyes on Fain. "I got some intel four hours ago about a group wanting to move a blonde American from Texas to Africa. They were looking to hire a plane and they needed a passport for her in case the airfield they would have to refuel at checked. The picture that came over the line was Mia's. I recognized her and realized they were moving tonight when the meet spot changed from Austin to Dallas about four hours ago. You are so lucky I was already on my way here."

Fain frowned but didn't seem like a man who gave a shit that he had a couple of guns pointed at his head. "I got the same intel. Why do you think I rushed in here like a crazy person? Why do you think you were able to catch me at all? I give a shit about that girl. If I didn't I would have realized the takedown had already happened and I wouldn't fucking be here."

Something about Ezra. Ten had told him something about Ezra.

Ezra was a dead man.

Did any of it matter when Mia was gone? He had to find her. He had to get her back. He'd promised he wouldn't let her leave again. He'd promised her they would be together.

"Case, sit down. You got hit pretty hard," Ian ordered. "Charlie's on her way. She had to drop the kids with Chelsea, but she's going to take you to the ER. You probably have a concussion. I've already contacted Drew Lawless. He's on his way, too. You understand that we have to keep this out of the press."

He was fairly certain he didn't have a concussion. He'd had a couple before. He was far too clearheaded to be hurt. But he did agree with Ian on one thing. No police. It was simply surprising the world around them had complied. "No one called after that fucking flashbang went off?"

It had to have shaken the floor, rattled the hell out his neighbors.

"Your microwave went on the fritz and exploded. Just some smoke and noise. Derek sent out a friendly to explain to the neighbors," Ten said.

A friendly would be a cop who Derek Brighton trusted. He was their DPD contact. When they needed police cover, Derek was their go-to guy. He liaised with the chief when it came to sensitive issues.

None of it mattered because Mia was out there.

And Ezra was here. Why would Ezra be here?

Something about Ezra. And Chelsea. Maybe he wasn't as clear as he thought he was.

"I'm going to ask again," Ian began, his voice dark. "One good reason I don't kill you."

Whoever had taken Mia would want money. Lots of it. He had to stay here, stay with Drew and her brothers and negotiate with whoever had her.

He was going to have to let Ian handle Theo because Mia came first. It's what he'd promised Ian. If he was going to love Mia, she had to be the most important person in his life. He had to choose her now and always.

Ezra had been going to the top of the building—to the penthouse. That's what Michael had said. Ezra had snuck up to the top floor where any visitor needed a passcode and there were only two residences to visit.

Michael had thought Ezra was spying on him. What if Ezra had merely been doing his job?

"I'll give you one, Ian. You can't kill him because the Agency would be pissed if you killed Mr. White." It had all fallen into place just before the door opened. "He's Mr. White. Take a picture of him and send it to Si and see if he'll confirm it. Chelsea can't. She would be guilty of treason if she did."

Ian shook his head. "Simon's under some pretty heavy contracts about Chelsea's work with the Agency. I've always known he had to stay neutral or there could be trouble. It's the only reason they're allowed to live here while she's working for them. But I'll go with your instincts on this one. I'll buy that he's an Agency fuckhead. He has that look."

Ten's brows rose. "We have a look?"

"Definitely," Ian shot back. "And no amount of gluing poodle hair to your face can change it."

"It's a beard, motherfucker," Ten shot back.

He ignored them. Sometimes Ten and Ian were like a bickering old married couple. They should get divorced, but they couldn't quite quit each other. While they argued about the state of Ten's facial hair, Case had to think.

Why would Mr. White be after Mia now? He'd spent months with her. According to Mia, he'd been the one to save her from multiple near misses. If he wanted to take her, why not do it when he'd been alone?

Fain's face went hard as he looked up at Case. "I'm going to get fired. Burned more likely. Thanks a lot, Taggart. You just cost me my career. You couldn't handle one fucking flashbang?"

Ian's fist shot out, catching Ten square in the face. He immediately backed up. "Wait. That shouldn't count. That was a professional punch."

Ten snarled and held his nose. "It counts. You're done. I've got witnesses."

Ezra shook his head. "I do not get them."

"Long story," Case replied. And apparently one that was over until the next time Ten did something so shitty Ian punished him with random punches in the face. It had been interesting since Ian liked to save them for holidays, but had sworn to keep that last one for a special occasion.

Ten cursed and holstered his gun. "Fuck a duck. I'm sorry, Tag. I've never met this asshole."

Ian stared at Fain, his weapon still ready to go. "Which begs the question why he would choose a name you did recognize."

It would be easy for Mr. White to change records. Hell, he could have ordered Chelsea to do it for him. Chelsea was Mr. White's asset.

If Chelsea thought he was going to hurt the team, she would break ranks no matter what the cost. She would have said something. He trusted Chelsea's instincts. If she hadn't warned them, she wasn't worried about the man they'd called Ezra Fain.

Fain stared mulishly ahead, but Case wondered just how much truth the other man had told him. One particular story seemed to ring true. "Ezra was your brother, wasn't he?"

Fain's jaw tightened. "My half brother. He was older than me. I knew going into this particular op that I was likely being an idiot idealist. He was the most idiotic idealist I knew. He gave everything for his country. Looks like even in this he was better than me. Fine. I'm the operative known as Mr. White. I was sent down here to oversee Chelsea Weston. Believe it or not, it was a demotion of sorts. I used to be a field operative."

Ten's jaw dropped. "Holy shit. You're Beckett Kent. You killed that general against orders. I should have recognized you."

Kent's face went tight and the man practically snarled. "There's no proof of that, but I was relieved when the bastard was killed. No one deserved it more. He was raping his way through villages. It made me sick that I had to stay close to him. Luckily someone put a bullet through the fucker's heart."

Ian backed off. "I did hear about that. The Agency wanted intel from the guy. I take it they couldn't prove you assassinated the fucker or they would have burned you."

"A lot of people hated General Mambasi. He had many enemies. I was brought back here for my failure to protect him," Kent replied. "I was assigned to relay messages of importance to and from the asset known as Chelsea Weston. Information that required sensitivity."

Information no one wanted written down. "Why the job with Ferland?"

"Cover. And because I wanted to watch McKay-Taggart. I wanted in on taking down The Collective. The Agency still has that as a low priority. When I became aware that 4L Software was working with McKay-Taggart and that gossip linked the case to Mia, I had her on my radar. When she went looking for a bodyguard, I was ready and in place."

Case was confused. "So if you were trying to get Mia, were you behind the kidnapping attempt on the plane?"

"Your brother's slow," Kent said to Ian. "Of course I wasn't behind that. Nor was I behind the three other attempts, but I did manage to stop the man who *is* trying to take her. Mia thinks they were random street crimes. I know the truth."

What the hell was going on? None of it made sense.

Unless the original kidnapping attempt was about more than mere ransom.

Unless Hope McDonald wasn't working alone. She'd already proven she would send her "boys" out to rob banks for cash. Why not kidnapping? Why not lure out a ripe target? One already known to The Collective.

Fuck. It was Santos. He'd lured them out to Colombia, but he'd been aiming for Mia. "Did you know it was Santos all along? What does he really want Mia for?"

"I told you it was Santos on the phone," Ten said, shaking his head. "Does anyone ever listen to a word I say?"

Case rolled his eyes. "The reception from your chopper sucks. I heard about half of what you said. Tell me it's not on top of my building."

"Of course it is," Ian tossed back, finally setting his gun down and freeing Fain…White…Kent…god, he wished Agency assholes would pick one name and stick with it. "He might have left the CIA, but the dude still likes to make an entrance. And Case is right. When you called me earlier tonight I wasn't sure if you were telling me my brother was in danger or if you were ordering a pizza. Your cell service sucks. Are we talking about Tony Santos? The asshole who only likes blondes? The last I heard the Agency was putting him out to pasture for mental health reasons."

Kent nodded. "He's a crazy motherfucker. Or at least he wanted everyone to believe it. I think he would have taken Mia on the beach that day in Colombia, but I let him see me."

Case ran a hand over his hair, trying to force himself to think. Panic sat in his gut, but Mia didn't need that right now. "Santos is a former CIA operative, right? So how much would he know about Hope McDonald and the drug?"

Kent stood, stretching his long arms. Case would bet Ian hadn't been kind in this particular bondage session. "He would likely know everything. I've been tracking him. I think he was a Collective plant, but he got out before I could get any evidence on him. It was right around the time Smith got burned and I was pulled back to the States. Things were a little chaotic and they're only now beginning to calm down. Tell me something, Smith, were you in DC to try to get Agency backing for the Sierra Leone op?"

Ian frowned. "How the hell do you know about the Sierra Leone op?"

Fuck. Everyone listened to his messages. "When did you get hold of Mia's phone?"

Kent sent him a sympathetic stare. "On the plane from Austin to here. She spent a lot of time on her other line talking to someone named Kori. It was fairly easy to get the private phone in my hands. I only listened to the last message, but I get it. I really do. She's an amazing woman. I'm going to do everything I can to help you get her back."

Ian's head shook Case's way. "I told you to talk to the woman, not lay out all our secret plans to her in voice mail. Why? Why do all my best agents lose their freaking minds the minute a nice pair of breasts walk into the room?"

"I do not need your sarcasm." Mia was in danger.

Ian sobered. "I'm sorry, Case. I know what she means to you. I'm surprised she was here though."

"I wanted her with me when we went to get Theo," Case admitted. "I wanted her with Charlotte and Erin. I know Grace isn't coming with us, but I wanted her with the rest of our…wives."

Ian put a hand on his shoulder. "Of course you did. I'll stop being such an ass. We have to get to the office and get someone over to Chelsea's to take care of our girls. I need Charlie and Chelsea trying to figure out where Santos would take Mia."

Ten had already told them. Case forced his hands to stop shaking. They still had the advantage. He turned to Ten. "You said you got some intel about Mia. Was it random?"

Ten shook his head. "No. It was a hacker. At least he said he was. He said he'd been searching the Dark Web and he had some stuff he thought I should look at. I've been trying to build a new network now that I'm no longer with the Agency. It helps that I'm not with a big firm either because I'm less likely to be able to track someone down. Sometimes even the bad guys have consciences about certain things. As this asshole proves."

Ten was gesturing to Kent, but Case wasn't so sure he was a bad guy at all.

Kent stared at him. "Are you thinking what I'm thinking?"

"Hutch." He was still in there. He was doing his best. He'd lain low and waited for the time he could help his team. Hutch was out there asking if he could come home now.

Ian took a deep breath. "Why would Santos take her to McDonald?"

"For the money she'll bring in," Case replied. Drew would pay anything to get his sister back. "McDonald needs money. For protection and to keep her experiments going. They can't steal enough to make themselves comfortable. Mia is a big payday. Drew will write a check for a hundred million and not blink an eye."

"Why not steal her in Colombia?" Ten asked. "Obviously Santos was trying to lead you to a place where it would be easier to take her."

He had to shrug at that one. "Theo didn't let it happen. I don't know. He was willing to let them take Hutch but not a female. You know how protective Theo can be about women. I guess no drug could take that out of him."

How much had Theo paid for that transgression? How much blood had he shed to keep Mia out of hell?

"So now we're going to rescue two family members," Ian said, his jaw firming with surety.

"I want in." Kent's shoulders had squared.

Ian started to say something, but Case put a hand out, stopping him. He looked Kent in the eyes. "Are you trying to get back in the Agency's good graces?"

"I'm trying to stop a crazy woman from developing a drug that could be used against us," Kent replied. "And you have to know that the Agency isn't going to help you out of the kindness of their hearts. Every intelligence group in the world is looking for that drug and they won't care how they get their hands on it. You need me. I can help you because if we don't get the formula to that drug, guess who the Agency is going to turn to? Going to study?"

"Theo," Ten said between clenched teeth. "They'll try to use him to figure out what she did and reverse engineer the process. It's why Santos is working with her. I'm sure she promised him a cut or that he could be the one to sell the formula for her. He always was a wily son of a bitch."

"I'm not letting the Agency take my brother." He would fight.

Kent looked him straight in the eyes. "Then let me be your Agency contact. I won't inform them of the mission until we're in the air and there's nothing they can do to switch me out. If you take someone else, I can't promise they'll help you the way I will."

"Why should we trust you?" Ian asked.

Case knew the answer. "Because he loves Mia, too."

Kent's eyes closed as though he couldn't stand to look at him.

"She's a very lovable woman." His eyes came open again and he stared at Case. "I know she doesn't feel the same way about me. You don't have anything to worry about. And it's more than Mia. It's about Ezra, too."

His brother. Case understood that. And he couldn't find the will to work up jealousy. Mia was his. All he could feel was some sympathy for Kent. He wouldn't get the woman he wanted, but he could help save her. "You're in. We fly out at six and we're going to have to deal with one seriously freaked out billionaire."

Ian pulled out his phone. "I'm going to call Alex and see if he and Eve will take the twins so Chelsea can work on this. I assume with Mr. White's approval she can answer to me without being a traitor. As for the rest of it, this is your op, Case. I'll follow your lead."

Ian turned and started to dial.

It was his mission. He intended to make sure he got his girl and his brother back.

* * * *

Mia wished she wasn't in a bathrobe. Clothes. They were super helpful when one was kidnapped.

How long had it been? Hours at least. Maybe a full day since she'd clung to Case and prayed that this had all been a shitty dream.

Granted, though, she'd been drugged for a while so her sense of time could be fucked.

She had no idea what had been done to her while she was out. It made her feel ridiculously small.

Don't think about it. Take stock of where you are.

She kept her eyes closed because she had no idea who was watching her. There was a hum all around her, a vibration beneath her body and a definite sense of motion.

"I know you're awake. You might as well sit up. It's almost time to land and this hunk of junk is going to descend pretty quickly. I've got a bag ready for you," a voice said over the whine of the plane's engine.

Mia opened her eyes and had to contain her shock.

Theo Taggart was sitting in front of her, his blue eyes staring down with absolutely no recognition in them at all. She gasped a little as she realized that wasn't the only thing that had changed. He had a long, angry scar that ran across his face. It started right under his left eye and wove its way down to his jawline. It had to have happened sometime right after she'd seen him because it was already healed to a nasty pale pink. He held a hand out.

She took it, allowing him to help her up. Her mind was foggy, her stomach not exactly still.

The last thing she remembered was holding on to Case and then a man in a mask hit him and jabbed a needle into her arm and everything had gone dark.

"Where am I?" She shifted the robe so nothing was hanging out. It looked like someone had also covered her with a blanket. It draped across her lap, but while she'd been lying down it would have covered her body.

It was a stupid question because she was obviously in some kind of a cargo plane. She was sitting on one side and Theo on the other. As her eyesight came back into focus, she could see the metal all around her. It looked like they were in the back of the plane.

"You're about to be in Sierra Leone," he said over the hum of the engines.

"Are you going to give her a full report and maybe plans to the compound so she can escape?" Tony Santos strode over and slid his lean body into the seat beside Theo's, his eyes finding Mia. "He got that scar the hard way. It was punishment for what he did to help you last time. You'll find he's been properly trained to obey during this op."

Fucking Tony Santos. Oh, damn it to hell. Case was going to slap her ass silly for this.

"So you're working with McDonald?"

Santos sat back, crossing one long leg over the other. "I worked for her father for a very long time. When it became obvious she was in trouble, I came to her aid."

Theo frowned. "How did I help her? I've never met her."

Santos's lip curled up in a vicious grin. "The doc is still working on the right mixture for him. It's a little different for everyone. He's proven to be stubborn when it comes to bending to another's will."

"So you cut him up?" She wanted to reach out and grab Theo's hand. He looked so much like Case. His face had been almost identical, but now there would be no one who would ever mistake them again. Another crime to lay at Hope McDonald's feet.

How many more scars did he bear? Did he even know why they were there? Or did he wake every morning and simply accept what he saw in the mirror?

"I was angry at the time," Santos allowed. "He had strict instructions. He tried to lie, tried to say his comm unit wasn't working and the last thing he'd understood was a kill order. The kill order was for your boyfriend. I was very explicit in my instructions concerning you. You were to be brought back with the hacker and taken with us. Yeah, I think he was hoping we would be so busy getting the hell out of there that we wouldn't notice. Sometimes it helps that the poor fucker can't remember much past a day or two."

"Why would I lie?" Theo asked, his eyes tight. "Why would I go against direct orders?"

"Stop trying to remember and it won't hurt so much, buddy." Santos put a hand on Theo's shoulder as if they were friends. "You know you're not very good at thinking. It's not your talent."

"It is," Mia countered. "You're quite good at it, Theo. When you were a Navy SEAL you weren't a grunt. You had to think your way out of tight situations."

His face went hard. "I was never in the military. This has always been my home. Excuse me. I'm going to check with the pilot. I don't trust him as far as I can throw him. Fucking mercenaries. Why Mother didn't allow Victor to fly us I have no idea."

He stood and strode toward the front of the plane, his hand briefly going to his head.

"You can't get him that way." Santos regarded her with curious eyes. "He's been trained to think of certain things when the memories start to surface. First there's the headache and then his brain goes to its safe place. He's always been here, always had his brothers around him."

"His true brothers will find him someday and then you'll get a real taste of his family." Mia didn't mention that the day might come sooner than they thought.

If this plane was going to land in Sierra Leone, then they had no idea Case had laid a trap. She wasn't about to give up that piece of information. Her man would need every conceivable advantage he could get because he was going to flip his shit when he woke up.

If he woke up.

What if they'd killed him?

"You just went pale," Santos observed. "Are you just now realizing how precarious your position is? You're going to be in a foreign country with no one but me to protect you. My partner can be a bit unstable at times. Maybe it's best if you stick close to me."

Eww. "No, I wasn't worried about myself and don't expect me to play the wounded doe. If you come at me expect to get your balls handed to you because I'm not about to trade my body for protection. So let's call it what it is. Rape. You going to get rapey on me, Santos? Because if you do, you better kill me afterward. I won't keep quiet and my family might be so happy to have me back alive and whole that they concentrate on me, but if I'm damaged in any way, they won't stop hunting your ass down. Do I make myself clear?"

"As crystal." He shrugged it off as though it was no big deal. "No romance then. Tell me something—are you involved with both Taggart and Kent?"

"Kent?"

He waved a hand. "Sorry, I believe you know the man as Ezra Fain. He's a CIA agent. I recognized him because I worked briefly with him on an operation in Indonesia. Kent preferred to work alone. Mostly because he's one of those idiots who tends to feel a bit ashamed of his crimes. He shouldn't. He's an excellent killer. Clean and precise. He was an assassin for a while before the Agency decided to see if he was smart enough to turn into a real field agent. Smart man, but he couldn't quite stop that conscience of his."

She was going to have a long talk with Ezra when she got back home. "Sounds like a good thing to have."

"Not when you're a spy, pretty girl. When you're a spy it tends to get in the way of the job. But I remember how much the man enjoyed the kill. It's why I didn't take you on the beach that day. I saw him. I think he let me see him. That was when I realized I had to try to get you to the clinic. You were the real target. The hacker was a bonus. We didn't have one of those. When it became apparent you had no idea who he was, I realized Kent was playing an angle. You were his pawn. Now I have the queen and I intend to get paid."

"So you're going to ransom me back to my brother?"

"Of course. And I'll attempt to keep you intact. I suspect getting in a war with your brother could be tricky. I don't want to have to slit his throat in the middle of the night. He's too high profile a target. But he knows the game. He'll pay and then we'll be done."

"Until the next time you need a little cash."

He shrugged slightly, not denying the accusation at all. "Hopefully we won't. The doctor believes she's almost at a breakthrough. The new drug has completely wiped Victor's mind and he no longer requires daily doses. Only Theo seems to be holding out. Once he no longer reverts to form, we'll be ready to sell. Then we'll never need money again."

"I suspect you'll need a good lawyer at some point."

"There's no FDA out here, and once we've sold the protocols and formula we'll all disappear completely."

"What about Theo and the others? What happens to them when you and the fine doctor ride off into the sunset? And what do you mean by reverting? How does Theo revert to form?"

Santos glanced down at his watch as though checking to ensure he was on time. "We've still got a bit of time to kill and I suspect Dr. McDonald will erase your memories of this incident anyway, so why not talk? Theo was her first experiment and he's proven to be her most difficult subject. If he goes off the meds for more than a few days, his memories begin to surface. Dr. McDonald believes she's handled the problem. You see, after the incident in Colombia, she realized she had to break him or kill him. She refined the drug and the protocols involving young Taggart. She'd been too easy with him. She preferred to attempt simple psychological manipulations. I knew that wouldn't work so I gave him pain, indescribable amounts of pain. The drug made it seem longer, worse than it was, though you should know it was bad enough without the drugs."

He was a monster. "You hurt him. What did that prove?"

"Effective is what it proved to be. Once the subject realized he would die if he didn't submit, his episodes of rebellion became less and he's able to go for longer without the drug. Dr. McDonald gave him a massive dose two months ago and he's had no issues since. His memory is wiped clean. Who he was is completely gone and he will be who we train him to be."

She felt sick and it wasn't because the plane was shuddering. How could a person's memories be lost? They couldn't be completely lost. There had to be a way to bring him back. When she'd mentioned the SEALs, he'd had a reaction. That had to mean something. "So he'll go with you when you head for the hills, so to speak?"

"If by 'hill' you mean my own private island, then yes. We'll need guards we can trust and they also serve as examples of how our product works. You would be surprised at how effective a killing machine a man can be when his humanity is utterly erased. Another issue we have with Taggart. We still have issues with that pesky conscience. He was the one to cover you up and watched over you to ensure no one touched you while you were drugged. He was quite insistent. And I thought we'd been doing so well. The minute a female who isn't the doctor enters the scene, Taggart struggles to remember who he is. Robert as well. He has some of the same issues as Taggart. I've tried sex therapy with all three of our boys, attempted to get them to view women as a sexual outlet and nothing more. It hasn't gone well, though at least with Robert sex seems to ease some of his discontent. Our problem with him is entirely different. Robert wants to keep all the prostitutes we bring in like they're teddy bears or something."

She remembered how Robert had wanted to keep her, how he'd tried to hold on to her. "And Theo?"

"He won't touch them. Says they're not right."

Because they weren't Erin. Because deep down, under all the pain and drugs and treatments, he was still there and still in love with the woman who'd borne his son. "Good for Theo. I suppose Victor got an A plus in screwing over hookers."

"Victor always strangles them after he's done. Messy, but it tends to make him happy. I was the one who pointed out that perhaps selecting soldiers wasn't our best bet. Victor was my experiment. I picked him out of a prison. With no morality to wipe away, all we had to do was train him not to bite the hand that feeds. Truthfully, if I had my way, I'd terminate the other two. I still think they're dangerous but the doctor is fond of them, and harming Robert is an effective way to keep Taggart in line. Though please call him Tomas. Calling him anything else tends to give him a bad headache."

She'd never hated anyone quite the way she hated Tony in that moment. And she was a child who'd lost her parents over the greed of others. Somehow Santos's sins seemed worse. He and McDonald were keeping good men in hell so they could make a profit.

"I'll make sure not to give him anymore pain than he already has," she returned. "Should I even ask where we're going to be staying? I don't suppose it's a nice hotel."

"Hardly, but then you don't mind it much when you're fucking that boy toy of yours." Santos's eyes narrowed. "I watched you with him. Should I perhaps offer you to Theo and see if you can change his mind about sex? We know he's your type."

Case was her only type. "I'm fairly certain I'm not his."

"Still, it would be a fun way to fuck with Case Taggart. Perhaps he would enjoy a postcard with a lovely picture of you in bed with his brother."

"I'm sure he would have something to say about it." Thank god he was alive. He was alive. She could breathe again.

"So it was Case you were worried about," Santos said with a nod of his head. "You thought I'd killed him. I won't anger Ian Taggart more than my partner already has. She was insane to think she could take a Taggart brother and they wouldn't find out. Believe me, if I had a say in the matter, I would give that kid back and pray the tiger didn't strike. Perhaps one day I'll have more of a choice and then I'll make a deal with the Taggarts to end this needless war we find ourselves in."

She could read between the lines. So the minute he no longer needed the doctor, he would kill her and try to save his own skin and keep all the cash. It wouldn't work. He was severely underestimating Big Tag's desire for revenge. He wouldn't be satisfied with merely getting his brother back. He would ensure the people who'd taken Theo could never do it again.

It was the mistake Santos was making with her as well. Drew would get her back, take a deep breath, and then likely hire an assassin to murder Santos. Drew didn't forget and he never forgave.

Never.

Santos stood, stretching himself out. "As for your accommodations, well, we're going to be hosted by a clinic. I'm sick as shit of clinics, but the doc enjoys playing around with the patients. I suspect you won't be there long. I've already sent your brother a note requesting payment. Naturally he wants proof of life. We'll settle in at the clinic and then make him a little video. You'll be home in a few days and we'll have the cash we need to finish the project. Victor! Come back and keep an eye on our guest, will you?"

Great. She was getting left with the serial killer.

Theo was the one who showed up. "Sorry. Hutch is flying the plane and Robert is watching him. I'm afraid the turbulence has affected Victor. He's busy puking. I can handle one small female."

Santos stared at him. "You know Mother will be disappointed if you screw this up. She's going to meet us in a few days. That means you're under my command. If you think Mother can punish you, you don't want to know what I'll do this time."

"If you'll send me the report of how I screwed up last time, perhaps I won't do it again." Theo stood at attention, his shoulders back, his feet aligned. His handsome face was blank, but his tone firm. He was a soldier seeking orders, wanting guidance.

"Just obey and all will be well," Santos said with a shake of his head. "Watch her. It's not like she can go many places. We'll be touching down in an hour or so. Mother will meet us in a week. She's got some tests to run. Until then you're my soldiers. Is that understood?"

Theo nodded. "Yes, sir. I'll sit with her. I don't particularly like to be around the new guy. His voice makes my head hurt. I want to stay away from him at the new headquarters."

Santos touched his shoulder. "I'll see to it. Behave and you'll see that you can have many privileges, Tomas. You'll see. Everything's about to change. Once we sell her back to her brother, we'll have what we need and Mother will be happy with you. That's what you want, right?"

"Of course," Theo replied.

An hour until they reached their destination. An hour until they landed and went to meet the person who would provide them with shelter.

Was that Case's plan? She knew they'd been going to Sierra Leone. How far ahead of McDonald and Santos were they?

She had to trust in Case. She had to be ready for anything.

Most of all, she had to survive and get back to her man.

Theo sat down beside her, his body stiff.

But maybe, while she was surviving, she could help her man's brother. She stared at Theo for a moment. He was so rigid, so tense. His jaw looked like it was made of granite.

"You don't like Hutch?"

He turned, one brow rising over his eye. "He's annoying to me."

Likely because he reminded Theo that he wasn't Tomas. It wouldn't do her any good to come at the situation directly. If she did that, Theo would walk away. "Does he still like candy?"

She asked the question with a smile, with none of the seriousness of before.

Theo shook his head. "He requested sugar in the beginning. We're not allowed sugar. It's not proper in our diets. We have to be in top physical condition to do the work we do."

That was the company line. She needed to go a bit deeper. She gave him a soft smile. "I like chocolate. I can't help it. It's an addiction. But I have a friend who loves lemon. Everything lemon, especially sweets."

Big Tag was a sucker for lemon anything.

Theo's lips tugged up. "Like donuts."

Exactly like donuts. They were Ian's favorites. No matter what Santos said, Theo was still in there. "Yes, my friend loves lemon donuts. The filled kind. He's got two baby girls. They're so cute. Kala and Kenzi."

Not an ounce of recognition crossed his face. "That's nice."

"Have you ever thought about having a family?"

"I have a family. I have brothers and Mother. They're all I've ever known."

She wanted to argue with him, but that would only make him

ache. She needed to get around those harsh barricades the drugs and therapies had created. "I love my brothers."

And I love your brother so very much.

"You'll be back with them soon," he promised. "I won't allow any harm to come to you. I've already spoken to Robert. He understands you're off limits. But you need to stay away from Victor. I can try to protect you, but Victor enjoys hurting people, especially women."

Santos was high if he thought he could ever break Theo Taggart. There was a core of honor in the man that no drug could erase.

"I'll do my best," she said.

He was quiet for a moment. "Did I know Hutch?"

The hair on her arm stood up and she turned to him. He was staring straight ahead. "The new drugs don't work any better than the old ones, do they?"

"I have moments where I know I shouldn't be here," he admitted. "But don't trust me. Not for a second. I'm conditioned to respond in a certain way and often I can't help myself."

"Do you remember Erin?" She wanted to tell him that his brothers—his real brothers—were on their way. She wanted to promise him it would all be over soon. But he was right. She couldn't trust that any lucidity would last. He'd shot Case without a second thought. Just because he seemed to understand something was wrong now didn't mean he would remember it later.

His face went tight and he had to put a hand on his head again. Theo's skin flushed to a deep red and he bent over, though he made no sound at all.

She reached out, putting a hand on his leg. "I'm so sorry. Forget I said anything. Let's talk about something else."

Thinking of Erin physically hurt him. God, she had to pray that would go away once the drugs were out of his system. How would Erin handle the fact that just the thought of her made Theo ache?

He reached out and she thought he would push her away, but

his hand came over hers and threaded their fingers together, holding her tight as he seemed to ride out the end of the wretched episode.

She held on to him, giving him as much comfort as she could.

When he sat back up, he was a little pale, but he took a long breath and a smile went across his face. "That was a rough one. I get bad headaches. Mother gives me medication for them though. I'm glad to have her. I have no idea what I would do without someone watching out for me."

Her heart sank. It was like the previous moment hadn't happened.

"Yeah, you're lucky." She didn't want to cause him more pain. When she tried to pull her hand away, he squeezed it, holding her tight.

"I don't love landings. Do you mind?"

Despite the scar on his face, he looked so much like her Case in that moment that she couldn't do anything but hold on to him. "I don't like landings either."

"I feel oddly comfortable with you. Don't think I'm trying anything. I'm not. It's weird. It's like we're connected, but I don't know you."

Case had talked to her about those weird twin things. Somehow, someway, Theo was still connected to his brother. Theo could feel Case's connection to her. "I feel the same way."

"I'll protect you. It's going to be all right. What was your name again? I'm bad with names. I have short-term memory problems. Long-term ones, too. I hit my head one too many times on missions I think."

She didn't argue with him. He'd been through enough. She simply sat there and held his hand and swore that she would protect him, too.

CHAPTER SEVENTEEN

Case looked at the woman standing in front of him. They were in the office of the small private airfield outside of Freetown, Sierra Leone. She was a petite woman who he knew was thirty but somehow managed to look like she should be in college partying with her sorority sisters and cramming for midterms. Dr. Stephanie Gibson had her hair up in a ponytail, her face makeup free. She was wearing a Captain America T-shirt and jeans.

He hoped he wasn't about to get her killed.

"You sure you're up for this?"

Her brown eyes lit up. "For the whole spy thing or for getting potentially shot by super soldiers with memory issues?"

"I think the spy thing leads into the getting shot thing," Ten said with a nod as he set down a duffel bag that Case was pretty sure was filled with weapons. "So you should make sure you're ready for both. Though being bad at the spy thing could make getting shot inevitable."

"Don't scare the doc," Ian said with a frown as he strode in.

"Or I'll have to take you out meself." Liam O'Donnell followed Ian. The Irishman got a big grin on his face as he caught sight of the doctor. "Hello there, darlin'."

Stephanie smiled and practically ran into his arms. "Li! It's so good to see you. How is Avery? And the baby? She told me Aidan was having trouble with ear infections."

Li hugged her and then stepped back. "Aidan's fine. He's growing like a weed and Avery's already on me about giving him a sibling. She's going to be here in a few hours with Erin and Charlotte and Kai. I'm sorry we had to move things up on you. And Case is right to be worried. This is dangerous."

She held a hand up. "I know. I have already been lectured on what I'm supposed to do. I walk in, let them see me, maybe make some small talk, and then I hide behind my bodyguard. I'm going to be fine. You know I would do anything for Avery. Anything."

A moment passed between Li and the doctor, one Case could only guess about. Stephanie had been a kid when she'd caused the accident that had killed Avery's young husband and baby. From what he understood, the woman standing in front of him had gone into a deep decline, her guilt nearly causing her to take her own life. It had been Avery herself who brought her back, Avery who found forgiveness for a girl who'd taken everything from her.

How odd that an act of kindness so many years before would save everything Case loved now. It had been Stephanie's solid base here that had tempted McDonald to take the bait. Had Avery chosen a different path, they likely would have no chance of saving Theo in the near future.

"I'll do anything for Avery, too," Case said quietly. "And you, Doc. You can't understand how much this means to me."

Stephanie turned and gave him a smile. "I can and I'm more than happy to help. Besides I've liked having the big guy around. He's taught me some moves I didn't know and the kids adore him. Though they all swear he speaks a different language."

"Not me. I'm a right proper speaker, I am." Brody Carter leaned against the doorjamb. The Aussie was the single biggest man Case had ever seen. He had a good two inches on him and probably an extra fifty pounds of muscle.

He worked for Damon Knight out of the London offices and

when they'd decided on this course of action, they'd sent an agent down to train Stephanie and watch over her. He was undercover as her bodyguard. He'd played the heavy on occasion and cemented his reputation with the local bad guys as a man they didn't want to mess with.

He would make sure the doc didn't die in the fight they were about to go into.

"Sure you are, buddy," Ian said, shaking the big guy's hand. "And I'm not sarcastic at all."

"Everyone move back." Sean shook his head, bringing up the rear. He hefted the bag carrying the body armor they would all wear. "Lightning's about to strike. Do we have any confirmation on when they're going to land?"

"We've got roughly a half an hour to set up," Brody replied. "I've already dealt with the locals. They've been paid and they agreed to stay in the mechanic's office. I pulled all their mobiles and there's no Internet access. I locked them in with an Xbox and two bottles of rum, so they're perfectly happy."

"Smart man," Ian said. "Lawless will pay for any damage to the structure. You explained that to them?"

Brody nodded. "They're good. The rest is just me being cautious. We won't have trouble with the locals. You get the memo I sent?"

Case nodded. Once Brody had been notified that the op was being moved up and changing locations, he'd quickly sent them a detailed report on the small private airport Santos was using to smuggle Mia into the country.

Luckily Brody had known the exact place since he was Santos's contact. Santos was expecting Doctor Stephanie Gibson and her enforcer to meet them in half an hour. Stephanie was to be paid more for not asking questions about the blonde they were bringing with them.

"Do we have any idea if Theo's on that plane?" Sean asked.

It was what they'd worried about on the long flight over. They'd taken the 4L jet, which moved far faster than the cargo plane Santos had hired. Santos's plane had required a refuel. The high-tech Bond Aeronautics jet Drew flew on had not. They'd beaten Santos in, but they'd been forced to come with a smaller team than Case would have liked. Now the plane was hidden in a separate hanger.

"I couldn't exactly ask him. I only know that he's bringing five people with him and we needed to provide him with a place to lock someone down for a few days. Where's the spook? Shouldn't he have some intel?" Brody asked. "And who's the suit? I don't recognize him."

Case looked out to see who Brody was talking about. Drew Lawless was stepping off the plane. It had been a fight to keep it down to one Lawless brother, but space had been an issue or they would have brought Alex and Jake along with them. Simon would fly them in later this afternoon along with the women and Kai, but hopefully the deed would be done by then.

He prayed it would be done. The alternative was they failed and Santos managed to get away with Mia. He would run with her and possibly decide she wasn't worth the trouble. He could dispose of her like so much rubbish and try to find an easier mark.

His body ached at the thought of her cold and unmoving. Mia was so alive. He needed to see her again, needed to hold her so he could assure himself she was alive. "That's Mia's brother and the CIA asshole is still on the plane trying to download some Agency reports. He said Chelsea was sending him some intel and DC had a message for him."

Kent was putting his career on the line.

"Or he's doing secretive shit that will blow back in our faces," Ian muttered.

His brother wasn't a fan.

Ten slid the zipper on the duffel open and started to unload a seemingly endless supply of weapons. "I don't think so. He was kind of legendary in the Agency. Very private dude. He was the agent you would send to study other agents and take care of them if they needed to be taken care of. I never met him but I knew his boss. Good man. Kent was a little like his Big Tag. The operative he could count on. I suspect that's the only reason he didn't get burned after the stunt he pulled with the general."

The fact that Ten could call the assassination of a man a "stunt" made Case feel good about having gotten out when he had. "I feel comfortable with Kent. And if he steps out of line, I'll feel comfortable murdering him."

"That's my baby brother." Sean high-fived him. "If it means anything, I think Kent's on the up and up. I was watching him on the ride over and he seems solid."

"And like you said, if he's not solid, we can turn him into a liquid," Ian said with a nod as he looked to the door. "Speak of the devil. What do you have for us?"

Kent walked in, Lawless hard on his heels. The billionaire looked worse for the wear, but Case would give it to him. The man wasn't about to stand down. He was willing to go to the ends of the earth to save his sister.

"Mia's on the plane," Lawless said, his eyes on the guns on the table.

Kent placed his laptop on the desk. "She was caught on a private airfield camera being carried onto the cargo plane. Chelsea used that big brain of hers to figure out where they would have taken off from and cut into their security feeds." He turned the laptop toward them. "And look who's carrying her onto the plane."

Case breathed a deep sigh of relief. There was no way to mistake his brother's familiar face. Theo was cradling Mia's still form in his arms, holding her close to his chest. Theo had Mia.

"What the fuck happened to his face?" Sean had flushed a nice shade of red.

Case felt his heart twist a little. Kent had frozen the screen and magnified the image. There was a horrific scar splitting his twin's left cheek. Someone had fileted his brother's face, but it wouldn't matter. Erin wouldn't care. Nothing mattered except the fact that he was alive and he was watching over Mia. Case would bet that scar was there because Theo had protected Mia before. While Case had been watching over Theo's son, Theo had taken pain for Case's wife.

Why the hell was the world going blurry?

"He's going to take care of her." Ian put a hand on Case's shoulder. "She's going to be okay."

"They couldn't break him." Sean stood at his other side.

His brothers, surrounding him with support. Why had he ever fought this? Why had he thought for a second that he didn't need these men in his life, to mentor him, to fight beside him, to be his brothers? He'd fought them. He'd wanted to remain the leader. Years he'd spent being the leader of the two of them—him and Theo. He'd wanted that to stay the same, but god, it was so much better now. He wasn't alone. He didn't have to be perfect. He just had to be here.

He'd spent years struggling, years when it had only been him and Theo, but now any way he turned he saw someone who gave a shit about him. They were obnoxious and loud and insane and they were his freaking family. Every single one of them.

"His face doesn't matter." Case had never been more sure about anything in his life. "All that matters is Mia and Theo and Hutch."

Sean nodded. "All that matters is getting our people back."

Kent flipped the laptop back around and stared down at the screen, his hands moving on the keyboard. "They refueled in Morocco and according to satellite data they should be landing soon. But there's some bad news. Dr. McDonald isn't on the plane. We have no idea where she is and she'll very likely figure out her whole operation has been compromised quickly. My boss wants to stand down and allow McDonald to join her crew before moving in."

Ten sighed. "Damn it. Why isn't she with them? We need that intel. We need to apprehend McDonald or she'll just set up another clinic in another country and continue her research."

Stephanie stepped up. "I'm ready. Brody and I have been working the last couple of weeks to make sure we can deal with this situation."

Brody stood beside the doctor, his big frame looming over hers. "We've got the rooms ready and everything. You can monitor the situation while we wait for McDonald."

"No." Lawless faced the big Aussie. "I'm not going to let my sister stay here. If you won't save her, I'll walk away right fucking now and hire someone who will." He turned to Case. "Come on. I'll get you all the backing you could hope for, Case."

He'd come a long way with that family. The fact that Drew Lawless just assumed immediately that Case's first priority would be Mia meant he'd properly settled into his role as Mia's future husband.

"We're not going anywhere," Ian said. "Stop slinging your big old wallet dick around. You should know that we're backing Case and Case won't allow his wife to be used as a pawn."

"Or my brother." It seemed like everyone knew him pretty well. It settled something deep inside him. Mia was almost here and she knew him, too. She would be waiting for him to save her. She wouldn't be crying in a corner and praying. She would know damn straight that her man would come for her.

His only problem would be the fact that his Mia would try to look out for his brother and Hutch, too. She was fierce and she would be a warrior.

Kent looked at him. "You know what you're giving up."

Revenge on Hope McDonald. It was an easy choice to make. Revenge or his loved ones. He would choose them every single time. "I know that I'm getting my wife and brother and friend back. That's a good fucking day in my books."

Kent nodded. "Well, I'm sure I can figure out a way to explain it all to my boss. I'll probably get stuck with babysitting duty for a few years, but I've gotten used to Dallas."

Brody got a big smile on his face and he put a hand on Stephanie's shoulder. "Told you we wouldn't really be needed, luv."

Stephanie grinned up at him. "He did. He got the report this morning and told me my time as a spy was almost done. It sucks. I was so ready to play Mata Hari. I was going to seduce someone."

Kent frowned at her. "I don't think you want to seduce any of those guys. One of them was in prison for murder, two of them probably qualify as mentally ill at this point, and Santos was a walking venereal disease when he was with the Agency. Now he's a traitorous walking venereal disease."

Stephanie sighed. "It seems so glamorous in the movies. Like that one about Pierce Craig."

Everyone else groaned but Ian perked up. "I know. That dude's awesome, right?"

Sean's eyes rolled. "I curse the day Serena sold that book to Hollywood."

Because that book had been loosely based on Ian's life and Ian never let them forget it. Luckily that one had a happy ending.

"Let's suit up. This is going down soon," Case said.

He was going to make sure this op ended happily, too.

* * * *

Mia was shaking by the time the plane taxied toward the hanger. Cargo planes didn't land quite the same way corporate jets did.

"You all right?" If Theo had been bothered by the landing, she couldn't tell. He seemed perfectly steady.

She was fairly certain she'd gone a nice shade of green. She managed to nod his way. "I'm good. Do you think I could get some clothes soon?"

He grinned. "I was going to ask you why you were in a robe. Are you one of the girls Tony brings in? Robert's going to love you, but you have to stay away from Victor. He's my brother and I care about him, of course, but he's not great with women."

She bit back a groan. This was what it was like to talk to Theo. He seemed almost normal one minute and then he forgot what she'd told him not ten minutes before. The only thing he seemed to keep a firm grasp on were his orders. He hadn't left her side once. She'd even tried to ask for things like a bottle of water to see if she could get a minute or two alone, but he wouldn't move.

"Maybe you should stay close to me," Theo said, his voice grim.

"I will." She was definitely going to try.

The plane rolled to a stop and Mia's stomach took a dive. They were here. She had no idea how long it would take Case to reevaluate and reorganize the operation, but she was sure he would be here as soon as he could. It was up to her to stay alive until then.

That's all she had to do. Stay alive.

"Tony wants us to gather our gear and get ready," a dark voice said.

She looked up and it seemed as though Victor had gotten over his motion sickness. He loomed over her, his eyes staring down.

Theo stood up. "I've got my bag. I'll handle the girl. Why don't you grab the computer equipment?"

"The geek's getting that," Victor said dismissively. "He's going to take care of the plane and then grab all his crap. I don't know why we haven't killed him yet."

"Because none of the rest of us can do what he does," Theo replied simply. "Mother wants him alive. He stays alive."

She saw Hutch move through the plane's wide hold. He was thinner than she remembered and there was a hollow look to his eyes. He stared at her for a moment before grabbing a bag and turning his back.

What had he gone through? Something horrible, certainly. It was like his light had gone out and he was a husk of his old self, walking around.

She wanted to call out to him, to say something, but Victor was watching her like a rabid lion waiting to pounce.

"Stay away from the girl." Santos strode from the front of the plane. He had a shoulder holster over his bulky body and Mia could see the big gun nestled in there. It looked like Santos was ready for a fight since he also had an AR-15 in his hands. "I told you she's off limits. She's worth more alive than dead. A lot more. If you touch her, I'll cut off your balls and feed them to you."

Victor's body went rigid. "Yes, sir."

Theo turned and offered her a hand up. "I'll find something for you to wear."

"But she's so pretty like that." Robert was armed to the teeth, too. He settled a light jacket over his torso, but she'd seen the guns he was wearing. "And I've heard it's pretty hot where we're going. Although it might be fun to dress her. I think she'd look good in blue."

Dear lord, now she was going to be Robert's Barbie doll. Still, she was surrounded by men with guns who might or might not know what they were doing. She gave him a smile. "Blue's my favorite color."

She was going to have to depend on Theo and Robert's better natures. Victor didn't have one and Santos would kill her the minute she wasn't worth more alive than dead. And she wasn't sure what was going on with Hutch. He seemed so different. She would do anything she could to save him, but she wasn't going to count on him.

"Stop playing with the girl. We need to move. It looks like our contacts are here. Victor, finish securing the plane. We paid enough for it. It will be good to have a way out of here if we need it. Especially now that we have a pilot. I think Mr. Hutchins has been properly trained."

"A few years of torture will do that to a guy," Hutch muttered under his breath as he walked by.

So they'd done to him what they'd done to Tennessee Smith. The drug in small doses made hours seem like days, made the smallest pain into something monstrous. One of the potential future uses of the drug was in prison systems, to ensure criminals did their "time" but to keep crowding to a minimum. The prisoner would experience the time as if it was going by, but would come out of the drug's influence to find only weeks had passed.

Hutch had gone through that. There was no telling how much

pain he'd experienced.

"Let's go and meet Dr. Gibson," Santos said. "She's off limits, too, but you can do what you like with the villagers around the clinic. I know you boys need to blow off some steam. Just wait until Mother gets here in a few days. She'll wipe the girls' memories so there won't be trouble."

Awesome. Now McDonald was wiping the memories of the victims of rape.

"I'll make sure she has plenty of test subjects." Victor winked Mia's way, sending a shiver down her spine.

Theo put a hand on her arm. "Come on. Stay close to me or Robert and you'll be all right. Don't talk to the new guys. Tony won't like it. We'll have you in a room to yourself very soon. One of us will make sure to watch over you the whole time."

Until they forgot to. She was going to figure out a way to defend herself. She silently thanked Ezra for all the training. After what happened in Colombia, she'd realized she'd panicked, and no amount of self-defense lessons could fix that. So Ezra trained her, made her stronger, more confident. If Victor thought she'd be an easy mark, he would find out she was a quick learner.

She followed Robert off the plane, her bare feet hitting the metal of the stairs that led to the concrete floor. She was in some sort of hanger, out of sight. Hutch was standing to the side, his gaze on the two people waiting to greet them. His eyes were wide and his shoulders had straightened.

He recognized them. Or at least one of them. Her heart started to pound. How far gone was Hutch? How much had they brainwashed him? She knew he hadn't had the same protocols and memory wipes as Theo and the soldiers, but he was obviously complying with orders. Would he give up the game? Would he call out and tell Santos what was happening?

Hutch's eyes averted, but he didn't say anything.

Yet.

"Hello," the brunette with the ponytail said. "I was surprised that you moved up our agreed upon date."

She was frowning, her hands on her hips. It was probably easy to be aggressive when one had a massive, truly scary-looking dude by her side. The man standing next to the doctor was a mountain of muscle with what looked like a bad attitude. He had a gun on his hip and he wasn't trying to hide it.

Santos shrugged and seemed to attempt to look charming. "You know how these things go. Sometimes opportunity knocks and we must answer the door. I explained that we would certainly be more than happy to give you a small percentage of our latest endeavor."

Yeah, Mia just bet they would. Or they would put a bullet through the doc and take over her clinic. She doubted there was truly honor among these thieves. If Hope McDonald thought her research would be served by murdering her business partners, she would do it in a heartbeat.

"Is everything arranged?" Santos asked, looking around.

The doctor nodded. "Of course. We've got a small holding cell for your new friend. I take it Dr. McDonald isn't with you. I was so hoping to meet her."

"We all were," the mountain said in a thick Aussie accent. "She's kind of become legend around these parts. There's apparently a bunch of people in Liberia who definitely know her name."

McDonald's first trials had been on unsuspecting patients at her sister's clinic in Liberia. Faith McDonald Smith had thought she was saving a small part of the world and her sister had been using her patients.

Santos's eyes tightened slightly and that relaxed set to his body suddenly wasn't so casual. "She'll be along in a few days. I'm surprised. I thought there would be a few locals. Don't we need someone to help with the plane? We need to make sure it's ready to go at all times. That was part of our arrangement."

The mountain moved in front of the doctor as though he could sense the change in Santos, too. "We thought you would want privacy for the girl."

They stared at each other for a moment.

What was happening? Mia's heart threatened to beat out of her chest. There was some tension running through the room that she didn't understand.

"Tomas, would you please escort our guest back on the plane. Now." The gun made an appearance.

Theo's arm went tight around her waist and he started to back up.

What? Why were they getting back on the plane? She couldn't get back on the plane. Case would come for her here. If she got back on that plane, he wouldn't know where she was.

"Why? What's wrong? Our orders were to settle in here and wait for Mother." Theo simply picked her up when Mia tried to drag him down.

"This isn't right. Something's off. I don't think we're alone," Santos said.

"Well, you always did have excellent instincts, you fucker." Ezra stepped out from behind a barricade of boxes.

She felt her eyes widen. "Ezra?"

Santos, Theo, and Robert suddenly had guns pointed at her bodyguard, who was likely going to give her a pretty stern lecture.

"Ezra was his brother," Santos said, his eyes firmly on his target.

The mountain of man with the doctor backed away, covering her as they retreated to what looked to be an office. When the door opened, she saw someone she never expected to see.

Her brother was standing there. Drew was here in Africa, waiting for her.

That meant Case was here. Tears pricked her eyes. He'd come for her. He was here and now she could practically feel him.

"Give me the girl. I brought her brother with me. We can split the money. He's ready to transfer funds as we speak. You don't give me the girl and that big guy will kill Drew Lawless and you get nothing," Ezra said, his voice flat.

She went still. Could he be telling the truth?

Santos's whole body was tense, ready for action. "I'm supposed to believe you're turning on the Agency for money?"

Ezra didn't seem freaked out to have so many guns on him. He strode forward. "Why not? I'm never getting back in the field. Fuck 'em. Isn't that what you said? I thought about trying to get my hands on the drug, but there's too much heat on McDonald. So when I realized you'd nabbed Mia, I decided it was time to make some cash. It was easy to tell her brother that I would arrange the transfer. He got on the plane himself. And it was very easy to figure out that you had to be dealing with Dr. Gibson. The Agency's been looking into her, by the way. We suspect her of arms dealing."

Bullshit. This was Case's plan. What was Ezra doing?

He was trying to get her out of the line of fire. Case was trying to ensure her safety before he fought for his brother.

It would have been easier for the Taggart brothers to simply overwhelm them. They would have had the element of surprise, but Case had chosen to risk the entire operation to ensure she wouldn't be stuck in the middle of it.

He was choosing her. Somewhere in this big hanger was a superhot cowboy who was so getting laid as soon as they got out of this mess.

He was getting married, too, because she was never letting that man go.

"Yes, she's in trouble with some of her clients," Santos replied. "It's why she was willing to cut a deal with us."

"Now she's cut a deal with me because I might have mentioned just how big this deal would be. They were surprised since you'd promised them a five percent cut of a million. All I had to do was mention that 4L Software was involved and suddenly they were very open to a new partnership." Ezra clapped his hands together. "So what do you say? Let's reunite brother and sister and get this thing done. He won't transfer the money until he's with her. Let her join him in the office and we'll talk about how we're going to split the money. Let one of your guards take her. How about the blond one?"

Theo stiffened behind her. "I can handle that asshole."

Santos moved back, though he never took his eyes off Ezra. "I suspect there's more than one asshole waiting for you. Damn it. Does the bitch have a tracker on her? I never thought to look."

"Give me the girl, Santos, and you might make it out of here alive." Ezra lined up his shot.

"Back in the plane, boys. We're leaving now," Santos ordered.

A shot crashed through the hanger and Ezra's body jerked around and he went to the ground as Theo dragged her back. Victor was on the stairs of the plane and he hopped down, ready to fire again.

Ezra was down. Oh god. She hoped Case stayed somewhere safe. She was right back where she'd been in Colombia and all she wanted was for Case to be safe. She would go with Santos, do anything, endure anything so Case would live.

And she suddenly realized he was out there thinking the same damn thing.

Case wasn't going to protect himself. He was about to make himself a big damn target. And that meant she couldn't get on that plane.

Ezra sat up and took his own shot and then chaos reigned.

Her world suddenly filled with gunfire as the team came out of hiding. She caught sight of Sean and Ian Taggart, but she didn't see Case.

He would be there. He would be right in the thick of the fight.

Theo's arm tightened around her waist and he hauled her up and back as he began to retreat.

To her right, Robert rolled away, firing as he looked for cover.

She had to get to cover, too. She needed to get to that office. It was where Ezra wanted her to go so that meant it was where Case wanted her. Out of the action so he could do his job.

He would sacrifice Theo to save her. She had to take herself out of the equation so her man never had to make that choice. She loved him too much to make him sacrifice.

Unfortunately, that meant getting the fuck away from Theo.

"Stay calm," Theo whispered in her ear. "I'll have you safe in a moment."

Theo popped off two quick rounds his oldest brother's way. Ian Taggart moved quickly for a big man. He rolled off to his left to the safety of cover the Humvee he'd been hiding behind offered.

Theo was the real danger because no one was willing to take him out, but he was damn good at his job.

She thought about everything Ezra had taught her. Defense wasn't hot. It wasn't emotional. It was a cool decision to win a battle.

She let Theo drag her, giving him nothing at all to work with but her dead weight.

"Damn it." Theo forced her up, managing to get her to the stairs.

Mia watched as Victor laid out a pattern of fire to allow Theo to haul her up. She brought her elbow up and back, hitting his solar plexus hard. Mia's knees hit the concrete. No time for pain, though it flared through her system. She had to make it to that door where the intensely large Aussie was no doubt holding her brother back. Thank god. The last thing she needed was Drew out here trying to get to her.

She shoved off the ground, trying to sprint for the door.

An arm wound around her, dragging her back up. "We have to get back to the plane."

He was so stubborn. Just like his brother.

"Erin! Erin loves you. Erin misses you so much," she screamed over the wail of gunfire.

It was mean, but she knew how to hurt him. Nothing affected him so much as the very sound of Erin's name. She heard him hiss, but he kept moving. He dragged her up the stairs.

"Erin had your baby, Theo. She had your son and she's on her way here." She couldn't let up. She wasn't as strong as Theo, but she had other weapons at her disposal. "Erin wants to see you so badly."

He stumbled back, briefly letting her go.

She immediately took off. The office. She had to make it there. If she could only make it there.

A dark object came out of nowhere, shoving straight into her gut. She heard someone scream, a masculine voice calling out her name. But she was falling backward, all the air whooshing from her lungs in a single, painful rush. She felt herself hit the ground and then she was looking up, the world a bit unfocused as Theo gripped her, hauled her up. Someone—she thought it was Robert—was giving him cover. Her world upended as Theo tossed her over his shoulder like a bag of grain. She had the briefest glance at what was happening around her and then her whole world stilled, slowing down and focusing on one point. Case. He was running toward her, his face a mask of horror as he tried to get to her.

And then he stopped and dropped to the ground as a bullet hit him squarely in the chest.

Mia screamed as she watched him fall.

Theo moved more quickly this time. Mia used her fists, pounding at his back, her only thought to get back to Case. She held her head up, trying to see what the hell was happening. The gunfire was rapid, filling the world with rage. She watched as Victor's head ripped back and his body fell. Liam O'Donnell was advancing, a gun in his hand as he took down Victor and seemed to be heading toward Case's body.

His body. That had been a solid heart shot.

Someone was screaming. They were louder than the damn gunfire. That wail was terrible and she tried to close her ears to it.

"Please stop." Theo shoved her down on the seat she'd occupied before. "Stop screaming."

She looked up at him. His face was white and there was blood on his shirt. She wasn't sure where it had come from.

"Theo, please." Her voice sounded cracked and tortured even to her own ears. "You have to help Case. Your brother is out there. Please." She couldn't stop the tears that were streaming down her face. "Please help him. Let me go to him. I love your brother so much."

"Hutch, get this bird started," Theo said, holding his head. "We have to get out of here."

She hadn't realized Hutch had gotten back on the plane. He was standing there, his eyes completely hollow.

Santos stepped in, firing out the door of the plane. "Get us moving, now."

Theo turned back. "Sir, Robert isn't here."

"Robert's been shot and Victor's dead. Get this fucking plane moving or we will be, too." Santos fired out again.

She looked up at Theo. "Please. That's your family out there. They're trying so hard to get you back, to save you. Please don't let them take us again. Your brother is lying out there. Your twin. His name is Case and I love him. You have a woman who loves you. You have Erin."

"I don't know who the fuck you're talking about," Theo growled. "I don't know anyone named Erin. Stop it. Stop talking. It hurts."

It sounded like the world was coming to an end outside the airplane.

She couldn't stop. Santos was pulling the stairs up. It was obvious he'd been hit, but he was still moving.

He closed the door and turned that gun on Hutch. "Get us out of here or I'll kill you." He turned toward Mia. "As for you…I'm going to shove your dead body out at our next stop and maybe then they'll think about fucking with me."

He lifted the gun and Mia knew she was about to die. She took a deep breath and all she could think about was Case—the way he'd held her, the way he'd touched her, those messages on her phone, how he'd held them together even over the distance. She'd been loved. It was all that mattered. She could see him again. She could be with Case.

And then Santos stopped, his body shaking as he looked down at the bullet that pierced his chest. He stared at it dumbly before looking up at Theo. His mouth moved, but it made no sound, and he finally hit his knees and then the floor.

Theo stared for a moment as though he couldn't believe he'd pulled the trigger on his own teammate. His face was pale as he turned to her.

"I'll get you to Mother. She'll know what to do. Hutch, we need to leave."

His inner soul, that piece of himself that lay unchanged, couldn't handle allowing her to die, but he reverted to his training very quickly.

Hutch groaned. "Or you can take a fucking nap."

Hutch brought the case he was carrying down on Theo's head. Theo spun and then slid to the ground, unconscious.

Hutch stared down at him. "I've wanted to do that every fucking day for months. He's the most obnoxious Patty Hearst clone in the history of fucking time. I want a goddamn milkshake and a fucking raise."

Her hands were shaking as she stood.

The door came open with a thud. "Mia!"

Case rushed in, his eyes wide as he looked for her.

She stood and found herself in his arms in a heartbeat. "I thought you were dead."

He held her tight. "Body armor, princess. I don't leave home without it. I get shot way too often to do anything else."

Ian Taggart's massive body came through next. "Who killed the douchebag?"

"Theo did," Hutch said. "He wouldn't let him kill Mia, but then he was an asshole and I knocked him out. My shit better be where I left it."

Ian put a hand on his shoulder. "Everything was taken care of, brother. And I've got a pound of Milk Duds calling your name. Come on, man. Doc is looking at the wounded. I want her to take a look at you, too."

"I love you," Case said, wrapping his arms around her. "I thought I was going to die without you."

All that mattered was she was alive and in his arms.

CHAPTER EIGHTEEN

Case didn't mind the ache in his chest. It just proved he was alive and that no matter how good the body armor, a bullet to the chest still hurt like hell. All that mattered was the woman in his arms. He sat with Ian, Ten, Liam, Drew, and Kai around a small conference table that the hotel they were staying at had offered them. The hotel was being very accommodating, likely since they were taking up more than half the rooms. Since the women had gotten in, Riley and Bran Lawless had shown up, and they'd had to deal with a couple of Kent's CIA pals who weren't particularly happy with how he'd handled the situation.

The one person who was not in the country? Hope McDonald. She'd gone deep and Case was worried it would be a while before she surfaced again.

Mia cuddled against him as Kai continued his lecture.

"What Theo needs is a little time to allow the drug to get out of his system." Kai looked like he hadn't slept for days. "He's calm right now, but I think we should wait until we're about to head home before letting Erin get close to him."

Ian frowned. "Do you know what that woman can do to you?

You're telling her that. Not me. Sean's with her right now. I could have him tell her. He doesn't need his balls anymore. Grace is pregnant for the last time, he tells me. Charlie wants a big family and I want way more boys out of that woman."

Sean was with the women, talking to home and visiting with their families. It would be another few days before they could go home, so Sean and Erin and Charlotte were using the Internet to talk to their kids. Even when their babies couldn't talk back. He'd been surprised Ian had made this meeting, but then Kai had said it was important.

Theo was in trouble.

Kai rolled his eyes. "I think I can explain it to her. He's in a precarious state right now. When he came to he tried to get away. I had to sedate him again. I need a few days with him. I think it's going to help that Robert will survive. Stephanie was able to stop the bleeding. I've got them in the same room. Being near him seems to calm Theo."

The idea that some person he didn't even know could calm his brother down rankled. He'd been to visit Theo, but his brother hadn't known him, hadn't remembered a thing. He'd stared at Case for a while and then seemed to be in some sort of pain and Kai had asked him to leave.

He'd gotten his brother's body back, but he wasn't so sure about his soul. It seemed so very far away.

Mia's hands ran over his shoulders, soothing him.

"Don't you think you should sit in your own seat?" Drew hadn't gone home yet. His future brother-in-law seemed damn determined to stick around until his sister was ready to go home, too.

Didn't he have like revenge or something to plan? The ruthless bastard seemed to have forgotten that he had his own life.

Case tightened his arms around her. He wasn't letting her out of his sight or his lap. He needed her. "She's fine where she is."

Mia chuckled and cuddled against him. "I'm afraid it's going to be a while before I'm willing to disconnect. I thought I watched him die. I need to keep hands on him."

He was all about keeping his hands on her. It had been two days since he'd seen her being hauled away by his brother in the middle of a firefight. Two days since he'd been sure he was going to have to kill Theo to save his wife. It felt like a lifetime. He'd had to watch as Theo was shackled to a bed because they were worried he would run away.

He wished they'd done the same for Hutch.

"Do we have any intel on where Hutch went?"

Ten ran his hands over the keys of his computer. "I tracked him into Europe and then he disappeared. I've got some feelers out, but the Agency is pretty damn pissed at us right now. Damon is going to keep his ears open, too. I think we can bet that Kent is going to go quiet for a while. So I'll have to try to find Hutch myself."

Ian groaned. "Do what you have to do. I know he's hurting but he needs his fucking family right now. If I have to drag his ass home, I'll do it."

"Me, too." Case wasn't about to leave Hutch out there on his own.

Mia sat up. "So Ezra's in trouble? I mean Kent. The Agency isn't going to burn him, are they?"

"If they do, he can come and work for me," Drew offered. "He did a damn fine job trying to save you. He's got a place at 4L."

"Or he can remain with the CIA." The last thing Case wanted was Kent hanging around his girl. He was grateful to the guy and all, but he wanted Mia to himself. He had to head to New York in a few weeks to help her brothers take down their enemies, but he couldn't share her with anyone else.

She wanted a big white wedding.

He intended to get her drunk in Vegas and make sure she was his forever.

"He's pretty good at talking his way out of things," Ten said. "And I'm going to back him up."

Ian sighed and sat back in his chair. "They're planning on

blaming me. I'm willing to take that particular flack. If the Agency no longer wants to work with us, I'll cry into my beer. By the way, I'm going to go find a beer. We're all going to need one since it seems like Theo is playing out his own personal version of *Memento*."

Kai held up a hand. "His short-term memory is already better. Long term is going to take a while. But my PTSD protocols call for a few days when he doesn't have to think about what happened. He needs to distance himself. We'll let him rest and then take him and Robert back to Dallas. This is a long-term project."

"But he's alive," Mia whispered.

She was his light. She always pointed out the important things. Theo was alive. They had won the fight for his body. Now they started the battle for his soul.

It was one he was sure they would win because Theo had a lot of love around him.

Case kissed his almost wife. "And we'll bring him back."

There were tears in her eyes, but she was obviously resolute. "Yes, we will."

She would be there. He wasn't alone.

"We will bring Theo back," Ian reiterated. "All the way home."

Case held on to Mia and realized he would never be alone again.

* * * *

A week later, Tomas sat in the hotel bar, a beer in front of him. Theo. He forced himself to remember. His name was Theo. "I like this?"

He understood that he'd been conditioned to respond in certain ways. Apparently he had a whole other life outside of Mother.

The man who was said to be his twin brother had told him that calling "that woman" Mother was super creepy and more than a little perverted.

Theo wasn't sure that Case Taggart was really his twin. After all, he was way more attractive.

But he definitely liked Mia. She was sweet. He wasn't attracted to her on any level. She felt like a sister. Which was good because according to the reports he'd been given, she was about to be his sister-in-law.

He'd always said he had a type. When asked to describe his type, he's always said he would know her when he saw her.

Of course his version of "always" apparently was about a year.

His life was kind of confusing.

"Yes," his twin said, slapping the bar with his hand. "You like beer. And bourbon, but we're going to start with beer. From what I can tell it's been over a year since you had alcohol so we're starting light."

Robert had already hoisted his glass and taken a drink. "I do like it."

He felt better with Robert around. He knew somewhere deep inside that he'd killed Victor. He'd been taught that Victor was his brother, but he'd always known there was a darkness in that asshole that went way beyond brotherhood. No amount of drugs and torture could make him think that Victor was a reasonable human being.

He'd read the reports of his torture, too. Apparently under hypnosis he talked a lot. He had a whole life that had been taken from him. Kai had told him that. He was learning to trust the dude with the ponytail. He was pretty cool.

Kai had told him he didn't need to follow Mother's orders anymore. He didn't have to follow anyone's order according to Kai.

He both liked that idea and was totally terrified by it.

New experiences. He needed them. The last few days had been illuminating. He was remembering more and that felt good. According to Kai, his memory should get better every day. Maybe in a few days he would remember his own fucking name and Tomas…Theo…was calling it a damn win.

He stared down at the amber liquid and made his decision. Decision. It was kind of cool to make a few of those himself. He couldn't recall a time when he'd made his own decisions.

Shouldn't he make his own decisions about food and whether or not he wanted a beer?

It was stupid, but it stressed him out.

Still, he was going in. It was time. He was a freaking man and he wanted to see if he liked beer.

Why was one beer such a damn hassle? Robert seemed perfectly happy. He was following Case and the other Taggarts around like an overgrown puppy.

Drink the damn beer.

He took the tankard in hand. It was cool, the glass nice under his skin. He brought it to his lips and took a sip.

Not bad. He could get used to it.

Case was staring at him like he was a toddler taking his first steps.

Theo nodded. "It's good."

Case hopped off his barstool. "I told you."

He would have said something, but he caught sight of someone he hadn't seen before. His twin was a massive man and he tended to take up all the space. Now he saw what Case's big body had covered up.

A woman sat at the end of the bar, a glass in front of her. Fiery red hair curled around her shoulders and she was wearing a white tank top and jeans.

Oh, that was his type. Fuck, yeah.

"I'm going to make sure the car is on its way," Case said. "You ready to head home?"

He was going back to Dallas. Why could he remember Dallas and not that he'd lived there? He could get a picture in his head of a house with a fire pit and comfy chairs, but he couldn't say he'd lived there.

He was all kinds of fucked up.

He gave his twin a smile that didn't reach anywhere close to his soul. "Sure."

Case took a deep breath. "Don't run away. I'll be back."

"Where does he think we'll go?" Robert asked as Case walked out.

Theo understood the issues. "I think he worries we'll run out because we want to get back to Moth…Hope McDonald."

Robert shivered. "I don't want to go back to Mother. She was mean. Best thing I ever did was get shot all to hell by your brothers. They're nice. And I totally like beer. And Xbox. War is way more fun in a video game."

He heard his brother, but his eyes were on the girl. He had no idea why he was different. Victor and Robert had been sex crazed. They'd been utterly desperate to have a woman, but Theo hadn't felt the pull.

Until now.

"Holy shit," Robert whispered. "She's nice. I think I'm going to go talk to her. We have an hour or so."

Rage welled. He wasn't sure where it came from but he had to tamp it down because he suddenly wanted to rip Robert's throat out. "No. I think that one is mine."

Robert's eyes went wide. "Seriously?"

Such a pretty girl…

The words swept over him and he shivered for a moment, a memory shimmering like a ghost he couldn't catch.

He shook it off. The dude with the ponytail had told him that for now he shouldn't try to remember. For now he should try to find the present. There would be time enough to find his past.

That girl at the end of the bar looked like a damn fine present.

"Yes. I'm calling dibs." He grabbed his beer and tried to find his swagger. He moved down to the seat next to hers.

Red hair, pretty skin. She looked a little lonely. Maybe he could fix that. He gave her what he hoped was his brightest smile. "Hi, my name is…Theo."

She turned to him and he saw a sheen of tears in her eyes.

Such a pretty girl…don't cry. You never cry.

He shoved the thought away because he could feel the migraine coming on. He didn't want that. He wanted to sit and talk to the pretty girl—the only girl to catch his eye that he could ever remember.

She thrust her hand out. "Hi, my name is Erin."

A pain flashed in his head. He forced it back. It wasn't going to control him. He took her hand in his.

Erin was a nice name.

Theo, Erin, and the rest of the McKay-Taggart crew will return in *Submission Is Not Enough.*

And Case and Mia will be joining the Lawless brothers in New York City in *Ruthless*, coming out August 4, 2016.

AUTHOR'S NOTE

I'm often asked by generous readers how they can help get the word out about a book they enjoyed. There are so many ways to help an author you like. Leave a review. If your e-reader allows you to lend a book to a friend, please share it. Go to Goodreads and connect with others. Recommend the books you love because stories are meant to be shared. Thank you so much for reading this book and for supporting all the authors you love!

Sign up for Lexi Blake's newsletter
and be entered to win a $25 gift certificate
to the bookseller of your choice.

Join us for news, fun, and exclusive content
including free short stories.

There's a new contest every month!

Go to www.LexiBlake.net to subscribe.

SUBMISSION IS NOT ENOUGH

Masters and Mercenaries, Book 12
By Lexi Blake
Coming October 18, 2016

A fallen hero reborn

Theo Taggart lost everything the night he died. His family, his beautiful Erin, and worst of all, he lost himself. A twisted doctor brought him back from the brink of death, but reprogrammed his identity to serve her will. Rescued by his brothers, he must fight to reclaim the man he was and the life, and love, that were stolen from him.

A love worth fighting for

Erin Argent thought she'd lost Theo forever. When he walked back into her life, it was nothing short of a miracle. Months of torture and conditioning at the hands of Dr. Hope McDonald have done damage to Theo that may never be mended. He has no memory of her or the life they shared. Breaking through to him, and helping him rediscover all he lost, will be the toughest mission she's ever faced. Luckily for Theo, Erin loves a good fight.

Their reunion under siege

Unfortunately, Hope is far from done with Theo Taggart. Obsessed with her prize experiment, she will do anything to get him back. If the only way to finally break him of his past life is to kill Erin and his son, then she's only too happy to oblige…

RUTHLESS

A Lawless Novel
By Lexi Blake
Coming August 9, 2016

The first in a sexy contemporary romance series featuring the Lawless siblings...

The Lawless siblings are bound by vengeance. Riley, Drew, Brandon, and Mia believe the CEO of StratCast orchestrated their parents' murder twenty years ago to steal their father's software program. And there's only one way Riley can find some solid evidence...

Heir to the StratCast legacy, Ellie Stratton hires a new attorney to handle a delicate business matter—and she's shocked by her attraction to him. Over the course of a few weeks, Riley becomes her lover, her friend, her everything. But when her life is threatened, Ellie discovers that Riley is more obsessed with settling an old score than in the love she thought they were building. And Riley must choose between a revenge he's prepared for all his life and the woman he's sure he can't live without...

Reviews

"Smart, savvy, clever, and always entertaining. That's true of Riley Lawless, the hero in Ruthless, and likewise for his creator, Lexi Blake. Both are way ahead of the pack." ~ *New York Times* bestselling author Steve Berry

"I love Lexi Blake. Read Ruthless and see why." ~ *New York Times* bestselling author Lee Child

With Ruthless, Lexi Blake has set up shop on the intersection of Suspenseful and Sexy, and I never want to leave. ~ Laurelin

Paige, *New York Times* bestselling author

Ruthless is full of suspense, hot sex, and swoon worthy characters -- a must read!" ~ *New York Times* bestselling author Jennifer Probst

* * * *

Riley turned and got his first glimpse of Ellie Stratton. Pictures didn't do the woman justice. In her pictures she was serious, even somewhat severe. She'd had them done to go out with newsletters and in business journals. He'd found her to be a bit boring, a couple of pounds overweight.

Those extra pounds were in all the right places. Ellie Stratton had that brownish blond hair color that looked dull in photographs because no picture could catch the subtle variations of color that the midmorning light could. Her hair was down, flowing past her shoulders. Blond and chestnut and sable strands vied with a few shades of mahogany. She'd ditched the severe suit she wore in pictures in favor of a wrap dress that clung to her curves. No pantyhose. Her legs were round and feminine, descending to four-inch heels that would look nice wrapped around his neck.

Where had she been hiding that rack?

His brother cleared his throat, a sure sign that Riley was fumbling the ball.

"Ms. Stratton, it's a pleasure to meet you." He was going to have to figure out how to handle her. He needed to get close, to gain access to the building and the offices and, more importantly, to the data Drew hadn't been able to find. He needed access to everything StratCast had to offer, and the closer he could get to Castalano, the better.

Revenge was only one part of their plan. Justice was another.

He held out his hand and she took it. She had a firm grip, but when she was about to pull away, he placed his other hand over hers, trapping her. He looked right into her eyes. They were brown with flecks of gold in them. Pretty eyes. Another thing she tried to hide in those business pictures. She wore glasses, likely trying to make herself look serious. "I want to assure you that we're here and you'll be satisfied with our services. We're dedicated to our clients, and I'll make sure this buyout runs as smooth as clockwork."

Her eyes widened and he saw a flare of awareness go through her.

It was a revelation to meet her in person. It was likely difficult to be the female boss in a male-dominated industry. She would have to hide her femininity, to cloak it in a coat of chilly intellectualism in order to be taken seriously. It was obvious that she felt at home here in her own office.

In the real world, she likely had very carefully placed walls.

Poor Ellie. He was going to have to break them down.

She smiled at him, and it turned her face from serious to stunning in a second. When Ellie Stratton smiled, it was like someone had turned a light on in a previously dark room.

"Thank you." She seemed to realize what she'd done and pulled her hand out of his. Her cheeks had a pretty blush to them. She was divorced, according to the dossier their security firm had worked up on her. He would know more this afternoon when Mia got back from Dallas for their briefing. "I'll be honest, I'm actually quite happy to have found a new firm. My father's lawyers were oh-so-stuffy. I'm not sure they knew what to do with me."

Castalano smiled her way. "You're a force of nature, sweetheart. They should let you do what you do."

She smiled for the disgusting old man, and Riley felt his heart rate tick up. "You're too nice to me, Steven. And not everyone thinks the same way you do."

"Then they can take a long hike," Castalano said with a smirk. "You're going to do great here. And don't worry about the lawyers. This will all work out. I promise."

"It's only a formality." She stepped back and nodded Riley's way. "If you'll follow me, we can get started. Steven, if you'll excuse us. I hope your day goes well."

Castalano suddenly seemed bright. Well, as bright as his craggy, florid face would allow. "It's wonderful, Ellie. I'm going to grab my clubs and meet my friend at Chelsea Piers for our weekly session. You look like you're in good hands with these two. See you later, dear."

She gave him a wave and then began walking toward the executive wing. "If you'll follow me, gentlemen. I was so grateful you could take me on. I know it was short notice, but I'm very appreciative."

Riley walked slightly behind her and wondered if she knew how the dress she was wearing clung to her backside. She had a spectacular ass. Little Miss Prim and Proper turned out to be someone entirely different than he'd thought, and she had some serious junk in her trunk. What had seemed like a mission of sexual martyrdom suddenly looked like something else entirely. He might very well enjoy the next few weeks.

"Come on, brother," he said quietly. "Let's get this thing started."

They'd waited twenty years and it was finally here.

ELEGANT SEDUCTION

Trinity Masters, Book 6
By Mari Carr and Lila Dubois

A CIA asset, an heiress and a corporate mediator

Sebastian has dedicated his life to upholding the ideals of the Trinity Masters. However, when his best friend, Juliette, is named Grand Master, he knows secrets he's harbored will be revealed. While he expects Juliette to be angry, he does not expect her to call him to the altar, to bind him to a stranger, Grant, and to Elle, the woman who's haunted his dreams for years.

Then Juliette reveals a secret of her own. There's evil at play in the secret society and she needs him to root it out. Sebastian has no choice but to go undercover to spy on his own trinity. As the danger surrounding the trio grows, Sebastian is forced to choose between loyalty and love.

Because reluctantly bound to Elle and Grant or not, Sebastian can't deny the pair have earned their place in his soul.

* * * *

"We're going out to dinner," he said.

She turned slightly, before returning to face the mirror. "Oh. Okay. I guess I'll see you later then."

Grant smirked. She wasn't getting out of it that easily. "*We're* going out, Elyse. You, me and Sebastian. Grab your coat."

Elyse turned around at that, responding with annoyance to his imperious tone. Good. She had a fighting spirit. It gave him no joy to see her sad, to see her struggling. If he had to piss her off to spark a little life into her, he'd do it...and love every minute of it.

"Excuse me?"

He leaned against the doorjamb. "You heard me. Grab your coat. I'm hungry."

"I think maybe we need to get a few things clear, Mr. Breton. I don't appreciate being told to do anything. I'm not a dog who heels and I'm not a soldier under your command."

He grinned. "So noted. And I agree with you. We don't know each other. Closed doors and silent treatments aren't going to help that. Am I right?"

Elyse appeared chagrined. "You are."

"You like Mexican?"

She nodded slowly. "Yes. I do."

"Then that makes three of us. I'd say we're well on our way to finding quite a bit of common ground." Grant walked into her bedroom and picked up the coat she had dropped at the foot of her bed. He'd been a gentleman thus far, keeping his distance, but he'd be damned if he would resist the urge to touch her a minute longer.

Elyse turned so he could help her into her coat, and then sank back without hesitation when he tugged on her shoulders, pressing her back to his chest.

"You're very beautiful, Elyse."

She looked over her shoulder and smiled at him. "Thank you. I'm sorry I snapped at you. And I'm sorry I closed myself in here. I just needed a few minutes to myself."

"Understandable. We've all just experienced a life-altering event. Takes time to adjust." With any luck, Grant would have a big portion of the walls standing between them knocked down by the end of the night.

"Ready to go?" Sebastian stood at the doorway, watching them with an expression Grant couldn't read.

Jealousy?

Given Sebastian's actions at the altar and his comments earlier, that feeling seemed unlikely. And yet…

Grant was a man of action. He'd spent too many years dealing with people who'd made dragging their feet an art form. It was time to see exactly where the three of them stood.

Keeping his hands on Elyse's shoulders, he turned until they both faced Sebastian, then he bent forward and placed a kiss on her cheek.

Sebastian's eyes narrowed.

Yep. Definitely jealousy.

Elyse didn't attempt to pull away, though Grant felt her stiffen slightly, surprised by his actions.

Upping the ante, he drew his hands down along her arms before wrapping them loosely around her waist. Elyse's breathing accelerated, but to her credit, she held her ground.

They were virtual strangers. And yet, they were about to embark on a lifelong relationship. That knowledge drove Grant to push the limits far faster than he would have if he were merely on a first date with someone.

Sebastian remained silent, still as a statue by the door. His gaze followed the motion of Grant's hands.

"Grant," Elyse whispered.

He kept his arms around her, though his attention was on Sebastian. "We all knew this day was coming. Knew what it meant to join the Trinity Masters. We understood what we were giving up. And what we were gaining."

He tightened his grip, letting Elyse feel exactly how much she was affecting him. His cock had hardened the moment he'd seen her lying on her bed, looking so lost and lonely.

For years, he'd worried that he wouldn't feel an attraction to his spouse or spouses. Sex was something he enjoyed a great deal. His desires were darker than most, stronger, hell—kinkier. So, he'd spent the past seventeen years indulging them…just in case he was matched with less-adventurous souls.

"You're going to be my wife, Elyse," Grant continued, his hand rising to cup one breast. She gasped in surprise, but the nipple budded and her body relaxed under his hands.

More common ground.

"Our wife," Sebastian said, drawing their attention back to

him. “She’s going to be *our* wife.”

Up until that moment, Grant had gotten the feeling Sebastian was still resistant to the union, determined to buck the Grand Master’s edict.

And for the first time since he’d taken her in his arms, Elyse tried to pull away.

Also interesting.

She didn’t have a problem being Grant’s wife, but she wouldn’t accept that same declaration from Sebastian. Whatever came between them in the past was still an issue. They had their work cut out for them.

There was a delicate balance to be met if this relationship was going to succeed. It meant all the players needed to be invested. They needed to accept it.

Grant refused to let go of her. He tightened his grip on her breast until she moaned, her hips pressing against his crotch in a way that betrayed her need for more.

“Our wife,” Grant repeated.

ABOUT LEXI BLAKE

Lexi Blake lives in North Texas with her husband, three kids, and the laziest rescue dog in the world. She began writing at a young age, concentrating on plays and journalism. It wasn't until she started writing romance that she found success. She likes to find humor in the strangest places. Lexi believes in happy endings no matter how odd the couple, threesome or foursome may seem. She also writes contemporary Western ménage as Sophie Oak.

Connect with Lexi online:

Facebook: www.facebook.com/lexi.blake.39
Twitter: https://twitter.com/authorlexiblake
Website: www.LexiBlake.net

Sign up for Lexi's free newsletter at www.LexiBlake.net/newsletter!

Made in the USA
Middletown, DE
10 June 2016